EL GÜERO

D1737282

TIM HARRON

PAGE PUBLISHING, INC.
New York, NY

First originally published by Page Publishing, Inc. 2016

ISBN 978-1-68289-625-9 (pbk)
ISBN 978-1-68289-626-6 (digital)

Printed in the United States of America

ACKNOWLEDGMENT

To my mother Joan Christina Harron. Starting with thanking you would mean there was a beginning and an end. You chose to give me life, love me, be there for me through the highest highs and lowest lows. Over the years I couldn't understand why I was protected more times than good fortune should allow. I came to the conclusion I had a guardian angel and I've come to the realization it was you all along.

To my father James Francis Harron. The man that instilled in me characteristics, character traits and character that continues to extend further than even I understand. You taught me the importance of a man's word, dedication and devotion. There are so many intangibles that to this day I continue to discover and am thankful for. Most of all I'm proud to claim you as my father and I, your son.

To my friend Jacqueline Denise Key. Unwavering, unapologetic and unmistakable you epitomize an old New York adage of "show and prove". You have shown me your friendship and proven it time and again.

CHAPTER 1

THE EXODUS

"What's that?" Agent Coppola said into the microphone attached to his wrist.

Agent Coppola's radio could only hear garbled noises and intermittent words. He pressed the earpiece in his right ear, attempting to drown out the ambient noise of the holiday travelers. As he stood just inside one of the departure terminals at John F. Kennedy International Airport, the noise from the crowd and perhaps some interference from other electronics made hearing what was said through the earpiece a bit problematic.

Standing one inch taller than six feet, Agent Coppola was every bit a member of the Federal Bureau of Investigation. From his freshly cut hairdo that looked like he cut it himself with a Flowbee to his generic suit that looked like standard-issue attire for the bureau, Agent Coppola was all in. He was seasoned even though he had only been in the bureau for less than ten years. His first stint fresh out of the academy was in Washington, where he formulated his department and interdepartmental connections. Longing for the ultimate prize of being home in his childhood residence of Brooklyn, Agent Coppola was dedicated. Finally being approved and promoted to run a task force in the bureau's organized crime section, he was back where it all began for him—Bensonhurst, Brooklyn.

As a child growing up on the streets of Bensonhurst, a young Coppola had grown disdain as he witnessed men of respect in the neighborhood flaunt their power and prestige over *normal*, law-abiding citizens. Now in his early thirties, the young agent looked much more hardened and aged than his birth age would have indicated. It almost seemed as if he was aging from the inside out at a more rapid pace. Even the dark bags under his eyes seemed to peek out from behind his patented cookie-cutter federal sunglasses perched atop his larger-than-normal-sized nose, which looked as though he had been in a fight or two.

"I'm getting static in this damn thing. Repeat that." Agent Coppola's frustration was mounting, and that New York temper began to rear its ugly head. "No, the information I got was, he would be traveling alone," he said as he simultaneously looked down at the photos attached to the clipboard in his hands.

Agent Coppola's clipboard had a few pictures, one a picture of the Department of Motor Vehicles and the next, a grainy black-and-white surveillance picture. The surveillance picture appeared to be taken from some distance and was not of the best quality, while the DMV picture looked a little dated. The DMV picture was of the man in the surveillance picture, but apparently, it was taken some years earlier. There was another more up-to-date mug shot that was front and center on the clipboard.

"No, shit, I know the pictures aren't the most ideal, but it's what we have to work with. And we don't have much time. Focus on the latest mug shot picture." Agent Coppola struggled to keep his composure as his New York temper reared its ugly head. "Just keep your eyes open and mouth shut, unless you see the target," he said again into his wrist microphone.

It was 6:49 a.m., and Agent Coppola's frustration was mounting. He didn't know when or even if this was the place to be. He knew it was a long shot, like looking for a specific needle in a stack of needles. He didn't know if he was being played for a fool, but for now, this was a viable tip he had to pursue.

CHAPTER 1

THE EXODUS

I never enjoyed flying. I preferred driving over flying even though statistically, I was at a greater risk of injury, fatality, or law enforcement scrutiny driving than flying. Sometimes in life, decisions are made for us and we have no choice. This would just be another one of those times in my life where a decision was made for me. I had to make the best decision in the worst of conditions.

From the backseat of the black-on-black Lincoln Town Car, I admired the view of New York for what I thought would be the last time, taking mental notes of the scenery, seeing things I had seen before but never paid much attention to but were now etched in my memory bank. I even had the tinted window rolled down partially, partly to let the billowing smoke escape and partly to let that unmistakable New York air circulate. As I puffed on my Hoyo de Monterrey Cuban cigar, it felt like my lungs were filling with the sweetness of the Cuban soil and the crispness of a New York winter. The sun was just passing the tops of the building-riddled skyline, attempting to add some warmth to the subzero temperatures of the awakening city.

"Terminal 2, Departure Flights, John F. Kennedy Airport," the sign read. That would be my exit as my driver turned off nearing the end of my ride. As the driver neared my curbside drop-off, I tried to enjoy the last few puffs on my cigar. Eyeing the hustle and bustle of JFK, I waited for my driver to come around and open the door for me and retrieve my luggage from the trunk. My door opened, and I slid off the leather interior, simultaneously reaching into my right dress pants pocket with my right hand for a tip. I peeled off a fifty-dollar bill and, with my left hand, carried out my attaché case. The cold pierced through my dress shirt as I put on my suit jacket, exiting the Lincoln. Nothing short of a parka would begin to shield one from the arctic wind. I took a last long drag on my cigar, making this one count, as I knew I would be smokeless for some time. Savoring the taste before exhaling, I discarded the butt in a nearby receptacle. My driver had my luggage ready for me on its roller, and with an even swap, I handed him his fifty dollars and he handed me my luggage. We shook hands and parted company. I peeled back my jacket sleeve to look at the time on my watch, 6:46 a.m.

Wheeling my life with me, I made my way through the cold to the glass doors in front of me, into the warmth of the chaos inside. Christmastime 1997, and I knew the airport would be at its peak a week before Christ's birthday. As I approached the motion-censor doors just past the baggage attendants' booth, I felt the warmth inside rush upon me, and as I passed through the entranceway, I noticed the entire scene inside resembled a Chinese fire drill. People hustling here or there, bumping into one another, trying to figure out which maze of crowd-controlling ropes to join. Others panicked because they chose the wrong ones, while others were stuck on stupid, not knowing what to do one way or another. Travelers were fumbling for their documents, some sitting in the sparse number of chairs that weren't nearly enough to satisfy those that had either missed their flights, were waiting for a connecting flight, or whose flights were delayed because of the weather. The worst of them were the travelers that resembled zombies, those that were completely overwhelmed by the process in general and whose minds were on sensory overload.

I took about ten paces inside as the doors automatically closed behind me. I felt the warmth of the commercial heaters above me blast down my freshly shaved head. I was no stranger to shaving my head and felt it the best way to change my appearance. My head was where I started, but I had also begun tanning heavily to change the Irish-white pigment of my skin.

Starting from my immediate right, I began scanning the room with terminator-like action. I was processing, analyzing, and assessing threat levels, storing them in my mind, categorizing them in order of importance. I began learning this skill on the streets of New York, growing up fast and maturing young.

Off to my right shoulder was a series of pay telephones with one occupied by a woman having an animated conversation. There was a little walkway and then a row of seats filled with what seemed to be a family in various stages of exhaustion, the father staying awake, watching his flock.

My head continued to move to the left, scanning people as they moved in all directions. It wasn't long before my eyes locked onto someone who was out of place. What made him stand out was the fact that he was perfectly still in the midst of the madness. He stood just in front of one of the check-in lines between me and the passengers moving from side to side. He was a good fifty feet away and still stood out—at least to me he did. He had what appeared to be a clipboard in his hand. His attire was composed of a dress suit, the kind I had seen before, the cookie-cutter type of a federal agent. The suit was just the cherry on the top. His steadied purpose, patented sunglasses, standard-issue haircut were the telltale signs of a threat that I took a mental note of. He stood just over six feet tall, with an average build; nothing about his stature stood out. His back to the counter agents, he was scanning the crowd and appeared to be speaking to others through his earpiece and microphone under his sleeve. I spent only a few moments locking all this into memory, and not wanting to make eye contact, I finished my scan for anything else that needed my attention. Finding nothing else on my radar, I wanted to be on the move and get to where I needed to be and not stand there for longer than twenty seconds and possibly draw unwanted attention. I would have to pass his vicinity, having spotted the airline ticket counter I needed to reach. My hope was that he wasn't there for me and my change in appearance was sufficient enough to pass muster.

I made my way into the line designated for my airline and realized I would be passing ever so closely to the man in the suit. As he moved forward in line, out of the corner of my eye I caught sight of a plastic piece embedded in the man's ear. He seemed to be pressing on it, undoubtedly to drown out the noise around him. I hoped my freshly shaved head and the itchy beard I had been growing the last couple of months would be disguise enough to slip detection. The voice in the back of my mind was wondering, *Was this guy here for me? How did he get onto me?* I'd process all that information at a later time. For now, it was business as usual and time to blend into the chaos.

As my line weaved down, the agent I had passed was just off my left shoulder. Not long after entering my line, I came upon my turn to check in. The agent was about fifteen feet away, but so far, so good. All the ticket agents looked normal, but even if they weren't, chances are, I wouldn't know it until it was too late. I was at the point of no return as I was motioned over to an available ticket agent.

This was one of the many life-changing decisions I'd made before not just for myself but also for others. Sometimes, choices are made for us. The paths we choose in life form the decisions we come to make and carve out the future we may one day look back on and wish we can change. Those are the moments of solitude and reflection that men in my position try to avoid like the plague. Nothing good ever comes from reflection when I'm always knee-deep in madness.

Rolling my suitcase, attaché case in hand, I walked the twenty-five paces to the ticket agent awaiting me. I reached the counter, placed my attaché case on the ground next to my left leg, and reached inside my left breast pocket for my travel documents, passport, etc.

I looked up to see the agent typing something into her computer and waited for her to give me her attention. She was in her midforties, brunette, her hair six inches past her shoulders, with bangs. She was a bit overweight, probably from having multiple children and working long hours. A couple of buttons from the top of her uniform were unclasped, where one's attention would be drawn to her name tag, which was conveniently placed where one would have to notice her large DD breasts, giving one the excuse of having to look at her name tag repeatedly.

"Miss, oh, excuse me, Ms. Herrera. Good morning," I said as her eyes were still locked onto what she was doing on the computer. I placed my documents on the counter for her to get, as she needed them, so she wouldn't have to inquire about them.

As Ms. Herrera stretched her hand out to take hold of my documents, I saw a ring on her finger, signifying she was married. "Excuse me, I didn't know you were married. My mistake," I said, noticing the small but obvious wedding ring.

"Oh, you're quite observant, but it's *miss*. My husband passed away near a year ago, and I just can't seem to find the courage to take the ring off," Ms. Herrera said, looking like she was almost trapped in some flashback of her lost love while staring down at the ring, as if the event had just occurred.

I gave her a moment before I said anything as it seemed as if she were really reliving a deep memory.

"Pardon me. I didn't mean to be presumptuous," I said, trying to snap her back into the task at hand.

"Not at all. It's about time I move forward. This was the last barrier I had to overcome." As she spoke, she slipped the ring off her finger and slid it into her pocket.

Ms. Herrera began to work on my papers, entering the information into the computer as she spoke. Looking down at my passport, she said, "Mr. B——, I want to thank you for being so observant." She had obviously noticed my name on my passport.

"My pleasure," I said, unable to get any more out as she was about done with her job now and was moving fast; I guessed it was her self-defense mechanism so she wouldn't break down in tears.

Just like me, Ms. Herrera had been immersing herself with her work, giving herself less time to ponder about the decisions she had made, the events that had occurred, or life in general. She was on autopilot in her self-imposed safe zone so she could function daily and not be derailed. I guess we all do that on different levels.

"Just one bag to be checked in, Mr. B——?" she asked, giving me my cue to place the bag on the scale for weighing.

"Yes, just the one," I said, placing it on the scale between Ms. Herrera's counter and the next.

Ms. Herrera placed a tag on it and lifted it in one motion. She was strong and able, lifting the bag—nearly fifty pounds in weight—effortlessly off the scale onto the conveyor belt directly behind her in one fell swoop. That conveyor led to the workers in the back, who would add my luggage to the others going in the same plane as I.

With her eyes focused on the tasks at hand, Ms. Herrera was emanating a language that was almost robotic in nature.

"Business or pleasure?" she asked, still typing away into her computer and finalizing the transaction.

"Pure vacation," I replied and, wanting to keep the conversation going, elaborated. "This time of year works best for me. Aside from a little extra traffic at the airport, the hotels have some great deals. Where I go, the crowds are thin."

All I could hear in my head right then, standing there at the ticket counter, was my attorney's voice resounding like the bells of St. Patrick's Cathedral.

* * *

"You're doing what? You're leaving? For where?" My attorney sounded like he was struggling for words, quite the polar opposite of the calm, cool, and collected attorney I'd known nearly my entire life.

Frank D'Fellippo was my attorney, a man I had known since my teenage years, when I first needed the assistance of counsel. He was every bit the Italian New York lawyer representing the average folk as well as the upper echelon of organized crime. He was a man I had come to think of so fondly that I entrusted my life to him on numerous occasions and considered him family. He was not a tall man, but at about five feet, nine inches tall, what he lacked in height he made up for in confidence, ability, and bravado. With a full head of jet-black hair, always impeccably dressed, and the confident swagger of a mob mouthpiece, Frank was direct and to the point. A workaholic, he even had a treadmill in his office he would use while listening to tapes his wife, and secretary, had made for him so he could work and exercise at the same time.

"You've finally gotten to a place where you've wanted to be and you're going to leave it all behind and give it up?" Frank said in his tone, a mixture of surprise, shock, and fatherly-type concern.

I was sitting in Frank's office, a place I was no stranger to. The decor was composed of solid oak furniture, pictures of Frank's large Italian family, and New York Yankees memorabilia. Growing up in the Bronx, Frank was a die-hard Yankee fan, and it showed. Frank proudly displayed the autographed pictures, balls, bats, and all types of merchandise that spanned the many years of Yankee dominance in the baseball world. A season ticket holder, Frank used the tickets both personally and for business, which had come in handy on more than one occasion. Gotta love the Yankees.

Sitting behind his large oak desk with me on the other side, Frank couldn't continue without getting to something first.

"Hold on a minute. I know I need a drink," Frank said, standing up and making his way to the right-hand side of his desk.

Frank headed to his bar. Another masterpiece in appearance, it had a bar cabinet on the bottom and a glass top that was a see-through humidor, any man's treasure. I knew where he was going, so it was my turn to break out my gift for Frank. I never showed up anywhere empty-handed, and I proceeded to hand him a couple of boxes of Cuba's finest earthy cigars.

"Frank, while you're there, why don't you add these to your collection?" I said, reaching down next to me, picking up two boxes from a bag I brought in with me.

Frank looked at them intently, and a smile broadened from one ear to the other as he knew what they were and noticed that these were certainly not the easiest to obtain.

"The ones on the top are Bolívars, and the ones underneath are the Cohiba Limitadas, the limited editions," I said, letting Frank know which was which and also just to voice out what gift I had brought.

I learned at a young age to never show up anywhere empty-handed and to always know what the person or people are interested in. It's just not polite to show up at someone's business or home and not present a gift, even if it's a small token. I was blessed to have great men in my life that taught me directly or indirectly how to act in the society. Frank and I had many things in common, clothes, cigars, alcohol, and the role of being a man's man. He always told me to keep my mouth shut and call him if there was ever an issue. Frank was my attorney, friend, and more. We had a professional relationship, but the personal relationship, I valued highly. The attorney client-relationship allowed me to tell him things that I would have never mentioned to anyone besides my inner self. Needless to say, Frank knew more personal information about me than any other man, making us quite close.

"You always outdo yourself, T——," Frank said, opening the first box of Cohíbas, letting the earthy aroma of Cuban soil waft into his nostrils.

Frank clipped a couple of cigars from his older selection and handed me one and himself, the other. "Two aged Montecristos would do the trick just nicely," he said.

Then he proceeded to pour two fingers of tequila, his drink of choice and one I wouldn't pass up. I wasn't much of a drinker at the time, but my Irish heritage allowed me to partake with the best of them. I tried to keep my drinking to occasions or holidays, where celebration was the order of the day. Frank always had a New Year's Eve party at his house, an occasion where drinking was the order. We celebrated after a favorable ruling in court, another time for the spirits to flow. This was another occasion, a farewell of sorts, and both Frank and I knew that this would probably be our last time seeing each other, at least in this setting.

We lit our cigars, enjoying the first couple of pulls, savoring the earthy tones of tobacco heaven. Raising our glasses, we toasted to each other, clinking them together. "Salud." This tequila wasn't for slamming down as shots but for slow sipping, and we enjoyed the aged agave splashing around our palates and mixing slightly with the taste of the cigar. I had introduced this tequila, Tres Generaciones, to Frank some years ago when I first ventured into Mexico as a twenty-year-old kid. I returned from that first trip with not only cigars and tequila but also a wealth of experience and contacts.

Frank took another sip, finishing his drink before he could muster what it was he wanted to say. Frank was never at a loss for words but was rather quite careful with them. I knew it must have been something more in-depth, what he wanted to say, the words of wisdom he would bestow on me. Frank never straight-up chastised me for the decisions I had made or the decisions I was going to make. That wasn't his way. He was a great listener, and without saying a word, he spoke volumes.

"Now, what's this again?" Frank said, leaning forward in his chair, pouring us both a second round of what would be many.

Frank seldom repeated himself, but the shock of my words took him off his usual unshakeable self. He processed what I said but wanted clarity of my words.

"I tell you, Frank, I'm just getting a bad feeling. Something's telling me to move on. I can't explain it. It's like the time in Jersey and I was on the run. I got that feeling to move on and just picked up. Then the feds were there bright and early the next morning, wanting to question me about some Philadelphia nonsense. I've come to learn that when I get these types of feelings, I have to listen to them even if they seem off the wall or erratic. I barely escaped that one there in Jersey, and on more than one occasion where events would have gotten life threatening, my inner voice has saved me. I never know what my gut feeling is telling me or exactly the purpose, but my gut feeling has never let me down. The other side of the coin is, I'm getting burned out here in New York. So many things are happening, and I can never really take a break. Even when I take a vacation, it never seems to be enough or relieves my stress levels for very long. You see it with other clients, that they never know when to change up, quit, or move on. I'm not quitting. I simply have a feeling that I have to act on."

Frank sat back in his high-back black leather chair, listening to me open up more so than I ever had. When we got together, it was usually about a case, work related, or just to goof off and blow off some steam between us. I had never before spoken about how I felt about this or that, so Frank was absorbing my words, words that he had never heard before and wasn't expecting.

"T——, you've taken this last pinch and did it the right way. It's elevated you to a whole other level. You're walking away just at the time when you should be capitalizing on your…well, fortunate misfortune," Frank said, reaching for the Mexican nectar.

"That's just it," I said, taking a sip from the second round of many that night. "All levels are elevated. I'm more on the radar now than I ever was or cared to be. Law enforcement's radar and the radar of those I would prefer to remain separate from. Frank, you know this more than anyone else. While the Italian's respect me, I'm not Italian. I can't be made and will always be on the outside looking in. All the old guys I grew up with are either retired, in the can, faded in power, or fading in power. Mind you, being made was never something I wanted, but everyone else knows it's not an option for me and can use that against me. I'll always be that outsider looking in no matter my skill set. Shortly, I'll be losing my power position with the older guys, and then what's next? I can't even get with the Westies because I'm not fully Irish. I know that sooner or later, I'll end up expendable in someone's eyes and dealt with. Shit, you see what they did with Anthony? Anthony was Italian from head to toe, and they killed him for nothin', for nothin'. He was the most loyal guy I knew. He would do anything for a friend and then some. They killed him just because maybe something might leak out about something that really didn't matter anyway. So who am I? What makes me so special? I've just been lucky so far. As far as me taking the latest pinch, shit, that wasn't even much of an option, and you know that. That decision was made for me the minute Michelle was arrested with me and charged. Yeah, I had options, but anything other than pleading out and accepting full responsibility would have been unhealthy." It seemed like my own mini tirade, the kind of which was reserved for close friends or confidants.

With "being made," I was referring to being a full-fledged member of an Italian Mafia family. Those who were made members had to be full-fledged Italians, with their ancestry traced back to Italy. That wasn't the only reason I couldn't be made. I had a family member that was a cop. My grandfather was one of the top cops in New York; hence, that would've been another hurdle to overcome even if I was

Italian. The Westies were an Irish gang in New York mainly based in the Hell's Kitchen part of the city. I only had one associate, a *friend* of mine that was a Westie, and they took way too many risks for me. I grew up with Irish and Italians, but it was the Italians that I gravitated more to, and they were the ones doing the organized crime that attracted me.

Michelle was my girlfriend at the time of my latest arrest and had been for the previous couple of years. She had thick auburn hair that ran down the middle of her back. Her eyes were a lighter shade of brown. Her face was round, dimples apparent, making her appear very youthful. Not tall by any means, she stood just a tad over five feet, and the heaviness of her large breasts had her tipping just over the one-hundred-pound mark. Italian in every sense of the word, she was. From her light-olive skin to the volatility of her personality, she was full-blooded dago.

My and Michelle's arrest was the debilitating factor in our roller-coaster relationship. I can't even say she was to blame for the relationship's failure. I know I was no walk in the park, never have been. I'm demanding, egotistical, spoiled, cocky, abrasive, selfish, narcissistic, stubborn, and those are my good traits. Then again, I'm not the typical nine-to-five guy—I never wanted that. Loyalty, respect, devotion, and dedication are traits that were deeply instilled in me since birth by everyone around me, friends, family, and associates. That is what I value, and that is what I have in me. I always had relationships with females, but those relationships never lasted no matter where my intentions were going. They were all good women, and the various twists and turns in my work and personal growth were usually the kiss of death for the relationship.

Michelle and I met through an associate of mine. I had been on the run in New Jersey for about the last year and a half. Until the heat could blow over, I could not return home to New York. The case was an older one, but a case that was just coming to court. I received a subpoena to testify, and that just wasn't an option. Picking up my dogs and arranging an apartment through an ex, I was able to reside there in New Jersey in relative obscurity. While I wasn't one of the main targets of the investigation, I was still of interest to the government. It was just shortly after Anthony was murdered, and tensions were high. Anthony asked me to do him a favor, and reluctantly, I did. But it was only because it seemed important for him to show his worth to the mob guys he had known his whole life and ultimately wanted to become. A man of respect and honor was just part of it. He loved the lifestyle and everything about being a member of Italian organized crime. Being a made member of the organization fit him as much as he wanted to fit it. Anthony was loyal to the core, and he had that devious insanity about him that was the mold for all up-and-coming gangsters. I didn't have any doubts that he would be a rising star, but rising stars also have the tendency to burn out too fast. Such was Anthony's fate.

I hadn't been a few months into my exile in New Jersey when I got a page from my lawyer. My pager, like every identifying marker that could lead to my real identity or to my real name, was in a false name and address. I didn't have another phone, certainly not a home phone of any kind. When I received a page, I would always drive to a pay phone about thirty minutes away from where I was living to make the call.

One of the tools to my trade was my pocket tone dialer. The designed purpose was the convenience of programming numbers into the phone so it can automatically dial the desired numbers with the ease of pressing a button. My purpose was a bit different. I was able to program the tones so that the pay phone would recognize the sound as if change was being deposited for the call. The first button was programmed for twenty-five cents, the second for fifty cents, and the last, a dollar. The device came in handy when using pay phones to call my associates as well as for any international calls I made. I had international connections and associates, so I gave them one so that their calls were made easier and safer to their people. There were times when we had cloned cell phones, but I used those sparingly as I still didn't trust them and only used them for convenience, when getting to a pay phone was out of the question. One of my associates in Philadelphia had a cloned-phone operation, so I would buy one from him from time to time.

Hiding out had its ups and downs. The beach in South Jersey was amazing at any time of year when I was able to enjoy it. I believe this was where I developed an affinity for beach living. The smell of the salty air was so refreshing. Watching the waves roll in while taking in that unpolluted air was idyllic. I was on the run, but I was still working. I wasn't working as much and certainly not in the open, as when I was operating in New York. I had to curb a lot of my business practices and limit my interactions with associates and common folk. My contact with associates back in New York was limited to one person. Not only a person I trusted but also someone I knew could assist me where I needed it most, on food and information. His family owned a restaurant I frequented, which was almost like a second home to me. I was at the beach in Wildwood, New Jersey, and for me, the food was terrible, to say the least. So every couple of months, I would have my associate deliver a fresh supply of food from his family's restaurant, just enough that I could freeze it and make it last. My favorite, which I had had brought down in large quantities, was penne vodka sauce, the true nectar of the gods. So along with the food, he would deliver news from back home, and we would conduct business. I looked forward to each of his visits on many levels. I longed for the news and the food but the like-mindedness of someone from back home.

I received a page from my lawyer handling this case back in New York. Having been on the run for a few months now, I hadn't heard anything about the case since I decided to hide out until things blew over. This lawyer wasn't my usual legal counsel. This was a special situation that required a lawyer that was familiar with this case and the agency involved. It just so happened that this case was led by the same agency my grandfather was the commander of some years ago. They investigated organized crime, and so the more personal I could make this type of case, the better position I would be in. The new lawyer I hired was in fact the son of the commander of the agency in charge of the case and had recently retired. His father and my grandfather were close friends, and our families, quite friendly. I was hoping the agents on the case wouldn't be so apt to pursue me if their old commander's son was involved in the case. The day the agents came to question me about the case, I arranged it at my new lawyer's office. The agents arrived and saw who my counsel was, and their demeanor was certainly different from what it was over the phone and the dealings I previously had with them.

I completed the nearly thirty-minute drive to a pay phone, what I considered to be sufficiently enough distance between where I was staying and the call I needed to make to my lawyer back in New York. The pay phone was a safe-enough distance if someone were tracking or listening to the call.

I didn't have to look down at the pager for the number to dial back. I dialed the number like I had many times before, and when prompted, I placed my pocket tone dialer to the receiver and pressed the dollar button three times, and the call was made. I got the receptionist, and when she asked who was calling, I simply said, "He would know."

"Hey, where are you?" my lawyer started.

"You know better than that," I said in a short response.

"What are you doing?" he said, asking another question that didn't need to be asked.

"There's about forty-five seconds left for this call, so don't ask me questions you don't need to know the answers to," I responded, needing to bring my lawyer's line of questioning to a screeching halt.

"I received a call this morning from the assistant United States attorney prosecuting the case. He says that in exchange for their helping you in a prior case in Connecticut, you're going to testify for the government in this case," my lawyer said with a hint of questioning my criminal loyalty.

I could only say the first thing that came to my mind, especially knowing that someone might be listening to our conversation. I wanted my stance to be well-known and unwavering.

"I'm paying you, right?" I said in a more stern tone.

"Yes, you are," my lawyer retorted.

"Then I want you to call the AUSA who said that to you and tell him from me to go fuck himself. If he wants me so bad, he can find me!" I said this and didn't even wait for a response, as one wasn't necessary.

My instinct about leaving New York when I did was correct. The general public believes that the federal government fights fair and that there's equal justice for all. Well, I'm here to tell you that the feds bend and create laws that are so slanted in their favor that our rights as citizens of the same country are slowly being taken from us. When those tactics fail, the feds will resort to levels that resemble the very criminals they are trying to put behind bars, except they do it under the veil of justice.

This particular federal prosecutor knew the information he was putting out for public consumption was going to have consequences one way or another. Saying to my lawyer that I was going to testify was the same as stating it publicly. Shit, I was on the run and left the state to avoid charges, the very same charges. The fact that the government was claiming they assisted me in anything was not only completely false but also a danger to my existence. This federal prosecutor's goal was to put the word out that I was assisting them so either I would do that very thing or the guys on the street would get word and kill me. Little did the government know I already chose what was behind door number 3. I was going to hide out until things blew over and everyone I knew understood I did the right thing. Nobody in my line of work waits to see if it's fact or fiction. Their motto always is "Better safe than sorry" and "Why take a chance?"

Now if I had gotten killed behind the misunderstanding, who would have been responsible? The feds didn't care; it was win-win for them. I would come in and testify against the guys or get killed as a suspected informant. The government would get information, or they'd get more indictments against those that perpetrated my demise.

Anthony, who was my best friend, was shot to death a few months before I decided to go on the run. The Italians were trying to clean up loose ends, or at least what they perceived to be loose ends. At least that was what I surmised. Better safe than sorry. Bullshit. Anthony wasn't even the kind of guy to be a loose end. He was dedicated to the lifestyle and looked forward to being a lifer in the business. Anthony lived, breathed, and slept the Mafia lifestyle. It was embedded in his very core. When I found out he was murdered, there wasn't much I could do, and soon after, the feds amped up their court schedule. Their concern was especially with witnesses, potential witnesses, and suspects dying and disappearing. I believe Anthony was so gung ho about being a made member of the organization that he lost sight of who was around him and underestimated the deviousness of those he believed in. I had my own crew I was working with in another borough. Anthony was based out of the Bronx, and I out of Brooklyn. Aside from the small favor I did Anthony, I wanted nothing to do with his crew. They were into drugs and some other aspects I didn't agree with, and I was content with my people and associations. Now I would freelance from time to time, but I never wanted a steady partnership aside from what I already had in Brooklyn.

It took about two years for everything to blow over back at home before I felt comfortable enough to venture back to New York. It started slow and at night. I would venture back to the restaurant my associate owned and where I felt the most comfortable. The restaurant was really decked out, well designed, and Italian in every sense of the word. The staff along with the owners spoke mainly Italian, as well as a number of the patrons of the establishment. The food was to die for, and I was treated like family, which meant more to me than anything. There was seating for about a hundred people, and often, the seating capacity was tested. I usually went at off times as crowds were never my thing.

I would get a hotel room to rest in for the evening and make my way back to Jersey in the midmorning traffic. I believed those off hours were best for driving, and I didn't want to drive after the wine and Sambuca had been drunk as well. I was testing the waters, and what better way than to get a great meal at my favorite restaurant, where I felt the safest. The restaurant was a neutral place for all walks of life involved in underworld activities. There were arms dealers, made members of the Italian Mafia, associates, hustlers, businessmen, and nobody disrespected the establishment. This eclectic group was, oddly enough, harmonious. I felt safe there, and with no advance warning, I would just show up under the cover of darkness and slowly work my way back into the mix.

The case I was on had already been adjudicated and sentences handed down. I wasn't a major player, so the government was not on to me so much as if I were the main target of the investigation.

The second evening I ventured back to New York, I had a meeting scheduled with another associate of mine I hadn't seen in two years. This time I brought my then girlfriend with me for the ride and a dinner out. She was the girlfriend I had while being on the run. Arriving at the restaurant, I found out my associate was there with his lady friend, and we proceeded to sit down to a meal and a little talk about the goings-on from his point of view. The seating at the restaurant was both formal and the informal seating in the bar area. This particular evening we sat in the more-relaxed side of the bar area, where there was table seating as well as the bar.

Arriving after my associate, my girlfriend and I made our way inside, stopping to pay our respects to the owners and the various others I knew. It was good to see friendly faces, and hearing the New York accent again was even better. The family of my associate that owned the restaurant spoke broken English, Italian being their native language. I introduced my girlfriend, and then we made our way to the table my associate had already occupied. I had only been back once since my hiatus, so some of the hellos took a little bit longer than would be normal.

My associate was there with a bright big smile on his face. Everyone I associated with had not only a name but also a nickname that I usually gave or, sometimes, one that was already tagged to him or her. The associate I was dining with I nicknamed Pete the Killer. He was a bit off mentally and was on psych meds but very loyal and dedicated, something you can never have enough of. I met Pete at a gym I worked out at, and we became friends, associates. I owned a restaurant before going on the run, and Pete would assist me in the kitchen and made the best sauce for pasta—I loved that sauce.

"Petey!" I said, approaching the table, and before any other introductions were made, I had to give him a hug and kiss on the cheek, as was customary for our greetings.

"T——!" Pete said, embracing me with long-lost affection. "Great to see you again. You look good, tanned, and in good health," Pete continued, looking me up and down.

I got into the introduction of my girlfriend, and Pete did the same with his lady friend. She was a short little thing, about five feet tall, and was a little over one hundred pounds, had DD breasts, long auburn hair almost touching the top of her ass, brown eyes, and was wearing a skirt and top that accented all her voluptuous assets and olive skin. Michelle was her name, and from the onset, I felt a connection to her and vice versa. Throughout dinner I kept getting glances from Michelle that were more than friendly, and it made me wonder if I had known her before. The evening wound down, and Michelle and I found ourselves alone at the dinner table. She made her intentions a bit clearer.

"I know you from somewhere," Michelle said in a lustfully wine-filled leer, never taking her full brown eyes off mine.

"You look familiar too, but I can't quite place you," I said in response.

I didn't want to be too forward, not truly knowing the relationship Pete had with her, and my girlfriend wasn't too far away in the bathroom. In our world you don't get involved with another man's wife or girlfriend; it's not only bad business but was also a punishable offense, depending on the parties involved. We had a little banter back and forth with both of us trying to place each other, at least that was what I thought. With the evening concluded, we all decided to make our way to a hotel to spend the night, each couple to a room. We were all a bit tipsy from the wine and drinks, and at the hotel, Michelle made her intentions even more known by coming onto me there. I brushed it off and went to my room with my girlfriend, and Pete and Michelle entered theirs.

The following weekend, I headed back to New York, to the same restaurant, with Pete again. Pete told me that he wanted to double-date with me, Michelle, and a friend Michelle had for me. It turned out Michelle had other plans for that evening. When I arrived, it was just the three of us, and by the end of the evening, Michelle made it clear she was only interested in me and never planned on introducing me to another woman. I came to find out that Pete never slept with Michelle and they were merely friends. I'm sure Pete wanted more, but Michelle wasn't interested. From her account, they had just met not long ago and were just friends. No claim was made or relationship consummated, so then there would be no real transgression on my side if I pursued it. We ended up at another bar that evening with Michelle pretending to introduce me to a friend of hers. The evening wound down and Pete called it a night, and that left me with Michelle and her friend. I ended up taking both to a hotel and spending the night with them.

It was more common than not for me to have girlfriends in whatever state I had business. My main business since the late eighties had been selling steroids. First, when I was in college, playing football, then even after that, the business snowballed and expanded. Now, after this encounter with Michelle, I had a female friend in New York again and still with my other in New Jersey. I wanted to get back to New York full-time and be back to working in the area I felt most comfortable in. A few months after I started easing my way back to New York, I made the decision to leave Jersey. The decision wasn't something planned out or something I knew I would do. One morning, I awoke with a feeling, a feeling that could only be described as a gut feeling, a hunch, or just basic instinct. I had learned at a young age to follow my instincts and hunches and not to ignore them. I was packing my belongings and loading them into my car when my girlfriend came home from work. She was more than surprised and shocked to see me in the final stages of packing up my car. I never was one to explain myself or give anyone a heads-up on what my intentions were. I was always of the belief that the less information someone had about what I was doing, my actions, or intentions, the better off it was for everyone. Deniability is a good thing and also helps if someone wants to do something that may jeopardize one's freedom or health. The other side of the coin was, how could I explain a gut feeling I had if I didn't even know what the gut feeling was pertaining to? It was usually a feeling that came over me to change direction or to do something or not do something. All I could do was finish packing and have a small talk with my girlfriend. I didn't want to spend much time saying good-byes as the good-byes in these moments would be long and drawn out. I didn't know when the gut feeling I had would take form, so the sooner the better to move on and not waste time.

The following morning, bright and early as usually was the case, the FBI showed up at my girlfriend's apartment in New Jersey. Apparently, I showed up on a surveillance photo with an associate of mine in Philadelphia. He was associated with an organized crime faction in Philadelphia. Unbeknownst to me, he had robbed a series of businesses along an entire city block. He and a crew that went from rooftop to rooftop, looting the stores. They disabled the alarm systems and entered the businesses and establishments one by one. One such store was a high-end bicycle shop. I was dealing steroids at the time, and we ended up trading some products I had for a couple of the bicycles he had stolen. He met me in Jersey, where we did the transaction, and apparently, that was where I appeared on the FBI's radar for something that wasn't even a business of mine. I guessed the FBI wanted to question me about something related to the robberies, but I had no idea about them. As mad and upset as my girlfriend was that I took off, she didn't say anything about where I was or what I had been doing. She was too distraught to have much of a conversation with the feds anyway. I got rid of the bicycles a day after I got them, and that was some months previously. My girlfriend understood more about why I left, and for that matter, so did I. That gut feeling I got saved me again.

Michelle and I had gotten closer over the months before I returned to New York. She didn't have a really steady job to speak of, which made it easier for her to travel with me when my travels weren't anything dangerous or heavy. We had a lot of common interests and vices. One such vice was gambling, which we both did rather often, and it was always blackjack. My main business then was selling steroids, which I had been doing for nearly the past decade.

I was staying a couple of nights a week at my parents' place in Westchester County, New York, and the other nights in random hotels with Michelle. I also had a crash pad in Brooklyn that I was given, but that was just for me and not for bringing women or anyone else over. Just three people knew I lived there, and that was just the way I wanted it kept.

Inevitably, as tradition would have it, Michele's Italian family wanted to meet me, the man their daughter and granddaughter was dating. A day was decided on when I would meet her family, and the location was her house. The house was located just above the borough of the Bronx in Westchester County. It was a split-level type, with her parents and siblings on the bottom and her grandparents living on the top portion of the house. The neighborhood was middle-class, and their duplex was quite nice.

Arriving at the house, I was prepared for the typical Italian greeting, but this one was a bit more than I expected. Michelle was waiting for me as I rang the doorbell. She was dressed more conservatively than she would have ordinarily been, but that was to be expected especially on this day. I wore a dark pinstriped suit, as was my typical attire for going anywhere. I always wore dress clothes at a bare minimum and a suit normally. She led me through the doorway and foyer to the left, entering the bottom half of their duplex. As soon as I entered, I noticed there were people everywhere. I was introduced to everyone, cousins, siblings, and the parents. I brought gifts for the parents, as was customary, flowers, wine, and coffee. Michelle told me ahead of time what her mother's favorite flower was, so I delivered that and her father's favorite wine and then an overall gift for the house—some fresh gourmet coffee. One never goes anywhere without bearing gifts, especially on a first-time visit to the house; it's just disrespectful and ill-mannered. The inside was donned with traditional Italian furniture and design right down to the plastic coverings on the sofa. I finally made it through the living room before meeting the parents, and then it was time to meet the grandparents, the key to the family.

Her grandmother was a frail thing, standing about five feet, two inches tall, and looked to be in her seventies, with silver hair. The matriarch of the family, even before she spoke a word, she was a woman of class and character, I just knew. She was well dressed and clad in some very expensive jewelry that let me know she was of money, more to the point her husband was. I paid my respects to her grandmother, presenting her with flowers as well. This was my second to the last introduction and test, so to speak. The final test stood in the kitchen at five feet, eight inches tall, with olive skin, appearing to be in his early seventies, dressed in slacks and textured, woven Italian short-sleeve dress shirt. He exuded power and respect before he even uttered a word. From his steely-eyed stare through his sagacious coffee-colored eyes, you knew he was a man of respect and one to be taken seriously.

I stretched out my hand, and in the course of having my handshake reciprocated, I was met with a firm hand and gruff voice speaking to me in Italian. Now I was familiar with Italian and could understand a bit of it, but this was neither the time nor the place to venture out and make a mistake.

"Piacere di conoscerti, benvenuto," the grandfather said, shaking my hand and greeting me.

Taken off guard a bit but not wanting it to show on my face, I kept calm, poised, and responded without hesitation.

"With all due respect, I understand and speak a little Italian but not enough to be respectful," I said, not relinquishing his hand before I finished speaking.

We let our hands go with her grandfather responding. "Oh, I thought you were Italian, ah, from the north of Italy, with the blond hair and blue eyes," her grandfather said as he made gestures with his finger, signifying the northern part of Italy, where men with blond hair and blue eyes would be found.

"No, sir, I'm Irish," I said in response.

When dealing with men of power and respect in the underworld, I have learned that they have their own agendas and for sure have done their homework well before they have a meeting, especially with someone dating their granddaughter.

"What's your mother's maiden name?" her grandfather asked with an immediate response, letting me know he was prepared for me and had done his homework.

The question, some may think, was odd or out of place, but like everything in his life, there was a purpose for his words and actions that had a deeper meaning. Michelle's grandfather was a cautious man who thought ten moves ahead, a tribute to him spending very little time in prison and still breathing free air.

"G——," I said, giving my mother's Irish maiden name.

There was a very short couple of seconds before he responded, pointing his finger at me in an acknowledgment of the name I had just given him.

"I know your grandfather. Give him my regards," the old man said with reverence and respect.

"He passed a few years ago," I said in response.

Still not wanting to show my emotions and my utter awe that this man not only researched about me and my family but also held my grandfather in such high regard, I kept my composure.

"My condolences. He was a good man." He paused while wagging his finger. "Tough, but fair."

It was abundantly clear I was researched and assessed. This didn't bother me as I had nothing to hide and was quite proud of who I was and my family lineage. I had no regrets or the slightest to be ashamed of. Not only my name but also my family name could withstand any test at any time. I actually preferred to be scrutinized by those seeking to distinguish whether I was a man of respect and righteousness or a man of contempt and deplorable character.

My grandfather was a New York State trooper for years. He started out on a horseback, when that was the style and mode of transportation. He grew through the ranks to become the deputy chief inspector of the New York State Police. He was also the commander of the Bureau of Criminal Investigation. The BCI is a division of the state police that investigates organized crime. Like most of the policemen back when my grandfather joined the force, one had to be six feet tall or over and Irish. That suited my grandfather to a tee. He was well over six feet, topping about six feet, three inches in height, and every bit an Irishman, with his roots tracing back to the old country. He was an intimidating man from his impressive stature to his massive hairy hands. He had passed many traits unto me through my mother, and I was glad he did. His character was first and foremost, physical attributes aside. He had a couple of rules that he never wavered on, which were no drugs and nothing that had to do with children. He had dealings with organized crime back in the day, and that's not to say they were affiliated but rather that he had an understanding about what was tolerated and what wasn't. There were clear lines that, if crossed, you would know the consequences of your actions; it was pretty routine. So when Michelle's grandfather, who just so happened to be a semiretired organized crime boss, spoke about my grandfather in high regard, I understood a little about where the reverence was coming from. It was reverence but also respect, and respect is something that is earned over time.

Michelle's grandfather and I had many interests and characteristics in common. I felt comfortable in his company, a man's man. His wife was a special lady, and I soon learned what she enjoyed and would always bring her something each time I was there. I always said my hellos and paid my respects to the grandparents upstairs and Michelle's family downstairs. No matter if it was flowers, coffee, wine, or something from the bakery, empty-handed I never was.

Michelle and I were big gamblers, another toxic part of our relationship that made us jell well together. Blackjack was our game of choice, and whether she was just watching me or us together at the tables, we spent many days and nights on the felt. As it would happen, Michelle's grandfather was an avid blackjack player, and when I found this out, through Michelle, I invited him to come and play with us. I drove the three of us from Westchester to the casinos in Connecticut. Hell, I figured if Michelle and I were already going, why not take her grandfather with us? I did this especially when Michelle used to tell me that he was dying to get out and have some action. Being semiretired, he was yearning for the action he had all but left behind him. For him to feel that blood coursing through his veins was everything to him. Back in the day, he owned part of a casino in Cuba, so gambling was well in his blood. That was back in the day when the mob had their flag firmly planted in the heyday of Cuba's capitalism. The many times the three of us we went to the casinos together, I never saw the old man lose. I mean, never did he have a losing trip. He would roll out of the casino being up thirty to fifty thousand every time. He was the only steady winner I ever knew, and like everything he did, he was mum about his system. I attempted to pay for as much as he would allow and never asked him for anything in return. Michelle told me he spent a lot of time in the house and was always looking to get out and hit the casinos. I knew as much as she did that a man who was used to being on the go, commanding men and demanding respect, would be suffering sitting at home in his retirement. I enjoyed his company, and just being in his presence was enough for me. A man of respect, a fellow gambler, and someone that was still seeing life with fervor even when his family members thought otherwise, I could relate to and admire.

Michelle would tell me about a year later that her grandfather liked and respected me. Apparently, I was the only boyfriend she ever had that never asked him for anything, quite the contrary. I looked forward to taking him places and stopping by the house and delivering my salutations to him and his wife.

Michelle and I had a tumultuous relationship, which I can admit was a good amount my fault. I was not as fully committed to the relationship, at least not as much as she was. I was more focused on work than making a relationship work. I was a mature adult but was certainly not open with my feelings to anyone, Michelle included. Perhaps a byproduct of my work environment and the volatility of the nature of the business. I was just not able to let emotions take over me, not with anyone; it just wasn't a luxury I could afford.

I enjoyed Michelle's company, and we had so much in common that it was easy for me to take her with me when I had work to do that wasn't heavy. As much as I preferred conducting business by myself, there were times when having a woman with me was advantageous, was enjoyable, and suited me. Typically, I would leave her somewhere as I went out to do what I had to do. Most of these ventures were out-of-town rides where having her with me driving was much appreciated. I never had her meet my people as that wasn't necessary at all.

A good portion of my work at this point in time was selling steroids, a business I started back in my first year of college. I played football, and in my first year, I weighed about 175 pounds, playing middle linebacker. For my weight I was strong, benching over 315 pounds, but compared to some on the team, I pressed a shameful amount of weight. One day in the gym, I saw a 280-pound lineman bench-pressing over 500 pounds. I was in total awe of his power and was immediately curious about how this was possible and how I could achieve such power.

Not long into my inquiry, a teammate broke it down for me. I heard about steroids before but never knew what they were, how they worked, where to get them, or how to use them. Shortly after my first season, I started my first cycle of steroids. A cycle is typically the length of time a person uses the drugs, which can go from six weeks to endlessly. I came to know many people that never went off the drugs. All they would do is either switch up drugs, change doses, or a combination of both. The teammate who told me about the steroids got me a cycle, one injectable testosterone and an oral Winstrol, which was typically a veterinary drug for horses but was also used by humans. I gained twenty pounds and shaved two-tenths of a second off my forty-yard-dash time, which was amazing and unbelievable for me. All this was done in less than two months. I quickly came to the conclusion that I didn't want to pay for my cycle again; rather, I would purchase more than my cycle, sell the rest, and hence, mine would be free. This endeavor grew and slowly became a business for me. Over the coming years, my business grew to encompass importation from other countries and purchasing large quantities both in the United States and abroad. As my business grew, so too did the laws change and become more stringent over time. For my first go-around with steroids, there weren't many laws at all governing the sale of steroids, and they were fairly easy to obtain if you knew where to look. Like in most everything, our government decides they will be the judge, jury, and executioner of all as to what is legal and what isn't. They decide what we can and can't do with our bodies. The laws governing the possession and sales of steroids were enacted after my first year in business.

Nine years later and many more changes to the legality of steroids, I grew tired of the business. Six months before I was to exit the business, I took on a new customer, something I didn't do often and attempted to steer away from. This particular newcomer came recommended by an associate of mine. From the start, he was a decent customer and showed promise. He was located further up north of New York City, and with a market that small and untapped, there was a lack of product. The prices I was able to charge made the relationship worthwhile, or at least it seemed to be.

Generally speaking, I had one customer or associate in a particular market or state. This was my work model designed to control and limit damage. If I were arrested or charged in a particular market, then I could reasonably deduce who told the authorities about me and enact damage control, understanding somewhat what law enforcement might have on me.

One such occasion was the latter part of 1997. Michelle and I were in White Plains, New York, a city just above the Bronx. We were shopping for a dress Michelle needed for her cousin's wedding, which we were invited to. The weather was a bit chilly for a late-September day. A few stores into our search and I received a message on my pager from a number I didn't recognize. It was just after noon, and I was already tired of dress-shopping. With a pay phone nearby, I returned the call with my pocket tone dialer and waited to hear who was reaching out to me. The person was the new associate of mine in the northern part of New York. Coming onto the tail end of a nine-year run selling steroids and building my business, from being a kid in college to becoming a man arranging steroid shipments from multiple countries via boat, plane, mail, or courier, I was growing weary of it. This new associate was whom I looked to for taking over my business. I figured, with some grooming on his part, I could sell the business along with all my contacts around the globe and still receive a small percentage of the profits without doing any additional work and leave the risk alone.

"Yeah," I said into the receiver of the phone when I heard the other party pick up.

"It's me. I need to see you, and can we meet?" my new associate said into the phone.

"Yeah, but it'll take me at least a couple of hours. Where at?" I said, anxiously wanting to cut the dress-shopping short.

"Off the freeway. Take exit Fourteen, and I'll meet you on the side of the road there." My associate told me where because I wasn't that familiar with the area, so I left the location up to him.

"Give me a couple of hours and I'll be there," I said before hanging up.

I already knew more or less what he wanted and already had an assortment with me in the trunk of my car. I informed Michelle that after we finished up here, I would have to make a drop-off and that we could do that after we finished looking in another store or two.

The drive up was uneventful, and seeing the beginning changes in the color of the leaves already meant fall was underway. I knew the area we were to meet in. The freeway was a major one, and I knew the side of the road had a large area to park the car in.

Just shy of two hours and I was nearing the exit to the meeting place. Michelle was half-asleep from the long ride and the tiring day of shopping for dresses. I saw we were about fifteen minutes early and decided to relight my cigar and wait. I looked over, and Michelle was in and out of sleep. Smoking my cigar, I also felt a bit sleepy, and I must have dozed off for a moment as I dropped my cigar on the floor of my car. I bent down to pick it up, and as I was in the process of sitting up in my seat, all hell broke loose. I saw an older sport utility vehicle pull right up in front of my car, stopping ten feet from my bumper. Two men exited the truck, one from the driver's side and one from the passenger side. Before they could make it more than a few feet from their vehicle, I already had someone on my side of the car pointing a 9mm inches from my temple. There was another man next to Michelle with the same scenario happening to her. I didn't see anything that told me these guys were cops. They were dressed in plain clothes, and the one I saw exiting the truck in front of me from the passenger side had a black mock turtleneck sweater on and slicked-back black hair, looking quite Italian. I simply closed my eyes, accepting my fate and waiting for the impact of the bullet.

"Don't you fuckin' move!" the voice next to me said, with the gun trained on my temple.

"Hands, let me see your hands! Place them on the steering wheel." The voice next to me began giving me instructions on how to proceed.

A sense of relief came over me, knowing that the lesser of the two evils—the police—were barking their orders. My first thought was a hit, and I couldn't help but show relief with a small smile on my face. When the mob does their hits, there are never any words or yelling; you rarely see it coming and, most times, don't feel too much.

Michelle and I were taken out of the vehicle, searched, hand-cuffed, and placed in the back of one of the undercover police vehicles. I took that time to reassure her not say a word and be patient. I knew she already knew but thought it prudent to mention it in that moment.

"Shut up. Don't say a word to each other," the detective barked at me for speaking to Michelle.

Apparently, Michelle and I weren't supposed to speak to each other. What were the cops going to do, arrest me again? Then they shouldn't have put us next to each other in the same car.

I knew where my problem originated—that was for sure. I only knew one person in this area, and that was my new associate. These cops were local sheriff's department detectives and not the feds, which meant the events must be something relatively new and not that far-reaching in scope. I was well north of the city, and these local cops treated my arrest like the crime of the century. They had already searched the back of my car and trunk and pulled out the gym bag that contained the steroids I had brought. The ride to the sheriff's station was a blur for me. I had to focus on the next set of moves I had to make, assess the damages, and run damage control.

Entering the sheriff's station, I felt a little claustrophobic. The place was so small it was not to be believed. The amazing part was how it was all self-contained. The station had holding cells, four to be exact, and lined up one next to the other. There was a desk in the middle where the sergeant or duty officer was stationed. There were a couple of offices or interrogation rooms on the left side of the building, just past the holding cells. There was only the desk sergeant in the room at the time with me, Michelle, and the detectives. We were placed in cells next to each other as we waited to get processed and booked. Being allowed one phone call, which turned into a few for me, I phoned my lawyer. I gave him the basic rundown and was told to sit tight. I then was able to phone a couple more people, associates of mine, to warn them I was arrested and so they must beware. I had other numbers for them that didn't trace back to their personal lines.

Whatever was happening and going to happen, I wanted it to end with me and for others to clean up their loose ends and be on alert.

The holding cells had no doors, just bars, and we were able to see everything that was happening. I just couldn't see Michelle, but I would know if she was going to be let out of her cell or vice versa.

I was booked first and then Michelle. They charged us with the same thing, knowing full well that she had nothing to do with the steroid business or any business of mine whatsoever. It was the cops' way of trying to put pressure on both of us to talk. I certainly wasn't going to say anything, and with Michelle's family lineage, I was pretty confident she would remain silent. I didn't feel good having Michelle there with me, being fingerprinted and having her mug shot taken, but it was totally out of my control.

Michelle and I had been sitting in our respective cells for about two hours when the associate I had just taken on, in handcuffs, was led past me. Tears were rolling down his eyes; he was noticeably upset. He looked at me and said, "It wasn't me. I didn't say anything." His voice cracked as he spoke.

All I could do was shake my head in disgust. I shrugged my shoulders and gave him the "oh well." This large man, who was in his early twenties, had tattoos, and was muscled up, was a far cry from the tough guy he had been portraying. His words felt more like he was trying to convince himself that he didn't rat me out to the cops and flip. Reality was setting in on his circumstance as he schlepped by my cell. He was led to the county jail cells that were attached to the back of the sheriff's office.

I had given my associate, as I did all my associates, my attorney Frank's business card. In case of being arrested, they could contact my lawyer for counsel. All my associates had to do was call the number on the card and tell my lawyer they were referred by me. This way, I knew all their legal issues, and in turn, they would be represented by quality counsel. The last thing I told this associate here was that there was nothing he couldn't get out of, but if he chose to go on a different route, ignore my assistance, and cooperate, then there was nothing I could do. Whatever happened after that was out of my hands. Had he done what I instructed him to do, this event would have never happened and I could have been out there, helping him get through whatever situation he was involved in. Instead, I now saw a man shedding tears. These weren't apologetic tears or tears of sadness; they were the tears of a man coming to grips with his fate. The realization that his life wasn't worth the betrayal he perpetrated.

Some months later, I found out that my associate had come upon some bad luck while being held in the county jail and was stabbed to death inside his cell.

Three hours had passed, and the desk sergeant came for Michelle. He handcuffed her and led her out of her cell into one of the interrogation rooms about thirty feet to our right. I didn't want to say anything to her and didn't feel the need to. She knew what to say and what not to say and how to act accordingly. Michelle was taken inside the room, where she was followed by a plainclothes detective. This detective I didn't recognize and wasn't one of those that arrested me. The sergeant soon came out, and Michelle was alone in the interrogation room with the interrogating detective. The interrogating detective was in his early fifties, had salt-and-pepper hair, was five feet, nine inches tall, and was overweight, most noticeably by his jutting gut, which was partially covering the gold badge on his bulging waistline.

I didn't have too much to worry about with Michelle being interrogated; after all, she didn't know much of anything. She knew little about my steroid business and even less about my other work ventures. The worst case was, she could mention people, but I doubted that she knew real names or last names and bits and pieces of things these local yokels had no idea about. My main concern was getting her out of this jam and back, free, to her family without them knowing she had been arrested.

It didn't take very long before Michelle was coming back out of the interrogation room, and I could hear why she was only there for a short time. The detective was fuming, or at least that was what he was portraying, coming out of the room.

"Yeah, we'll see how tough you are," the detective said, leading Michelle out and putting her back in her holding cell.

I was the next on his hit parade, and as soon as Michelle's cell door closed, the detective came for me and opened my cell, handcuffing me and leading me into the same room he and Michelle had just left.

The interrogation room was small, about sixty square feet. There was a metal desk and a chair at the far side of the room and another chair just as you entered it. The chair at the far side was metal and had a metal pipe attached at the base so the detective could handcuff me to the chair, which was firmly planted in the concrete of the floor. I was locked in, and the detective brought his chair a little closer to me and then began his form of interrogation, his interview.

"Your girlfriend didn't want to speak with me. She doesn't care about you."

As he spoke to me, neither one of us batted an eye. We both stared straight at the other. Just as the detective said the last word, I spoke. I wanted there to be no misunderstandings and to let my intentions be clearly understood.

"I'm represented by counsel. His card and number is with my effects. I've already made my phone call to him." I wanted the detective and whoever else might be listening to our conversation to know in no uncertain terms that I wasn't going to speak to anyone without a counsel present.

"Yes, you're welcome to have your attorney. I just have a couple of questions for you."

The detective had his agenda regardless of what I said or what my rights were. Since the detective was ignoring me, I thought I could repeat myself in another fashion and see what buttons could be pressed. I already knew he had some temper issues, so I thought this could be fun.

"I don't know what part of 'I'm waiting for my attorney' was difficult to comprehend, but I've retained counsel."

My response wasn't the response the detective was expecting, judging by the change in his body language, tone of voice, and the losing of control. I could see his heart rate quicken under his shirt. His face turned a bit flusher, and his forehead wrinkled.

"You want to be a wise ass? By the time I'm finished with you, I'm going to charge you in the state, and then I'm going to charge you federally!"

The detective, in all his mediocrity, exposed his ignorance. I couldn't help myself yet again and responded, "I'm no lawyer or anything, but how are you going to charge me with the same crime twice? What kind of cop are you?"

That was the last straw. He nearly lost his ever-lovin' mind and blew a gasket. I got the desired response, all right. The detective hurriedly uncuffed me from the chair, cuffed me up again with my hands behind my back, and ushered me out of the interrogation room at a quick pace. The whole time I could feel him behind me, breathing heavily in his frustration at me and my cool responses. He was telling me things like I was going to regret this and was muttering things under his breath. I couldn't help myself and responded with a sly smirk. I got my desired result and knew these cops were not only amateurs but also didn't have too much on me aside from the assorted bag of steroids they took from the trunk of my car and the phone call I made to my associate arranging to meet.

It was about nine thirty at night now, and Michelle and I were about to be arraigned. A slight man with dark hair and unassuming features came into the sheriff's station. I quickly surmised it was a judge there to arraign us. I didn't think they would awaken a judge on a Sunday night to come down there and do all this, but again, this must have been a big case for the sheriff's department. First, the judge read the charges to Michelle and formally charged her, and next, it was my turn. The charges we both received were possession of a controlled substance and possession of a controlled substance with the intent to distribute. I was a bit surprised that in this small town, they would awaken a judge to come to the jail and arraign us. I thought that would have been saved until the morning. This was another sign that this arrest wasn't the normal occurrence, or I believed there would have been a more-effective way to effect the process than awaken a judge on a Sunday. Either that or they thought it a priority to charge me fast.

I made arrangements for bail but knew that nothing would happen until the morning anyway. Hell, it was Sunday and already now going on close to ten at night.

After being arraigned, Michelle and I were given the standard-issue county-inmate T-shirt and green jumper. We had to shower and delouse before putting on the standard-issue clothing. As we were escorted back to the county jail attached to the back of the sheriff's department, I told Michelle not to call anyone or do anything and that by morning, I would have her out on bail. My main concern was getting her out. Our bail was set at ten thousand a piece. I didn't mind my being where I was, but it was paramount to get Michelle released as soon as possible. The phones in the jails let you call, but all calls were collect calls, unless you dialed from an officer's phone, which wasn't going to happen. If she dialed the pay phone and her family on the other end hears it's a collect call from an inmate at whatever correctional facility, I would not be in a good position. To her grandfather I would be considered the cause of Michelle getting arrested, and even though it was over steroids, you can't tell an old-school Italian gangster that it's not drugs. The end result was, my life would be worth less than zero.

Michelle was off to the women's section of the jail and I, the man's section. I noticed some offices on the left before I made my way into my section, and I gathered those were the administrative offices and the officers' offices.

This particular county jail wasn't as large as most—well, most of the ones I had been in in my short life span. Not only smaller but also not as populated, from what I saw. I was brought into the section where I would be staying. Walking in the first set of doors, I noticed there were eight cells in a row, each with its own door. In the state and county system, most facilities have electronic door openings. The federal system has the old key system where each door must be locked and unlocked with a physical key. From what I've gathered, if the electric were to go out, then the feds would still be able to operate with less issues with their lock-and-key system. Each door to the cells was visible from the walkway, which was solely for the officer's use, and completely safe from interactions between inmates. In between the walkway the guards used and the individual cells was another row of bars that made it even harder for an inmate to get out. If someone were to escape, he would have to get through the individual cell door then through another set of bars and yet another to get to the guards' walkway. The walkway connected the different units of the building. At the end of the tier was a pay phone. If our cell doors were opened, we could potentially use the phone while still being well secured on the tier. The inmates would be allowed to use the pay phone when it was the proper time indicated by the jail. My cell was the last one down at the end of the tier. I reached the seventh cell and realized someone was occupying it. I stepped inside it, and the door behind me closed. With a metal bed with no pillow, blanket, or amenities to speak of aside from my own sink and toilet, it was far from the Hilton. It took me a moment to get my bearings, and then a voice from the cell next to me let me know exactly where I was. The guard had just left the unit, and I heard it.

"Hey, what you in for?" the voice from next door inquired.

I said the bare minimum to get the guy off my back and to also put the conversation to an end quickly. "I don't know."

"You don't know why you're here?"

"No!" I said with a firmer tone and then headed to my bed, for lack of a better term.

I wouldn't put it past the cops to put someone in the cell next to me to get me to admit to something or speak on something that the cops could use against me. I never spoke about anything even to my own people, so why would I speak to some skell that was either some degenerate at best or a cop at the worst?

"Well, you have to know something about your charges." The skell couldn't just let it die.

"No offense, but I'm not in the mood for conversation." I let it die right there, and that was the end of the brief chat.

I found it odd that in the entire facility, this guy would be next to me when there were a lot more open cells for him to be in. Then right away, I got bombarded with chatter. Jail 101 is, never ask why someone is there and what they did to get there. This guy both didn't know jail etiquette or knew it and was a cop. I never asked questions to anyone outside in the world past the necessary ones that pertained to business and my life, safety, and freedom.

The lights never fully went out and the guards walkway was always lit especially for their hourly round of checking on us. To say the least, I wasn't going to be getting a good night's sleep. The "mattress" was only a couple of inches thick and was very flimsy. It was like sleeping on an autopsy table. I stared at the gray ceiling, in and out of a light sleep. I didn't know when the next count was, losing track of the minutes in between the hour check. The count came at the top of every hour when a guard would enter the tier and count the inmates and make sure everyone was accounted for and still breathing.

The second guard count of the night and I was sleeping, although very lightly. My body and mind were tired from the ordeal, and any sleep I could steal, I tried to. Unexpectedly, the door to the tier opened, and automatically, I awoke from my semislumber. Not wanting the guard to know I was awake, I didn't stir. Then I was forced to move when something happened that was never a good thing: my cell door opened. This was well after midnight, and there was no good reason why my door would be opened. I immediately got up. Jail's no place for unexpected activity on either side. There wasn't much space in my cell and there certainly was nowhere to go, but I wanted my back to the wall, or in this case, the back of my cage, in case someone was planning on coming in and giving me an unwanted surprise. The guard who walked on the tier saw me and, in one motion, put his finger to his mouth, telling me to be quiet. Then he put is hand to his face, signifying as if a telephone were in his hand and he was speaking. He pointed to the pay phone at the end of my tier. He was six feet tall, white, but looked Italian and had me thinking of other scenarios, none of which had a happy ending for me. The guard didn't look menacing. I was still a bit in shock and could not believe what I was being told. I cautiously stepped to the front of my cell and peeked out. Nobody else was on the tier besides the guard, the skell who was also waking up, and me. I saw the guard walk down the walkway and out the other door. The skell, of course, asked me yet again who I was and why I was allowed out of my cell and he wasn't. Shit, I didn't even dignify that with a response; I was still trying to figure this thing out. He was as surprised as I was, and I had no time for him. I peeked my head out of my cell, looking like I was trying to cross a busy street expecting, traffic. Cautiously I made my way out of my cell, down past the skell and at the end of our tier to the pay phone.

I still had a few other associates I wanted to reach out to that I had the safe numbers of. I also wanted to reach out to my parents and let them know where I was. I did that not for anything else besides a little insurance policy. I didn't trust my associates much, and I was in a situation where I was still unsure the jail I was in was totally safe. If something nefarious were to befall me, at the very least I wanted someone I knew that had my best interest at heart to know where I was and to let them have some idea of the circumstances. You can never be too cautious about anything, especially in my lifestyle. I never put anything past anyone anywhere at any time under any circumstances. People's actions under stress, pressure, or payoff are at times unpredictable, so I expect the unexpected and plan for the worst-case scenario while planning for the best-case scenario. I called my attorney again just because of the circumstances and informed Frank why I was calling. I knew the call would be recorded some- where in a log as well as with him, and I tried to cover every base I could. With all my loose ends cleaned up, I went back to my cell before the guard came back for his next round. The guard entered a few minutes after I was in my cell. He didn't bat an eye or miss a step and went about his usual routine. He passed through the tier and out the other door as usual, closing my cell door electronically.

I got to sleep a bit better and wasn't so much on edge as before I was let out to use the pay phone. It had been a few hours more when again, I was awakened by my cell door being opened. This time, the guard spoke. It was the same guard, except this time he told me that there was a call for me in the sergeant's office. I walked down my tier to the end, where I was let out by the *friendly* guard. I asked him the time, and he said it was nearly 6:00 a.m. I didn't want to ask many questions but had to ask this time as I was led out.

"Can you tell me about this phone call?" I asked the guard and thought he would be a little forthcoming if he could, being that he let me out of my room and broke policy.

"I can't tell you too much. They wouldn't tell me anything besides to bring you to the sergeant's office. I know you have a call there, and that is about it."

I could tell the guard was speaking honestly and that he was a mere pawn in the game. Why was I receiving calls in jail? Why was I able to use a pay phone in the middle of the evening? I didn't voice my questions; rather, I decided to keep them limited to my inner voice.

The guard and I exited our block and went back the way I had come in. A series of twists and turns, through a door, and we were at the group of offices I saw as I came into the county jail. To my surprise, Michelle was there as well, standing against the wall opposite the offices. She had her head down and looked visibly upset. She didn't lift her head to see me coming even though I knew she felt my presence. Not acknowledging me was a telltale sign that something was tragically wrong. I knew we weren't supposed to be speaking with each other, but again, what were they going to do, arrest me?

"You all right?" I asked as I was just a few feet from her, waiting to enter the sergeant's office.

I didn't get a verbal response. What I got was Michelle lifting her head, and I saw the tears cascading down her olive cheeks. I didn't say anything further, and then for some reason, it hit me. In my heart of hearts I knew what would make her cry like that.

"You called home?"

Michelle's response was a heavier flow of tears. My question was rhetorical as I was fairly certain of the answer, and her physical response was proof enough. Subconsciously, I knew the answer and perhaps was hoping against all hopes I was wrong. My heart sank, leaving me with a whirlwind of thoughts and emotions, none of which had a happy ending. I had to hold my composure as the sergeant called me into his office.

"Sit down. Have a seat." The sergeant instructed me to sit in a chair across the desk from him, with the guard that brought me in standing next to me.

My mind raced through what I already expected Michelle's grandfather had had set in motion; after all, he was a very resourceful man, to say the least. Her grandfather and entire family now knew she was in county jail with me and knew I was the cause. But that was not the worst of it; her grandfather would now already know the charges and would consider it a drug offense. None of my deductions comforted me in the slightest. This man was old-school in his ways. Michelle was his pride and joy, and here I was, getting her in trouble with the law in an offense I knew he would consider a death sentence for.

"There are detectives at your house, and they're attempting to gain access to it. They have a search warrant but say there are dogs there. Do you have dogs?" the sergeant queried.

"Yes, I have two dogs."

"I'm going to call the lead detective there and let him know you're here with me, and we'll see how to get the dogs out of your house so they can proceed with the search."

The detective proceeded to dial the phone as I tried to formulate a way to get my dogs out of the house from where I was. I owned two pit bulls that were not only fiercely loyal to me but also quite protective of both my property and me.

"Yes, I have him here with me now. Okay, I'll pass him over to you," the sergeant said into the phone.

The sergeant passed me the phone, and I lifted it to my ear. "Yes?" I said into the receiver.

The voice I heard on the other end of the receiver wasn't as pleasant as the ones I was just hearing, but I expected as much.

"We're outside your home right now, attempting to effect this search warrant, and if we're not able to gain access, we're going to be forced to enter and shoot your dogs if we have to. Is there anyone you can contact to get here and contain the dogs so we can enter the house?"

"Yes, I have my brother or father I can reach, and they can get my dogs."

"Well, they need to hurry because we're not waiting long to do this search. Hurry up!"

I handed the phone to the sergeant, not wanting to even dignify the detective's response with an answer. I merely told the sergeant that I needed to make a couple of calls and see where either my brother or father were and get them to go to my house. This location the cops were at was my parents' house, and their business wasn't far away. I used my parents' house as an address where I lived, at least to the authorities. I didn't keep much there, and most of it was stored in a safe I installed in the basement. I did have some odds and ends of steroids in the house, mostly in my bedroom, with some human growth hormone in the refrigerator. I hid my silencers in the basement safe along with some bombs I had built. I had other explosives in different stages of completion, and the majority of that was in the safe. I wasn't sure what the scope of the search warrant was going to be and couldn't just ask the cops either. Not even my parents knew of the safe, and I wasn't going to volunteer any information about it. That just wasn't me at all to speak much on anything I was doing, did, or going to do.

I was finally able to locate my brother, and he was at the house as he answered his phone. My dogs were safely put away, and the search was underway.

I would classify this as a low point of my life on every level. I was now in custody, my girlfriend's well-connected grandfather was aware I was the reason she was in jail for what he considered to be drugs, and to top it off, I had some of the tools of the trade at my parents' house, which was being searched. My parents and family didn't know details of my life, but they weren't ignorant. They knew I was involved in something, but we never spoke about it. Don't ask, don't tell sort of thing. My family is like that in every sense of the word. We're all adults and responsible for our own actions, good, bad, or indifferent.

I thought that if certain items were found, I wouldn't be getting out anytime soon, let alone getting bail. This was a particularly dark time for me, and the light at the end of the tunnel was but a pinprick in the darkness. Whether I made bail or not, I figured the value of my life was now worth diddly-squat. I was in danger whether I stayed in here or whether I got out. My main concern was getting Michelle out as fast as possible. I didn't even want to get out, at least not before getting her out first.

I was escorted back to my cell and sat there for about another four uneasy hours. Every second felt like minutes and minutes like hours. I was helpless, a prisoner of my own thoughts. In my mind I didn't know if it was safer for me to get bailed out or to sit locked in this cage. My options were limited, and the unknown was my enemy.

A quarter after nine in the morning, and the guard entered the tier. The count and hourly check were already done, so I knew it was something else. Sure enough, my cell door opened, and the guard proceeded to tell me that I was getting bailed out. I got to the door of the tier and, right before exiting, asked the guard if Michelle was getting bailed out, and he told me that she was. Not until I reached the property clerk's desk to gather my possessions did I learn who had bailed Michelle and I out. My father's' signature was on the paper-work, allowing Michelle and I to walk out of the sheriff's station. My father and I had differing views on most everything. We did, though, have many of the same traits and characteristics that I would come to realize much later in life. He and I butted heads so often because we were so much alike in character, so he was the last person I thought would have bailed me out of jail. We didn't really have the best of relationships, both of us being so strong willed and stubborn. Looking back at our relationship now, I can see I would have acted in the same manner as he did through most of everything. My father was responsible, either directly or indirectly, with instilling me the characteristics of being a man, which I couldn't realize until I was able to understand them and him.

I remember walking with Michelle out of the sheriff's station, not knowing if I was going to get killed going to my father's waiting car. I couldn't help but think that having Michelle with me walking out upped my odds of living, if even temporarily. My father was driving, and my eldest brother rode shotgun. I was hoping someone else was going to bail me out if I had to be. Not for anything else besides me wanting to do things on my own and not having to involve my family in my affairs or be beholding to my father. In the end, my father acted as many fathers would do and how most would hope their father would, protecting their children.

Now that I was released, my concern switched to getting back to my house and seeing what was found and what wasn't. Damage control was the number-one priority. The next moves I was to make depended on what had transpired and who knew what about which things. If the detectives did their job, I wondered why I even got bail in the first place. A part of me knew they didn't find the main instruments that would've probably made my bail so high that getting out wouldn't have been an option.

I got home, and my brother brought me a copy of the search warrant and explained to me that the police searched my bedroom only. Apparently, because I wasn't the primary owner of the home, the search was limited to the space that was entirely mine, and that was my bedroom. I breathed a sigh of relief, knowing that what was in my bedroom was just some odds and ends of steroids.

In the bedroom, there were some drawers turned inside out, clothes strewn about, and my closet in a little bit of disarray. The small amount of steroids that was taken and marked on the inventory list of what the detectives took wasn't anything that would add new charges to me. I next wanted to check my refrigerator, which had a dozen or so boxes of growth hormone in it, and after I opened the door, I saw it was not disturbed at all. The final inspection was of the basement, where I had the items that would have landed me behind bars for a lengthy period. By some stroke of luck or divine intervention, the cops didn't venture down to my work area. My safe was untouched, and with the tools of my trade undisturbed, I felt more confident that not only my case but also the worst of my legal woes had not been realized. The worse of my personal woes was yet to reveal itself, and reckoning would soon follow.

My silencers were untouched, and I was thankful, as each carried a seven-year sentence. I never had my silencers and guns in the same place at the same time unless it was time to go to work. I was currently fitting my .380 automatic for silencers and had some of the pieces to the gun at my home, but the barrel was in the shop where I had the silencers made. The shop was at a fellow associate's basement. He had an out-of-the-way, quiet, rural place, where little suspicion would be brought to me and my arms-making activities. Each individual silencer matched one particular gun. My associate and I would take the gun, disassemble it, take the barrel, and bore it out so the silencer we crafted would screw into the front of the barrel, hence making each gun and silencer a one-of-a-kind match. This would mean the cops would have to have the gun and silencer in the same place at the same time in order to prove the piece of metal was an actual silencer and not just a lightweight piece of metal.

The process for making the silencers was relatively easy once the materials and knowhow were there. My associate worked for a company that did work with NASA, the space agency. The company had an extremely lightweight metal alloy that was perfect in size and weight for crafting silencers. We figured out a way to pack the silencer with a material that would muffle the noise of the bullet passing through the gun and exiting through the silencer. Through practice, we discovered that seven shots were the ideal number of bullets that could pass through with a limited amount of noise made. Slowly, the packing of the silencer would blow apart, making each shot a little noisier than the last. After the seventh shot, the noise would become more recognizable. My associate and I both felt that if more than seven shots were needed to be used, then you were either a bad shot or in the wrong line of work. I did, however, have one person I crafted silencers for. He had a unique type of gun. I knew him from the gym where I trained, and he was a man of respect. We became friendly, friendly enough where the topic of weaponry came about. We met one evening after working out, and he asked me if I could fit a gun for him. We went to his truck, where he had the weapon he wanted to show me. He proceeded to show me a Uzi submachine gun. I had never heard of an Uzi with a silencer. Silencers were generally used for close-contact use and for a more accurate kill to occur. I didn't understand the purpose for fitting Uzi's with a silencer, but then again, it was none of my concern what he did with it, nor did I care to know. He saw my puzzled face as I examined his weapon. I took his weapon and brought it to my associate's shop to see if this was possible. My associate gave me the same look I had given the owner of the Uzi. The only difference was, my associate and I could speak freely with each other. He asked me the question I had in my head but didn't ask. That was "What the hell is the reason of fitting an Uzi with a silencer?" Hell, I had no idea and got right to work. I did as I was asked and returned it to him in less than a week. Shortly thereafter, I got his order for an entire case of Uzi's he wanted fitted in just the same manner.

It had been a week since I had been let out on bail, and I slept in a different location each night. I couldn't stay in my home, where my parents were, as I didn't want to have any heat or violence to be brought there. There had been enough aggravation already at my parents' home, and they didn't need to see or be involved in anything further. I had other locations to stay in, but those didn't feel safe to me, and I thought that moving around was my best option for remaining healthy. I slept in random parking lots, at the back of my friend's gym that was a day care during the day, or at another associate's garage and never in the same place twice. I didn't know what Michelle's grandfather had planned for me, and there was nobody that could intervene on my behalf. Michelle kept telling me that her grandfather wanted to see me and sit down with me. Since the day after we got bailed out, she had been sending me messages that her grandfather wanted to meet with me. There was no reason for me to go meet him as we didn't work with each other, and I felt I didn't owe him anything. Aside from dating Michelle, I felt no obligation to her family. In my mind I was going to do the right thing and take the weight of the charges, whatever the case, but he didn't fully know that. So a meet, yes. A talk? Well, I was not so sure there would have been a lot of talking. Michelle acted as if it wasn't such a bad thing to just meet him and talk about things. She was either being naive, in denial about who her grandfather truly was and what he was capable of, or facilitating my murder.

The week following our getting bailed out came to an end, and Michelle's insistence continued; I felt pressure and was worn down from the stress. I didn't want to duck and dodge her grandfather any longer. I ignored the overtures long enough and finally caved in. I called Michelle and told her to arrange the sit-down with her grandfather. A *sit-down* is a meeting between two parties that either have a dispute or differences, and at the sit-down is where those issues are worked out and generally through an intermediary. An underworld sit-down can range the gambit of choosing sides, dividing up assets, a decision on one side or another, or the worst-case scenario, death. Being that we had no business dealings, there were really no sides to take. I was facing either a severe tongue-lashing or the worst-case scenario. With me out of the way, the case would fall apart, and her grandfather's uncertainty of what I would do would be resolved. I wouldn't be able to tell from Michelle which side of the fence her grandfather was on. He wouldn't reveal his feelings or intentions; probably, the opposite would be true. When someone is marked for death, the path of least resistance is used in getting the job completed. The closest ones to you are usually the ones that are used to facilitate the task. The target of the murder is meant to feel comfortable, relaxed, to let his guard down and be lulled into a false sense of security. How many times was I on the other side of the hunt? Perhaps some of the hunted from my past felt the same way I was feeling now. The emotions I'd been experiencing the past seven days were some of the lowest moments I had. Either way this meeting would go, I wanted closure. I'd never been one to avoid this type of issue and didn't want to start now. Head up, head on, and straightforward!

The sit-down I agreed to was set for the following day after I told Michelle I would meet her grandfather. Her grandfather chose their own family house for the meeting. This was a location where I felt comfortable at, was familiar with; yet again, it was not a good place to meet in as her grandfather knew I would feel comfortable.

I arrived at Michelle's house by myself, as was expected, and also unarmed, which was not an option. I didn't notify anyone besides Michelle about me going there and decided to let the chips fall where they might. I was already resigned to my fate. Michelle's house was almost always alive with some activity or people about. Another part I felt uncomfortable about was that Michelle had picked me up and dropped me off. That too was part of the events that made me more than concerned. There wasn't even a car to dispose of if the sit-down went bad for me.

I didn't even have to ring the doorbell. As I got to the door, it opened before I could knock or ring the bell. Expecting her grandfather to be there, instead, I was greeted by Michelle's father. Her father was a hulking mass of a man who, to the best of my knowledge, had nothing to do with the underworld, but now, I was having second thoughts on that. He didn't even say a word to me but, instead, just held the door open for me to pass through and enter into the downstairs half of the duplex where Michelle lived with her parents and siblings.

The first thing I noticed was the eerie silence of the house, and once I entered the doorway and was into the house, there stood Michelle's grandfather. He was standing directly behind a high-back chair. The chair was positioned on top of a plastic covering the carpeted floor. I had never paid too much attention to the plastic before, but now it was what drew my attention. I couldn't help but think that the plastic would be a great drop cloth. Typically, if there's some sort of drop cloth beneath where you're sitting, that's the telltale sign you're fucked.

Michelle's father instructed me to sit in the high-back chair, and he took his position just off to my right, out of direct sight. Her grandfather, still in silence, stood directly behind me. There was a period of silence that had me thinking this was it. The first thing that came to my mind was to put my head down and close my eyes. The last sight I was going to see was the heavy plastic beneath my feet, so I preferred not to look. My eyes closed, I resigned myself to my fate and awaited my judgment. I was there out of respect for Michelle's grandfather, and while my trespass was simply having his granddaughter with me, it was, in his eyes, an offense he needed to address personally.

Would I hear the hammer fall down? Would I be that lucky to get it over with swiftly, or was this one of those long, drawn-out, torturous affairs?

"What the fuck were you thinking?" a voice came across my left shoulder. It was the distinctive gruff voice of Michelle's grandfather. I didn't act at first or even move. It took me a few moments to do anything at all besides keep my head down and eyes closed. I opened my eyes after a few seconds and lifted my head a few inches and proceeded to endure the rhetorical rant.

"You got my granddaughter involved with this junk? Did you ever use her for anything or have her work?" Michelle's grandfather continued saying.

I still wasn't out of the woods. The old man wanted to know if she was involved or if I had her involved in anything at all. He knew she was with me a couple of times in Mexico and thought that I might have had her smuggling steroids back. He wanted to hear it directly from me and then decide whether I was lying to save my ass or telling the truth. He would ultimately decide one way or another what he considered fact or fiction.

"No, sir," I said with the only response that was appropriate.

This was no time to elaborate on answers; a simple yes or no would suffice. I only wanted to answer in the shortest form possible the questions that were asked. My life hung in the balance, and regardless, I was going to tell the truth. I had nothing to hide in my actions, and I let my character and the man I was stand the inquisition.

"The only reason you're not dead right now is because you didn't rat on that other case."

I assumed he was referring to the case I was on the run for in New Jersey. The old man and I never spoke about anything about my allegiances, alliances, my work, or cases I was involved with. True to his character, he was very well-informed and more informed, as I would soon find out as he continued his verbal tirade.

"I never tell a man how to make his living, but you got my granddaughter involved with this junk."

To the old-timers, everything that was even remotely classified as drugs was considered junk. Yes, it's true that there were guys involved in the drug business, and there were top gangsters that looked the other way and took money for it too while pretending not to know what was going on. Michelle's grandfather was true to the letter of the law and abhorred all drug dealing and banned it from anyone that he interacted with or worked for him or the organized crime family.

"You're going to do whatever you have to do to get her out of this. No more newspapers or publicity."

When Michelle and I were arrested, we were in the local newspapers for the case. My brother saw me on television. Even my brother's wife heard the event on the radio the following morning as she drove to work.

Michelle's grandfather was old-school mafioso and believed in staying out of the news and the public eye. I agreed with his sentiment as well; we were from the same school of thought. I had no control over the matter, but he wanted to voice his position, none of which were optional. He wanted a quiet solution to the current situation, of which I was in total agreement.

"Yes, sir, I will." I felt the need to chime in and let him know I was still listening and on board, as if I had a choice.

"You have a place to hide out until this thing blows over? Maybe that place in New Jersey."

True to form, Michelle's grandfather was a wealth of investigated information. He already knew of everything and was even aware of things I had forgotten about and had not thought of.

"Yes, sir, I do."

"That place down in Jersey, you still have that?" he said, asking but knowing the answer.

I still had a place down in Jersey that I owned. It was a piece of property I took off a guy that owed me for a loan-sharking debt he couldn't pay. The property had a little shack on it but was prime real estate. How the fuck he knew about that, I had no idea, but nothing surprised me about the old man.

"Yes, sir, I do," I said.

"Good, when I need to, I'll reach out to you. Until then, you lie low and don't get into any more trouble. If you have to go away to prison, you'll be taken care of, and you'll do your time."

"Yes, sir." I again was keeping my answers short and respectful.

"You're not going to rat anyone out in Brooklyn either, are you?"

By *Brooklyn* he was referring to the Mafia family I worked for there. A different family than his, but still he knew all. I wasn't working as much as I had been in years past but was still working and living part-time there. Informed, he surely was. I wasn't out of the woods yet; more key questions were coming up, and not only the old man but others as well apparently wondered if I was going to talk to avoid going to prison.

"Never, sir, never," I said emphatically.

Respect and reputation were the mainstays of a man of my lifestyle. One must conduct oneself with elevated character as it followed you in and through some of the strangest places and when you least expected it.

My case was winnable, but that meant going to trial and more publicity. Something I was specifically told not to do. Had I taken the trial route, I never would have made it to the trial in the first place and, hence, find out if I would have beaten the case. The point was moot anyway. I was to get the best deal possible, admit my guilt, and take blame for everything, which included Michelle's charges, stacking them with mine.

Michelle was right; her grandfather respected me as a man. I handled my business while keeping my mouth shut, even if at my own detriment. I viewed it another way. I made my choices in life and lived my life a certain way. I did the best I could to avoid issues, prison, or otherwise, but when they are upon me, I must be true to my character and conduct myself as a man. If one sticks to basic codes, ethics, and character, he is a man of respect. When events change and challenge you, it's just par for the course.

My character and record withstood the grilling, and the old man was satisfied with my responses because I walked out of the sit-down healthy and unscathed. This wasn't the outcome I was expecting, but sometimes it feels good to be wrong.

The following months were a series of trials and tribulations with vast life changes. This current arrest put me on the radar of law enforcement when prior to it, I was a mere blip on the radar screen. To the best of my knowledge, I wasn't a target of any investigation before this arrest. I thought I was a cursory figure at best in the eyes of law enforcement. The conclusion of the sheriff's department that arrested me turned out to be a fifty-page report. Fifty-page report. What the hell was there to report on that needed that many pages in the first place? The report was full of speculation and hypothesizing in those pages, but fair to say, they weren't too far off the mark. The sheriff had squeezed information from my associate that flipped, but he didn't know names, dates, or times, simply bits of pieces he knew and threw at them. Most of what he gave was speculative, put together from our dealings. The report attempted to link my dealings with foreigners based on the origin of particular steroids. Some were correct, although the cops had no facts other than the language written on the boxes and packaging. Then the report also gave some references about my organized crime connections, mainly from past associations given to them through other law enforcement agencies they had spoken to.

I was referred to as a menace to society, the largest steroid dealer in the tristate area (New York, New Jersey, and Connecticut). To be honest, I didn't even drive into Connecticut that often, let alone sell steroids there. New York and New Jersey, that was a separate issue altogether. I was a larger dealer but didn't consider myself the biggest, but then again, it could have been true. Perhaps that was my attempt at modesty. After all, I had been building my steroid business over the past decade, and I had forged many international relationships along with those in the United States. I still did work for the Italians, but not so much daily.

While my case was in limbo, I couldn't shake the uneasy feeling I felt. A feeling that my associates with both the Italian and/or Russian organized crime groups were sensing I could be a potential lose end. That maybe they didn't want a loose end around, just in case. The old adage among us was always "Why take a chance?" I couldn't blame them for thinking it, and hopefully, I was more valuable alive than dead. My friend Anthony fell in the loose-end category, and from my point of view, it wasn't true. I was neither Italian nor Russian. Irish, for the most part, was my lineage, but I had some German in me. I made money with and for the Russians but wasn't Russian. I worked with the Italians and, for some time, was their go-to guy for special jobs. I saw firsthand when both dealt with a potential problem or a question of whether someone might turn to an informant.

What exactly is a man's value or future value? What's the risk versus the reward? Who decides the fate of others? I was constantly judged by my present activities and my future-day value. All the while, my fate was being weighed against the risk of harm to those that decided people's fate. The random pat-downs and strip-searches by my associates didn't bother me in the slightest. To me, those cautions meant I was still useful and my associates and crew were just being cautious.

The next sit-down with Michelle's grandfather was set in a restaurant he chose that was relatively close to his house. I wanted to have a little more security, so I had Michelle drop me off a block away from the meeting spot. I did all I could to make sure I would leave alive. Just because I had walked away from the first one alive didn't mean I was going to walk away from the next one alive as well. This next summit was called by the old man under the guise of discussing a strategy for the case. In this instance, my lawyer, Frank, would be present, and he decided on bringing Joey, a young lawyer who worked for Frank at his firm. I had known Joey since he began working at the firm four years prior.

Joey was probably about my height, six feet tall. He was slender, though, and to me had more of a geeky look to him. His suits looked like they were off-the-rack. His look appeared to be something trapped in the eighties, complete with a hairstyle that matched. He was every bit Italian, but definitely more on the legal side than anything else there could be.

The old man picked the perfect spot to meet in that was completely beneficial to him and left me at a disadvantage. The front window of the restaurant allowed him to see outside from where he would be sitting. He could see someone entering or passing by the restaurant with ease.

I walked through the front door at exactly fifteen minutes before eleven in the morning. I knew the lunch was scheduled for eleven, but I had to be at least a couple of minutes earlier and certainly did not want to be late. I wasn't alone. The old man was already there, positioned at the table he chose to be most advantageous. To the left of the door was a separate dining area, but that was empty. To the right were eight tables of which the old man was sitting, facing the door and window. Our table was near the back of the room and dining area. The bar was in another back room with some tables and was partially enclosed so it appeared each room for dining was its separate spot.

It was a bit early for lunch, but to not have anyone in the restaurant at all was a bit odd for me. I saw one man exit the back room and walk toward us as I greeted the old man. I made sure I approached him directly and gave him a hug and a kiss on the cheek. The kiss signified a sign of respect and acknowledgment. Whatever the circumstances, I didn't hold any kind of ill will toward him. He was in the right, and I had no ground to feel otherwise.

We each had mutual respect for each other; even though this incident with the arrest happened, that was no cause for respect to be lost.

"You sit here next to me," Michelle's grandfather said in his gruff voice. "When I have something to say to you, I want you close to me, and I don't want anyone else hearing what I tell you. You got it?"

"Yes, sir," I said.

The old man had a way of getting his point of view across with his raspy, broken English. He never spoke directly about something, a language that I understood completely.

I took the seat to his left and waited for the moment when it was proper to speak. This was a completely different world with a completely different set of rules. I learned the rules young and understood protocol almost instinctively. It was almost as if this lifestyle chose me.

He offered me a glass of wine and then proceeded to tell me, boasted even, about the wine and other aspects of his lifestyle. I think part of it was him inviting me into his world a little more while posturing his status and well earned respect. None of this was needed for me, but he wanted to speak, so who was I to say anything?

"Here, try some of this. I have them stored downstairs in the wine cellar for me for when I'm here," the old man said as he poured me the wine the waiter just brought.

The waiter, I later surmised, was the "owner" of the establishment. I say *owner* because what I also surmised was that Michelle's grandfather owned this restaurant and many more throughout the tristate area.

We drank our first sip of wine, toasting to each other. He was right; this was an extraordinary vintage, and I understood why the old man had an affinity for it. He also wanted to let me know how much the wine cost, and at over $800 a bottle, we ended up going through four bottles that day. He told me the wine cellar was filled with this particular wine, and I had zero doubt about that.

As we concluded our first glass together and we had our small talk, my lawyer, Frank, walked in with his protégé, Joey. I greeted both Frankie and Joey with hugs and kisses on the cheeks, as was the correct greeting. Joey had picked up his dress a bit more especially since the four years since we first met. Frankie must have advised him on upping his game and that this was a meeting that he couldn't slouch on.

Italian music echoed throughout the surround sound of the eatery. With the ambience of the restaurant, the wine being poured, the four of us were in the midst of our conversation. Well, really three of us, as Joey was on the sidelines, really, listening with rare instances of input.

Our third bottle of wine just being poured, we we're finishing appetizers when I noticed a man pass by the window of the restaurant. The case was being discussed, and seeing the man pass by the window had me feeling a little uneasy. As far as I was concerned, the case was cut-and-dried. I couldn't go to trial and would have to plead guilty to whatever the best deal possible would be. Michelle's charges would then be dropped and dismissed. The man passing in front of the restaurant looked in the window and seemed surprised at what he saw inside and proceeded to walk in, heading in our direction.

Five feet, nine inches tall, of stocky build, early fifties in age, with black hair mixed with a little gray running through it, dressed in slacks and a long sleeve dress shirt, the man caught the old man's attention right away, and it was obvious they knew each other.

"Hey, what are you doing here?" the stranger asked, focusing his remarks and attention at the old man.

"We're having a little lunch. Why not sit down and join us?" the old man said as they hugged, kissed, and exchanged their apparent mutual respect for each other.

The old man always took the lead, and it was quite apparent that everyone bowed to his will.

"Why don't you sit down here in between us?" The old man directed the stranger to sit between him and me.

I moved one chair over as the new arrival sat between me and the old man.

"I was in the neighborhood, passing through. I had a couple of errands to run," the stranger said as he sat down, and we were introduced by the old man.

"Why not have a glass of wine with us?" the old man asked. Even when it sounded like there were options, the old man wasn't asking; he was telling you politely.

After we were introduced, I can honestly say I couldn't remember the stranger's name, and in retrospect, it probably wasn't even his real name anyway.

We had a little small talk and drank a bit. Not too much longer, the old man got up from the table, excusing himself to use the restroom. Just as he passed the corner and was out of view, the stranger leaned in and had me lean into him so he could whisper in my ear. He put his hairy-knuckled left arm around the back of my chair. With his mouth a little less than six inches from my ear, he spoke in a soft, gruff, direct tone. He didn't waste time or mince words.

"I just got out of prison. Did twenty-five years. You're going to get that girl out of trouble. We'll take care of you while you're away, but you will take care of this, or I'll kill you. If you understand me, just nod your head yes," the stranger said, waiting for my response, which was given immediately.

The stranger spoke as if I had any other options. While in my view, this wasn't necessary, apparently, the old man thought otherwise and brought this knuckle-dragger in here to have a heart-to-heart with me.

"Now lift your glass and drink your wine as we toast to each other," the stranger said as he lifted his glass, keeping his eyes locked on mine.

The old man returned shortly after the stranger and I toasted and drank. A brief couple of minutes and my newfound friend, the stranger, excused himself from the table, saying he had some errands to run.

"You have to leave so soon?" the old man said, as if he were still reading the script to the play that was over.

"Unfortunately, yes," the stranger responded, keeping with his copy of the script.

I don't think anyone else at the table knew about what just transpired, least of all Joey. Joey was new to these types of meetings, while Frank wasn't. I could tell Frank was trying to break Joey into being not only an attorney of quality but also an attorney that specialized in special cases involving the underworld. By the looks of it, Joey was still green around the gills and didn't quite comprehend certain scenarios. Frank represented a good number of organized crime figures, and this was a perfect training ground to bring Joey in and show him what to expect and how to conduct himself. Frank being of Italian descent from an Italian neighborhood made that portion of his clientele that much more comfortable hiring him. Not to mention the most important fact that Frank was one hell of a counselor. It seemed that he always had a solution to a problem and knew a lot of people in all facets of the legal system.

Frank first introduced Joey to me one day when Frank came to see me about some legal assistance I inquired about. This was about four years prior, when I was twenty-three and had hustled together about a hundred thousand and built myself a health food restaurant. I built it from scratch, where the building I rented was just four walls.

I was in the middle of my steroid business, still working for a Mafia faction in Brooklyn, but all in all, I wanted to have a legit business and distance myself from criminal activity. I was at the point when I was building my restaurant and operating it that I spent more time in the legitimate entrepreneur world and less time in the criminal entrepreneur world. I wanted a legit business, something I could call my own, and perhaps one day leave the underworld behind me.

The theme of my restaurant was health food. I constructed the restaurant in an old fifties style, complete with checkered-patterned flooring, antique fifties radios that donned the walls, and a juice bar with six stools so customers could eat there or get their orders to go. The juice bar had a cappuccino/espresso machine with a large golden eagle on the top. I had eleven tables inside that sat about thirty-two people comfortably. I had a couple of tables for outside dining when the weather permitted. The kitchen had three doors, one in the back and two in the front, one leading to the hallway and another that led to the juice/coffee bar. The kitchen was fitted with all the top-of-the-line appliances and everything a gourmet chef would crave.

My menu was created so that everything you ate would have a complete breakdown in calories, fat, carbohydrates, and protein. I opened seven days a week, serving three meals a day, which meant I never closed until late and was always opened before the sun even thought about rising. My concept was thought of partly because a guy I knew was opening a large chain gym and thought a health food restaurant might do well. My best friend Anthony went out west and told me of some of the healthier restaurants out there, and with these combined, my idea was realized.

Perhaps I was a bit ahead of my maturity when I opened my restaurant. My aspirations of having a *regular* existence and ignoring the street life might have been a bit premature.

I hadn't done any steroid deals since opening my restaurant. I only ventured to Brooklyn to get fireworks or on the rare instances when the powers that be there wanted me to do a particular job. For the most part I was, twenty-four hours a day, trying to make my restaurant work. My restaurant was in Westchester County, above New York City. I wanted to get as far away from the city as was possible to make a good, legit business.

Four months into having my restaurant, I found it tougher than I anticipated, but I was as devoted as ever to make it work. I was getting decent traffic from the new gym that opened behind me, as well as the large train station located across the freeway less than a quarter mile away. Location, location, location!

One morning, a man walked into my restaurant. He'd been a regular customer and was a man I knew from the gym. He placed his order, and while waiting for it, he and I got to talking, as it was a slow day and I was available.

Mike was his name, stocky, five feet, five inches tall, with a powerlifter's build. He had curly black hair from his Italian background, but he was not a connected guy or had any dealings with organized crime; he was a civilian.

"How did you manage to get your restaurant opened?" Mike inquired.

Mike's question took me a bit off guard. He and I never spoke long and especially never about anything that was in-depth. I never spoke about my connections, sources of income, or involvement with crime at all to anyone. When I completed some work, I left my work where it was and did so as quietly and cleanly as possible. Well, sometimes not so quietly. I gave Mike the generic answer his question deserved.

"Hard work," I said, wanting to end the conversation right there.

"Yeah, I know hard work, but how did you make the money?" Mike was persistent and had his agenda, which was obvious. "I want to do the same thing," Mike said again before I could answer, as I had paused, trying to formulate the proper response.

Mike knew on some level I was involved in steroids but didn't know much else, which was the general consensus of most that knew me on a cursory level. These are the types of questions civilians ask. They are so curious and not aware of what to say or not to say, so they speak freely, ignorant of what may be offensive.

"You know, people in the gym and who's around that crowd. Why don't you buy some yourself and sell them? It shouldn't be that difficult. Look for some good connections, buy in bulk, and have a customer base ready to go. Then you build your business from there," I replied, speaking around the question.

Without saying what exactly I did, I gave Mike the very broad recipe for success. I knew he wouldn't know what to do, or he would have done it already. That wasn't my concern, and I wasn't going to get too into any subject of me and my illegal activities with him. I was apprehensive to delve further into any details. I wasn't concerned that Mike was there to get me jammed up legally, but I was already out of the business. To me, Mike wasn't the sharpest tool in the shed, and ignorance can be just as detrimental as any flaw, weakness, or ineptitude.

"The problem is, I don't know where to go to get them," Mike said, staying the course.

Mike was prompting me to respond. I should have inquired more, but instead, I brushed him off with a statement I thought would be helpful and not a far reach for me to do. "I'll see who's around, and if it's a possibility, I'll make the introduction, and the rest is up to you."

My thought was that Mike wasn't capable of going to Mexico, or anywhere else for that matter, and getting steroids, and I certainly didn't want Mike anywhere near my contacts. I thought that if there was a supplier in New York that had good prices and quantity, then I could join them with Mike and they could do their business, and I could either collect a favor or get a cut somewhere without getting involved. The other part was, I didn't think Mike was serious about making steroids a business for himself.

"When I have the right people, I'll let you know," I said, extending my hand to seal the deal.

"Thank you T——," Mike said, smiling, a content look on his face.

My girlfriend at the time worked for a large local gymnasium chain. She and I had been dating about a year. We had a lot in common, and she had been in her current position for a couple of years now. Before she had her position as sales manager to the gymnasium, she was an airline stewardess. One of her many junkets was New York to Moscow. Her many trips to mother Russia produced friendships between the flight attendants and some of the shady male citizens of the pre- Berlin Wall tumbling Soviet Republic. Some of my girl-friend's coworkers married Russians in order to bring them to the United States. The marriages were mutually beneficial, and my girlfriend, five-plus years later, still kept in contact with some of them. At the time, the Russians had little access to activities outside Russia, and any chance they could to better their situations, they did so.

My girlfriend knew I was in the steroid business previously, but not to any particular extent. She had picked me up at the airport once on one of my return trips from Mexico. She had also taken a cycle (duration of time one uses steroids) of steroids that I provided her with.

Not long after I had my morning talk with Mike, I had a revelation. I approached my girlfriend about asking one of her Russian friends to meet with me. The vast majority of Russian immigrants that came to New York ended up settling in a section of Brooklyn known as Brighton Beach. The late eighties and now early nineties saw Brighton Beach turn into little Moscow. I had a good suspicion that one of her old acquaintances could steer me in the right direction for Mike.

Lo and behold, my girlfriend came through and provided me with a number to call.

The next day, I made a call from a pay phone to the number my girlfriend provided for me. It was one of her Russian friends, who spoke broken English, but his English was sufficient enough for both of us to get our points across, and the call went smooth. A meeting was set for a few days, and my restaurant was the chosen location. I wasn't sure who exactly was coming, and my restaurant was as good a place as any, especially since I spent the majority of my time there, including at times sleeping on the butcher top in the kitchen.

Sunday rolled around, and it was one of those mornings when the sun was powerful. My girlfriend and I were having breakfast outside as the breakfast crowd had all but dissipated. We had time for a meal before the lunch crowd was to arrive, and I knew that shortly, my invited Cold War companions would be arriving.

My restaurant was right in front of the parking lot of the shopping center, and when my guests arrived, my girlfriend noticed them before I did. I had never met them before, but it was obvious by their dress and facial features that they were foreigners. Three men stepped out of a gold-colored Lexus. The closer the three approached, the more apparent it was that they weren't from suburban Westchester. Their fashion sense was a little off and appeared to be what they considered trendy. It was stylish, but magazine stylish, which doesn't always translate well once you're dressed in it. Their haircuts and facial features clearly had them pegged for Eastern European at least, if not Russian in particular.

The trio reached close to our table as my girlfriend and I stood. The first of the trio to greet my girl was apparently the one I spoke to and the one she was most familiar with. He was about my height, six feet tall, and had a slender build, but I could tell he exercised before and was no stranger to the gym in one fashion or another. The other two men were introduced to her, and in turn, she introduced me to the first man and then to the other two by him. I shook the first man's hand, the one I spoke with on the phone, and automatically noticed some tattoos on his hand and arm. My girlfriend then excused herself as the four of us sat at the table and got comfortable. I had my waitress come around and take their orders for some food and drinks, and our meeting was underway.

Alexi was the emissary of the group partly because he spoke the most English out of the three. Alexi introduced Vladimir next, a man of smaller stature, about five feet, eight inches tall, that didn't look anything like someone that worked out, at least not with weights. Vladimir had a pudgy face and belly to match—nothing gluttonous, but certainly not an athlete. Vladimir's English seemed better than Alexi's, but apparently, he wasn't the negotiator and was more on the bottom rung of the criminal ladder. Vladimir wouldn't speak much unless there was a language issue or something of less gravity to speak on. The third man didn't speak any English at all and only spoke Russian. I think he understood some of what was being said and was simply playing the role of a boss, which turned out to be the case; he was the boss of these other two and others both here in New York and back in Moscow. The boss's name was Bogdan, which means "given by God," which certainly matched his personality. Bogdan was dressed classically with dress shoes, shirt, and pants and was clean-shaven. He was overweight as well but a bit huskier than Vladimir. I saw immediately that he was all about business and never really had many moments of levity in his life. I attributed their being overweight to enjoying the food and lifestyle of being in the United States. Bogdan was treated with respect by the other two, and it was obvious he was deferred to when it came to making decisions. Bogdan's lack of English was no deterrent to having business negotiations. He relied on Alexi for translation and being the intermediary. Alexi was doing the negotiating while having some rein to make decisions, but if a vital decision was needed to be made, Bogdan would be making the decision.

We ordered some food, I on my second round, and then got to the point after some minor feeling out of one another. I decided to kick off the point of the meeting.

"You guys have steroids over there?" I was speaking to all three, looked at all three, and waited for a response.

The key to these types of meetings is eye contact, speaking frankly, and being confident. Like sharks in the ocean, they can smell blood, and weakness is preyed upon.

"Yes, we have steroids. I was Olympic powerlifter. The government give us steroids as part of our routine. In military they give us also, but more for athletes," Alexi said and translated what I was saying.

Alexi then pointed to some of his tattoos and described them to me. One in particular was the one on his arm. "This I get in military. I was in special military branch. Most Russians before was in military."

Alexi saw me looking at the tattoo on his right hand in between his thumb and forefinger. He proceeded to speak about it proudly. "This is a tiger mean I always available to do work. Each dot above the tiger is for each year in prison." Alexi's tone of voice spoke volumes about who he was and his pride of self.

"My brother is in prison. He is there for life. Me, I get out and come here to this country," Alexi said while he looked directly at my girlfriend inside the restaurant.

Alexi spoke so matter-of-factly about the tattoos and their meanings. As I got to know Russians through the coming months and years, I came to realize they were quite cold and indifferent even when it came to situations involving family, close friends, or personal matters that regular Americans would revere. I was used to my associates being cold and callous, but theirs was another level entirely, as my time with them would attest.

"What kind of steroids do you have there?" I brought the conversation back to its main focal point.

Alexi consulted with his two cohorts, and they seemed a little indifferent to the question. "I don't know names, but I know we have."

"What about a price?" I asked, trying to get some idea of numbers and quantity, knowing that there probably wouldn't be an answer to that.

Alexi spoke to Bogdan, and they conversed back and forth for a few minutes. I was totally new to this language, so I was relying on Alexi to convey the true sentiments.

"Six grand," Alexi said, businesslike, with no other words or explanation.

"What's that for?" I said quizzically.

"For my trip, expenses, and I bring back steroids."

I didn't want to show weakness or uncertainty. I had every confidence that this would be profitable and something I should pursue.

"Deal!" I said. "About how long do you think it will take to happen?" I asked, wanting some sort of a timeline so I could plan things out.

"I leave Friday and say, like, two weeks," Alexi said after a few words with Bogdan.

It was now Sunday, but I was already counting on this deal to happen in some form, so I made sure Mike had money ready and waiting for me when I called upon it. Alexi spoke to Bogdan, and he shook his head yes in approval of both the deal and the time frame.

"You guys finish your food, and I'll bring the money," I said, excusing myself.

There was a pay phone not far from my restaurant, and that was where I used my pocket tone dialer to make the call to Mike.

"Mike. Yeah, it's me. Six, now. I'll meet you at the supermarket. Okay, thirty minutes." I hung up the pay phone.

I had made arrangements with Mike to have money ready for this day. I didn't know the amount or time but just to have it ready for me. I didn't want Mike to have direct access with the Russians in fear that if something went wrong, I would be held responsible for his transgressions, and that could potentially be life-ending. I was now entering a situation I thought I had been out of, and lo and behold, here I was right back in the thick of it. I assumed risk on both sides. If the Russians took the money and didn't produce, I was responsible on Mike's side for the six thousand. I was also on the hook with the Russians. If Mike didn't come through with the money, my reputation would take a ding, and perhaps I would lose a great contact for a multitude of business ventures. For all intents and purposes, the Russians thought it was my deal and we already agreed on the terms, so I was on the hook on some level.

America and, especially, the United States federal authorities weren't prepared for this type of criminal that post-Communist Russia would produce. The Russians that entered mainstream America were ex-military, ex-cons, and/or ex-KGB. Of course, there were others that led normal lives, but a large number of the immigrants from Russia had some sort of criminal or government background. The immigrants were hardened, trained, and thirsty for a different way of life. The Russians were a tight-knit group. They had their own customs, language, and dialects that had been forged over years of oppressive control. The new Russian criminals had camaraderie (derived from the word *comrade*). Many were friends since childhood, relations forged from a sense of needing one another and operating in groups and bands to stay alive and survive. Russians stayed in their neighborhoods aside from when they had to do their military service or when incarcerated. They were raised together, trained together, stole together, went to prison together, and killed together. Anything to survive under some of the most oppressive regimes the world had ever known. The Russians would rival the twenty-year Cuban exile and that of the southern Italian immigrants from the 1880s. Each was oppressed and fled to the land of opportunity. Opportunities were realized, and the United States, in all it's infinite wisdom, was unable to see forward to the organizations and criminal enterprises that would form.

There wasn't much law enforcement was capable of doing, at least not right away. The feds underestimated the incoming Russians' thirst for capitalism and their capabilities. The United States government was so fixated on the downfall of Communism that it had very little resources, let alone the knowledge, to combat the new group of criminals. Outside a few in the spy world, there were a minimal number of agents that spoke Russian, let alone their varying dialects. The intelligence information for who was who in the Russian underworld was murky at best. Another great example of American foreign policy getting way ahead of itself. Not every country is capable of functioning in a democracy or free market.

The feds found it increasingly difficult to penetrate the Russian underworld. When a member of the Russian underworld was arrested, the standard interrogation tactics and American penal system weren't an effective deterrent. What was a possible deterrent for Russian organized crime? Certainly not our prisons. Russian prisons were generally situated in the harshest climates Russia could manage. Their quality of food and medical treatment was below adequate, to say the least. Interrogation? C'mon now. Torture was the steady course in the Russian Gulag. The United States gives you the steady dose of good cop, bad cop, praise, then a yelling session. Not even close in comparison between the two countries.

The Russians feared reprisals from their group more than anything the American government could dream up. What would flip (turn into a government informant) a Russian? Answer: nothing. His or her family would be at risk, and most Russians living in the United States had family still back in Russia, and they could be brought into the equation if it was deemed necessary to keep a person from talking to the authorities or keep him in line, period. The fear of reprisal kept the criminal cooperation with law enforcement at an almost nonexistent level, at least in the beginning years.

I returned to the meeting with the money, and my three Russian guests were waiting. We completed the first part of our business together. With the three now on their way back to Brighton Beach,

I was back at work at my restaurant, waiting for the call from Alexi that I believed would be coming in the coming couple of weeks, as we had spoken about.

A couple of days past the two-week mark, and I received a phone call from Alexi. He was arranging for himself, Vladimir, and Bogdan to make the drive again to see me. The trio pulled up, and I had a table arranged for them to sit at while Alexi and I went elsewhere to complete the transaction. I went with Alexi, and as he drove, he told me that the bags in the back of the car were mine. When I turned to look in the backseat and saw a shopping bag, a duffel bag, and a suitcase, I thought they must be packed with something or that the steroids were in some hidden compartments.

"Which one is mine?" I asked Alexi with a bit of hesitation in my voice. I wanted Alexi to tell me again or get a little more specific.

"All three," Alexi said again.

We continued driving and made the short five-minute drive from my restaurant to my apartment in no time. We took them to my apartment as I wanted to open them inside, out of the way from anything or anyone. Upon opening the first one, which was the shopping bag, I noticed it was filled to the top with Russian dianabol, a drug used for gaining size and strength. At the same time I was discovering that, Alexi opened the suitcase, and it was filled in plain sight with vials of testosterone laid out on masking tape so they wouldn't break. There were mats of thirty to a side. Thousands of them were lined up. Lastly, I opened the duffel bag, and it too was filled with the same dianabol on one side, and the other side was filled with human growth hormone. The growth hormone Alexi brought was of the human variety, which had been extracted from cadavers, as opposed to the other type, which was synthetic in nature. The Russian dianabol was in cellophane strips of ten per group and rubber-banded together in packs of ten, equaling one hundred. I was in awe without showing it. I couldn't believe the quantity and had to try to figure out the catch or what the circumstances were.

Before I even got to count the lot, I had a few questions I needed answered. "This is very good and a good amount. What is the cost of each one?"

Alexi gave me the prices, which I thought were not only good but also a little hard to believe. I had been selling steroids since 1988, and now it was 1993, and this by far was turning out to be the best connection I had, factoring in the door-to-door delivery and price.

"Can this be an ongoing thing, or is this a one-shot deal?" I said, thinking forward.

I wanted to know because with these prices and quantities, I was thinking this could be quite lucrative, especially when I knew these particular products were not seen in the US market, at least not that I had seen or heard of. There were other forms and variations of these drugs, but these particular ones were new, and new products are quick sellers especially if people are getting quality results.

"No problem. We get all the time," Alexi said as we counted the merchandise.

I normally don't ask questions about too much, but with Alexi not being in the business and, in less than three weeks, producing something like this, I was curious. I needed to know it would or could be a regular event so I could plan on where to go with this newfound connection.

"How were you able to bring so much product in a short period of time?" I asked Alexi, stepping out of my comfort zone and asking a question that wasn't the norm to ask.

"No problem at all. We go to factory, put gun to head, and load up van." Alexi spoke in such a matter-of-fact tone, continuing to count the inventory.

That was as much information as I needed to have. The fact is, Alexi and whoever else was involved were quite resourceful. Whatever needed to be done to complete the task, I knew it would get handled. I enjoy and prefer these types of associates as I do whatever is necessary too, and our being on the same page businesswise was a great start.

I took out a bunch of the steroids for myself, both for personal use and for selling a bit on the side to some longtime friends that I knew would like them. I wasn't looking to get into the business again and was thinking that even if this were a one-shot deal, it was a good little score for myself, and I was able to facilitate Mike in getting going. Perhaps there would be some favors I would be owed, whether realized or not. I repackaged the steroids into other bags, giving Alexi back his duffel bag and suitcase, then we headed back to my restaurant to join the other two Russians to speak about the future and what other possibilities there might be. We spoke and planned on meeting up again very soon to discuss more business and other ways to make money. I loved the Russians; they were all very businesslike and were very opportunistic. They found business from nothing and made it something. They always had a solution to a problem and made things work.

I went to a pay phone and called Mike. I had him meet me away from my restaurant to do the handoff. I knew he wasn't a cop or setting me up because it would've already happened, so I felt comfortable in the transaction.

I handed Mike the bags, to which I saw the same expression and feeling I had when Alexi and I opened the bags together.

"This is a lot of stuff," Mike said in a surprised tone, saying the words he was fumbling for.

"Yeah, it is. This should get you more than on your way and the best of luck with it," I said, thinking that the transaction was over and Mike would be on his way.

What I wasn't ready for was Mike's response to my delivery. Another rule I broke was involving citizens into my world.

"This is too much stuff. I don't know if I can sell it all," Mike said as he gazed on the haul.

Now, I'd never heard that before. Too much stuff? What the hell was that? This was where I questioned again if it was a setup of some sort because nobody in their right mind would say it was too much unless they had an ulterior motive of some kind. I didn't think anyone could be that ignorant or that much of a nonbusinessman. This suburban bumpkin, I was guessing and hoping, fell into the latter category.

"Too much stuff? C'mon, man, you asked me how to make money and I told you. Then you asked where and how and I delivered. Now you're really telling me that this is too much product? Go out and see how it goes. I'm not in the business anymore, as I stated.

I reached out and did you a favor and don't want any further involvement in the matter. I'm not responsible for your end of the deal. Now I have some work to do, as do you," I said, wanting everything clear and understood.

Mike took possession of the bags and went his way, and I went back to my restaurant. I still couldn't believe what I had heard, but as soon as it was over, I forgot about it and went back to focusing on my restaurant.

A week passed, and Mike came into my restaurant. I asked him what he wanted to eat and got his order together. While that was going on, Mike proceeded to tell me the same words as when we had parted ways the last time. That the quantity was too much and he wasn't able to sell much. I didn't have much patience for this type of stupidity and ignorance. I leaned into Mike so he could hear what I was saying and not have it broadcasted to the other patrons in my establishment.

"You asked me for the tools to become successful, and I arranged those for you. If you couldn't do the business, why did you start the business?"

I didn't realize that Mike had brought the steroids back to me in the bags. As I spoke, he motioned to his side where they were, and I got a bad feeling about it. Mike wanted to return the steroids to me, minus what he had sold or was selling.

"You didn't say anything when you agreed to the deal or when you knew what was expected of you," I said, making my point clear and concise as I despised repeating myself, a pet peeve of mine.

Mike continued with the same rhetoric, completely unabated. I knew I shouldn't have given in and should have put the kibosh on Mike's insistence. Partly, I wanted Mike out of my hair, and there was another part of me that understood there was a good amount of money to be made. I would have to reestablish some of my old connections and customer base. I would have to put some feelers out there, especially with a product that was new to the market. I couldn't do that full-time with the restaurant and all, and it would certainly take longer than any other time. Being out of the business, even for a short stint of time, I had not been in touch with what was happening, who might have been in trouble or was still around. This process would have to be a bit longer than any normal time.

"All right, all right. I told you I was out of the business, so it's going to take me longer to get rid of things. I have to get in touch with people and running my restaurant at the same time. I have little time to devote to selling. I'm not promising you anything, but I'll try. I'll reach out to you when I'm ready and have some progress."

Mike took some steroids for himself, and aside from the little he sold already, the amount was near the same as what I gave him a week ago. Mike agreed with what I said and took his order of food to go, and I went about my business.

The first week of me being in possession of Mike's stash didn't produce much at all. I was just getting to my feelers and contacts with one person buying some to see if they were going to fly in the market. I understood, at times, this was the case and collected only about five hundred dollars. When word had spread and the results had come back, then the product would sell fast.

Less than a week into the last time Mike and I spoke, he was back in my place, asking me about progress and how sales were looking. Not even a week in, and he was questioning me about doing the job he was incapable of doing. He ignored the part of our last conversation when I told him I would contact him when I had progress to report on.

"I told you I would reach out to you," I said not in a rude way but certainly more cogent.

"Yeah, no pressure. I was coming in for a burger anyway and thought I would see how things were coming along."

Mike used the food as the excuse to pressure me on the money. Mike ate at my restaurant regularly, but the steroids were his agenda.

"I'm getting the word out and sold only a small amount. It's not even been a week yet, and these things take time, as I already mentioned to you," I said, hoping to put a rest to Mike's questions and future questions.

Mike looked at me oddly as I handed him the five hundred from the sales. As he took hold of the money, I could tell that he wasn't pleased with it and was looking as though there should be more there than what was in his hand.

"I thought you would have sold more by now," Mike said as he took the money and placed it in his pocket.

Now I was feeling disrespected, taken advantage of with a hint of anger and resentment. I was attempting to remain patient but saw where this was going. "I don't want to hold on to your product or money any longer than I have to." My tone was growing increasingly agitated. "You're welcome to take it all back and do it yourself," I said, pointing down to a bag that contained some of the product, but Mike didn't know how much was there.

"It's all there minus what I sold and paid you for. I'll let you know when I have more money for you. There's no need to ask me about it again," I said, not wanting Mike to have any confusion of how the process worked or having this progress report conversation again.

"Okay," Mike said in a bit of a huff with a slight shrug of his shoulders and rolled his eyes in obvious dissatisfaction.

I sensed a problem was about to unfold, and I held my composure very well. I was trying to do the right thing with the restaurant and do the right thing by assisting Mike with getting a business going for himself. Under different circumstances, I would have acted and reacted differently, but I was trying to go to another path. I had a restaurant to run and an inner struggle to not revert to the man I had been repressing for close to a year now.

During the course of the next week, I received calls from Mike periodically to check on the progress. Even in code, I despised speaking on the phone about anything. I was taught young that speaking about any illegal business over the phone is off-limits. I didn't even call from my home or have anything in my name that was associated to me, like my beeper, which was in another name. I was trying to keep cool and certainly didn't want to speak or yell at Mike over the phone and cause an issue.

Not even another full week, and Mike was again at my restaurant bright and early when nobody was there. He began questioning me about money from across my juice bar. I was more surprised and shocked that I was able to keep my patience in this situation, but that was now coming to a head. I leaned into Mike from my side of the bar, and instinctively, Mike leaned in with me. I wanted to whisper what I was going to say. I didn't want my chef or waitress to hear it, or anyone else that could have possibly been within earshot.

"I've told you before multiple times that I would call you and contact you when I had something for you. I told you not to contact me and that I would reach out to you. You've not only ignored what I asked but you've also ramped up your persistence."

Mike had a quick response to my words, and he showed his cards from what he was feeling the entire time and where his mind was at.

"I want my money," Mike said in a short tone.

That was about all I could stand, and the patience I was clinging too had run its course.

"You want what? You come into my restaurant and make demands on me? You come to me and ask me how to make money? I gave you the roadmap, and you couldn't figure it out. Your ineptitude had me doing the entire transaction for you, knowing I was retired, and you didn't care. This isn't my problem. Now you're here demanding your money. Let me tell you, you have the wrong guy! You're not only shit out of luck with the money but you're also not getting any product either. Now get the fuck outta' my joint!" I said, looking directly into Mike's eyes as I pulled back from him.

As I leaned backward from Mike, I wanted to have some distance between us as I reached with my right hand for my .380 automatic holstered on the small of my back with a chambered round at the ready.

This was about where I saw this episode going, and by the looks on Mike's face, it was not what he was expecting. Mike was short and stocky but certainly out of his element here. There would be no intimidation or, perhaps, what he thought all along, that I was soft.

Mike wasn't a total idiot; he saw my hand behind my back and knew he wasn't in a power position at all and was not in his environment. Mike took a step back and said what came to his mind.

"We'll see about that."

I stayed focused as Mike backpedaled out of my restaurant. I didn't take my finger off the trigger until Mike was out of the door, just in case and to continue to show him I was serious.

I slowly eased my finger off the trigger of my trusty .380 automatic, my weapon of choice. "Never leave home without it" was my motto. I possessed other weapons and, at times, sold weapons, but I always kept my .380 on or near me. I had a couple of weapons that I kept on the steady, my SKS Chinese assault rifle and a sawed-off twelve-gauge shotgun. I never wanted to be caught dead without a weapon on me.

Two days passed, and I got the follow-up visit from Mike, which, on some level, I had been expecting. He entered with two guys from the gym I knew in passing. Mike's next move was to press me and bring the cavalry. The three approached the juice bar as I was inside and they were outside, approaching.

"We want the money," the biggest of the three said, taking the lead.

"We, now it's *we*. I'll tell you what I told Mike. You're not getting a penny or an ampoule. If Mike had done his job and held up his end of the deal, we wouldn't be having this conversation," I said with a swift response. "He's so inept that I had to do all the work and then have to get constant pressure about me doing favor after favor. Why would I part with anything? I warned Mike to let me handle it and it would take time to complete, and he ignored me. Then he wants to come in here to my place and demand money from me, and now you guys want to demand money from me. I think not!"

As I finished my statement, I slowly reached my hand behind my back. The three men insisting money knew I carried a gun and were in no position to do anything besides bark. I was outnumbered, but I had position and the best of all things, my equalizer holstered and ready.

The bigger of the three's name was Paul. Paul, the tallest, stood six feet, two inches, had black hair, and was muscular, the body of an ex-boxer who's past his prime.

The third man, I had seen before in the gym as well, but one I never had a conversation with. At five feet, seven inches tall, he too was athletic to muscular, had dark hair, and stayed quiet throughout the entire event.

I wasn't threatened by any of the three, and aside from their lame stares and half-assed demands, which were more comical than threatening, I had the upper hand.

Sensing that they too were not in a power position, Moe, Larry, and Curly backed out of my restaurant with a few parting words that sounded like the teacher from the *Peanuts* cartoon: "Waaaaa waaaaa waaaaa."

Three days past this last encounter, I was in my kitchen at about eleven in the morning and preparing some stock for my lunch rush. I was nearly fifteen feet from the door of the kitchen leading to the hallway when the door opened. I was on the other side of a large butcher block and prepping station. A man entered my kitchen, someone I had never seen before, and he certainly wasn't invited. After being initially taken off guard by the intruder, who apparently bypassed my waitress and just walked right in, I snapped to alert. I quickly scanned him for a threat assessment. I didn't sense anything threatening, but for him to walk into my establishment, he had a good deal of confidence.

With slicked-back jet-black hair, standing six feet, two inches tall, not muscular but big in stature, he was wearing a suit that was a pinstriped black with a black shirt and pastel-colored tie, topped off with a pair of wing-tipped shoes. It appeared this character had watched too many old gangster movies and had spent too many hours in the tanning booth.

I had an idea why he was there but was willing to give the intruder the benefit of the doubt on the slim chance he was representing someone or was connected to someone and was there for another reason. I would be willing to look past what I considered a matter of disrespect in some rare instance. The disrespect was entering my restaurant, let alone my kitchen, without an invitation.

"T——?" The intruder directed his question at me.

My right hand had plenty of time to reach behind my back, draw and fire, and at minimum, get a round or two off before he could reach me.

"Who's askin'?"I said, not taking my eyes off his.

"You T——?" My new, unwelcomed guest stayed his course.

"Yeah, I'm T——. You are?" I was stern and stayed focused, waiting for him to make his fatal move, my hand inching closer to the small of my back.

"I'm here to collect a debt," the tanned intruder said.

Now I knew why he was there, and I preferred it this way. In the underworld and in organized crime, when there's a dispute about money, property, or a perceived trespass, parties higher up in the organizations are called upon to mediate the dispute and rule. This is done for a few reasons: one, it cuts down on the amount of violence, business isn't halted, unnecessary law enforcement attention isn't attracted, and most of all, the flow of money isn't interrupted. Once the meet is agreed on, the dispute heard, and the ruling made, the decision is final. The beauty of this way of mediating disputes was that the entire matter was out of my hands and was in the hands of people I knew had my back. If the beef (dispute) was even remotely close or a decision was in the air, the people representing me would side with me. I was still valuable and never had a blemish with my underworld associates. The meeting is also referred to as a sit-down. The parties involved on both sides must agree on whatever the outcome is, and if that is broken, then repercussions are certainly delivered swiftly without reprisal. This guy coming in like this was representing an organization, at least that was what I assumed. It was either that or he was freelancing. One way or the other, I was with people, and now that this business dealing had reached this phase, the path was clear.

I wanted my new visitor to say what he was there for even though I knew full well why he was there. Just saying the debt wasn't good enough; I wanted details on what he thought was owed and what the terms of the collection he was going to set were.

"What is it?" I said, looking for those details.

"It's seventy-five hundred. You can make weekly payments, and we'll charge you six points. Your payments will be four hundred and fifty a week, and I'll be collecting that vig [an underworld term for an interest payment and short for vigorous] every week," the stranger responded, his intentions clear.

Now, the original money that was used to purchase the steroids was six thousand, and with five hundred dollars already paid, this guy was now two thousand over the original disputable money. This didn't even include the vig, the interest payments, which doesn't come off the principal amount. I wasn't mad at the attempt to collect the disputed money. My issue came from the intrusion into my restaurant. I wanted to follow what I'd been told since I entered the underworld lifestyle and kept my composure.

"You with anyone?" I said even before questioning the terms and amounts of the debt he said he was there to collect.

The term *being* with someone in the underworld means that the person involved in the dispute is in a criminal organization and that those people he's represented by are of a higher rank who are in positions to negotiate across organizational bounds. This also means that the disputed debt that is collected is sanctioned by members of higher rank in the organization. If both sides to the dispute have people they can call on, then the matter is referred to them for a decision. Nothing more is to transpire between the parties in question, and when a decision is made, then it's to be upheld and the matter is closed. These decisions are made via sit-downs or through their underworld channels. This process is preferred most times to avoid bloodshed and chaos while creating some sort of order in a world that can be tumultuous.

"Yeah," the intruder quickly retorted.

"Don't say you are if you're not, because I am. I run a restaurant and don't get involved in these types of things. So if you're not, now's the time to say so," I said, responding just as quickly as the intruder spoke.

"Yeah, I'm with someone," the intruder said again, reaffirming what he already told me.

Whether it was his pride getting the better of him and he didn't want to go back on what he previously said to me or he was truly represented by higher-ups of an organization, he spoke confidently.

"Okay, I was just making sure and giving you an out because I'm with someone, and we'll now let them handle it."

I reached for my cell phone and made the call to my people back in Brooklyn so the process could begin, and all this I did in front of the intruder so he knew I was not only serious but also truly with someone. My people knew I was always on call for them, so here was my call. They left me alone to make sure my restaurant would work and prosper, so hearing me call, especially about something like this, they were less than pleased and not with me, mind you.

"Hey, it's me," I said without saying my name on a cloned cell phone.

"Hey, how's the joint doin'? You all right?" The thick Italian New Yorker voice garbled on the other end after answering the call on the second ring.

"Restaurant's going well. Hey, I have someone here that's trying to collect on a disputed debt. He says he's with people." I didn't have to say much more than that as the person I phoned knew exactly what I was speaking about and what would happen next.

"Oh yeah," my guy in Brooklyn said. My guy in Brooklyn sounded like he was both pissed and excited to hear the news. Pissed someone was bothering me and excited to get involved and see who his people were. "Give him my number and have his people contact us. We'll straighten it out. When he leaves, call me back."

I hung up the phone and wrote the contact number down for the intruder to take with him and pass on to his people so the situation could be dealt with. Now that we were on this level, I asked the intruder his name so I could pass that as well and also for my own knowledge.

"What's your name?" I asked the debt collector.

"Vincent Florida," he said.

"Vincent Florida it is. Okay, Vincent Florida, it's now in other people's hands, and what they decide will be final."

I wrote the number of my guy in Brooklyn down on a piece of paper and handed it to Vincent. Vincent looked a bit shocked and disarmed. He realized, whatever the outcome, it truly was out of our hands and was a decision for the higher-ups to make. Vincent left my restaurant without much fanfare, and I resumed my duties for a few minutes before calling back to Brooklyn.

"Hey, it's me," I said, calling back to Brooklyn.

"So tell me about this," the same voice on the other end said and was that of the guy who brought me into the organization I was currently still working for, just not as often as before I started my restaurant.

Richie was someone I met in Long Island some years back, when I was living there. He was from Brooklyn but had some relatives out on Long Island. It was a month before the Fourth of July, and when I met Richie, we had an instant liking for each other and a mutual understanding that we were both men of the lifestyle. Richie was a shorter man at five feet, nine inches, had a pockmarked face, and who chain-smoked Marlboros and lived on coffee, espresso, or whatever form of caffeine he could ingest. Richie was older than me by about four or five years and looked like he was double that, a real picture of ill health. Richie would be my introduction into the Mafia family I ended up working with, which started out fast and furiously. The relationship started with me purchasing fireworks from him and then escalated. Soon I was being introduced to some of his people back in Brooklyn, and in short order, I was finding new revenue streams and rising among those in the organization. I was selling fireworks, which were supplied by the organization, the largest supplier of fireworks in the tristate area. Before the Fourth of July, I was introduced to Richie's boss, Ricky, and my assignments and involvement grew. Fireworks turned to me running the annual fireworks show they had every year in Brooklyn, to bodyguarding the old-time mafiosi, then to me doing collections, extortions, and bombings, and the violence progressively accelerated. I soon had the respect of the higher-ups in the organization because of my willingness and effectiveness at whatever task I was assigned to. Their trust in me and my abilities grew steadily. I carried out all instructions to the letter, and there was never a question of my loyalty. I was an outsider, yes, but I came recommended, and from the first interaction, I had done my job and kept my word. I had respect for the chain of command, said little, minded my own business, and accepted assignments without hesitation.

I gave Richie the rundown about the deal Mike and I made and how we came to the point where I had to make the call to him. I didn't get into specifics, solely the deal, money involved, Mike, and his friends.

"It'll be handled. You just mind the restaurant. When that guy Vincent reaches out, I'll let you know what the decision is," Richie said, being direct and to the point.

The afternoon crowd was just dissipating the following day when Richie called me.

"Hey, that guy Vincent called."

I could hear the ambient sounds of Brooklyn behind Richie's voice. "Okay," I said, wanting Richie to elaborate.

"Yo, that guy's a clown," Richie said with a bit of a chuckle. "So I'm walking with my guy and a friend of ours, Stevie, that runs all the nightclub security and some other aspects of the nightclubs in the city for us. Vincent calls, and I pass the phone to my guy so he can hear the dispute and speak with Vincent's guy to work things out. Right away, Vincent starts to get a little mouthy with my guy. I can see my guy's blood boiling, and he is getting heated fast. My guy then demands to know who Vincent is represented by. You wouldn't guess who Vincent claims as his guy."

"I have no idea," I said in anticipation.

"Stevie," Richie broke out laughing. "This douchebag claimed one of our guys as his representative. Stevie's not a member and on the bottom rung. Now my guy turns to Stevie, who was only there for a meeting about some other things, and asks him who the fuck this Vincent Florida is. You should have seen Stevie's face when he realized he was in the middle of something he had neither any control over nor even knew had happened. Stevie tells my guy that Vincent is a bouncer at a club that he runs security for and for us no less."

Richie was trying to contain himself, but it was too late as he was reliving the incident in his head, and now, sometime removed and away from his guy, Richie could express himself more.

"That's not the end of it. My guy proceeds to take my cell phone and punches Stevie in the face with it. While Stevie is recovering from getting a phone slapped in his face, my guy tells Vincent that Stevie is with him and now for nothing Stevie did. Stevie was in trouble because his name was used when it shouldn't of been. He was in trouble because Stevie's named was used when it shouldn't have been. My guy passes the phone to Stevie and is told to speak with Vincent. Stevie tells Vincent he is in trouble and has to come in and see him that evening. My guy takes the phone back from Stevie, berates Vincent some more, then hangs the phone up."

When someone is sent for, it's not a good thing, and in Vincent's case, he violated multiple codes of the underworld. He knew, or at the very least, he should have known, that he was in violation. He gambled and now had to pay the cost of losing the gamble. Vouching for someone is one thing, but claiming someone or claiming to be a part of something and not is even worse.

I hadn't really seen Richie that much in the last year because of the restaurant and my responsibilities there. I still worked with Richie and the family but was mainly on assignments I would get that could be handled on my time, working late at night and generally by myself. I did get my orders through Richie, but the last couple came directly from Ricky. The guy Richie used for this incident with Vincent, I didn't know and did wonder why he didn't choose Ricky in this case, but it wasn't in my character to ask or question why things were the way they were. Ricky's father owned a social club in our section of Brooklyn, and now that Richie was speaking of someone else, I was afraid there had been some drastic changes in the leadership or power of the crew I was in. I would have to feel Richie out the next time we'd meet because it was obvious I wasn't being let in on things. I never wanted to be on the wrong side of things or having others think I was on the wrong side or join a side when for me nothing had changed. This is the potential danger of not being around all the time; things change and power shifts.

Stevie and Vincent were both in a bad position, and I would come to find out how bad when I would meet Richie's guy. Stevie and Vincent had to sit there and take it with not many options available. Stevie said he never gave Vincent permission to use his name, but that mattered little in the grand scheme of things. Stevie was in trouble, but the brunt of the problems now rested firmly on the tanning-bed-tanned shoulders of Vincent.

There was a lull between the lunch crowd and the dinner crowd that would be filing in in a couple of hours, so I spent that time resting a bit and prepping in the kitchen. My waitress was cleaning the tables and sweeping up outside when she came into the kitchen.

"Excuse me, T———, there's a man here to see you."

"Who's that?"

"He said his name is Vincent, and he was asking if he could see you."

I couldn't believe Vincent wanted to see me. I figured I was one of the last people he wanted to see aside from maybe Stevie. This was a stark difference from the last time he was here, when he just sauntered into my place.

"Have him come in." I directed my waitress to have Vincent come into the kitchen.

In walked Vincent, fresh from his verbal tongue-lashing from Richie's guy. This time, Vincent was quite meek and humble. He looked like a dog fresh from being neutered. His eyes were down, his shoulders slumped, and he was walking as if he were tippy-toeing through a minefield. I didn't say anything when Vincent walked in. Part of me wanted him to sweat more than he was and torture him a bit; the other part was curiosity about why he was here again, especially after the verdict didn't exactly go the way he had planned. A minute or so had passed, and for Vincent, I knew it must have seemed like an eternity.

"T———, I wanted to come here in person and apologize to you," Vincent said submissively.

"Remember when I asked you if you were with someone and you said yes? I even gave you another opportunity to change your answer, and you insisted on sticking with your story about being with someone," I said, giving Vincent my I-told-you-so moment.

"I know, I know, I'm just very sorry for any inconvenience and disrespect I may have caused you." Vincent continued to plead his case, which was falling on deaf ears.

I wanted to rub it in even more but wanted Vincent to know that his current and future issues had nothing to do with me.

"No need to say sorry to me. I believe you have more pressing matters to be concerned with," I said smugly.

"Uh, yeah…ummm, I'm leaving town now but, again, wanted to see you before I left and apologize in person." Vincent's mouth was getting ahead of his mind as he fumbled for words, which seemed to be a pattern of his, his mouth getting ahead of his brain.

"Your apology is duly noted," I said, looking at the man whose mind was already racing down the parkway to parts unknown and had left his body behind.

Apparently, Vincent called Stevie later that day and was called in for a sit-down. It was apparent that Vincent was forgoing that sit-down and getting as far away from New York as possible. He saw the writing on the wall for him, and the writing spelled a horrible ending, one he didn't want to face. What a coward. That's no man at all. Make your decisions and face it like a man is what I say.

To my amazement, not two days later, into my restaurant walked Mike, still trying to collect on the disputed money that apparently wasn't ruled in his favor. Mike took a seat on a stool at my juice bar, while his two cronies lurked about outside in the parking lot. It was apparent that neither Mike nor Mutt and Jeff were going to abide by the ruling that was sent down.

I approached Mike from my side of the juice bar and leaned in where again he and I could hear each other and nobody else.

"Didn't Vincent give you the verdict?" I said to Mike in a sarcastic tone of confidence.

"I wanted you to know I'm going to collect my money!" Mike retorted as if he had grown a set of balls over the last couple of days.

My eyes squinted, and my tone was even more confident than the last statement. "You couldn't collect before even with that banana head dressed in his best throwback gangster outfit. If you insist on pressing the issue and going against the ruling, I won't be held accountable for what might happen. Do what you have to do," I spat out my last words and turned my back on Mike and went back into my kitchen.

I called Richie immediately, advising him that the matter was still unresolved. When a ruling is sent down and ignored, it's more than a violation; it means the party that has been ruled against is either ignorant or telling the favored party that they don't respect their decision and are not afraid of the consequences. Now, it's not just the ruling that's on the table; it's the validity of the party involved. And if decisions aren't upheld and are ignored and the trespass left unaddressed, then the family loses face, and their power position dwindles. Future rulings will come under scrutiny, or others will look at my family as weak and vulnerable. Weak and vulnerable, in my world, was not a position Richie or anyone else could let pass.

"I'll see you tomorrow for lunch," Richie said in a tone I had heard before, which had never ended in a peaceful outcome.

Richie would now be in suburbia and totally out of his element. Richie was the epitome of Italian Brooklyn, and I knew he wouldn't be coming alone. This was exactly what I was trying to avoid. I wanted to leave Brooklyn in Brooklyn. *Just when I thought I was out, they pull me back in.* A phrase that couldn't have been more spot-on.

With my lunch crowd just finishing up the next day, I was behind the bar, going over receipts and getting change at my cash register. I turned toward the front to hand a customer her change when I noticed something out of the ordinary. A black stretch limousine was parked in front of my restaurant horizontally. There were a few minutes of nobody entering or exiting the limousine. I didn't go outside or move from behind the bar because I couldn't see any of the occupants through the dark tinted windows.

The first to emerge from the limousine was Richie. Now him, I recognized, and I now knew it was friend, not foe. Seeing Richie, I came from around the bar and made my way outside to greet him. As I made my way outside and Richie and I made eye contact, two more men emerged from either side of the rear of the car.

The man that exited the rear passenger side of the limousine made the car raise a few inches as the first of his large legs hit the asphalt. The second leg hit the pavement, and the car lifted again to where it was supposed to be in height, taking the stress off the rear shocks. The man was easily 350 pounds, appeared to be near fifty years old, and was sweating even though the temperature was mild and he hadn't even exerted any real energy yet. He appeared to be just an inch over six feet tall, had thinning black-and-gray hair, and stood out in the suburban area just as much as the limousine did. Dressing more casually in a jogging suit made life for him a bit easier, I imagined. The larger man joined Richie on the driver's side rear of the limousine as the third man exited the vehicle. The third man was about six feet tall tops and dressed in slacks, a cream-colored Italian dress shirt, Italian shoes, and had a stride of confidence and power in his step. Richie was dressed in his slacks and dress attire as he led the other two to my front door, where I met them. Richie and I greeted each other with a hug and a kiss on the cheek, and I was summarily introduced to the other two men he brought with him. The customary kiss on the cheek and hug, I gave to the other men, and Richie introduced Antonio first and then the larger Ronnie, who looked like he was one cannoli away from coronary heart failure.

The introduction to Richie's guy, whom I had never met before, was odd, and I wondered how I had never met him before in Brooklyn and, more to the point, why Ricky wasn't involved in the process. Richie introduced him as Antonio, and since Richie introduced me to him first, I knew this was his guy. Antonio was stone-faced with eyes that looked directly through you. Antonio was in his early thirties and was all business all the time.

"This is T——, and this is his joint." Richie directed his words mainly to Antonio about me.

"Nice joint you have here," Antonio said to me as his eyes surveyed my restaurant, nodding in approval.

"Yeah, T——, you did a great job with the place," Richie chimed in.

I directed Richie and the others to a table near the juice bar, where we could see everything from that vantage point and where our backs were to the walls for the most part. As we sat, my waitress brought us some menus to look at and for my guests to choose what they wanted. I gave some suggestions and told the trio I could have my chef whip them up something special. Antonio spoke for the group and said they would order off the menu. With little changes, we placed our orders.

I understood that the Mafia family I worked for was rather large and stretched throughout the East Coast and beyond, but these two, I had never seen before. I was in no position to speak my mind and never would. I was sure everything would come to light, and the process was what it would be.

Antonio began to speak to me once we had some drinks and everyone was settled in. "I've heard some good things about you. Richie and some of the others speak very highly of you."

I looked at Richie, and in true Richie form, he said, "Obviously, I haven't told him everything." Richie's comment had us all laughing, except Antonio, who stayed true to his character.

"I've been away for seven years and just getting back into things." Antonio then spoke about just coming home from prison. "Ronnie was with me during my stint in Sing Sing," Antonio said, slapping Ronnie on the shoulder.

Sing Sing is a notorious prison on the Hudson River, not far from where we currently were situated with my restaurant. Sing Sing not only has a reputation for housing some of the most-violent offenders in New York but it actually is a place for those whose crimes are violent or those who have committed violent acts in other prisons and have been sent to Sing Sing for further punishment. The prison was where the first electric chair was used, when New York had capital punishment. The first and only Mafia boss was sentenced to death there. A good amount of inmates who were incarcerated behind those cold enormous walls simply disappeared and were never heard from again and died under mysterious or ominous means.

"I'm out now and looking after things," Antonio said, not wanting there to be any confusion about where he stood or what his position was or would become.

A few months later, I would be made aware that Antonio was the nephew of the current boss of the family, who was serving a life sentence. Antonio hit the ground running, making up for those lost seven years. He was putting everyone on notice that he was back and taking what was his before and taking what he thought was rightfully his, having done his time the right way.

This was a delicate situation, to say the least. I didn't think I would feel comfortable under Antonio, and my allegiance was still with Ricky. If there were to be a power struggle in the family, I would have to choose a side. Being perceived to be on the wrong side or choosing the wrong side could be fatal. Not knowing the politics of what was going on and being far removed now from the situation, I wasn't informed on the goings-on, and that wasn't ideal. Over the years, I had been careful to avoid these types of pitfalls. My preference was to be called when there was work to be done. Give me my assignment to fulfill and let me work. I was very cautious about being left out of the politics and staying out of the limelight. Now, Antonio might feel I owed him my allegiance for what was going on, and Ricky would expect me to side with him, being that we had had a relationship for about three years or so now. Then there was Richie, who was my guy coming into the family, but now I was unsure what was going on with him and what his intentions were.

Our meal was coming to an end and dusk was falling when a man appeared outside the window of my restaurant. He was about thirty feet away in the parking lot and was taking pictures of what appeared to be my restaurant and us in it. The flash of the camera set Antonio off, with the four of us being in full view of the camera lens. Antonio didn't even have to instruct Richie to handle the situation; Richie was on the move as soon as the flash happened. Exactly more of what I didn't need, which was more publicity. Richie was already out of his chair and halfway out the door as Antonio finished what he wanted to say. Instinctively, Richie knew what to do and was on his task immediately. All we could see from our vantage point was Richie speaking to the man with the camera. The man didn't exchange many words; knowing Richie, he wasn't letting the man speak and intimidated the hell out of him. Richie extended his hand, palm up, and the man placed the camera in Richie's hand. The camera was in Richie's hand for all of about one second before Richie slammed it to the concrete and stomped on it. The expression on the man's face was total shock and astonishment as his disposable camera was shattered into tiny pieces. Richie handed the man a twenty-dollar bill for his troubles, picked up the camera, retrieving the film, exposing it to the fading light. Richie then turned and walked back into the restaurant. Apparently, the man was in the wrong place at the wrong time. He said he was thinking of renting the store next to mine, which was vacant, and was taking pictures to do more calculations before making a decision. Being in the wrong place at the wrong time can be fatal at times.

We had ourselves a good laugh about the scene, and then Antonio opened up a bit more. He let me know the reason why he was away for those years and then also a little more about him and Ronnie's apprehension about being photographed. They were both on parole and both had just been released less than a month ago. One of the restrictions of their parole was they weren't allowed to travel outside of Brooklyn without permission from their parole officer, and Westchester County certainly qualified as being out of their restricted area. Then the other restriction they had was, they couldn't be in the company of convicted felons or known criminal associates, which Ronnie and Antonio both were. Richie didn't have a conviction, but a known criminal associate, I'm sure that category fitted him.

After our meal concluded, Antonio made it clear that he was going to make sure his decision would be adhered to by any means necessary. If a decision is reached, not obeyed, and no retaliation is forthcoming, then there's no reason to even have the sit-down or for anyone to respect it or fear it. The message would be enhanced with Antonio wanting to reassert himself into the power position of the family.

I had a few pictures of Mike and his two buddies that I passed to Richie. I didn't want there to be any mistake about who was who if conditions got hectic.

"Keep to your restaurant and make sure that someone is always with you. The next few days, the three of us will be around," Antonio said to me, and then we all said our good-byes.

The following day, I was just finishing up in the kitchen and heading out to clean the tables and sweep for lunch when I barely noticed Ronnie enter my kitchen. To not notice Ronnie, I must have been busy, distracted, tired, and half-dead. I had my chef take a break and step outside so Ronnie and I could speak about what was going on as it looked like Ronnie had something he wanted to say.

"The boxer, when does he leave the gym and through what exit?" Ronnie said, referring to the biggest member of Mike's group, who was supposedly a former navy boxer.

In our group and for most of us, we never spoke names but rather nicknames and codes that represented the people we were referring to, especially under these circumstances.

"About one thirty, he leaves the gym through the side of the building. He parks his white Lincoln on that side, where there are never many people at all. It's blocked from all views, and there are no cameras there," I said, getting to all the points I knew Ronnie wanted to know without needing to ask me.

"Good," Ronnie said as he huffed, taking a handkerchief out of his pocket to wipe the sweat from his brow, leaving the kitchen.

I waited some minutes before going out to the dining area to give Ronnie some time to get where he needed to be. Apparently, my guys clocked the trio entering the gym and had their plan in motion.

Later, I found out that Antonio was pretending to be on the pay phone on the opposite side of the building at the other exit. His hand was in his jacket pocket, his finger on the trigger of his .22 equipped with a silencer, something Antonio was quite familiar with. Antonio's prison sentence was for possession of silencers.

Ronnie went to his post, where I described the boxer would be exiting. That left Richie, who positioned himself parked in a car a hundred feet away, lying in wait. He was in prime position parked exactly next to the third member of Mike's trio's car.

I didn't know that my guys would be here today, but then again, I didn't want to know, and it was better that I didn't and acted as natural as possible. Whatever the plan, it was in motion, and I was staying out of it and, as Antonio said, staying to my restaurant.

Another thirty minutes had passed, and Ronnie came back into my kitchen, looking like he had just seen a ghost.

"All set?" I said to Ronnie, fully knowing that it wasn't and, apparently, something had gone awry.

"I was there and ready for one in the trunk, but the boxer came out of the gym with two little blond twin girls on either side of him," Ronnie said, and I could see him visually shaken.

"And?" I replied with indifference, not knowing what would cause Ronnie to have such angst.

"I'm not going to kill no kids. I swore if I ever got out of prison, I wouldn't do that again. Here I am out now not even two months, and I'm right back in that position again. I just can't do it. I don't care what you guys want to do to me. I can't kill no kids," Ronnie said adamantly.

Ronnie had his car parked on the side of the building just in front of the boxers, and if the situation was as it should be, the trunk of Ronnie's car was lined with plastic for easy access to throw the boxer's body in the trunk, close it, and take off.

Apparently, Ronnie had completed an assignment that ultimately killed a child in the process. Although it was not done on purpose, Ronnie was convicted of it, and that was what he was in prison for for a quarter of a century. Just making it out of that gladiator hellhole he was in for that time gave him time to think about things, and I could understand his trepidation. The many nights he had to sit in that cage and relive the nightmare of that child's death. In our lifestyle, we try not to include family members, especially, children, but through the course of events, sometimes things that are out of our control happen, and accidents happen. I didn't have the same feelings that Ronnie had about the situation, not that I had a feeling one way or another about it; I was just indifferent. My concern was just to make the matter disappear. In my estimation, sometimes there is collateral damage. I knew that Ronnie was in the right, but I still wasn't pleased and wasn't going to show him that I was on his side in the matter. I needed Ronnie to remain calm and focused. Noticing my disappointment, Ronnie reiterated his position.

"I just can't do that again. I'll take whatever punishment I have coming. I can't go through that again."

Ronnie knew the punishment for walking away from an assignment, and it generally resulted in one's demise. He was willing to take that punishment rather than dish out the one he was ordered to do. I wanted to relieve the burden he carried on his broad shoulders.

"Look, just go tell Richie and Antonio what happened, and I'm sure there will be another opportunity to get this done," I said, knowing nothing else to say.

The call of what to do wasn't up to me anymore. Once Mike and his trio violated the order in the dispute, the matter fell out of my hands. I think Ronnie was just trying to win some sympathy in case Antonio wanted to punish Ronnie for walking away. I didn't know Antonio that well, but from what I had surmised from the little time I knew him, he was a pretty cold character.

An occasional annoyance from the trio over the next few days was par for the course and nothing that had me too alarmed. On Friday, the fourth day since the botched undertaking, it was like any other Friday for me. My breakfast crowd was dissipating, and I was about to settle in and eat my long-overdue first meal of the day.

As I fixed myself a double espresso at my juice bar, I could see out into the parking lot. Instinctively, I looked out and saw a man exiting a gray Crown Victoria with tinted windows. Everything about the man walking toward my restaurant screamed cop. Staring from the car that was unmistakably a cop car, I knew this visit wasn't going to be subtle. I noticed the man's walk had purpose from the first step onto the asphalt with the worn-out, discounted black shoes that supported his cocky stride. His suit was store-bought, off-the-rack charcoal-colored. His flattop dirty-blond haircut stuck with him even into his midforties. His entire six-foot-two-inch-tall frame headed right for my door. This cop had a purpose, and it wasn't buying a smoothie. I kept my eyes on the man until he opened the door and walked right up to me in my restaurant.

"Are you Mr. H——?" The cop wasted no time making a beeline for me at the juice bar and getting to the point.

"Who's askin'? I retorted.

The cop wasted no time reaching into his left inside jacket pocket. He withdrew his billfold, and out came his badge, credentials, and business card.

He leaned into me and showed them to me. I didn't really care about the credentials as much as I was curious as to what branch of law enforcement he represented and for what purpose he was there. With an outstretched hand, he offered me his business card. I let him leave it on the counter, not even wanting to accept it in my hands. I didn't want him to think I had the least bit of interest in having a conversation. He laid it on the counter and began his spiel.

"I'm Detective Sullivan with the district attorney's office," he said, keeping eye contact with me.

Before the detective could finish what he was saying, I backed up from the counter, wanting him to understand that I was neither interested in what he had to say nor going to cooperate with whatever he had on his mind or whatever he had to say.

I stood in silence, the detective's steely blue eyes doing their best to stare me down but to no avail. He would have to do better than that to get any kind of a reaction or response from me. I sipped my espresso, not taking my eyes off his.

"I'll leave my business card here," the detective said without breaking eye contact with me, placing the card on my counter.

He tucked his billfold back in his jacket pocket and continued to speak even though I never responded to his statement or to the question of even my name. He knew who I was, so there was no need to respond. Just because someone asks you something doesn't mean you have to respond, and in most instances, it's more prudent not to respond. Cops tend to ask questions they already know the answer to, especially a man in his position. When it's time for them to come and show themselves like this, then something has transpired, and it's best to keep your mouth shut and call the lawyer.

"I would like to speak with you about an incident that took place yesterday." The detective wasn't specific about who, what, where, how, and why and was vague on the when.

The detective was looking for a reaction from me and, if possible, locking me into a response he would later be able to hold me to. This cop was acting as if I'd never been questioned before.

"I have nothing to say and am represented by counsel. I would appreciate you exiting my establishment," I said in a low tone but direct and to the point.

I didn't want there to be any confusion about my stance and wanted the conversation to be over. I wanted to convey my message that he wasn't going to lock me into any statement and he wasn't going to be allowed to question me further or speak to me at all. More to the point, I wanted him to know his presence wasn't welcome in my restaurant.

Whether I conversed with the detective or not, it wasn't going to change whatever transpired and could only hurt me. Only bad things could come from responding any differently than I just did. Words you say paint a story, and truly not knowing the real reason why he was there lent even more credence to my lawyer's cardinal rule: say nothing, don't incriminate yourself, invoke counsel, and give him a call.

The detective almost expected my response, but it didn't stop him from being irritated with my words, or at least that was what he wanted me to think. It was almost like he was doing the "good cop, bad cop" all by himself.

"I'll leave, but I suggest you speak with me. Your name has surfaced in a recent homicide investigation," the detective said, giving me even more insight into what the purpose of his visit to me was.

Investigation, I thought, was an odd term, being that he said the incident happened yesterday, and that was pretty quick for my name to surface about a murder investigation. I knew it wasn't me; that was for sure. I felt good about not being directly involved, but for the life of me, I had no idea whom he was referring to. Once the detective mentioned *murder*, I certainly wasn't going to say anything. My name came up for a reason, and whatever the case was, that was not a good thing and was usually hard to shake. I said "usually hard to shake" because even if I weren't, that would mean I would have to explain myself and talk. That could only incriminate me in perhaps other legal issues, or they could twist what I said into something that would make me look guilty. Then there was the other part; if I didn't recall correctly and part of what I would say wasn't true and I went to change it, then I had lied, and that would make me look guilty. Keep quiet and act accordingly.

"What part of 'I'm represented by counsel' and 'exit my establishment' was difficult to comprehend?" I didn't want to be too rude with the seriousness of the potential charges, but I didn't want him to have the slightest hint that he could stand there and speak with me any further.

"You'll see me again," the detective said with his parting words.

I drank down the remainder of my espresso as I watched the detective walk out. He gave his best last-ditch effort to sway me, to no avail.

With the cop out of sight, I reached for my phone and called Frank, my lawyer, and told him we had to meet. Frank knew from my tone that it was important and that no conversation over the phone would suffice.

Before Frank could arrive, I received an agitated phone call from my girlfriend. She managed a health club at the time and apparently was in the middle of a meeting when she was interrupted by Detective Sullivan, who had just left my place. She was abruptly pulled out of the meeting and was attempted to be questioned. She didn't know anything outside of perhaps some acquaintances, which didn't bother me in the slightest. The detective was trying to pressure me from another angle. Whatever girlfriend I had was aware of my lifestyle and knew not to say anything just as I knew never to involve my woman with anything involving my work. My girlfriend was irate and vented in my direction, which I let her have because I understood her frustrations. After a few minutes of her venting, I calmed her down and told her to finish her day and come by the restaurant.

A good thing my lunch crowd was thin that day, as Frank was on his way to meet me not at my restaurant. What we had to speak about I wanted done away from anywhere someone, particularly the police, could listen in. I left the restaurant duties to be handled by my chef and waitress and exited. Frank knew where I wanted to meet, at a parking lot about fifteen minutes from my restaurant where we had previously made arrangements to in case we had to speak away from people and known locations.

Frank's car pulled up, and he was accompanied by a man I hadn't seen before. This would be the first time I would meet Joey. Joey exited the car, and he and Frank walked over to me, where I was introduced to him.

"T——, this is Joey. He is working in my office now. I wanted you both to meet so if in the future you had to speak to one another, you would already be familiar," Frank said as I looked at Joey, assessing him and the situation.

Joey extended his hand to shake mine. Frank immediately saw my disapproval. My disapproval wasn't at Joey in a particular way but merely of his presence at this particular occasion. I didn't reciprocate Joey's handshake gesture, and it wasn't meant in disrespect. This was no time for me to be meeting new people, especially new people I didn't seek out or know about.

"No disrespect or anything, but I don't know you, and I need to speak with Frank alone," I said to Joey, looking him in his eyes, with a respectful tone.

Frank jumped right in, knowing full well how I felt. That was Frank; he was very in tune with the gravity of situations and understood people well.

"Joey, take the car back to the office, and I'll meet you back there." Frank put his arm around Joey and handed him the keys. There was no further conversation about it, and Joey understood my position and his.

Frank waited for me to begin, and once out of earshot from anyone, I explained the need for this meeting.

"I got a visit today from some detective at the DA's office. He was asking me questions about a murder that supposedly happened yesterday. He says my name came up in the investigation. For a murder to happen and the next day I get a visit, that's quite a coincidence. It usually takes weeks for the cops to even think of a motive or suspect and usually never figure anything out."

Frank had his standard questions he needed to know in order to assess the situation and formulate a defense and strategy. "Did you say anything to the detective?" Frank said, knowing I wouldn't, but he had to hear it from me.

"I told him I was represented by counsel and to leave my joint."

Frank had a prideful smirk of elation as I did as I had always been instructed, especially under these types of circumstances.

"The guy's name is Sullivan." I handed Frank the business card the detective left on my juice bar.

Frank looked at the card as I continued to speak. It looked as if he were trying to place the name in his head.

"The Irishman kept trying to speak to me even after I told him I had counsel and wanted him to leave," I said as Frank studied the card.

"What else?" Frank said eagerly, trying to decipher everything that was said between the detective and me.

"I told him I didn't know what part of 'I'm represented by counsel' and 'exit my establishment' was difficult to comprehend."

Frank and I both had a good laugh about it. The seriousness was still there, but some time had passed, and thinking back, I realized my comment was funny, at least in my circles. Some levity in an otherwise serious predicament was needed. Finishing the laugh, Frank began to recollect more about the detective that visited me.

"Is he a big Irishman, dirty-blond flattop haircut?" Frank asked while picturing the detective in his mind.

"Yeah, Frank, that's him, all right," I said, validating Frank's recollection.

"He's an investigator with the district attorney's office in their organized crime division," Frank said with confidence now, starting to get a better idea of the situation.

"Well, how did he get to me so quickly?" I asked quizzically.

"That I don't know, but you did the right thing by saying what you said and contacting me. We'll find out more as the DA's office goes through their investigation and process. One thing's for sure, they don't have anything concrete, or we would be having this conversation through bars."

"Frank, can you give me any pretext to the cops coming to see me?" I said, still trying to find some answer as to why me and why this quickly.

"I would guess someone told the investigators that you and whoever is now deceased had issues, or a connection between you was a possibility for his demise. There could have been something on the scene that pointed to you, but I believe it's just some hearsay. You know I don't like speculating about anything. We'll just sit tight and see what happens. We need to nip this in the bud and get all our ducks in a row. I'm sure you have an alibi for yesterday." Frank wasn't only hinting that I had one, but if not, then this was the time to start formulating one.

"I was at my restaurant the entire day. My chef and waitress can verify the fact I never left. The only time I was out, and perhaps unaccounted for, would have been when I did my daily bank deposit. That was at two thirty. Round trip, I was back at the restaurant in thirty to forty minutes tops. I'm on camera at the bank, making the deposit, which I know is time-stamped. The rest of the afternoon and evening, I was at the restaurant and never left. I'm sure with credit card receipts I can have patrons of my joint verify I was there as well. Sullivan never gave a time of the murder, but I believe I'm all covered from before five in the morning until well after eleven at night."

"No need to ask your customers about anything just yet. Gather whatever you have about your alibi and hold onto it until it's needed. So far, I didn't see anything on the news yet, but there will be if not already. Stay at your restaurant and always have someone with you wherever you go. If you have to leave, make sure to take someone with you at all times. I don't want the cops having the idea they can harass you or otherwise," Frank said, giving me his best advice.

Frank's advice was always top-notch. He always seemed to be right and usually was. I trusted him implicitly with everything, and his counseling was invaluable.

"Thanks, Frank. You're the best. I appreciate everything," I said, giving him a hug and a kiss on the cheek.

"That's why I bill as the best," Frank said with his usual quick wit as we both laughed.

I drove Frank back to his office, and we spoke about the Yankees and our families, never anything in the car, ever. I dropped him off and headed directly to my routine at my restaurant.

With my dinner crowd just starting to file in, my girlfriend came into the kitchen and was visibly a bit frantic.

"Turn on the news!" she said, pointing to the television.

I had a small television in the kitchen that I used to break up the monotony of my days or for when there was nothing else happening and I was bored. I turned on the local news, and in short order, the anchorman for the local news channel was speaking.

"In the early morning hours, an explosion erupted in the otherwise-quiet suburban neighborhood of Ossining. A law enforcement source said a white Lincoln-model car was on fire when police and fire department personnel arrived on the scene. It took about thirty minutes for the fire to be extinguished. The damage was limited to mainly one vehicle, a white Lincoln. Other cars were damaged from what sources say was shrapnel sent into the air from the explosion. At the moment, police are saying that there is one fatality. He's been identified, but the name of the deceased isn't being released until the family has been notified," the anchorman said, giving some very broad details.

The camera then panned to a police spokesman, who was just beginning their mini press conference with some questions and answers.

"By *victim*, then you believe there's foul play involved?" a reporter asked.

"At this time, we believe the explosion was no accident. Some shrapnel was found embedded in other vehicles, but no other persons were injured. We don't have any further information to offer as our investigation is in its early stages. The arson investigators are finishing their report. We will be releasing more information about the exact cause of the explosion and the death of the individual once the proper procedures are taken," the police spokesman said.

"Is there anything you can tell us about a possible motive or explanation for the cause of the explosion and death?" Another reporter wanted more explanation.

"As I previously stated, we can't speak about any ongoing investigation, especially at this early stage in the process. I can tell you that the medical examiner will be releasing their findings to us as soon as possible, and then we can release them to the public once we have more concrete facts. One more question before we have to go. Yes, you in the back." The spokesman pointed to another reporter in the crowd.

"Detective, you mentioned *shrapnel*. Was there a bomb or some sort of device that was used?"

"Again, we're going to wait for a definitive word from the arson investigator. Some of the shrapnel found wasn't from the white Lincoln vehicle. We'll be forthcoming with information as it's made available to us and we proceed with our investigation." The spokesman looked as if he didn't want to respond any further, and certainly not to anything more specific.

The spokesman walked off, and the reporter continued with his broadcast from the scene. The scene was filled with police in a roped-off area where the explosion happened. Both sides of the street where the explosion happened were cordoned off with more investigators and officials. Even from the distance the camera was positioned, we could see the shell of a car and some other minor damage from the blast.

"It's apparent this was no accident. Cars don't burn like that without help, and with comments like *shrapnel*, it leads us to believe there must have been a device of some sort as the cause of the explosion. This is Sean Carver reporting from the ongoing investigation of a car explosion in Ossining. Back to Sue in the studio," the on-site reporter said.

I didn't want to show any emotion one way or the other. My chef and girlfriend were watching the report with me, and I needed to show my indifference. They had suspicions, and my chef only knew what I told him, which was "Talk to nobody and notify me if someone approaches you." He was no idiot, and being around me for almost a year, he had his ideas about me. My chef wouldn't be working in my restaurant if he didn't, on some level, understand his surroundings.

"How's the crowd shaping up out there?" I said to my waitress as she walked into the kitchen with perfect timing.

"It's just starting to get busy. We have three tables just sitting, and another was walking in as I was walking into the kitchen."

My girlfriend appeared to be in shock, and the best thing for that was to act as if nothing happened and we never heard a thing. She also knew when I wanted to speak on something or when it was best to move on from the subject. If these events and others that were part and parcel to the lifestyle I was involved in didn't occur, perhaps our relationship would have turned out differently. Most of my relationships fell victim to my lifestyle. Many women find my lifestyle attractive, but that came from a viewpoint of the Hollywood version they had fallen in love with or some peripheral sense they got when they saw all the good things and enjoyed the perks of the lifestyle. Some women want a bad-boy type, and there are characteristics that are appealing—that's undeniable. The worse the boy, the harder the personal relationship is to survive.

The coming weeks were more of the usual for me. With the revelation that the boxer, one of Mike's trio, was the person in the car, I received increased attention from law enforcement. I also learned that Mike was the one that went to the district attorney's office the day of the car bombing and spilled his guts about the beef he and I had. He implicated himself in the steroid business and told the authorities he feared for his life. All I could think was *What a jerk.* This guy came to me for help, and whether it was his intention to try to fuck me over or not, all he did was screw himself over and got a good friend of his killed for no reason.

Mike didn't have any specific information that I felt concerned about. There weren't any names, numbers, or locations he could offer law enforcement. The only reason I could surmise Mike went to the authorities was that Mike figured it was his only option, even if it meant exposing himself and his role. His actions never made much sense to me, so this was just another move he made that fell in line with his character.

Vincent was on the lamb (hiding out), and he didn't want any part of either end of the exchange, so that option for Mike was a dead end. There was no connection between my people and what was going on. My alibi was airtight, and so far, aside from some increased law enforcement presence, I wasn't in any danger of being anything more than a suspect. The increased law enforcement pressure wasn't something I enjoyed and was something I was hoping to distance myself from. I opened my restaurant to try to start a different way for myself.

Aside from my girlfriend being miffed at me, she knew some things were out of my control, and the topic never came up past that one day. She and I never spoke about the particulars, as was the norm for not only our relationship but also the lifestyle. The need-to-know basis was always in effect and was standard operating procedure. My girlfriend knew of some of my affiliations; hell, she introduced me to the Russians. She didn't know anything or anyone concrete, and that was how I needed it for everyone concerned.

Frank filled back up our glasses, and instead of speaking further on anything, he placed the half-finished-off bottle of tequila down and proposed a toast.

"Here's to our sixth sense and gut feelings. May they never steer us wrong," Frank poetically said.

We finished off that bottle and more of another as we spoke no more of anything besides good times, old times, and anything not associated with the knowledge that this would probably be our last time seeing each other.

* * *

"Sir, Mr. B——," Ms. Herrera said, snapping me out of my trance-like flashback.

Ms. Herrera had my paperwork in her hand and was looking at me intently.

"Is everything all right, Mr. B——?" Ms. Herrera asked, handing me my paperwork with a look of concern on her face.

"Yes, I'm fine, thank you. I'm not much one for air travel," I replied to Ms. Herrera as I took hold of my documents and paperwork.

I gave that as my excuse partly because it was true and partly because it was the first thing that came to my mind. Heights and sharks are the only two things I fear in life. I tried not to think of what I was leaving behind. A lifetime of work. Yeah, I wasn't even thirty years old yet, but I lived a lifetime thus far and busted my ass to get where I was. Where I was was what I thought I needed to leave behind. It sounds confusing, but imagine me living it; that's confusing.

"I totally understand that. It's a necessary evil. Mr. B———, have a pleasant flight and peaceful holiday. You'll be departing from gate 42 to your left, up the escalator, and follow the signs to your assigned gate," Ms. Herrera said in a soft manner.

Ms. Herrera then looked into my eyes, and before I could say anything, she spoke directly. "Thank you," she said with our eyes locked.

I didn't believe I did anything special aside from being observant and aware. I said it was my pleasure and wished her the best of the holidays. Sometimes it's the slightest bit of attention and attention to detail that counts. Little did she know that she did some of that for me, letting me relive a part I was leaving behind.

The federal agent was just off my left shoulder as I turned and made my way to the escalator. Just ten feet away now and making my way toward my destination, I noticed the agent's attention wasn't on me or anything in my direction but rather ahead and of those entering the airport. I caught a glimpse of the clipboard he was holding and a glimpse of one of the photos on it. I was passing behind him and didn't want to spend a lot of time looking in his direction. A quick glimpse, and I saw one was an old Department of Motor Vehicle picture and the partial of a grainy black-and-white surveillance photo. I kept moving without breaking a stride in hopes I passed the last hurdle of law enforcement.

I took as many precautions as possible, and only a handful of people knew I was embarking on my new journey. I wondered why these agents were looking for me and what agency they represented.

All this information I could process as soon as I was in a *safe* place, if there were such a thing. Nobody knew where I was going and when. I had been to Mexico so many times before, so the airport could have been the logical place to look for me.

Up the escalator I went and didn't even look back in hopes I was in the clear. Down a hallway to the next security station checkpoint would be my next hurdle. Here I would pass through the metal detector and x-ray machine checking my carry-on luggage, my documents, and at times, a pat-down.

I showed the security agent my boarding pass and passport. She proceeded to signal me through, and I placed my briefcase and laptop in a bin through the conveyor belt to be scanned. The rest of my odds and ends, watch, and change from my pocket, bracelet, belt, etc., went into a separate bin that I slid through the conveyor belt as well.

The security agent doing the x-ray screening had no pauses as he looked at the items going through his view. I passed through the metal detector and waited for my belongings to finish and roll down to me. While I was waiting for my briefcase, laptop, and odds and ends, there were two security personnel standing near me.

"Good morning, sir," one of the security agents said to me as I gathered my belongings and placed everything in its proper place.

"Good morning to you. I hope you guys aren't too busy on the holidays," I retorted with some kind small talk.

The tone of voice I was addressed with wasn't investigative, and no alarms went off in my mind. He sounded like he was merely passing time, and unless something out of the ordinary arose, he would be waving me through and not bat an eye.

"Business or vacation?" the other security agent asked me.

"Pure vacation," I said, knowing full well that this was where the security could still question me or do a more thorough search of my items if they so chose to. "I'm taking advantage of the low airfares and hotel rates while I can. Most people are flying in and staying away from the resorts, and that's where I prefer to spend my holidays."

"That makes perfect sense. I never thought of that. Have a great flight, sir, and be safe," the first security agent told me.

"You both enjoy your holidays and be safe yourselves."

The security agent's parting words in my mind read, "From your lips to God's ears."

I made it to gate 42 to see the board hanging down with red neon lights that read Flight 451: Belize City. The airport was pretty busy, and I did my best to blend in with my fellow holiday travelers. I got stuck looking at the flight board as a rush of other thoughts went over me. I began thinking this would be my last time being in New York—or anywhere in the United States for that matter. I looked down at my watch and saw I had over an hour until my flight was to depart. I wasn't much of a drinker, but in this situation and this scenario, I was going to the watering hole and having myself a couple of drinks. Not far away from and with my gate in site, I found the perfect location to sit, have a couple of drinks, and await my flight. I positioned myself near the back of the establishment with a clear view of my gate and whoever was coming or going in either direction, my back against the wall. I ordered a double Bloody Mary and eased myself into my seat, taking a deep breath.

An hour and ten minutes passed, and I heard the call for my flight over the loudspeaker come through. I took a bite of celery from my second drink and the final sip of my red cocktail. Paying my tab, I headed toward my gate as the first-class seating was called. Heading out of the bar, I again heard my calling. "Now boarding at gate 42, all first-class passengers bound for Belize City flight 451. That's flight 451, destination, Belize City, Belize."

Approaching the gate, I was both nervous and anxious. I was leaving everything I had known my whole life behind, including friends, family, and career. I was third in line getting onto the plane for first-class passengers and couldn't help but take in the sights of New York before boarding. I saw onto the tarmac the cold, snowy New York that I called home. There was nothing quite like New York. Born and raised here, you are certainly part of the city, the smells, the people, the experiences, the food, the character and characters, the sights, the sounds, and the ups and downs no matter where you go or how much time you spend away from it. People from around the world can recognize a true New Yorker not just by the sound of his voice but by his walk, his style, his mannerisms, his class, and his character.

"Sir, your boarding pass," the ticket agent said to me as I was again in a trance and snapped out of it when her voice hit my ears.

"But of course," I said, handing her my ticket and boarding pass.

With her smile and pleasantries out of the way, I walked down the jet bridge, the tube connecting the plane with the airport gate. Approaching the entrance to the plane, I was greeted by two lovely stewardesses. Right away, one stewardess caught my eye—just my type. They both said "Hello" and I said "Hello" in return, my eye contact with the one I found attractive, never leaving her almond-shaped brown eyes. I was escorted to my seat by the other stewardess and found the first class on this plane to be to my liking. A high-back wide leather seat that reclined almost all the way had me melting directly into it. I was arranging my laptop and briefcase with my head facing the window and my mind elsewhere when a sultry voice behind me brought me around.

"Buenos dias, senor."

I turned to find the stewardess that caught my eye. Five feet nine inches tall, long dark hair, just a hint of makeup on her smooth brown skin highlighting her full, natural lips. Although her uniform wasn't a pattern I would have chosen for her, it accented her full figure and childbearing hips. As much as the top of her uniform tried to hide her breasts, the DD beauties couldn't go unnoticed.

Her voice really struck a chord with me, and I was busy taking in her essence when she spoke again.

"May I get you something to eat or drink before we take off, Mr. B——?"

For a moment I must have looked like a deer in the headlights as I never thought, nor did I expect, this beauty to be serving me during my flight, especially when the other stewardess escorted me to my seat.

The stewardess leaned in so other passengers boarding the plane could funnel into their seats. Her name tag now in full view and more in my face, I read her name and responded.

"Good morning, Gabriella. That's a beautiful name and suits you perfectly. I'll have a double Bloody Mary thank you very much," I said, sitting down in my seat and accepting a menu that Gabriella handed me.

"I'll see about a food order when you return with my drink," I said, still studying her.

"Thank you, Senor B——," Gabriella said as she walked to the first-class galley, dismissing herself.

I browsed the menu and found what interested me. Not a few minutes passed, and Gabriella returned with my drink and took my food order. By now about half of the passengers were on board and adjusting their overhead luggage.

"Your Bloody Mary, Sir," Gabriella said as she was once again serving me and leaned in to turn down my food tray.

She placed my drink on the tray in front of me, and before I could muster a thank-you, Gabriella was already asking for my food order.

"Is there anything I can get for you from the menu?" Gabriella said, now putting some innuendos in the air.

Our eyes met and Gabriella couldn't remain in eye contact with me for too long, and I wasn't letting her off the hook just yet; I had to let what she just said sit there for a moment.

"I would like a cinnamon raisin bagel toasted with a little cream cheese. An egg white omelet with mushrooms, tomatoes, and American cheese. Half a cantaloupe with cottage cheese. Coffee, dark and strong, will do just fine with a glass of orange juice."

Gabriella kept pace with me, taking my order, as the preflight announcements were just about to come over the intercom system.

"Very good, senor." Gabriella was about to say something else before I cut her off.

"I love how the word *senor* rolls off your lips, but please call me J——. Senor B—— is my father, and I'm curious how J—— rolls of your tongue and lips."

Gabriella's guard came down, and inhibitions blown away. She smiled coyly and slowly spoke, making sure to enunciate every letter for me.

"Yes, J——," Gabriella said, highlighting the *J* while rolling it off her tongue and lips, making sure her lips were properly pouting.

Gabriella knew what she was doing and knew just what I wanted. I thought I was using my inner voice, but apparently, I said it out loud.

"Perfect," the only word that came to my mind that encompassed all my thoughts.

"I'll be back shortly with your order," Gabriella said as she turned to get to my order.

"Thank you, Gabriella." Three words were all I could muster.

The security procedures and general information were coming over the airplane intercom system. I didn't even realize the airplane had detached itself from the gate and began to make its way to the runway for taxiing. *That was fast,* I thought. I began to feel a slight unease in the pit of my stomach, realizing that in short order, the plane would be thrusting its way down the runway and into the air. I downed about half my drink and reached into my shirt to clutch onto a medal my grandmother gave me as a child, blessed by our family priest, my father's best friend. Both sides of my family are devout Roman Catholics, and my upbringing was steeped in religion. For me, Sunday Mass was a given, a family affair and tradition. The medal my grandmother gave me was a St. Jude's medal, the patron saint of the lost causes. Maybe it was my grandmother's vision of my future that caused her to gift me the medal. Whatever the case, I was taught St. Jude's prayer, which, oddly enough, comforted me in times of need, when everything else around me was spinning out of control and events that couldn't be reversed were already in progress. Closing my eyes, I began to recite.

"Sacred heart of Jesus, have mercy on me. St. Jude, worker of miracles, pray for me. St. Jude, the helper and keeper of the hopeless, pray for me."

I repeated this prayer over and over until I felt the wheels of the plane begin to lift and the distance between the aircraft and the ground grew farther apart. The plane was at a point where it wasn't as vertical as first taking off. I opened my eyes, drank the remainder of my Bloody Mary, and exhaled deep.

The year before high school, I was caught with a gun in school. I had a gut feeling I was going to have issues that day in school because I was shooting birds in the school parking lot, and that was at lunchtime. I didn't hide the fact that I was shooting the gun off, and for some reason, I wasn't concerned with what others saw. Before going back inside the school for the remainder of the day, I took the firing pin out of the gun so it would be rendered useless. I had a feeling someone would rat me out to the principal or worse, and I wasn't going to take any chances. Thinking back, though, I wonder why I wasn't concerned about police or school authorities, even my father, for that matter. At a young age, I knew my way around a gun. Lo and behold, I was called to the principal's' office not long after lunch break, and there was my father and the principal. Now, my father never took off from work at all. My father being there because of what I did was bad, but the worst of it was him having to miss some work because of me. My father was a hardworking man, and for him to have to miss work because of something like this, I knew I was in for it even worse. I knew I would have to hear that, and just hearing it would be the best-case scenario for me.

Being the gun wasn't operational, I escaped being dismissed from school and prosecuted. The long and the short of it was, my father gave me an ultimatum. I had two choices with what I wanted to do, reform school or all-boys Catholic prep school. Not much options for me, but I chose the lesser of the two evils, the way I saw it. My father already had the school in mind; it was where he went to school with most of his brothers, and my brother went there, but not because he was bad; it was his choice.

In my second year in high school, I was gravitating toward a more religious life. Seeing the priests and the dedication and devotion they showed was moving, to say the least. How a man can forgo all the pleasures / worldly desires and dedicate himself to a religion and calling of God were enticing. I saw it before in priests, but seeing it everyday and having the personal interactions that I did, I was becoming drawn to it. On the surface, I saw men dedicated to a calling, men with strong principles, men driven by a common belief in a higher being, men whom a large number of the world population entrusted to instruct them with the Word of God. Dedication, respect, honor, drive, passion were the base characteristics I was instilled with since I could remember. I held them dear to me no matter the circumstance or calling. A man must be dedicated to something and have principles he holds true and grasps onto especially in trying times. A man's beliefs, his core beliefs, will form his decisions and actions. They should never be compromised for anyone or anything for it will change his character.

I was a young man drawn to this type of dedication. By my third year in high school, I began assisting with morning Mass at my school chapel. I can't place the exact timeline as to when it happened. My best guess is when I injured myself in football and was nearly paralyzed. Between being severely injured, having a Catholic background, I was drawn even closer to God.

The top floor of the school was where the priests who taught in the school lived along with some more elderly priests who had retired. I was happy to see that the church took care of their priests, both present and past, and held them in such high regard.

One morning, I was early to school and went to our school's chapel and saw one of our resident priests saying Mass. I entered the chapel, sat in on the Mass, and was drawn to it. Something was driving me there; there are no such things as coincidences, and I was there for a reason. Soon I began purposely leaving my house early and getting to the morning Mass before my school day began. On Sundays, I would also assist with Mass at the local parish my family and I attended. Some months into my involvement with assisting with Mass, I began believing I could see myself devoting my life to this calling. I was seeing a dedication and way of life that others respected, admired, and people entrusted their families to. The power and respect these men of the cloth wielded were intoxicating. I was interested in going all in and adhering to the structure and regulations the Catholic Church mandated.

When I reached my senior year and my thoughts were turning to the seminary, I was more focused than ever. I don't know if it was me maturing or the fact that events were coming to a head at my school, but I began to notice some differences between the year before and my last. The chinks in the priestly armor were beginning to show themselves. I saw priests who were supposed to have taken a vow of poverty driving a classic Mustang, BMWs, and other luxury vehicles. The priest I assisted many Masses with those weekdays in our school chapel, delivering the Word of God, was a full-blown alcoholic. He was saying Mass a bunch of times, and I could smell it. Mind you, Mass was said and over way before eight in the morning. Corporal punishment was prevalent in my school, and there were times when out-and-out beatings with closed fists at the hands of the priests took place inside the school. What could possibly be the rationale for a grown man, a man of God, to closed-fist-punch a minor? After I graduated from high school, I heard the principal of my school was excused from his position for having sexual relations with some of the students. It was always rumored to be so, but I thought it was just boys being boys. Some of my fellow students would adjourn to his office, and the principal would take them on trips and such.

Why would I dedicate my life to something that others I encountered pretended to do? It was not that I saw every priest not adhering to his vows; it was just the ones I saw, the ones I was with for days, weeks, and years and had come to respect and admire. So when I realized the transgressions, I was totally turned off at joining the seminary, and I made a complete 180-degree turn. Where I grew up, the main choices of occupations were one of the three Cs: cop, criminal, or clergy. I was surrounded by all three of these polar opposite callings. My grandfather was one of the top cops in New York, and I never really had a desire to become a cop. My ultimate choice not to become a member of the boys in blue was when my grandfather told me to never become one and it wasn't worth it. Whatever his reasons were, I didn't know. To me, my grandfather was a godlike figure, and his words cemented the feelings I had on not making that a career path. Core beliefs I was instilled with and attracted to—

dedication, drive, passion, commitment, brotherhood—I found in the clergy. This I thought to be my calling. The priests I was around were empowering and imposing figures. I looked up to the priests as men of calling and the ultimate men of sacrifice. Forgoing all worldly benefits. For a young kid looking for dedication and devotion, the priesthood was the ultimate choice. When the years showed the human side of man in some of the priests I admired and looked up to, it was enough to have me do a complete reversal of mind-set. Not reversal in my core beliefs, but a reversal in my life's dedication. At the parallel time in my life I was choosing a life of God, I was around members of a different group. Those involved with organized crime. Yes, they were polar opposites, or at least so I thought at the time. The same characteristics I was drawn to, the wise guys had. As my teenage years progressed, I saw that the priests and gangsters had some similar qualities, except the gangsters didn't have the hypocrisy associated with their calling.

I still had my religion and carried it with me; it was my solace even if I wasn't involved in organized religion anymore. I prayed and had pieces of my religious past that I used and held on to that helped me in times when I much needed them later in life. The St. Jude's medal I was gifted and the prayer that I was taught, later in life, I learned the value of and the depth it represented. I had my relationship with God, and when my day would come, I knew I would have to reconcile with my maker. That was my choice.

I tried to keep my mind off the what-ifs, what could have been, and what would be. I was leaving behind my family, career, lifestyle, language, food, culture, friends, and associates. If I were to think long and hard about the what-ifs, I could drive myself crazy, lose focus, and expose myself to risk. It was this fleeting moment of solitude that brought these thoughts on. Thank God they were few and far between and actually quite rare. The wandering mind, if left to its own device, can be a dangerous and potentially deadly creature. A sound mind and learning to control one's thoughts and emotions are vital. Making sound decisions will cancel many of the what-ifs. Focusing on the tasks at hand from the planning to the goals and the execution should be done with a sense of purpose. Not every decision will go your way, but take your time and think before the decision is made. Thinking of every possible outcome and aftermath saves on possible negative outcomes. Once a decision is made, I take ownership of them and see it through to the end. Never apologize; it only shows ignorance and lack of thought, something a grown man in my world couldn't afford.

I had finished my deep breath but still had my St. Jude's medal in my hand and was lost in thought when Gabriella began placing my breakfast on my tray and opened the tray next to me for the rest of my order.

"J——," Gabriella said softly to me as she placed my order on the table and saw I was deep in thought.

"Thank you for breakfast, Gabriella. I was daydreaming a bit. Another double Bloody Mary, please, if you will," I said, handing Gabriella my empty glass.

"Of course, J——. Is there anything else I can get for you?"

"Yes, some orange juice as well. Thank you."

"I'll be right back with your drinks, *buen provecho*," Gabriella said to me to enjoy my meal.

"Thank you."

The in-flight meal was quite enjoyable, and the flight was smooth. I took my time with my meal and sat back, enjoying the ambience of first class. I had just finished my meal, and Gabriella's timing was as impeccable as it had been the entire flight.

"Can I take some of this out of the way for you?"

"Everything but my drink, thank you," I said, sitting back in my seat and letting Gabriella clear my plates and glasses for me.

"How was everything?" Gabriella said in her accommodating manner.

"Better than I expected, and better service than I could have hoped for. Impeccable," I said, looking directly into Gabriella's deep brown eyes.

"What's that word?" Gabriella said, turning around and placing my dishes on her cart.

"It means flawless, perfect," I said with confidence and enunciation, looking over my right shoulder, staring at Gabriella's round and shapely backside.

"Thank you, J——," Gabriella said, turning around, and me not flinching from looking in her direction.

"Totally my pleasure, Gabriella," I said quickly.

"Not yet," Gabriella said with a growing quick wit based on our burgeoning rapport.

Both Gabriella and I had smiles on our faces the remainder of the flight, a good thing for me, keeping my mind off what I left behind and the unknown I was soon to face.

With the flight about thirty minutes away from landing in Belize, Gabriella came to check on me.

"We are thirty minutes from landing. Is there anything else I can get for you?" Gabriella bent down this time and leaned in a bit and enunciated her words like music to my ears.

"Please. A vodka cranberry and the name of your hotel," I said, not batting an eye.

"Hotel La Paz. Gabriella Torres. Are you in Belize for business or pleasure?" Gabriella responded as if she were expecting me to take the lead, and she followed.

"Pleasure, pure pleasure," I said right back at her with conviction.

"I'm on an overnight layover. I'll be right back with your drink, J——."

Gabriella wanted it known that she was spending the evening in Belize, and after giving me her name and hotel information that quickly, I knew the feelings were mutual.

Gabriella returned with my drink, handing me a tourist card to fill out for customs and immigration in Belize. She told me she had some duties to attend to and excused herself. The copilot came over the airplane intercom. We would be landing in Belize City, Belize. The weather was eighty-five degrees sunny and pleasant. The local time was one something, and my mind began to consider all the variables. I sipped on my drink, tasting the fresh cranberry juice mixed well with the Grey Goose vodka. Feeling the plane drop even farther, I instinctively looked out the window to get a good look at a different world. I looked for a time until the uneasiness had me look away again. Friggin' hcights did it to mc every time. The water was an amazing shade of turquoise. The jungle below was a stark contrast to the snowy city skyline I had left just this morning. Gabriella intuitively stopped one last time to see if I was all right before heading to her seat for the landing. That was what I was attracted to in her; she was very attentive, even more than what her job required.

The sound of the landing gear dropping, the sight of the vastly different airport below—I almost forgot what I had just left behind.

With the wheels touching down to a thundering applause from the other passengers in coach, I was now focused on the task at hand, passing Belizean customs. It was my first time in Belize, so the waters were certainly uncharted, but not a situation I was unfamiliar with. I had an edge by being briefed ahead of time on the layout of the Belizean airport on how the agents and police operated there.

The plane came to a stop after a few minutes of taxiing. I undid my seat belt, gathered my briefcase and laptop, and walked toward the exit of the plane. I was a little excited to say good-bye to Gabriella. My excitement was that and also knowing that I would have some friendly company in a new country.

"Thank you for flying with us today. Happy holidays and have a great stay while in Belize," the copilot said to me as I exited.

"Thank you for flying with us, sir," Gabriella said with almost a sly smile, knowing I preferred J——, but she had to switch back to *sir*.

"Thank you for a pleasant flight, and have a great evening," I said.

My good-byes were spoken to all, but when it got to the evening part, my eyes went directly to Gabriella's. My meaning was escaping everyone but Gabriella.

CHAPTER 2

BELIZE

"Yes, he's here. I'm watching him right now. From the picture and what you described, it's him, and there's nobody else that even comes close to that. He came off the plane first, so I'm guessing he was in first class. He has a beard and shaved head, but it's him for sure. Just one suitcase and what looks like a briefcase and laptop computer. No, he's by himself and walking through customs now. He's approaching my area and will be passing by my window in a couple of minutes," the Belizean Army captain said, speaking into the receiver of a cell phone.

The captain was considered tall for his countrymen, standing well over six feet, three inches tall, was well dressed, and had impeccable hygiene. His uniform was clad with the insignia of the branch he served in, the collar with his rank. The captain's office overlooked the airport, and when passengers finished with their customs declarations, they needed to pass by his office before heading to the last security area before being allowed to enter the country.

"He's reaching me now and passing me to go through to the last security check," the captain said as he watched the man he had a photo of pass him by.

The captain then began laughing as he saw the man he was watching reach the checkpoint and press the button that determined whether or not he walked out of the airport or was questioned further and perhaps detained.

"He pressed the light and it came up red," he said with laughter. "Want me to intervene and grab him? No, okay, I'll keep you posted on what happens." The captain kept both eyes on his new arrival and spoke into his cell phone.

CHAPTER 2

BELIZE

As I stepped into the jet bridge, my body and face were hit with an intense temperature. Coming from the tundra of New York and the air-conditioning of the airplane, I felt this change in temperature right away. The heat was intensified by the sun's rays bouncing off the asphalt below, and although the temperature wasn't anything drastic, it was drastic for me.

The sixty feet of jet bridge I walked through led me to the airport, where again cooler temperatures hit my body. My first look into the Belize City airport, and I thought I was taking a step back in time. Off to my right were two luggage carousels, the closest of which began to spin. Directly in front of me, about a hundred feet off, were three immigration and customs booths. There was nobody manning them yet, but I saw some action behind them and knew the booths would be ready as the passengers came to them with their bags and documentation. The decor of the airport was drab and plain, with it looking as if it could use a renovation at least. Four military personnel were walking about, paired up in twos, armed with automatic weapons, patrolling the inside of the small airport. I could see off to my left, about a hundred feet, another security measure kind of like ours in the States where you had to pass the customs officials before being able to leave the airport. That area was cordoned off with a rudimentary chain with removable posts. It was clear you weren't allowed to cross the chain, as whimsical as it appeared to be. The entire airport inside appeared to be about thirty thousand square feet, give or take, and certainly what I considered small for an international airport.

Five minutes passed since I entered the airport, and the luggage from the carousel began appearing. Other passengers had already begun filing into the airport and positioning themselves around the carousel to retrieve their luggage. Apparently, we were the only flight that had arrived, not something that I would usually enjoy. I preferred when there were multiple flights so the customs and immigration people generally would speed up their process and wouldn't want to delve too deep into who was who and who was here for what.

My luggage appeared around the tenth piece that had dropped down, and I grabbed it as it made its half turn toward me. In one motion, I turned toward the immigration line that was just starting to form. Looking at the three potential agents that would be handling my paperwork and stamping my documents, I assessed each one quickly to see their demeanor and body language. There were other factors that came into play when I was assessing who was who in the immigration line. Their sex, age, manner of dressing, whether they were appearing tired or overzealous, etc. I had my passport and tourist card inside my left jacket pocket ready to go when the line would fall on me to be next. One agent was a woman and the other, two men. They didn't look particularly concerned about doing any more work than their shift called on them to perform, and so far, nobody had issues with any of them. All three looked quite robotic in action. I could see the top half of them through the glass partition and could watch their body movements and actions. The Belizean immigration authority seemed like a rubber-stamping authority more than an investigative one. There appeared to be no computers or technology that they used in determining passengers' paperwork's validity or its accuracy. Our flight brought in about fifty people, not including the crew that would have to go through this process.

A spot was opening, and I made my way to the third agent in the booth line, a male. He was short and appeared to be a little over five feet tall and had a mustache and uniform that looked worn for someone on the job as long as he was, being in his late forties. His face was a bit pockmarked and worn from the sun. The long hours he had to put in for very little pay were probably the cause for him looking outwardly tired. I presented him my paperwork so he didn't have to mention anything by the time his head elevated to speak. I wanted to take as many variables out of the way as possible. I said "Hello" to him in English and pretended to be a regular tourist there on a holiday, eager to be in a new country. He reciprocated very little as I knew his English would prevent anything further than the basic greetings.

In no time, my paperwork was stamped, and I was on my way to the last security location before leaving the airport. I tucked the paperwork back into my left inside jacket pocket and grabbed my luggage. I had to turn left to the waiting customs officials but first pass by a series of glass offices. Not wanting to look at the officials and agents in the rooms, I looked straight ahead at what lay in front of me. I briefly scanned the offices through my peripheral vision and made sure there was nothing out of the ordinary. I always had to be aware of what and who was around me at all times, a creature of habit. I noticed one man through the glass standing in the last room of the row. A few things that stood out for me was his height and the fact that he was on a cell phone and was an officer. I didn't know much about the Belizean military, but distinguishing rank wasn't that difficult to do. Just past this glass window with the officer in it, I focused on the last stage of the immigration process. It was about a hundred feet away, plenty of time for the agents to assess me and me them. There were two long tables, one for each line, and in front of each was an old-fashioned traffic light. The process apparently was to stop in front of the button and press it. The light would either come up green and you would pass or red and you would be delayed for a further check of your luggage and/or interrogation.

My heart rate remained normal as I knew I had secured everything quite well. I knew they wouldn't be able to discern anything with my paperwork, especially if the Americans couldn't decipher real from fake. I was pretty sure these guys wouldn't be any Dick

Tracys. I never got caught out of character and wasn't going to begin here.

The line I got in had three officers in it that waited for the light to turn its color. There was one male and two females. I could see two more soldiers near the exit of the airport, about three quarters of the way between me and the exit. I chose the line with more females, hoping that if my light turned red, I would have an easier go at it with female officers than male officers, who might have some jealousy or feel like they needed to prove something.

I approached the light, and one of the females told me in broken English to press the button. Standing in front of this thing, I felt like something from *Let's Make a Deal* and the model was moving her hand over the prize, giving me the body language that this was my prize. It was like a game show with two women on either side of me, showing more skin than they should be showing. The only thing was, this was reality, and what was behind door number 3 might be a Belizean version of a zonk, a nightmare. I must have been the topic of the two women agents' conversation the way the two giggled and looked at me. The officer who motioned for me to press the button was about thirty-three years old, five feet six inches tall, and had black hair, the front of which resembled a claw held together by at least half a can of hairspray. Her skin tone was brown and light in comparison to others. She was a bit overweight, and that's being generous. Her tight brown uniform highlighted the areas where she let herself go. Her brown eyes were transfixed on me, but not in an authoritative way. I stepped up to the light, following the officer's hand motion, placed my luggage on the floor, and pressed the light.

As I pressed the light, it turned red. In Spanish, the woman that motioned for me to press the button told me to place my suitcase and bags on the table just ahead of the light. I understood what she said but pretended I was having trouble comprehending her language. She pointed to my suitcase and luggage and pointed at the table. I responded by saying yes and doing as instructed.

"Ese guapo no entiende," the woman speaking continued in Spanish, saying that this good-looking guy didn't understand.

The two women had their giggle, and I knew they found me attractive, but there were other things in play now. How far would they go in searching me and my luggage, and would the male agent or others intervene and be thorough? The male officer stepped closer and began inspecting my bags, as did the women. I drew a little more attention from the soldiers but not because of anything else besides me being a larger American and the light turning red.

As the inspection of my bags began, I noticed the flight crew was walking through the inspection area and nobody was searching them. The crew was focused on walking out, and aside from the few second glances that Gabriella and I shared, none of the other crew members paid any attention and were concerned with exiting the airport.

"Vacaciones or negocios?" the male officer asked me as he opened my bags and moved around my items.

"Vacation," I replied, sticking to not speaking Spanish and playing the tourist role.

The five-minute search was nearing an end, and the trio couldn't find anything in my luggage that was out of the ordinary. I don't believe they were equipped to know what to look for. The other reason why the search was so cursory was because I was entering Belize from the United States, and the Belizean authority wasn't concerned about things entering their country. I mean, who would smuggle drugs or contraband into Belize, especially from the United States? The flow typically goes north, not south.

"Have a good stay," the male officer said with broken English as he zipped up my suitcase. It probably was the extent of his English.

Both the female officers had smiles on their faces and continued to speak as if I couldn't decipher what they were saying. Speaking others' language and not letting them know you do can be advantageous. In instances like this, I can get a better idea of what people's mind-set is and, hopefully, what their intentions may be. People are more apt to speak their minds if they believe their conversations can't be understood. Playing ignorant isn't the same as being ignorant.

The walk to the outside of the airport from customs and immigration was an exercise in evasion. I was dodging and weaving through the various Belizeans attempting to sell me everything from excursions, two-fors, discounts at nightclubs, handmade trinkets, and timeshares. There were plenty of exchange houses where you exchanged your money from whatever currency you had to their Belizean dollar. I wasn't halfway out of the airport, and before I felt the heat from the outside blowing through the open doorway, I had shunned off over twenty salespeople and a handful of others wanting me to use their taxi service or wanting to help me with my bags. I made it to the large opening leading to the warmth of the powerful sun. The key to walking through places like this and other areas where there are crowds of people who potentially want to violate your personal space is to walk with a purpose. Growing up on the streets of New York and the years in Mexico City prepared me for events just like this.

Stepping out from the air-conditioning of the inside to the steaming late-morning sunshine, I took a moment. As I closed my eyes, taking in a deep breath of fresh air that filled my lungs, the warm tropical sun fell upon my face, and a wave of satisfaction came over me. I felt relieved about so many things. I was alive, not in prison, in a tropical paradise. I had my health and not beholding to anyone for anything. A free man in every sense of the word was what I was.

The first leg of my journey was complete now. Breathing a sigh of relief and exhaling a lot of my angst behind me, I opened my eyes, and to my left was another money-exchange house they call casa de cambios. I decided that this exchange house was where I would exchange some money that I would need to get me through this leg of my journey. I also had to purchase a few calling cards, and just as luck would have it, they sold those there as well. I peeled off five one hundred-dollar bills from my pocket and presented it to the person behind the counter while asking for a few local phone cards for their public phones. I received my Belezian dollars while looking around me to make sure nobody was clocking me, sizing me up for robbery. This wasn't the richest country in the world, and the slightest opportunity was not something I wanted to give a potential thief or worse.

To my right, just before the row of taxis that were waiting for exiting airline passengers, was a row of pay phones. I made my way there and inserted the phone card. I called information for the hotel Gabriella gave me to see what rooms were available and to book a room.

I called the hotel and spoke to them in Spanish. I preferred speaking to the hotel in Spanish to let them know I understood their language and to attempt to ensure that they wouldn't try to rip me off or take advantage of someone they thought was an ignorant tourist.

"Good morning. Do you have a room? And if you have a suite, that would work better. It would be for tonight and possibly more, but for sure, tonight. I'm at the airport right now. How much for the night? A suite? Perfect. Can the suite be an oceanfront? And the higher the floor, the better. I'll take it and will be there shortly. No, I have a taxi. Thank you. Yes, my name is Mr. P———."

As I hung the phone up, I scanned the area for a taxi that suited me the most. There were regular taxis available as well as private taxis, where the owner owned his own vehicle and wasn't part of a company. I located one taxi driver that had a pretty decent vehicle and that wasn't too much of a man on a hustle. I didn't want a regular taxi; in case someone would later try to trace my whereabouts, a private car service would be harder to track. There was a man with a slim build standing about five feet, nine inches tall with cowboy attire like he lived on a ranch, complete with a belt buckle, straw hat, blue jeans, and cowboy boots. His mustache, bushy mustache, matched his curly, bushy black hair. He was standing outside his late-eighties four-door sedan. He wasn't actively looking to address people, and I preferred this type of man rather than one that was too eager to pick up a fare.

"You free?" I said in Spanish, approaching the taxi driver.

"Yes, where are you going?" the taxi driver said as my words touched his ears.

With any transaction, especially those in a third world country, one must negotiate all prices whenever possible before accepting a service. Nearly everything in these countries is open for a negotiation. If a price isn't negotiated beforehand, then it's a certainty that you'll be ripped off, being charged exorbitant prices.

"Hotel La Paz. How much?" Again, I spoke in Spanish so the taxi driver understood I had some knowledge of their system of conducting business.

"Three hundred pesos," the taxi driver told me.

This was the equivalent of about thirty dollars, give or take. Always know that the first price that's given is the starting point and always let the other tell you their price and go from there. Knowing the general price for the service is helpful. If you're unsure about the price, then the general rule of thumb is to take about 40 percent off the asking price. You'll either be accepted or another offer will be forthcoming.

"Two hundred pesos, and I'll pay you in American, twenty dollars."

The locals preferred taking American money, so while the counter offer was ten dollars under the original asking price, the taxi driver would be getting his fare in American. Quick to accept the offer, knowing it wasn't out of the realm of reality, the taxi driver agreed.

"Twenty dollars American is good. Do you have any other bags you need help with?"

"No, I have just this here with me, and I'll put it in the backseat," I said, not needing his help.

I never wanted my luggage and belongings separated from me incase things went bad in the taxi and I had to make a quick exit. I didn't want to have to get to the trunk to retrieve my bags in the worst-case scenario. There was plenty of room in the backseat for me and my luggage.

The driver opened the passenger side door for me, and I slid my bags, laptop, and briefcase inside as I entered after them. The driver closed my door and got into the driver's seat as we took off.

The upholstery of the vehicle was covered with a cloth texture that was more comfortable than the plastic or other material that didn't work well with the tropical heat.

"It's okay if I smoke?" I asked as I took out my cigar holder from my briefcase.

"Yes, why not?" the taxi driver said very accommodatingly.

My cigar case was capable of holding three cigars and another tube that was a built-in flask. I withdrew a well-aged Cuban Montecristo Churchill. I had to smell it as I did most every time I lit a new cigar. Depending on the crop and brand, I preferred Cuban cigars over any other cigar in the world. For me there was no other. The flavor of this particular cigar had hints of coffee, cocoa, cedar, and some other spices. Each brand cigar is different as is the particular crop. The soil of Cuba suited my taste buds just fine. My gold-plated cigar cutter in hand, I clipped the end, lighting it with my gold-plated butane lighter. I preferred using wooden matches, but they wouldn't be as effective in the taxi with the wind blowing. A few puffs on this slice of heaven, and even the driver was inhaling the earthy goodness with a smile.

The bumpy twenty-minute drive sure tested the shocks of the taxi. By third world standards, these shocks still had many more miles left on them, but my spine would say otherwise. The drive gave me time enough to open the bottom compartment of my briefcase, which held my other passport and identity papers I would use on this leg of my journey. I switched out the other passport I had just used and was now armed with a new identity, complete with matching credit cards. I didn't know if I were being tracked or followed and made every attempt to conceal my whereabouts as much as possible. If someone had followed me to the airport or knew about this leg of my journey, I didn't want there to be a surprise showing up for me at the hotel for the duration of my stay.

The fresh air coming in from the outside mixed with my cigar's aroma made the drive a bit more tolerable and took my mind off the constant up-and-down motion of the taxi. The scenery was mainly jungle with road signs letting the drivers know the mileage to the landmarks and hotels. I knew I was getting closer to the beach as I could smell the ocean air becoming more prevalent. I must have gotten caught up in the climate and unpolluted air because the taxi began to slow down. Just ahead on my right was the entranceway to

Hotel La Paz. As the taxi made the right turn into the hotel, I noticed the road was a good couple hundred feet in length until we reached the circular turn in front of the hotel. The taxi came to a stop just as a bellhop for the hotel exited the double glass sliding doors above a cascading flight of steps. The bellhop opened my door, introducing himself and welcoming me to the hotel. I handed the driver his twenty dollars and an extra ten as a tip. I made sure I got a card from him so if I needed a driver while here, I knew I had one I could count on and one that already knew of me a little. The tip was just good business and ensured that if I needed him for anything, he would be more apt to assist me in what I needed to do. I always believed and was taught that in any transaction, the compensation should be greater than the normal or standard amount, especially if the service or transaction was more than satisfactory and/or profitable. You never know who you'll meet or need again, and it's just good business to treat others with respect. I thanked the driver for the ride and told him I might need his services again for when I depart in a few days. I didn't want him to know the exact time when I was leaving; hell, I didn't even know when I was leaving. Enthusiastically, he told me to simply call and, with as much notice as I was able, he would accommodate my needs.

I handed the bellhop my luggage and took a moment to admire the hotel's outer appearance. The texture was fresh and painted smartly in a whitish cream color. The bellhop's uniform started off the whole color ensemble with a light-turquoise shirt and white pants all neatly pressed and cared for. I headed up the steps, the bellhop leading the way. As we approached the large glass double doors of the entranceway to the hotel, the doors opened automatically. I was unexpectedly surprised by the eye-pleasing decor of the hotel. The marble floors accented the large fountain in the middle of the reception area. To my left was the reception desk, and to the right were the elevators, a couple of public pay phones, and a small gift shop. Directly to the back of the reception area, I could see the pristine turquoise ocean and sandy white beach through the floor-to-ceiling glass. Statues, from what I assumed had something to do with the Belizean culture, were tastefully placed throughout the lobby.

As I approached the reception desk, the woman behind the counter addressed me even before I was fully in front of her.

"Good afternoon, sir. Do you have a reservation?"

She was a smiling beauty whose attentiveness and personality was where her beauty laid. Her uniform was more feminine than the bellhop's but still color coordinated and tastefully put together, with her name tag showing her name: Ms. Flores. Her long dark hair appeared to be still wet, and I didn't know if that was the look she was going for, but it fit her well. Her permanent smile accented her dimples.

"I called your hotel about thirty minutes ago from the airport. The name is P——," I said, looking directly at Ms. Flores's brown eyes and dimples.

"Senor P——," Ms. Flores said, clicking a few buttons on her computer.

"Yes. We have you in your suite that you requested."

As Ms. Flores was explaining the reservation to me, a waitress approached me and offered me something to drink. The waitress's tray had some red and white wines, champagne, and assorted juices on it.

"Sir, something to drink?" asked the waitress as she balanced the drink tray.

"A mimosa, please," I said, only averting my eyes away from the receptionist for a brief minute.

As she was pouring the drink, I knew I wanted to have some sort of fresh juice, and throwing in a little alcohol was never a bad thing. She handed me the drink, and in return, I thanked her and handed her a ten-dollar tip, knowing full well that that was what she was living on, especially when the drink was free.

"Sir, do you know how many nights you will be staying with us for?" Ms. Flores asked me as my attention was returned to her.

"For sure tonight, but I don't know how many nights more I'll be staying. I'm thinking about one or two more nights but haven't decided yet. Let me know if my suite is available for the next couple of evenings, and then I can make a better decision."

"Your suite is available the next couple of days. If you could just call down to the front desk and ask for me or someone else in reception before nine in the morning and let us know of your decision to stay longer or that you'll be checking out."

"Thank you. That's very kind of you to be so accommodating," I said with a smile.

"Will you be paying with cash or using a credit card?" Ms. Flores asked with her head down, arranging the paperwork.

"Cash," I said, reaching into my front right pants pocket, taking out the Belizean dollars I had just exchanged.

"I'll also need your identification and major credit card for incidentals," Ms. Flores said almost instinctually.

"I do have those but would rather pay cash for the incidentals and leave a cash deposit instead. Does that work?"

I let Ms. Flores see that I had pulled out what appeared to be a few thousand dollars, a mixture of American and Belizean money, in the hopes that her response would favor my position. I didn't want a paper trail in any regard. My identification and credit cards were impeccably done, but still, I didn't want to take any unnecessary risks.

"That shouldn't be a problem. Let me calculate that for you," Ms. Flores said as she was busy tapping away on her calculator, totaling the room costs and deposit.

"The room charges and deposit total three hundred and fifty dollars."

I saw from the sign behind Ms. Flores that the conversion rate was about the same I received in the airport, so I used American money for the cost of my room and deposit. I peeled off five one-hundred-dollar bills and handed them to Ms. Flores.

"Keep the balance on my account for whatever expenses I might incur. There's no need for change," I said as Ms. Flores reached to give me change.

"We have a twenty-four-hour room service available with a limited menu from midnight until six in the morning," she said, explaining some of the amenities of the hotel.

I flashed my identification for her to see without it leaving my hand, and she seemed okay with it, even though I know at times the hotel would want to photocopy it in case there were damages or otherwise. She printed out my receipt and pointed to appropriate locations for me to sign. As I was signing, Ms. Flores was handing me my room key.

"Suite ten twenty nine. Jorge will assist you with your luggage to your suite, Mr. P———."

I took my final sip of mimosa and thanked Ms. Flores for her assistance and kindness. I turned, took a few steps, then turned around as if I forgot I wanted to say something else.

"Has Gabriela Torres checked in yet? She's the person that referred me to your lovely hotel," I said, wanting to lend more credence to myself and also trying to get information about Gabriella and how I could locate her.

"Yes, I know her, and we aren't allowed to give out the room number. I can take a message for her, or you can leave a message through our operator by dialing extension 9 from your room."

"I'll leave one here with you as I know she'll receive it when it comes from you. Thank you. I would also like to leave a voice message and, if possible, from here," I said as I went back to the reception desk and wrote a small note on a piece of paper and used the phone to leave the voice message.

I thanked Ms. Flores for all her help and assistance and made sure to pour on some New York charm.

"You're very welcome, Mr. P———, and enjoy your stay with us."

I had to tip Ms. Flores something for her assistance in getting me the suite I required and making the entire check-in process go so smoothly. I tipped Ms. Flores fifty dollars, ensuring I would be taken care of in nearly any capacity I needed, including making sure Gabriella would be notified. She wasn't expecting it and was thanking me up and down for that. I don't know what receptionists make a day at the hotel, but I'm pretty sure that exceeded her daily rate. I wanted to leave enough impression to ensure I got what I wanted when I wanted, but I didn't want to leave so much of an impression that, if someone came in and asked about me, I would be easily found.

Jorge the hotel bellhop had my suitcase in hand, and I didn't allow my briefcase or laptop out of my control. I followed him to the elevator, and we both entered.

Jorge was a slight man in his early fifties and had dark hair and thick mustache. His uniform seemed a bit too big for him but was still impeccably kept. His body language was humble and respectful. The lines on his face were like that of an old oak that, when cut in the middle, shows all the tree's age. The lines were proof of Jorge's life and that he had lived one filled with ups and downs.

Jorge waited for me to engage him, and as the doors shut, I spoke to him. "What time do you work?" I said, speaking to Jorge and breaking the ice with some small talk.

"From nine in the morning until nine in the night, sir," Jorge responded with his humble tone.

"Do you have any days off?"

"Monday and Tuesday, sir. Sometimes I don't have any and work a full week straight. I would rather work than rest, sir."

Jorge seemed content with his work and thankful to have employment. I totally understood what Jorge was speaking about and where he was coming from. If there were money to be made, I would be there working. I am a workaholic as well and I have respect for those that have the same work ethic as I do.

We reached the top floor, where my suite would be, and the elevator doors opened. I followed Jorge's lead yet again. The hallway was well kept, had fresh paint and some distance between each room, letting me know the rooms inside must be spacious and just my style. My room was at the end of the hallway, as I preferred.

The unexpectedness of the hotel continued into my suite. Jorge opened the door for me, and I was taken aback at the luxuriousness of the suite. The living room was sunken down in the middle, a big screen television on the wall, couches on both sides, and what appeared to be authentic artwork decorating the walls. To my right were a dining room area, small refrigerator, and sink. The back part of my suite had a balcony that overlooked the beach and natural elements of a resort paradise. I had to walk to the back before seeing any other part of the suite. Opening the balcony doors full-on, I got the view I could only describe as perfection. Breathtaking views of pristine turquoise waters, sandy white beach, and the calmness of the view that I was intent on taking mental notes and pictures of. The ocean air was like a cleanser to my soul, wafting upward and running through me, filling me with serenity. Before my mind could completely wander away, I had to complete this transaction with Jorge. On the way back through the suite, I looked into the bedroom, and certainly, all was right with the world. This suite was just my speed, and I knew that just one night wasn't going to do it for me, with or without company.

"Senor, everything to your liking?" Jorge asked softly, awaiting my approval.

"Jorge, perfect!" I said, reaching into my pocket and peeling off a twenty-dollar bill.

I knew that twenty for this minor transaction was a bit much, but again, I believe in overtipping, especially watching the expression on the person's face when they receive it and it's an unexpected pleasure. Jorge was certainly humble and thankful for my generosity, which made me want to do more.

"Thank you, sir. Enjoy your stay with us," Jorge said, thinking we were finished with our transaction.

"Jorge, I have a couple of things I would like for you to do," I said, catching Jorge before he could exit the suite.

"Anything. What is it?" Jorge said with a little more anticipation and exuberance in his tone.

"Can you bring me a bottle of tequila—Tres Generaciones, if it's possible? If not, something of similar quality? I also need some small sipping glasses and maybe a couple regular glasses. I need a mixture of fresh juices, some bottled water, and a fresh-fruit assortment. I'll call down if I want something else for lunch, but for now, that works for me."

"Sir, please give me about an hour to bring you your order."

"Perfect! Also I, left a message for Gabriela Torres downstairs. If it's not an issue, can you get me her room number? I'll have a note ready for you to deliver when you return, if it's possible," I said to Jorge, giving me time to settle in and decompress.

Jorge was more than happy to oblige me in all that I requested, right down to delivering my message later. Jorge exited the suite, and I took my suitcase into the bedroom, turned on the light, and placed the suitcase on the bed. I put my clothes in the dresser drawers and hung up my suits and dress clothes. Once my suitcase was empty, I carefully opened the bottom part of my suitcase, the compartment that was skillfully designed for me and my journey. It was impossible to detect it, and it came equipped with a pinhole lock that, to the naked eye, couldn't be seen.

I had never sold drugs in the United States aside from steroids, which I didn't consider a drug, although technically, they were. I was rationalizing, but among most of my associates, steroids was a permissible offense. Now the old-timers back home thought differently about it, but that was a risk I was willing to take and deal with the consequences if they arose. The legal penalties weren't much to worry about, and truthfully, that was what the old-timers were worried about. Guys facing lengthy jail sentences would possibly look to reduce their sentences if faced with basketball-number sentences.

Opening the stash compartment of my suitcase revealed ten bundles of pills, ecstasy. I had wrapped the pills carefully, tightly, and in groups of two thousand, totaling twenty thousand. On my previous trips and stays in Mexico, especially in Cancun, I discovered a relatively untapped ecstasy market. I say *untapped* because the quality of the pills there weren't the best, and the availability was fleeting. I was able to befriend a couple of the local dealers and made arrangements to sell to them when I returned to Mexico.

Besides the pills, I had two stacks of cash, twenty thousand in each stack. I didn't know what I would find with me as far as marijuana was concerned, so I packed a small amount for a few days until I could reach my final destination. The marijuana was wrapped tight, vacuum-sealed, and I had it tucked into a small bit of coffee grounds to mask any smell from a drug dog. I wasn't too concerned as I had never seen a dog checking anything leaving the United States, and certainly, Belize wasn't checking anything arriving from the United States. The compartment was wrapped in tin foil, so when passing through the x-ray machines, the false bottom wouldn't be recognized.

Unwrapping the marijuana, I rolled myself a big joint to smoke as I took a shower. The bedroom was very nice, and the king-size bed was quite comfortable, to say the least. This paled in comparison to the bathroom that was cleverly designed with mosaic tiles, especially in the shower, where the large rain head made the experience of taking a shower the most relaxing. I smoked nearly the entire joint on the balcony overlooking the ocean before heading into the shower and turning it all the way hot in order to get more of a steam effect. Once a fair amount of steam was billowing through the bathroom, I stepped in, turned the hot water to a cooler temperature, and felt the soothing stream of water cascade down over me.

Between the weed, the relaxing surroundings, and the comfort of this incredible steam shower, I felt the stress of cold Brooklyn (not just the temperature) slowly depart from my anatomy.

* * *

My cell phone on the nightstand next to my bed began to ring. I was in a deep sleep and was startled into answering it. As I answered the phone, I noticed the clock was reading ten after seven in the morning.

"You up there?" the voice in my receiver said.

"Yeah," I said.

"Come down," the thick New York accent said.

"Leaving shortly," I said before the call was ended.

I knew the voice on the other end of the call. The voice and the call itself could only mean one thing: there was work to be done. It was Richie from Brooklyn, and neither words nor explanations were necessary. I stayed part of the time at my parents' house in Westchester County, above New York City. I only stayed a night here or there when I was in the area and needed a place to crash or get a home-cooked meal. I spent other nights in various hotels as well as in a crash pad I had in Bensonhurst, Brooklyn. I had prearranged meeting spots so nothing would be said over the phone in case someone was listening or a bug picked up the information. I never had any set schedule of where I would be staying; I never wanted to create a pattern and tempt the hand of fate. I fluctuated between places and states, keeping everyone, friend and foe, guessing on my whereabouts at all times.

I got my coffee brewing and, in the meantime, took a shower, waking myself up for what was shaping up to be a day where I would need my wits about me. I toweled off and got dressed while taking a second pair of clothes with me just in case there was a need. I poured my coffee in a thermos, leaving it as I preferred, black and strong. I walked down the steps to my basement. Off to my left was a hand-made wooden shelf lying flush against the wall. The basement was a bit colder, being all concrete and enclosed. I approached the shelf, and on the middle tier of five, I moved a bunch of old paint cans aside along with some cleansers and miscellaneous junk. The concrete block behind the shelving was quite solid and was where I had a safe built in. I had the safe designed to be somewhat camouflaged and look as if it were part of the wall. The only thing that was a little visible was the small digital pad for the combination information, but you had to really be looking for it in order to recognize it. I entered in the combination, and the concealed door opened. The door was less than a foot wide and six inches tall. The depth of the safe was about ten inches, and it sat inside the solid concrete. I took a rag from the shelf and proceeded to withdraw my weapon of choice, my .380 automatic, stainless steel, black handle wrapped with electrical tape to match the tape found on the trigger. I used the electrical tape in order to mask any fingerprints that could be taken from the gun in case I wasn't wearing gloves and had to drop the gun in the midst of a job. I wanted to be very careful in this regard and use any means at my disposal to assure my prints couldn't be lifted off the gun. I already had the magazine loaded and ready for business. For me, the .380 was the perfect weapon. It gave me the power I needed, the size I preferred, and the caliber that was sufficient in order to get my point across.

I locked up the house and exited through the basement of my parents' suburban homestead. I got into the little Honda that I used to make my trips and ride around. I always used a nondescript car, taking another precaution against showing up on the radar of law enforcement or anyone wishing to do me harm. When someone thought of a gangster or criminal moving in my circles and making very good money, one's mind automatically went to the flash and flashy lifestyle, all of which I shunned. I was taught well at a young age that being inconspicuous isn't the same as being irrelevant.

In my car I had some of my favorite music that I listened to, but the most soothing and the most fitting for me and my personality was *Ol' Blue Eyes*, Frank Sinatra. His voice smoothed out the bumpy ride down the West Side Highway of Manhattan. Sinatra made songs that touched on a man's life, lifestyle, values, and worth. Among my associates and I, Sinatra and the fellow crooners in his genre created the music we all clung to. Some of the older guys referred to Frank as Uncle Frank, knowing him personally. Uncle Frank was quite close to a lot of the older guys in my organization as well as those in other organizations. Organized crime permeated many parts of regular America and not limited to just illicit activities. Back in the days, when Frank was at his heyday, organized crime was also in its heyday, a perfect match.

The exits for Brooklyn began coming into view, and my mind was becoming more focused on whatever task I knew would be at hand this day. I came around a bend in the highway, and my exit was next. A few turns and stop signs later, and I was at my crash pad apartment in Bensonhurst, Brooklyn. Only a couple of people knew of my apartment here in Brooklyn, one of them Ricky, who arranged the apartment for me. Ricky was the boss over Richie and everyone else in my crew. He wasn't the boss in the neighborhood, but he and his father pulled a tremendous amount of weight. Ricky liked having me around just as much as I enjoyed being there. My dependability, loyalty, tenacity, never turning down a job while always going above and beyond when called upon were assets that Ricky coveted. Some five years into working for the organization, I was reporting directly to Ricky. Richie, who was my original go-between, was falling out of favor, and I was warned about staying away from him in certain instances. I still associated with Richie, but now when there were important matters at hand, Ricky would contact me directly. Richie was aligned with Antonio now while still working for Ricky. Even though we were in the same family, these events can happen and at times do, but spreading oneself too thin can be a dangerous game. Ricky had a decent-sized crew in Bensonhurst, but Antonio had the flash, name, recognition, and brazen style that some considered attractive and alluring. Richie always wanted to be the flashy kind, and with Ricky, I knew that wasn't going to cut it for long. I preferred Ricky's style and means of conducting business. Ricky's father had a social club in the neighborhood and was a man that was well respected. I liked Ricky's father a lot, and when events in the neighborhood would get a little crazy, I would watch Ricky's father and some of the other older gangsters in the neighborhood. I enjoyed that part of it because the old men treated me with a lot of respect, and they felt safe with me. Respect is something that's earned through good deeds, positive results, and one's word always being true.

My apartment was situated on the bottom of a house, the entranceway of which was only accessible through the rear of the house. This house in particular was owned by an elderly Italian woman who had lived her entire life in the neighborhood and the majority of that in this house. Her husband was lost to one of the Mafia wars that occurred way before my time. She produced one son, who was doing a life sentence for avenging the murder of his father. The woman knew I was there and never asked anything about it. Once the matter was negotiated and she agreed, there wasn't much to talk about with her new tenant below.

The apartment was a one-bedroom, which was more than sufficient to house me when I needed to be there. Walking down the steps, you came into the kitchen and living area. Of course I had a coffee machine and espresso maker for my coffee. I did have it decorated well even if I was going to be the only person there; I wanted to at least be comfortable. I had a wraparound leather sofa, a big-screen television on one wall, and a black-and-white picture of Frank Sinatra hanging on another wall. The painting of Frank with his fedora on, drink in hand, was just the "end all, be all" of being a man. I walked up to the painting and lifted the king of cool off the wall. Behind the painting was where I installed a safe, the same type I had back at my parents' place. I entered the digital code, and the safe opened.

Inside the safe I had a couple stacks of hundreds bound by bank bands indicating each stack contained ten thousand dollars apiece. I moved the money to the side so I could reach my silencers. I withdrew two of them. Each weighed less than an ounce and were silver in color from the alloy that I used, their length about three inches and an inch in diameter. The metal was an alloy I got from an associate who worked for a metalwork company that had a contract with NASA. We had a decent side business making silencers, but usually, I didn't charge for those. We made them for my use and used them as favors where we would fit guns for guys we knew. Anyone that had the talent to make a silencer that worked effectively was in high demand. The metal needed to be as lightweight as possible for space travel, which made it a perfect suitor for being turned into a silencer. My associate was a master machinist and steroid user. I met him at a gym, and we hit it off. I felt comfortable enough with him to speak on a couple of things, then one day, he shared with me about his work and the types of materials that were available. I thought about a silencer and how I could make them to fit an individual gun. We spoke about it back and forth, and I used my personal .380 for fitting the first one. We took it apart, bored out the barrel, and matched the metal to the inside of the barrel. Through trial and error, we became proficient. In short order, we could take apart, design, and fit each gun with three silencers in two days' time. I came up with a price for three silencers per gun that was sufficient, I thought, and when needed, I could make more but preferred the person bring me a clean weapon to be fitted. I didn't want to be in possession of a weapon that had been used in a homicide or any crime, so I insisted, but then again, I wasn't expecting an honest answer at all times.

Each silencer was packed with a material that would slowly blow apart as each bullet passed through the barrel. Through trial and error, we discovered that on average, seven bullets could pass through the barrel before the thudding noise would become a more-resounding sound. A small tapping sound was all that could be heard from the first until the seventh with a barely noticeable increase in volume. My feeling was that if you needed more than seven shots to kill someone, then you were just in the wrong profession.

The only time I had my gun and silencers in the same place at the same time was when there was work to do. If you didn't have the silencers in the same place as the gun, it was fitted, so not even the cops could charge you because it wouldn't fit another gun. The threadings of each gun were unique, and so would the threadings of each silencer be. The cops would have to catch me with both at the same time, and if that were the case, then I would have more problems than just a simple weapons possession charge.

I went to my bedroom, which was fitted with a couple of nightstands on either side of my king-size bed. My apartment had no windows, so sleeping here made for a very relaxing time. I preferred to always enter at night and parked away from my apartment for maximum discretion. This particular time, I was called in the early-morning hours, and so the cover of darkness wouldn't be my friend.

Closing up my apartment, I headed for Ricky's shop. The shop was a garage where a lot of our business was run through in one manner or another. The shop was our version of a social club because we spent a good deal of time there, and it was a hang-around spot. More than a social place, the shop had a multitude of uses, some of it seasonal. We housed our fireworks at the shop for the most part. We had other warehouses, but the headquarters and major storage was here. Our crew was a major player in fireworks distribution not only in Bensonhurst but also in the tristate area. If you were to buy fireworks in the tristate area in the eighties through the late nineties, chances are, they originated from my crew. We had a freighter park offshore and would periodically unload when needed. Other warehouses stored the fireworks scattered throughout the five boroughs. We separated the loads for safety and distribution purposes. I started selling fireworks when I first met Richie in 1990. Fireworks were my way into Ricky's crew and the beginning of my relationship with the Bensonhurst-based crime family.

Two years into me joining my crew, I was running the annual neighborhood fireworks show we held on the Fourth of July. We closed off both ends of the street and used the fenced-in playground to shoot off the fireworks. The show would start by sundown and go until a good eleven at night or longer. The entire day we worked and then a few hours before we would call it a day and begin to bring the fireworks to the houses around the park so when we needed them, we could run them out fast and never have a lull in the action. The fireworks were still sold by others in our crew, so business never ended. The day was for the kids, for sure. We had Richie dress up as a clown and run games and rides for the kids. We had free food and prizes for the neighborhood kids, and the old men would sit out and hold counsel. Our fireworks show wasn't interrupted for years until our new mayor cracked down on the activities, and by 1996, our annual show was no longer. For years we paid off the police, a practice that was more culture than anything else. Richie would drive, and I would deliver the packages. Strictly for the Fourth of July holiday, I would be delivering a brown paper bag filled with an assortment of fireworks and envelopes filled with money. Each cop got a payoff, but depending on your rank and position in helping our organization, your envelope would vary. Our route would be throughout Brooklyn, but the majority of the cops we dropped off packages for were in Staten Island. I don't know if these were all the cops we were paying off, but I know our car was filled with brown bags. Another thing for certain is, these cops were expecting their package as I assumed the deal was structured for. A lot of guys from the neighborhood had relatives that were cops, and most stayed local, so indirectly, we had multiple contacts and cops we could rely on to look the other way or assist us when necessary. It was just how things had always worked since the beginning of time. It was like clockwork; you didn't even think about it. Now times were changing, and we had to adapt to them or take action and change them by our methods. One thing for sure, business and the flow of monies wouldn't be stopped for anyone under any circumstances, and the Mafia family I worked for, like so many others, protected their assets by any means necessary. I started in 1990, and now it was 1995, and many changes were made all around me, most for the bad—at least that's how I saw it.

With fireworks being seasonal, the shop became quite versatile throughout the year and offered a wide array of uses. One such year-round business was chopping cars. We had a couple of kids that would scour the neighborhoods and boroughs for cars we needed. After stealing them, the cars were brought to the shop, where they were immediately chopped up into pieces we would sell. We usually had orders for parts, or we would stockpile certain parts for future orders, but that was at a last resort. The shop was so deep it could house two cars comfortably. The back of the shop was walled off, creating a separate room in the back of the shop that was even more private and out of anyone's view. There was a small door that led to this back room, and it took a couple of glances to realize it was even there. This back room had many functions. We used it to house fireworks and car parts, and it was a perfect, out-of-the-way spot to dispose of a body and body parts. The room was soundproofed so that it drew less attention and would drown out any noises that might emanate from it. The room was complete with an engine hoist, a device that we used for more than just hoisting car engines. Underneath the hoist was a drain that led out to the street and into the sewer system. Typically, we had a plethora of tools for whatever job we needed to complete.

I took my usual couple of laps around the shop, surveying the area for any law enforcement that might have eyes on us. The last couple of years, I hadn't been around the shop that much. I had my restaurant and wasn't in Brooklyn that often. Then I had to go on the run for a bit, so for sure, I couldn't be around the shop, and more to the point, I didn't want to. I didn't mind the occasional hanging around, but I felt that being located in one spot often brought about a pattern that either law enforcement or rivals could use against me. None of these two possibilities appealed to me, so I came when called and acted as instructed. My loyalties were already tested over and over, and I didn't need to be around every day in order to show or prove my worth. I parked a couple of blocks away, walking the short distance to the shop and my meeting. My apartment was only about ten minutes tops from the shop and strategically located.

As I approached the shop, the sun was almost at its apex, the temperature rising in the early-summer sun. The bay door to the garage was a quarter open so as not to show any direct view of what was going on inside from the street outside. I ducked down, and when

I lifted my head, I was greeted by Brutus, one of the pit bulls that inhabited the shop. He was actually half–pit bull and half-rottweiler. For his size, Brutus was very intimidating. He and I got along greatly and roughhoused whenever we saw each other. I'm a dog lover, and at this time, I had two dogs of my own, an English bull terrier and an American pit bull terrier. Brutus was dusty and dirty, but that never bothered me, and it sure didn't bother him in the slightest. I caught Brutus in midair as he leapt at me. I closed the gate behind me, and after a few licks from Brutus, I heard a distinctive voice.

"Big T——!" the gruff voice behind me said.

I recognized that voice anywhere. It was the same distinctive voice that called for me this morning. I hadn't seen him in some time, but it was good to hear Richie's voice. Even though he was now with Antonio, he and Ricky still worked together at times. They were in the same family but still were cordial. Richie always thought what was best for Richie and not anyone else.

"Richie, 'sup?" I said to Richie, greeting him with a big hug and kiss on the cheek.

There were a few other guys from our crew around the inside of the shop. I greeted a few more of the guys before Richie and I walked where we could whisper to each other away from the others' earshot and low enough to not be picked up on a bug.

"Ricky sent for you. He's got something for you," Richie whispered in my ear.

Richie and I engaged in a couple of minutes of small talk until Ricky came down the stairs from his office. Ricky's office overlooked the garage, and the long stairway to his office led to a door with a small blacked-out window where only Ricky could see out. Ricky was shadowed by the other pit bull from the shop, Tara. Tara was all black, a bit scarred in the face, and every bit Ricky's dog. She tolerated most people that frequented the shop, but I never trusted her; she was fiercely loyal to Ricky and had a bit of a temper when she wanted.

Ricky stood about six feet tall, maybe an inch taller, had brownish hair and medium build, was very soft-spoken most of the time, and rarely associated with many people. When I met him, Richie was directing Ricky's orders, but that had changed since Richie's move to another crew and some other issues I would come to find out later. Ricky's soft-spoken nature carried when he spoke to you. When it was very important, he would lean in and whisper, making his voice barely audible. This was due in part to his nature and the nature of what he was saying, not wanting to be overheard by anyone but the person receiving the message. Ricky's brown eyes looked directly at you and, at times, through you, all the while getting his message through loudly and clearly. Ricky didn't mince words and rarely joked. When business was very good or an occasion went his way, he would smile or smirk and perhaps laugh, but those displays of emotion were few and far between. Ricky had to be tough and all business, especially with this crew and in this neighborhood. Ricky didn't look like your average gangster, but then again, there was nothing usual about him. Ricky dressed the part of a workingman and not the flash so many others chose. This was one of my attractions to him and his crew. He was a blue-collar gangster and presented himself as such. He was a family man and had his children around when there was nothing incriminating to endanger them. Ricky split his time between the shop, his father's social club under the L train, and his neighborhood home.

"T——!" Ricky smiled as he approached me.

Ricky's hand was outstretched so he could begin our greeting. I moved toward him to show respect and to acknowledge him. He grabbed ahold of my hand and pulled me into him, giving me a hug and kiss on the cheek, greeting me with respect. Ricky smiled, so I knew this job, whatever it was, was going to be important and in my wheelhouse.

"Good to see you." Ricky's tone always had double meaning.

Ricky was happy to see me for me but was also happy to see me for work I was dedicated to and talented at. Ricky put his arm around my shoulder and led me away from Richie so he could speak directly to me. Whether Richie knew why I was there or not, Ricky never spoke openly about something with more than one person at a time. Out of earshot from everyone, Ricky whispered in my ear the broad message of why I was there.

"We have a problem." Ricky said *we*, and by *we* he meant us, the organization.

More and more, Ricky and the organization relied on me to solve some of their more-delicate situations. I was receiving work and completing it to the letter. My credibility was unblemished with my crew and its leadership. Even if someone didn't know me personally, they knew of me, my capabilities, and my reputation, which would continue to carry with me throughout my life. The first year or so, it was a series of progressing assignments that showed I was both trustworthy and proficient. I accepted my tasks without question or hesitation and was more than capable of thinking on my feet. I was quickly becoming the problem solver, and when necessary, I made the problem disappear. My crew in the shop came to realize when they saw me that it could only mean someone was going to have a bad day.

"There's a guy who's undercutting our bread business." Ricky opened up the conversation with the purpose of me being called down.

The bread business was just one of those businesses our organization had control of, one that was certainly not going to be relinquished anytime soon. The bread business we controlled was the delivery of the bread to all the local markets, stores, delis, and the like. Whoever bought bread and used it in their locations bought from us. The organization had its hand in anything that turned a profit and wrapped its arms around it with a voracious choke hold.

"This guy's been selling to our stores. He's been warned a couple of times. Richie's going to drive, showing you locations where this guy's been known to frequent and what he's driving. He's in the neighborhood, so it shouldn't be hard to locate him," Ricky whispered as I felt his breath on my ear; he was that close.

I didn't need to respond to what Ricky was telling me, and I read between the lines about what the situation was. This guy was warned—and not just once—and the warnings weren't heeded. I was being called in; it meant there would be no more warnings that he would be afforded.

I nodded in acceptance, and Ricky responded, "Good."

We hugged and kissed, and Ricky went back to his office, Tara close behind. Richie already knew the plan, or at least part of the plan. The rest of the situation was in my hands. I raised the garage door, and the hunt began.

The sun was just passing directly overhead, and it was a little past noon when our hunt began. Richie had a black-on-black Lincoln that attracted more of the climbing temperature now reaching the humid upper mideighties.

We had driven about twenty minutes, cruising through the neighborhood. As we made a right-hand turn onto Twelfth Avenue, the traffic was congested, and then we made a right onto Sixty-Eighth Street. We had come to a stop only about a quarter of the way onto Sixty-Eighth in between traffic lights when Richie spotted something.

"That's it, the white van." Richie pointed forward to a white van about four car lengths ahead of us.

Four cars ahead of us was our target. I took out my .380, locking and loading the first round in the chamber. I had the safety locked and began turning the silencer until it was snugly fitted at the end of the barrel. I tucked my pistol into my waistband and pulled my shirt down over it for concealment. The whole process took me less than thirty seconds. Richie and I didn't say a word as I exited the Lincoln. Immediately I clenched the St. Jude's medal, reciting the prayer that I sure would need this day.

"Sacred heart of Jesus, have mercy on me. St. Jude, worker of miracles, pray for me. St. Jude, the helper and keeper of the hopeless, pray for me."

Without hesitation, I walked calmly with purpose down the passenger sides of the cars in front of me. I didn't look at anyone in the surrounding cars but was still alert and aware of who and what was around me. The heat was intense this day, and my perspiration was accented by the fact that it was broad daylight and here I was, walking down the middle of the street, armed and about to do something out of my character. By "out of my character" I'm referring to such a public display, my face in full view of wandering eyes. My adrenaline was surging, not knowing who this guy was or what I would find when I confronted this man. There's nothing wrong with a little extra controlled adrenaline.

When I was able to see into the target's passenger-side mirror, I could only see there was nobody riding in the passenger seat of the van.

I counted seven cars in front of my target's van before I reached for the passenger door handle. In one swift motion, I opened the door and swung myself up into the passenger's seat. Before my ass was fully on the seat, my eyes locked in on the man I was sent to find, and my assessment of him, I formulated fast.

The driver's face wore a look of shock, not knowing who I was, what I was doing, or what he should do. His face was that of an Eastern European workingman that had some struggles in life. He was a bit paler in the face than normal and was getting whiter by the second. The short combed-to-the-front-look hairstyle showed his receding hairline coming on. The look that formed on his face was a look I'd seen multiple times before. He instinctively knew that whatever this was that was happening to him wasn't good and there wasn't much he could do about it. He wasn't an imposing figure in any manner. Medium height, slender build with light features, and appeared the little pigment he had to begin with was now history. His hands were frozen on the steering wheel and hadn't moved since the moment his passenger door opened.

Before he could speak, I withdrew my .380 from my waistband with my right hand. Just below dashboard view, I aimed the barrel at the driver's midsection, leaving my left hand free to block or stop the driver from attacking me with something or lunging at me. My left arm also protected my gun and would give me enough time to let off a couple of rounds before he could even get close to a range to get ahold of my weapon. There was no center console between the driver's seat and the passenger's seat, leaving a few feet in between me and my pale-skinned friend. It was obvious the driver wasn't wearing his seat belt, and that also made it easier for him to defend himself in such closed quarters if he were so inclined. He saw my weapon and began to openly panic.

"This my van!" the driver said with his broken English that made his Russian accent that much more prevalent in his current state of fear.

"Put the van in park now!" I said demandingly.

He nervously enough obliged, I think out of fear, and with a gun pointed at him, fear was just one of the feelings I'm sure he had. With the van safely in park, I let the first round off, hitting the driver just under his armpit. Just as the first bullet pierced the skin, the second bullet was on its way. The second muffled thud entered just under his rib cage. Upon the second bullet's impact, the driver's body naturally turned my direction, to where his midsection was now in full view of me. I fired two more shots in rapid succession, now having an even bigger target to choose from. Unfortunately for the driver, my two shots were on their mark, and at least one pierced his heart. The lifeless body of the driver fell toward me as I backed up, not knowing for certain if the driver was deceased. With his last breath and last bit of life he had in his lungs, the immigrant tried to grab my arm in desperation. With my left hand, I caught the top of his left shoulder and pushed him to the floor in between the two seats. There was no time to waste. I jumped over the driver's motion-less body and into the driver's seat as traffic began to flow. I placed my weapon in between my legs and leaned down to feel the pulse or lack thereof from the driver's right wrist. Lack thereof was a better way to describe it. I sat full up in the driver's seat, reached across my body with my right hand, and pulled the seat belt across, clicking it squarely into place. The flow of traffic had already begun, and I was a couple of cars behind. I didn't need any unwanted attention on me and quickly put the expired immigrant's van in drive.

Richie and I had a prearranged signal to let him know I was in command of the van and he was to follow me as close behind as he could manage. I tapped the breaks two times with a second break in between, then I tapped the breaks again a third time three seconds later. Making the right onto Eleventh Avenue, I drove the speed limit and periodically checked my rearview mirrors to make sure my escort was still with me.

The ten-minute-or-so drive back to the shop was coming to an end. Turning onto the street the shop was on, I moved over to the right-hand side of the road a bit and slowed down. This allowed Richie to now move in front of me and take lead. I needed Richie to drive the remaining eight blocks to the shop, get there ahead of me, and open the garage door so I could pull right in without hesitation.

I arrived at the shop, and there was Richie, right on cue, and the plan so far was on track. My tires never stopped as I crossed the street and pulled right in. The sliding metal door closed behind me, and I parked the van inside, turning off the engine as Richie locked the metal gate tightly. I took my pistol off the seat, double-checking the driver's pulse to make sure I wasn't leaving a live person in the van before getting out. Yeah, he was dead all right, not a pulse to be found. I exited the van, pistol in hand, and met Richie outside the back of the van. I unscrewed the silencer from the front of my gun, placing it in my pocket and the gun back into my waistband, safety on.

Richie was there, awaiting my instructions for what to do next. While Richie brought me into this organization, I had surpassed him in status by performing all my tasks the correct way and without hesitation. Some people had qualms about doing one thing or another, but for me it was strictly business. I didn't know why Ricky wanted Richie with me on this assignment, being that he was already with another crew, but mine wasn't to ask why; mine was but to do and try not to die. I didn't particularly feel one way or the other about an assignment. I felt that those that were involved in the lifestyle, business, game, whatever you might call it, everyone knew the rules ahead of time, or at least they should have known.

I had Richie open the rear door to the van, making it easier to carry out the motionless body. I would have loved to take the driver of the van alive and finish the job here, but I knew that wasn't going to be the case, and I didn't have the time to see if I could. Richie didn't know exactly what the state of the driver was, but I'm guessing he had a good idea he wasn't breathing. Richie and I jumped into the back of the van, positioning ourselves in the best way to get this corpse out and finish the work.

"Grab his legs, and I'll grab his arms. You can pull him out if you're too weak. I know all those friggin' cannoli have taken their toll," I said laughingly.

"Fuck yourself. He feels heavier than he looks," Richie grunted, dragging the body by the ankles out and I his arms.

While the driver wasn't particularly heavy, deadweight is more laborious. I was laughing, watching my out-of-shape friend struggle with the legs. We exited the van, Richie in the lead with the ankles of the driver in his hands. Walking around the van, we entered the back room and placed the body of the driver on the drainage pipe. Richie went to lock the backroom door as I went to work wrapping the driver's legs up in the hoist. The driver's ankles I wrapped in chains and secured him in less than two minutes.

"Hoist away!" I said to Richie as if the driver was a car engine.

Richie joined me at the hoist, and we lifted the driver's body to where his head was about a foot off the ground directly over the drainage pipe. Door locked, body in position, and time of the essence, Richie and I proceeded to strip the body of all clothes and jewelry. This was done to thwart investigators and not to leave any identifying traces of who the driver might be, making the identification process that much harder.

The bench behind the hoist was where we had tools of the trade, and especially tools for this work we had, at hand. Specifically, we had hacksaws, an electric saw for those times when it was very hard to saw through bone or the other saws break, which had been known to happen. We had a couple of large serrated knives, enough of each so we wouldn't have to leave and find other means to dismember the body. Richie got the hacksaw and took the serrated knife for starters. We began draining the body of blood, letting the first bit drain from the neck as I slit the driver's throat. I ran a hose so the blood and small fragments would run down the drain at a steady pace. Once the body was drained, we proceeded to carve the body into sections for further disposal, again, attempting to disguise the identity. Richie and I surgically separated the body into parts. The hands and head we would separate as they would be the most identifying of all parts. Once those were separated, Richie and I would dispose of the parts in different places, where detection and discovery were less likely. Those bodies that were found were usually meant to be found as a reminder and warning to others. This particular body had no elements where we wanted to leave a warning for others.

I had Richie pull the teeth and place them in a separate bag. The pulling of the teeth was another attempt to prevent identification. I placed the hands and head in separate satchels, and the rest of the body we wrapped into a body bag that we would weigh down with chains and weights. Everything we planned on disposing in the river, we weighed down. We poked some holes in it so that when we tossed it into the water, it wouldn't emerge anytime soon, and the creatures down below would assist us in the process.

I went back to the van and scoured it for any spent shell casings and to see if there was anything that I needed to take with me, wipe down, or dispose of. I found my casings, and nothing else of note was there for me to attend to. I took a plastic cloth and laid it down over the seat covering, wherever my body might have possibly touched.

The day had now passed into the early evening, and Richie and I proceeded to bleach down the entire back room and any possible trail of blood that we might have missed from the van to the back room. We even bleached and cleansed the drainage pipes, leaving the shop clean in case some DNA was still lingering around. I gathered the tools from the back room that we had used and placed them in another bag—no need to weigh that down. It was plenty heavy enough. We loaded all the body parts and tools into the van, and we were now at the halfway point in the process. Richie and I stripped down naked, showered, scrubbed down, and changed clothes, placing the work clothes we had in separate bags for disposal later that evening.

We had some time to waste before we thought it sufficient enough to leave the shop. The cover of darkness for this next stage was not an option. We lit up a couple of cigars and relaxed, puffing the Cuban tobacco filling our lungs. I made some coffee and grabbed some cold cuts from the fridge. We had worked up an appetite and had a few more hours to kill.

I kept the gun with me, the spent shell casings and all. I kept the gun loaded and with me until I was able to dispose of it myself with nobody else around. It was not that I didn't trust Richie, but I didn't trust Richie. I wasn't going to give him a loaded weapon with my back turned. I wasn't going to be the odd man out with no weapon, and I didn't want him to know where I disposed of my gun. In this lifestyle, anyone could be against you at anytime. I remember the words Richie told me the first time I was briefed by him about what was expected of me. He told me that this family came before any other in our lives. He told me that if there were an issue with my blood brother and I was told to kill him, I would side with our family's decision and kill my blood brother. If I was told to kill my brother, then that was what I would have to do without hesitation or thought. As odd as it may sound, I didn't even think twice about what he said it. I wholeheartedly agreed and truly was on board with it. Over the years, I saw how Richie lived his life as well as how those around us lived, and so handing him a loaded weapon under these circumstances would have been just ignorant. I didn't want the gun and casings in the van with me with the driver's body, but the other option was not an option. It was bad enough Richie was with me during this event. This was the first time I had eyeballs directly on me. I didn't know why Ricky set it up like this, but I knew somewhere there was a reason.

Richie exited first, opening the garage door for me to exit. Darkness was well underway, and Richie stepped out to make sure everything was clear for us to finish up our work. I put a large gas can in the passenger seat with me for later use. I pulled out to a "coast clear" sign that Richie gave me, and he closed the garage door behind me, locking it. I waited just a minute until he was in his car and led the way to where we needed to be, place by place. We drove first to dispose of the main body parts to an area close to us that we knew well and wouldn't attract much attention. Down Bath Avenue in Brooklyn to the water that was ideally called Gravesend Bay, we went first. This was where we got rid of the first parts of the job. We tossed the body bag with the odds and ends of parts into the water. The next stop was farther down Shore Parkway to a spot called the

Narrows, where we threw the satchel of head and hands into the murky water. That left the last bit of work to be done, which was making sure that the van couldn't be traced back to anything relating to us, and all contents of the van that had forensic evidence would have to be destroyed. We had a spot already picked out for ourselves where we could have enough time to do our business and leave undetected. Near the landfill in Staten Island, we had a spot we used as our dumping ground of sorts. Crossing over the bridge and not far, we had an out-of-the-way spot. I got out of the van as Richie was there in front of me. I doused the car with gasoline, inside and out and especially over the seats and the interior. I put our clothes inside and lit it up. The next step, we headed back to Brooklyn. Crossing over the bridge and with Richie being distracted in his own mind, I tossed the gun first into the water and then, farther down, the silencer and casings, one by one.

Richie and I didn't speak much on the way back to the shop. We were both thinking about things. I didn't know what he was thinking, nor did I care; I preferred the silence anyway. Through the whole day, we didn't eat much aside from the sandwich at the shop, and that just wouldn't do. We agreed it was time for a good meal. We lit another cigar on our way back to a favorite dinner of ours. Windows unrolled, puffing away on the cigar, we rode through the neighborhood, and all I could think was *Ahhhhh, the smells of Brooklyn!*

* * *

The sound of the doorbell to my suite rang, bringing me back to my reality. I toweled off a bit before putting on a robe and headed to the door. Jorge was at my door with a warm smile and a much-needed tray of drinks and fresh fruit. I thanked him for bringing the drinks and had him place them on the table by the door.

"Sir, I found that room of the lady you asked about," Jorge said, smiling.

I wrote a quick note down on a piece of paper and handed it to Jorge. I didn't want to leave anything to chance, making sure that Gabriella would know I was in the hotel and wanted to enjoy her company for at least an evening.

I handed Jorge a hundred-dollar bill and told him it was for the drinks and his tip, which was more than sufficient. I wanted to make sure by any means necessary my message was delivered and my service, top-notch. Jorge couldn't smile any more than he could at that moment as the Benjamin Franklin touched his palm.

With Jorge's exit from my suite, I poured myself a glass of tequila straight up. This particular tequila was for sipping. The first few sips of Tres Generaciones leaves your throat with a little burning sensation, and soon after the tequila begins to smooth itself out, it becomes a drink one can savor. I rolled another joint, smoking it as I finished off my shower, feeling the weight of my day's decisions being cleansed away.

My shower finished, shaved, I air-dried and went naked to my balcony. The sun was going down, and the most gorgeous sunset was taking place over the horizon of the turquoise Caribbean sea. Tequila in hand, I kept thinking to myself that I could get used to this.

A knock at the door to my suite had my insides churning and temperature rising. Instinctively, my body knew who was knocking and began reacting accordingly. It was funny; my heart rate wouldn't raise when placing a bomb or pulling a trigger, but a woman I'd never been with before sure did. With a look through the peephole, I was treated with the distorted beauty of Gabriella. I asked to hold on a minute while I put on my robe.

There was no more uniform for this beauty. Her attire was now a formfitting sequined miniskirt with a top that exposed her tanned midsection, slim waistline, and ample breasts. I must have been standing there ogling as I opened the door. I was taking in her beauty and was pleased that she was standing just outside my door.

"Good evening, Gabriella," I said, taking in fully Gabriella's beauty.

"Please call me Gaby," she said as I stepped aside and watched her enter, now taking in the rear view that my eyes automatically were drawn to.

"Gaby it is," I said, closing the door, pleasantly surprised. "I'm glad you accepted my invitation," I said to her as she stopped about ten feet into the suite, getting her bearings.

"You think I wouldn't?" Gaby quickly responded, turning toward me with an intent of lust in her eyes.

"No, I knew you wouldn't, which is why I made sure I could reach you and let you know I was here and wanting to spend time with you. You look stunning," I said, walking over to the table where the drinks were located.

"Thank you, J_____" You don't look so bad yourself. I liked you in your suit this morning. I told my coworker I wanted to serve your section of first class the minute I laid my eyes on you. Now you in your robe, I don't know which manner of dress I prefer." Gaby was talking as she had her eyes go from my eyes, over my body, down to the lower half of it.

Gaby continued to take in the suite, walking over to the balcony, where the sun was just past three quarters of the way under the horizon. I asked her what she liked to drink, and like me, she enjoyed her tequila straight up. I poured the two drinks of tequila for us and picked up a freshly rolled joint, joining Gaby on the balcony.

I reached around Gaby with my left arm, handing her her tequila and putting my left hand on her stomach.

"What a beautiful view you have here," Gaby said, scanning out the Caribbean.

"I sure do," I said, looking down at Gaby's ass.

She turned around, and we clicked glasses, toasted to each other, and took a sip. I put my glass down, putting the joint in my mouth and was about to lit it. Gaby didn't seem to be offended—quite the opposite. She took the joint out of my mouth and kissed me full-on. I felt her soft, moist lips touch mine, and then her tongue touched mine and my body reacted immediately. I pulled her close to me and took the lead. We kissed for a few minutes before detaching ourselves. She took the joint and placed it in between her luscious lips and leaned in for me to light it. I didn't even have to ask or query if she was a pot smoker; she made that clear. She took a few deep pulls and inhaled into her lungs. She exhaled and blew the remainder of the smoke out into the early-evening air. She handed me the joint, and the red lipstick she added to the end didn't bother me in the slightest; actually, it rather excited me further. We finished our drinks and the joint in the evening air as the stars began to appear in the sky above our paradise.

"Do you take E?" I asked Gaby, referring to the drug ecstasy.

"Tachas?" Gaby responded with her eyes a bit wider, referring to the term used by many Spanish people regarding the drug.

"Yes, tachas," I said.

"Do you have any?" Gaby said with an excited tone.

I excused myself for a moment and returned with a couple of the ecstasy that made their journey with me from New York.

"Are they good?" Gaby said, looking at them in the palm of my hand.

I usually got that response from someone that had never had any of the ones that I used. I never had bad ecstasy pills, and to the contrary, they were always top-shelf.

"The best, nothing but the best, especially when it comes to things that matter and are important," I quickly retorted.

"Are you trying to take advantage of me?" Gaby asked as she took one of the pills out of my hand.

"Yes!" I said with a mischievous smile.

We both chuckled and headed inside to take our ecstasy with some water to chase it down with. I put mine in my mouth, sipping on water to wash it down with, and then Gaby followed suit, taking hers down her sexy throat. The marijuana and tequila began kicking in, and I knew in no time, the ecstasy would be taking effect and the night would be in full swing.

"Your marijuana is very good. Actually, everything so far has been. I look forward to seeing what else of yours is good." Gaby was easing up more and more and settling into exactly who I knew she would be.

Gaby was just my speed. We matched in every way possible, at least from my limited involvement with her thus far; she was matching me thought for thought and had a touch of aggressiveness to her. She knew how to be aggressive and knew when to sit back and be led. We matched each other's thoughts to where verbal communication wasn't necessary, rather a mere formality.

One more drink and some small talk, and the ecstasy began to creep into our systems. Gaby and I on the balcony with the breeze, atmosphere, and drugs taking effect, we inherently began touching each other, goose bumps in full effect. First light touches, kisses, and then clothes began being withdrawn as our temperatures rose. Neither one of us had much to depart with. Me my robe and Gaby, a few articles of clothing that seemed to peel off quite effortlessly.

It was time to take this party indoors and get better acquainted. I turned on music appropriate to our mood and proceeded with anticipation. This erotic encounter wasn't to be rushed. We were in a trancelike state where the only two that mattered were her and I. We took our time with each other, and there was much to explore. If I were to create a scenario in which to start my new life, I wouldn't have been able to conjure up a story like this. I was able to relax and feel free. Free from the constraints of my associates and duties back home. Free from the pressures of having to produce and worrying about either being replaced or replaced permanently. Free from the burden of being the one that others relied upon to handle their dirty business for them. Free from all the politics and double-crossing that the business involved. I was ready for a near-complete 180-degree change that I was seeing in my new lifestyle. Yes, I was going to be selling ecstasy, but in the economy of a third world country, it was all part and parcel of the way of life. When maneuvered correctly and with the right people being aligned with, I thought it to be an easy avenue to go down. I felt free, and my guard, for the first time, was being let down. I never drank back home aside from the wine, some after-dinner drinks we would have, and of course, certain binges with my attorney. I never even entertained the thought of being in an altered state, especially among the wolves of the underworld. I knew that Armando would have something for me to do, but I considered that to be payment for anything he might be able to help me and my new life with. Could I not be on high alert 24-7? I had no idea, but I was soon to find out.

Gaby and I were finished with our first round of sexual activity and were lying naked with legs intertwined. Gaby asked me about the medal around my neck. The medal was the only thing I would never take off unless I was forced to do so and that at times, those asking thought it best to let slide. I never really spoke about it, and Gaby was genuinely interested, so I was more than willing to be more vulnerable and speak on it. My newfound life, the drugs, company, atmosphere, and geographical location had me in a different frame of mind.

"My grandmother gave me this medal when I was a kid, and it was blessed by my father's best friend. He was our family priest and took care of everyone of my family's religious events. My father's mother gave me this when I was young. For some reason, when I wear the medal, I feel another level of comfort and protection that I find a need for. It brings me back to my days before the life path I chose. It was a time where purity and piousness were what I felt. It's the medal of St. Jude, the patron saint of the lost causes. It wasn't until much later that I understood the meaning of the medal and for what it stood for. Still, all in all, I've always found comfort in it, especially when everything else around me seems to be spiraling out of control or I need that sense of calmness in my life. So between my grandmother giving me the medal, it's meaning that I didn't realize until later in life, the blessing bestowed upon it, and the sense of comfort I feel when I pray upon it, the medal is something I respect and treasure."

I knew Gaby wasn't going to comprehend all that I said, but that wasn't important. The important part was me opening up more than I ever had in the past, especially to a complete stranger. Well, not a complete stranger, but damn-near-complete stranger. To be honest, I never even said anything to anyone before about it and what it stood for.

"May I touch it?" Gaby asked me in a quizzical manner.

While that might have been an odd request in any other forum, this made sense, and her intention was genuine. We shared a lot in the short time together, and I wondered if this might be something that I could see myself in in the future.

"Of course you may," I said, letting Gaby wrap her little tanned hand around my medal, examining it.

Gaby held it and looked at it with a curious nature. Before letting go, she looked at me with almost a look of concern.

"Why lost causes?" she said, looking almost sorry for me.

"You know, I don't know why she did, and I never asked. She's passed now, and I can't ask her the reason why she gave it to me. I tell you, she couldn't have been more spot-on with me now at this point in my life. Maybe she saw something in me back then. Who knows?" I said, letting Gaby know I didn't want to speak further on the subject.

The sun was about to come up, and neither Gaby nor I had been to sleep yet. Our clothes were strewn about the room, and I arose to get some water and juice, replenishing some of the fluids I had lost the last ten hours. I couldn't help but take a moment to enjoy the first sunrise of my new life, and while I still had a shorter leg of my journey left, I felt confident that I would complete my travel without a hitch. *Peaceful* was the understatement of the year when describing all that I was surveying.

I felt the warmth of Gaby come up behind me, wrapping her soft arms around me. I couldn't remember the last time I had that in a situation where I could enjoy it.

"What a beautiful morning, baby," Gaby said, peeking her head around me, taking in the same scenery as I.

I put my orange juice glass in her hand as I thought she would probably be needing the same thing I did.

"Everything keeps getting better by the moment," I said, taking time to think that the truth of the matter was that things were getting better and better for me.

We sipped our orange juice until the sun was fully in view. Retreating inside, I called downstairs for breakfast and to confirm another night in my suite. I really didn't eat too much the night before, and after the night and morning I had, I knew I needed nourishment and thought Gaby was in the same boat as me. There was no way I was going to leave this paradise too early and needed another night to soak it all in. Gaby and I spoke about her staying another night. She made a call to a fellow flight attendant and switched flights so she could spend the extra night with me. I ordered breakfast for us both in the style I loved, and since Gaby and I were so simpatico, I knew she would enjoy it. Hanging up the phone, I turned to find Gaby back in bed, waiting for me to return, picking up right where we had left off. She was a machine, and again, we were thinking the same thing.

Gaby's body was near perfect to me, but more to the point, she understood me. Even with the language difference and terminology disparity, Gaby and I understood each other. She was accommodating and more sensual than the women I was used to. Not only a change of geography but also my first day out; a change in the type of woman I was used to was very refreshing, and if this were any indication of what my new life was to become, I was all in.

Jorge came to the door about forty minutes after I made our breakfast request. The cart he wheeled in was loaded with more than enough food for two. Fresh fruit, assorted juices, eggs benedict, bacon, bagels with cream cheese, cottage cheese, and coffee. Jorge noticed I had company, confirming the order that I placed. Jorge simply smiled, making little eye contact with me before laying the food on the table. I took the bill from Jorge and peeled off the money for breakfast as well as the money for the next night along with a nice tip for his services. I instructed Jorge to get the receipt for the additional night's stay and slide it under the door when he was in the vicinity of my room.

Gaby enjoyed my choice in cuisine, and we took our time letting the nutrients and calories replenish those we lost the past half-day-plus. Following the meal, we smoked a bit more weed and returned to the bedroom for another round before we both collapsed and passed out. Our bodies' batteries needed recharging.

I awoke after a few hours of slumber. The white sheets deeply contrasted Gaby's tanned, flawless naked body intertwined within them. Her perfect breasts were rhythmically heaving as she slept peacefully. I had to take a moment, making a mental note, taking a mental picture of the scene before heading to the shower. I let the shower run hot for some minutes to let the steam build so my pores would open up. I was trying to release some of the toxins I had ingested the day before and into the morning.

I was in the shower for about ten minutes, standing there, my mind half off in another place, when I felt the shower door behind me open. Gaby decided to join me for a dual cleansing. My shower time now just got a little longer, and I wasn't complaining.

We got dressed, Gaby with her clothes from the night before and I with my swim trunks, tank top, hat, and sandals. We agreed to meet at the beach once Gaby went to her room and changed her clothes to what I assumed to be a knockout bathing suit.

My build was that of an athlete. I played football in college and loved the competitive aspect of sports. When college football was no longer an option, I found that same passion for powerlifting. A week before a bench press meet where I was to go for the world record, I tore the tendon in my chest in half. I was told there was no protocol for stapling a tendon to a tendon, so I was left with a hole in my chest where the tendon was. I was able to return to lifting, but I was never able to get back to the strength I had before the accident. Not being able to push my body to the limits of strength any further, I tried my hand at bodybuilding. I wanted to see the transformation in my body as I shed body fat and gained muscle mass. I enjoyed the process but soon knew it wasn't for me aside from some local competitions I entered. I was muscled up and built but lacked a tan. I would lie in the sun and burn, which in a few days turned into a tan. That tan lasted what seemed to be a few days, then I was back to my white self. It was hard enough for me to get a tan, let alone hold one for any duration. I was looking forward to lying about, getting some of those tropical rays.

I put my weed and ecstasy away and out of view from the maid that would be around later to clean. The safest place was right back where it was when I arrived, in the stash compartment. The room safe was where I placed my passport and documentation. I took the loose money, phone card, towel, a big bottle of water, and tanning lotion that was going to be much needed. I had a stop I had to make before I would be able to enjoy nature's rays. I kissed Gaby, and she left for her room to freshen up and change attire.

Exiting the hotel, I realized it had to be in the upper eighties, and it wasn't even noon yet. I could feel the sun energizing my body and filling me with much-needed warmth. Across the street from the hotel was a pay phone I spotted when I had arrived the day before. There were a couple of pay phones in the hotel, but I preferred the one outside and away from any extra ears.

"Hey. Yeah, it's me. Well, part of the journey is over. No, I'll probably leave tomorrow. Yeah, everything is more than perfect. Hahaha. You would be correct, my friend. She's just my speed. This one required more than one serving. If something changes, I'll let you know, but I should be out tomorrow or the next day. Either ,way I'll call you the same time tomorrow morning to check in. Yes, yes, all right. I'll see you then. I will. Thank you." I hung the phone up and made my way to Gaby.

Through the hotel I walked onto the beach. Seeing Jorge in the lobby on my way out back, I gave him an order for Gaby and me, and our day was spent sunning ourselves. I was the first to arrive on the sand and got us situated for a day at the beach. I had some bottles of water on ice and some fresh fruit brought to us. There weren't many people on the beach, and I knew we would be able to smoke the three joints I rolled before coming down.

I laid out a couple of towels for Gaby and me down toward the water. I got us an umbrella to shade us, especially me, though. I wasn't on my blanket a few minutes when I felt someone approach. I looked up into the sun to see Gaby. I got up to get her situated and have her rub some lotion on my back and wherever else she wanted. Gaby's towel down, I was able to enjoy what she looked like in her bikini with a wraparound sarong. Even though I partook in Gaby's raw beauty since we met last evening, her curves still stunned me. She took her sarong off, and her orange thong bikini was stunning. The orange color played well off her tanned body. Jorge wasn't far behind, bringing us our order for our stint here. Even Jorge I caught looking at Gaby for longer than a glance, and I couldn't blame him one bit. Hell, I was proud that he took longer than a glance. It wasn't disrespect; it was human nature.

"Can you spend another evening?" I said to Gaby as she applied lotion on my back.

"I already made those plans," Gaby said, reaching her head around me and looking me in the eyes.

Aside from Gaby's incredible figure, we connected mentally as well. There were language barriers, and of course, my slang was lost on her, but for now, in this moment, I was enjoying her.

The rest of the day and night Gaby and I spent together was more of the same as before with a bit more of us getting to know each other on a more personal level. I half-thought that if this were any other time, Gaby would make a perfect partner. She didn't get too personal with me aside from what I was willing to part with. Gaby was about pleasing me and was across-the-board interested in everything I spoke on. My work and way of life always came first even to the detriment to my personal relationships. I made my decision when I was young with whom I wanted to be, what I wanted to do for a career and that certain sacrifices had to be made. My female relationships were always the last to stand the test of time, and I was okay with that. As much as I wanted to keep one and at times I truly tried to do so, my life choices always crept back in and made me realize I should be single. Life in my line of work was always lonely, which was why moments like this I longed for and, when found, tried to prolong. I could never speak to anyone about anything. I barely told my lawyer anything, but he above anyone else knew more.

The following morning, we parted ways. I took down all her information, and true to form, she never asked for mine. I believe she had some inkling of what I was about and what my way of life was. This suited me perfectly, to have a woman that understood me and who didn't pry much, if any. She was a bit emotional upon our parting, and that touched me. The two days and nights we spent together were intense, and emotions were to be expected.

Gathering my belongings, I secured the ecstasy in the bottom of my suitcase. I exchanged passports for the last leg of my trek. This passport was the same, with the exception of the personal data and different stamped-country information. I packed my clothes in my suitcase and policed the suite for anything I might have missed. I went to the balcony to smoke one last joint before I headed downstairs to settle my bill and check out.

Once I was all checked out and ready, I made the call from the outside pay phone to Armando, letting him know I was going to be there today. I didn't want to give him too much notice, but I wanted him to be prepared for me when I made it past all the checkpoints. I called the taxi driver that brought me to the hotel and made sure that he had a passport in order to travel across the border. I negotiated the price of the taxi ride ahead of time, as was the best way to conduct business in third world countries. I said my good-byes to Jorge and the rest of the staff of the hotel. I walked to the back of the hotel to take in the view of the beach again until my ride arrived. Puffing on my cigar, I blew the smoke into the Caribbean air. Jorge came to get me when my ride had arrived. I gave Jorge a tip for taking my bags to the awaiting taxi. The ride was going to be a good two-hour-plus drive, so I settled in for the ride and got comfortable.

The spice-flavored, earthy tones of my Cuban cigar flowed through the rear window of the taxi, lingering a bit inside the car. I was headed to Mexico and, more specifically, through the border crossing at Chetumal. The ride was a bit bumpy, but then again, these were highway roads, not heavily traveled or one located in a densely populated area, which was why I figured they weren't attended to. The first thirty-five miles or so were smooth sailing; the remainder of about thirty miles would be slower, going through some small towns and villages. The drive had me thinking back to over seven years prior, when I first ventured to Mexico.

* * *

The summer of 1990, I was taking a semester or so off from school and living in Long Island. I was making new connections in my steroid business, and everything was on the upswing. There was always a demand for product, and I was continually looking for a variety of inventory, better suppliers, and cheaper deals. Only in business a couple of years, I had made huge strides in networking and connections. What started as a way to take my cycle of steroids without paying money for them had turned into a full-fledged business. One such connection I made a few months prior started out smooth and promising. A couple of deals into the relationship, I placed an order for about fifty thousand dollars' worth.

The deal I made was for monies to be paid upon the sale of the product. I received the package without hassle. The steroid names I knew, but the brand I was unfamiliar with. I didn't know the exact date of arrival, but I knew it was coming. I gave myself plenty of time to arrange buyers for as much as I could sell. My reputation in the business had been established, so when people knew that something was available, they stocked up. I didn't sell to just anybody, and my prices were low enough for the product to be resold at margins where it made sense for my people to purchase in bulk.

Toward the end of the first day of sales, I had already sold nearly half the contents of the package. My customers came to know that I had good product, fair prices, and ready availability. Slowly I began to get negative feedback and questions of the product's effectiveness and/or legitimacy. By this time I had 75 percent of the product in circulation and a problem on my hand. I tested the contents of some of the bottles. The expiration dates smudged, the tops of the bottles weren't crimped down securely enough and were twisted; a few drops of each in the toilet showed that the substance dissipated on contact. I even injected myself with some of the drugs and felt nothing in the general time that I normally would if the drugs were legit. Until this transaction, I had never encountered counterfeits of any kind, at least not that I was selling.

Armed with my newfound discoveries, I called the guy I bought the package from. I told him the issues I'd been having with the product, and I agreed to pay half the cost that day. The rest of the monies owed wouldn't be paid. He couldn't say anything about the other half of the monies, knowing full well the cost of the shipment I was sent. I traced the fake anabolics to a homemade laboratory in Tijuana, Mexico. Now there were some homemade products that were effective and legit; this just wasn't one of them.

Now was the headache of reimbursing some of the money I had collected but even worse, satisfying a customer base that still craved product. I didn't lose many clients as they understood that these things happened and knew it wasn't my intent. I needed to find a legitimate, reliable source that was able to fill the orders I had and would have in the future. I wanted to oversee the entire process myself and create the network from the origin to my clients. With this in mind, I set out to get as close to the *source* as possible. My solution was the closest and most viable—Mexico.

From a pay phone I rang a travel agent I located in the yellow pages. When the woman that answered the phone asked me where I wanted to go, I responded, "Mexico." She asked where in Mexico I wanted to travel to, and I could only say the cheapest location she had. She seemed a bit confused and asked when I wanted to travel. I didn't have a specific date, but sooner rather than later was in my thought process. She gave me some travel dates within a week's time, and I picked a date a few days away. She came up with a flight leaving in a few days to Mexico City and asked if that worked for me. I wasn't even twenty-one years old, and this was a very new thing for me, to fly to a country I didn't know about. The language that I didn't pay attention to in high school was now haunting me. I told her I wanted to book the trip. Then she asked what day I wanted to return, and in my naïveté, I chose the same day, thinking I could land early and handle all my business in one day and return.

I had informed just one associate, and he was the only one who knew I was going there. I had him drive me to the airport and made arrangements for him to get me later in the evening. I had taken only one flight before, and that was as a child, from New York to Florida. This flight was uneventful, and my nerves were more geared toward my fear of heights than anything else. I made it to customs and immigration, which was not what I would have expected. There were two lines leaving, and no immigration or customs officials were stopping anyone entering Mexico. It was almost like a turnstile without interruption. Immediately, I noticed a large difference between the United States and what I was currently experiencing. The smell was a mixture of pollution and street food, the likes of which I had never smelled before, even coming from New York City. There were plenty of people around, and their manner of dress was lackadaisical and laissez-faire. The size of the airport was not what I assumed it to be either. Just coming from John F. Kennedy Airport, I was expecting something similar. I definitely stood out among everyone else that was around me. I was dressed in a suit, was taller than most, had blond hair and blue eyes, was muscular, and had athletic build, and I didn't see anyone that resembled that description at all. Hell, I didn't see one American there besides myself.

That summer day in Mexico City International Airport was certainly warm. I had made it past customs and immigration when I was bombarded by a slew of taxi drivers and others clambering for whatever service they were offering. There wasn't much security to speak of either, the complete opposite of New York. This scene was the first of many culture shocks to come. One taxi driver stood out as I was nearing the exit. He was taller than most, calm mannered, not hustling people, and standing as if to say, "Here I am." His nonaggressive nature drew me to him. When it came time for him to say something to me, as I was a few feet away, his broken English was enough for me to speak to him. He was a man in his early fifties, was well over six feet tall, had bigger-than-average build, and had curly black hair, plaid flannel shirt, knockoff designer jeans, and cowboy boots.

"Taxi, senor? I have my own car," the taxi driver said to me.

There was something about him that made me stop and inquire. "Yeah, where are you parked?" I asked.

"In front of the airport. I have a comfortable car."

Getting past the two chickens just outside the airport, I knew I was not in the United States anymore. The streets weren't kept well, and the immediate smell of the streets and pollution combined was a sign of differences to come. The smell of street food gave my nose a break from the other ambient smells I had been taking in. The four-door sedan I would be riding in was just a couple of cars down from the airport exit. Passing the obstacle-like course of Mexicans in the street trying to sell me something, we reached the sedan. The driver introduced himself to me as Fernando. Fernando's car matched him perfectly: older, a bit worn, comfortable, yet dependable. As Fernando spoke, his thick mustache moved with every word he uttered. He was common in every sense of the word, from his mannerisms to his flannel shirt. I extended my hand and introduced myself simply as T——, and my driver responded with his name, Fernando.

"Where to go?" Fernando said in his broken English as we entered his sedan.

"I need steroids," I said as the doors to the sedan closed and we were settled in.

"Oh, esteroides. I take you to farmacia," Fernando said as we left the parking space and began our journey.

I was now learning Spanish on the fly, as I did with most of the events in my life until I learned it firsthand. I saw some of the words in Spanish were similar to words in English. I didn't speak a word of Spanish and couldn't help but think, if I had paid attention more in high school Spanish or showed up to class more, I would have been in a better position. I did know what *farmacia* meant, as it wasn't too hard to decipher it was a pharmacy, especially when speaking about buying steroids.

Fernando gave me a crash course in Mexico, the way of the land, geographical lesson, history lesson, culture, economy, and language. Fernando was quite informative about things I needed and things I found valuable later on. I was soaking it all in and listening to all he had to say. He reminded me of my father, who would point out all the historic locations and history of sights when we would take drives. My father taught me history, so when Fernando was laying it down for me during our drive, I was excited to know as much as I could. There were Volkswagen Beetles everywhere, and was the car of choice for not only taxi drivers but also the public in general. I had never seen so many Beetles in my life, especially in one place. Every other corner had some sort of food vendor on it, and that's being conservative in my estimate. They had tacos, tortas (sandwich), meat hung from a spinning rack, ice cream and ices, etc. I could see the pollution hanging in the air from the factories. It was clear to me, and what I found out later, that Mexico had little to no standards for pollution control, and I surmised that if they had them, they weren't enforced.

Fernando's late-model Chevy took about twenty minutes to get to our first of many stops. Farmacia was the sign above the location we entered. From the looks I was receiving, the inhabitants weren't used to seeing many Americans. These looks would be the norm as my time in Mexico would progress in this trip and in the years to come. This was magnified as I would enter areas of Mexico that not only Americans weren't seen but also regular, everyday Mexicans, who would surely stand out. I had no idea where I was and what neighborhoods were what. All I did was go where business took me. Later, I would come to realize from other Mexicans that the places I was in were not the norm for a Mexican, let alone an American.

Inside the pharmacy, Fernando and I approached a man in a lab coat behind the counter. Fernando spoke to him in Spanish, letting the pharmacist know what I was looking to purchase. The pharmacist went to his stock and returned with a few different types of steroids. I recognized the steroids, but the quantity was a far cry from what I was expecting and requiring. I purchased them, of course, but I let Fernando know that I needed more than this; in fact, I needed hundreds of them. Fernando gave me one of the many stares I would come to coin as monkey stares. I equated it to visiting a zoo, passing by the monkey cage. The monkeys would have that patterned blank stare on their faces; no matter what you did or said, their expression was just a blank stare. This was the first of thousands of these looks I would receive in my years in Mexico.

"This will take much time to get. Not one farmacia will have all you want."

At this rate, Fernando was right. It would take more than the time I had allotted to purchase them, ship them, and return home. I bought what the first pharmacy had on hand, and we went to the next location to continue our hunt. I now knew I would have to delay my flight, but I didn't want to stop doing anything but continuing to purchase as much as I could. This was also part of my naïveté both as a young man and in being in a foreign land, doing business that wasn't new but a new way of doing business. Some pharmacies even asked for prescriptions, something I didn't think was necessary in Mexico; in fact, I thought it really was an option, not necessarily a must-have.

More than a dozen pharmacies later, time was running out for me to change my reservation, get situated for the night in a hotel, and make preparations for a full day of steroid-hunting the next day.

Fernando chose a decent hotel in the heart of the city for me to stay in. He dropped me off, and we made plans for him to call me later that night, and we'd go over the time he would be there the following day to resume the search.

The hotel wasn't the Ritz, but it wasn't half-bad either. It was in the heart of Mexico City and conveniently located for everything I needed. I settled into my room as the sun was going down. I got on the phone in my room and called the airline to change my flight, which wasn't as difficult a task as I thought. I packed lightly, with my clothes fitting in my knapsack snuggly—a couple of tank tops, sweats, shorts, socks, underwear, and my hygiene items just in case. I changed my clothes and headed to the streets to see what pharmacies were around and if there was a gym to get in a workout. I had no idea what type of food to get and what was safe. I always had such a fair palate, and the last thing I needed was to get sick in Mexico. I found a little spot and loaded up on some fresh eggs and chicken. The food was so cheap I ate like a king for very little money. After I ate I made a call back home to let my associate know I wouldn't be arriving tonight and advise him on when I would return. The next order of business was to get in a workout. I thought I could train a bit and also see if there were some connections I could make that would speed up my trip. I asked around for a gym and was pointed in a direction that took me about twenty one minutes to get to, walking. I didn't mind at all, as this city was filled with great architecture and seemed to be quite dated, a stark difference between Manhattan and here. I had to walk off all the protein I just consumed, so the walk did me some good. Wherever I was now and in the future, I preferred walking around to get my bearings and to see for myself what was around. It's the little things you miss when you're driving that you can't experience if you take the time to walk about.

The gym was a hole-in-the-wall place and walking in the entranceway, I noticed to the immediate left was a juice bar. The man behind the counter was the owner of the bar, weathered and in his late sixties, at least. I was definitely looking to get some liquids in me and sat down at the counter. More than anything, though, I wanted to get some information on what was what around here, and who better to ask than a man who had been here since the beginning of time. His English was good, surprising to me because of the location. Immediately he began to speak to me and asked what I wanted in my shake. While making it for me, he was asking me questions about why I was there and who I was. His questions were based on curiosity, which I came to realize was because there had been many Americans that traveled here and visited this gym. I noticed pictures of famous athletes, wrestlers, bodybuilders, and a bodybuilder that later became a politician donning the walls. The photos were all taken in the gym with the juice bar owner or the owner of the gym, who, I learned, was a former Mr. Universe. Being just under twenty years of age, I took in all this information of whom he knew in the past and why they came to visit. Apparently, Mexico City was a major player in events that were held for bodybuilding, wrestling matches, and pugilistic bouts. The old man's stories matched the eras and pictures, and all of it made sense to me. As we spoke, I wondered why these many athletes—and famous ones at that—would visit this little hole-in-the-wall, but I equated it to Venice Beach, California, when so many would flock there and train and congregate. The common denominator was hardcore training and steroids. The old man told me that Americans would visit, train, make connections, and purchase their steroids. I knew the guys in the pictures I was looking at were on steroids, but to hear it from a man who had been here since the beginning was validation enough for me. This was boding well for my need to find steroids in quantity. I now thought this might be a good place to find some connections in and speed up my process.

I went up the small spiral staircase to the gym upstairs. The gym resembled something from the seventies that I saw in the bodybuilding magazines, in black-and-white pictures. Again, there were more black-and-white photos on the walls. Some of the photos were of the owner in his heyday of competing. I walked around the gym a bit, taking it all in and surveying the equipment and deciding what body parts I wanted to train. I had to formulate the best plan for my workout and use what was available. The heat was all trapped in here; the central air-conditioning consisted of some half-open windows, hoping to catch a cross-breeze fueled by a few fans. The equipment was old, and some didn't work, but there was enough for me to get in a good power workout. I chose chest and triceps to train this day. I located a flat bench and made my way over to it to begin my chest routine. I approached the bench at the same time as another man. He was a few years older than I and was set to do the same exercise. We met at the bench and looked at each other. I didn't know if this man was Mexican or not. His skin was lighter, his hair short and jet-black, almost like a military haircut, and he was about my height, six feet tall, and had athletic to muscular build, as I had, just not as thick as me.

"Mind if I work in with you?" I asked, knowing that he wasn't on the bench yet, but I wanted to show respect for him, especially being in a foreign land.

"No, I don't. You want to go first?" The man spoke in English with a Spanish accent.

His English was pretty good, more than what I was expecting, and thankfully so because my command of the Spanish language was certainly in its infancy.

"Sure, thank you. My name is T——," I said, extending my hand to the man I would be working in with.

"My name is Armando," he said, greeting my hand and clasping it firm and strong, looking at me directly in my eyes, the sign of a confident man of respect.

The entire gym felt dedicated to their workouts. This certainly wasn't a gym of lavish decor and state-of-the-art equipment, but it was filled with men and women who took their training seriously. There were a few that were there training probably because of a lack of another location, but the atmosphere was hard-core. Atmosphere is everything for a gym, and this place had plenty of that. You didn't want to slack off here, and the atmosphere alone wanted me to push it to my limit. I was in the right frame of mind, and having Armando to train with helped me along. Being in the gym was no different than walking through the airport—or anywhere else in the city for that matter. People's eyes looked at me as if they were seeing an alien, and it was a look I came to become comfortable with over time.

"So what brings you to Mexico?" Armando asked as he lay on the bench to do his first set of bench press.

"I'm looking for steroids," I said without hesitation and without concern that by opening up to Armando, I was putting myself in harm's way.

"Steroids. Well, perhaps I can help you get some," Armando voiced his willingness as he repped out his first set.

"I need more than some. I need them in quantity, not just personal use," I said, making my needs and wants quite clear.

"When we finish working out, we can speak more about it. I have some people that should be able to assist," Armando said confidently.

Armando didn't seem surprised to hear why I was in Mexico. His matter-of-fact attitude had me at ease with offering up the purpose of my trip that quickly. I had neither time nor options to be wasting on investigating who was who at this juncture. I was relying on what I did so many other times, my gut feeling. Hell, it saved my ass more than once, and my gut was telling me that Armando was more than resourceful and was someone that I could rely on and trust. Mexico's laws regarding steroids were nonexistent, so there was no threat in any legal ramifications.

"Good, let's get this workout in then," I said, not showing any emotions either way, almost half-expecting Armando to say the very thing he did.

We continued our training and even trained triceps together, completing our workout with each other. Armando showed me the equipment, and I showed him some exercises for gaining thickness, as he was interested in how to pack on thick, dense muscle. We continued to spot one another, and our chemistry in the gym was off to a good start. We shared the same intensity for training, which wasn't easy for me as I generally preferred to train alone.

We finished our workout and went down the rickety staircase to the juice bar to replenish ourselves with a protein shake. I purchased the shake for us both, a sign of good will. We began speaking about what Armando had in mind for me and my steroid business. He wanted to know a little more about what I was looking for, and I sure wanted to hear more about what he had in mind and what his capabilities were. I gave him the steroids that I considered the top of my list and then mentioned that any steroid would do. I offered

Armando a dollar on each ampoule or box of one hundred pills he could arrange. The dollar was on top of whatever the price of the item was. Whatever quantity Armando could provide, I would purchase. I knew I didn't have unlimited funds with me, but I could always call back home and arrange more money or stockpile them and return to purchase if the quantity was that large.

I didn't know Armando's line of work and never even thought to ask at the time. My only concern was having enough products and making enough connections to make this trip financially worth it and making future trips profitable as well. I was never one to pry, especially at this juncture in our fledgling relationship. I took Armando's information, and I gave him the hotel in which I was staying, in case he needed to reach me there. There was some risk involved with giving him the information about where I was, but I weighed that against the possibility of making a really good connection. We agreed to meet at the gym again the same time, if not earlier the next day, and if something were to arise, we would contact each other.

The next morning came, and I awoke to ambient sounds of Mexico City outside my hotel window. I called Fernando to confirm our meeting in an hour, and he mentioned he had made some calls to some friends and scheduled us to meet them throughout the day. I showered up and went downstairs to see what establishment was close that I could get a quality meal to eat before Fernando would arrive to begin our steroid hunt. The front desk told me of a little spot around the corner where I could get breakfast, and I figured I could figure out the food when I got there. I wanted to keep it simple, nothing that would have me getting sick. I always heard about the food in Mexico and that definitely, drinking the water was a no-no. I couldn't afford to not be able to function or miss a day of work. I ordered a large egg white omelet and some grilled chicken. I figure that was safe enough and wouldn't cause me too many problems while getting in the share of protein I needed. I finished it off with some fresh fruit, freshly squeezed orange juice, and a bottle of water.

Fernando arrived, and he had already eaten so we could begin our journey. He began telling me some of the connections he had made and rekindled in regards to the steroids. Our first run was to a doctor he knew who owned his own hospital. I figured this to be a home run. I didn't know of an individual that owned his own hospital, but then again, I was learning a lot of new things I had never heard of before and just added this to the list.

The ride to the hospital was a good forty minutes, and upon arriving, I realized it wasn't exactly what I had in my mind when I heard of hospital. It was like no hospital I had seen in the States. It was a two-story building and was not overly large but still large for a private institution in Mexico. Fernando and I walked in and were met by a nurse and then the doctor who owned the hospital. We exchanged some words with Fernando translating. The doctor looked as pleased on the outside as I was on the inside to see him. Fernando introduced the doctor to me as Dr. Mevilla. The doctor took me inside and introduced me to his wife and staff. We first went to his office, and we spoke about what I needed. I explained to the doctor the dilemma I had was quantity and that this was not just for now but for well into the future. The doctor was slim and unassuming, a professional man of no particular characteristics that made him different from anyone else. I wondered why and how a doctor in his early forties could own his hospital, but then again, I wasn't going to speak on it out loud, just something I kept to myself. I bought what he had on hand and some other more-exotic drugs, like human growth hormone. We finished our brief talk and our getting to know each other. It was pretty cut-and-dried, with half the time spent with the doctor asking me questions about me on a personal manner. He had never seen an American around these parts, so his curiosity was on high level. His nurses also hung around a bit here and there as they were more than curious to know more of me on a personal side as well. I was given the tour of his facility. The doctor explained the various rooms, and from top to bottom, I thought I was trapped in a 1950s time warp. The IVs, nurses' outfits, hospital beds, rooms, and technology reminded me of a scene from *The Godfather* when Don Corleone was hospitalized after being gunned down in the street. For me, much of Mexico City had me feeling like I was taking a step back in time, or two steps, as the case might be.

Over the coming years, the doctor would prove to be a reliable source and one I could always count on. After this first meeting, I was dealing directly with the doctor in future deals. At times, when my trip was short and I had to see the doctor, I even slept in his hospital. I was now collecting my contacts like stacking cordwood. I had Fernando tell the doctor that I needed as much as he could muster and would be leaving in a few days. I would return in two days' time to gather what the doctor had and make arrangements with him for my next go-around. The doctor even wrote me a bunch of prescriptions for steroids that I knew where in high demand back home.

Fernando and I left the hospital to continue our search of larger pharmacies. I had some time before I was to meet with Armando, and although I had some success, I was still running into issues with obtaining quantity, and at times, I still was asked about presenting a prescription.

The day was coming to a close for Fernando and me. He drove me back to my hotel, and we spoke about the next series of events for us. We agreed I would call him tomorrow morning to have our day mapped out. I wanted to see what Armando had in store for me before I made definitive plans either way.

I had an early dinner or late lunch, depending on how you looked at it. I was to meet Armando at the gym and needed some quality food in me before even entertaining a workout.

Armando and I were at the gym within ten minutes of each other's arrival, and we wasted no time getting to the business at hand. Armando and I had some qualities in common; sugarcoating things or not getting to the point wasn't among them. Over the years, I would find out just how much we had in common, similarities in character and eerie uniformity of our mind-set.

"T——, I have some good news. I spoke to my cousin who's a veterinarian. She said she could supply us with and write prescriptions for steroids."

Armando had my full attention now as we continued working out. I loved veterinary steroids, and they were in high demand back home. His cousin being able to write more prescriptions would satisfy part of my problem. Things were looking up for sure.

"I thought of something that can get us more steroids with the help of my cousin. We can go to Tepito and print out copies of prescriptions and go to pharmacies," Armando said resourcefully.

"Tepito, what is that?" I said more than curiously, not knowing if Tepito was a person, place, or thing.

"Tepito is a barrio located in Colonia Morelos in the Cuauhtémoc borough of Mexico City, bordered by Avenida del Trabajo, Paseo de la Reforma, Eje1, and Eje2. Most of the neighborhood is taken up by the open-air markets, which drive the majority of the economy for Tepito. You can buy or locate whatever goods or services you are seeking and even some of those that you haven't even thought of yet. We can print copies of the prescriptions there. I know some people that live and work in Tepito. I want to introduce you to my people there and see what we can do. Tepito is the spot that will get us what we want. If we can't find it in Tepito, we won't find it anywhere." Armando's confidence and legwork were impressive.

Now my mind was racing as Armando did his set and left me to contemplate on the possibilities. I was quite impressed with Armando's hustle and contacts, more traits we had in common. If the market was as Armando was saying, I knew I would find more than what I desired in product and contacts.

We finished our workout and headed downstairs for a much-needed protein shake. We spoke more in-depth about Armando's plan. We scheduled it out and decided to go to his cousin's office first and get what I could at the veterinary hospital, including prescriptions. His cousin was going to wait for us this evening so we could get started. They knew time was of the essence for me, and I appreciated their understanding of my schedule.

I was able to obtain some good veterinary steroids and enough prescriptions to get a decent quantity in the hours after we left the office. Pharmacies in Mexico were open late, not all, but enough to add to my existing supply. I paid her for the steroids, and Armando and I went about our business. It was then that Armando told me that tomorrow, we had a busy schedule. He wanted to go to Tepito to a printer in order to make copies of the prescriptions and make our own. That was just part of the plan. He was going to introduce me around and let me purchase whatever I could from the "vendors" there. I was excited to see this new angle. I had the doctor now, knew of pharmacies that were cooperative, and looked forward to what tomorrow would bring. We said good-bye, and I went back to my hotel to call Fernando and get a much-needed good night's rest.

I called Fernando, letting him know that I wouldn't be needing him tomorrow. Perhaps the following day, I would meet with him in order to get to the hospital. I didn't want to take up much of his time, and especially if I were paying him, I wanted to make it count. Fernando didn't have anything new on the agenda—good timing for me to go to Tepito with Armando.

The next morning came before I knew it, and a much-needed rest for me was well received. I asked for a wake-up call at 6:00 a.m., giving me enough time to shower, eat, and prepare myself for a long day of work. Armando was on time at eight in the morning—plenty of time for us to get to where we need to be and accomplish our goals for the day.

Our first stop was some old-fashioned printing presses on the outskirts of Tepito. I brought my prescriptions with me and handed them to Armando. The owner of the press took a script from each doctor and duplicated them with specific typeset and ink. We printed up a few hundred, more than enough that would handle the task I needed for the remainder of time I had left. Mexican pharmacies didn't keep track of the scripts—it was more a formality than it was an enforced law—yet some insisted on them. I began filling them out and signing them as the printer was finishing the others.

Our printing completed, we began our walk into the market of Tepito. There seemed to be hundreds of vendors selling anything one could imagine. Not only were there products from Mexico but also a large contingent of products from the United States. Most of the products I saw were fakes or really good knockoffs, but none of that was my concern. My eyes went past the perfumes, electronics kitchen appliances, and Mexican trinkets that you would expect to see. I was there for one reason and one reason only: steroids. Some of the vendors had steroids to sell right out in the open; others made calls for them to be delivered. Armando introduced me to his people, and luckily he did because here, of all places, I stuck out more. Not many ordinary Mexicans entered Tepito, let alone an American. It was like nothing I'd ever seen before, not that I had seen a ton, but for my young age, I'd seen a lot. Tepito, as it was explained to me, operated like no other city I knew of. The entire place policed itself. If something happened in one area, word would spread like wildfire so the other end of the market would know of the matter in moments. There were no police or government agencies that governed here. It was like a country unto itself, and everything had a price, including one's life. I was told that coming back tomorrow would be ideal as most of the people I had met would make sure they had products for me to purchase then if not now. I left instructions to stockpile as much as they could, and if I missed them this time, the next visit I would purchase whatever they brought forth.

Cash is king and solves most people's concerns, and Tepito was no different. I moved around Tepito like I belonged there, and the inhabitants made me feel as if I were a local. It helped that Armando vouched for me and that my money was right. That was a good start to any relationship, a good word and money. Growing up in New York helped put me at an advantage when it came to conducting myself in the proper fashion. I was blessed to have the upbringing I did, and the key was to be aware. To always be aware of my surroundings was driven home like Babe Ruth in Yankee Stadium. Always be aware of who's who and why things are the way they are. I had to walk with a purpose and not look as though I was lost or unsure of things. I was there in Tepito for a purpose and proved it. Show and prove—another New York adage that continues to arise. Show what you're about and prove it through actions and deeds over time. A real man can travel with his word. His word will follow him and precede him. A man's word slowly develops into his character and reputation. I was taught well at a young age that one's reputation was most valuable, and the strength of his word, the most coveted. Through my experiences I learned and experienced that my reputation followed me whatever country or whatever situation I found myself in. I could always resort to stating my name or referencing an associate that could vouch for me.

I left Tepito armed with a whole slew of contacts, products, and orders placed for larger quantities. I was also leaving with a new name, El Güero; in English, it roughly refers to a person of blond hair and/or fair complexion American. The name fit me for sure, being of fair skin, dirty-blond hair, American and none of that was changing anytime soon. I didn't see anyone else in the city that fit the description but me, lending to my name spreading like wildfire. Whenever anyone heard of El Güero, they thought of me. I for sure couldn't fuck things up because my name, as distinctive as it was, would identify me.

My subsequent trips to Mexico City and the nickname stuck with me, as most referred to me as El Güero. My second trip to Mexico City had me renting an apartment in Tepito that served me well in the years to come. I found comfort in living in the heart of the action and found it odd that the everyday Mexican would hear the word Tepito and cringe with concern.

As we were leaving the barrio of Tepito, Armando and I began discussing other forms of business that he thought I might be interested in. He discussed marijuana and cocaine being purchased and delivered to the United States. I didn't want him to think me scared or concerned that he was asking. I simply mentioned that it wasn't my business. I didn't get into details about why as I didn't know if he would understand and thought explaining myself would only complicate the issue. I told him I had never really seen those drugs, let alone dealt them. I knew back home that dealing drugs was considered off-limits, so I stayed clear of them. Armando wasn't particularly telling me to do one thing or another; he was merely throwing ideas out about what else we could do together, and I appreciated the brainstorming.

I knew there were guys that were in the drug business and there were factions of the Mafia that dealt in drugs, but with me being on the lower end of things, I certainly wasn't going to rock the apple cart. I generally identified and associated with the older men of the organization, and the old men preached a drug-free work environment. I was concerned about how some viewed the steroid trade. I knew some of the old guard would consider it drugs regardless of the fact that it had only been illegal recently. I also wanted to keep it under wraps because I didn't want to kick money upstairs to guys that had no financial stake or other involvement in my business. The less everyone knew of my business dealings, the better off I would be.

Coming up on my last day, I was running out of time and money. I met with the doctor in the hospital, Fernando, Armando, the veterinarian, and more. I was rushing around to get my entire product and never really thought about how I was going to get it back to New York. Faced with a dilemma of what to do, I made the decision to physically bring the steroids with me on the plane. Luckily, I passed through the Mexican customs without concern. The next test was John F. Kennedy International Airport. The law making the possession of steroids illegal without a prescription was in flux, but there were still laws in place that made it a felony to import steroids with the intent to distribute, which was what I was surely doing. It was a risk I was willing to take especially when my options were limited and time was not my friend.

I approached customs with my one knapsack of street clothes, the box containing the steroids, and me wearing the suit I had departed New York with a little less than a week prior. My box was about two feet in length and about two feet high, maybe a foot and a half in width. I wanted to look more business than touristy when traveling in attempts to throw off customs from stopping or search-ing me. I wasn't even twenty-one yet, and all this was certainly new territory for me. Hell, this was my first trip anywhere besides the one plane ride as a child I could barely remember. I surveyed my sur-roundings and spotted a customs officer I thought would be an easier passage for me to exit without instance. The agent was older, about fifty years old, and had thinning gray hair, his uniform a little less tidy than the others', and I thought that in the worst-case scenario, if he were to stop me, I could explain away the product I had with me. While it wasn't a ton, it was a decent amount and something that was certainly a punishable offense.

Being in Mexico even for this short stint, I had to get used to the stark difference between the two countries.

"Good afternoon, sir," the customs agent addressed me as I was now just a few feet away.

"Good afternoon to you," I said, handing the agent my birth certificate, license, and declaration card.

"What was the purpose of your trip?" the agent asked as he finished reading my paperwork and then looked directly in my eyes as he spoke.

"A good vacation," I said, knowing that business might not be the most believable answer.

"Vacation it is," the agent said as he assessed his protocol in his mind.

The agent was looking at my box, and I knew it. I was pretending the box wasn't even there.

"What's in the box?" the agent asked. Knowing now that I would have to open it, simultaneously, I began formulating responses to the agent's actions and deeds.

"Medicine," I said matter-of-factly, not knowing another word to describe the potential jail time I was facing.

"Can you open it for me?"

I didn't skip a beat and pretended what the agent was telling me was a bit of a surprise for me to be hearing. I opened the box nonchalantly, paying attention to the agent's response and demeanor. The agent leaned his head over the edge of my box, looking inside. He began moving some of the contents around, trying to make heads or tails of what he was seeing. He moved aside the boxes of syringes, ampoules, and pills. The initial look on the agent's face wasn't alarming to me. Quite the opposite was true; he looked puzzled, as if this were something he had never seen before.

"What's all this?" the agent asked me, finishing his question, looking at me for a response.

"Medicine. It's for gaining weight. I have a hard time gaining weight," I said quickly, not knowing what else to say.

My response wasn't alarming to the agent and looked like it made sense to him, even though I was trying so hard to believe it myself, especially outwardly. The key is to not stumble on your words when asked a question and have answers formulated that make sense and something that is believable when circumstances dictate otherwise. I wasn't nervous, anxious, or anything besides calm. There was nothing that I could do now. I couldn't rewind Father Time. I couldn't go back to Mexico and send the package by mail. I had to deal with what was now directly in front of me and act as if everything the agent was seeing was not only completely normal but legal.

"What about all these needles?" The agent became more inquisitive as he tried to discern what was really going on.

"The doctor in Mexico gave me instructions that I was to use one needle per injection and usage, or I would risk infection or worse," I said, knowing I had at least five hundred needles in my box. "I have prescriptions for each one of these here," I said, reaching into my knapsack, attempting to show the agent that what I was doing was legit.

Armando's idea of printing prescriptions turned out to be a great idea on many levels, and whether it worked or not, I was giving the agent more ammunition in order to give me a favorable pass.

"That makes sense to me," the agent said as a bit of calming came over me that I wasn't totally screwed.

Now the odds of me not being arrested for trafficking tipped more in my favor. I was always an odds guy, weighing the odds for or against something. I was now thinking that I might even have a shot of leaving with my product. He kept pausing, moving items in my box, as he contemplated what to do.

"I'm going to have to ask someone about this. I just don't know if I can let you pass with all this," the agent said in an even tone.

The agent looked puzzled and hit the button near him, in turn making the light go on above the line I was in. The light was meant to call for assistance from other agents. This wasn't the most ideal option for me, but then again, it wasn't the worst event to take place. The agent wasn't alarmed or in an aggressive manner, merely looking for guidance in my situation.

Another agent came over and was as puzzled as the first agent when it came to knowing what exactly they should do. The same conclusion was reached, and hence, the light was pressed again. Some other officers came over as my situation became a bit of a sideshow. My process was taking up more time than was logical to the agents. When there were a handful of agents either in front of me or approaching, a supervisor made himself known and took charge of the scene. Astonishingly, the supervisor derived the same conclusion. The supervisor, looking every bit the part, came up with a solution that was near the best-case scenario for me.

"Let's take this back to my office, count it, inventory it, and see where we go from there," the supervisory agent said, giving the definitive word of the ordeal.

I picked up my box, confidently walking with the agent to his office. Nothing was complicated about his office, and there was nothing personal to make me think he spent a lot of time there or it was something permanent for him. I sat opposite the agent as he took up his position behind his nondescript desk. He had me take out the contents as we both sat there and inventoried the contents of my box, done on a triplicate form.

"What's your address and telephone number?" the supervising agent asked me.

I gave the proper information and left my parents' address as my main address. I had not been at my parents often but didn't want my real residence to be known. Customs already had the address that was on my license, and there was no sense in complicating matters with giving false information. I was planning on spending a few days at my parents anyway in the next couple of days, so I left that to fate. Leaving the address wasn't putting anyone in danger, especially if I were to be released from the airport. Being released was what I was hoping for in the best-case scenario.

"Okay, that seems to be about it," the supervisory agent said, looking over all the papers he had in his hand.

The agent handed me the papers to sign, agreeing that the quantity and amounts matched what we had just inventoried. I was given my copy of the inventory, and the agent gave me some parting words.

"I'll have to speak with my superiors and see if we're able to release this to you. In the next couple of days, we'll be calling you, and if you're cleared to receive the box and its contents, we'll let you know. Don't lose your copy of the inventory, and we'll be in touch soon."

I was almost bowled over that I wasn't in handcuffs at this point. I made my way out as fast as I could without bringing attention to myself or the box I had just left behind. I couldn't help but feel I was going to be tackled from behind before I was able to exit the airport. I found a pay phone close by and called the associate who was to pick me up. He was smart enough not to leave the vicinity when I was late, instead waiting for me to exit or worse. It took him a few minutes to reach me as I jumped into the passenger seat as he pulled up.

"Drive, go," I said, jumping into the car, closing the door as the wheels were already in motion.

I looked behind me to see if anyone was exiting the airport, realizing his or her folly.

"What's up?" my associate asked as we exited the airport and all seemed to be clear.

I mentioned what happened and that although my box was lost, it was only a cost of some thousands. More important were all the contacts I had made down in Mexico and what my brain was thinking, my next trip to Mexico. In a short amount of time, I made solid contacts and had left instructions for them to gather as much product as possible so when I returned, I could handle my business in short order. I would call them ahead of me coming to ensure that they were prepared and I knew more or less what to expect.

A few days later, I was at my parents' house, and the phone rang. I answered the phone, and to my surprise, it was an agent with the customs department. He introduced himself as Agent Willis. He asked me my name to make sure who I was. I was positive I was being recorded at the very least and didn't want to give anything besides brief yes-or-no answers to his questions. Agent Willis informed me that my box was ready to be picked up and cleared by customs. I wasn't going to fall for the banana-in-the-tailpipe act. I declined ownership of it and said it was okay. Agent Willis didn't take my answer for what it was. He insisted that it was okay for me to come to customs and retrieve my box. Politely, I declined his offer, and when the agent knew he wasn't going to get anywhere, he excused himself, and we concluded our phone conversation. My merchandise being ready for pickup was a joke, and I was good on that. I kept the call respectful but direct to the point. Customs realized their blunder, and there was nothing they could do about it. I had too many loopholes to use if they were to legally pursue this matter. The problem was that even if customs didn't make this an issue, I would now be on customs' radar and in their database for whatever that looked like.

My first venture into Mexico wasn't a complete failure. I now knew where to go in Mexico and had numbers, addresses, and names of everyone I made contact with that was a connection or a possible connection. The others that I didn't have information for, I knew where to go and visit them. I was also speaking a little Spanish, a lot more than I did before, which was zero Spanish. Overall, I was feeling like my trip was a success and looking forward to and planning my next trip, which was set for a few weeks later. My only X factor was how to get the product back to the United States safely.

I didn't waste any time getting my next trip ready. I began making my calls to Mexico and making arrangements for the people there to gather up quantities so I wouldn't waste so much time there. I knew there would be more work to do, and I would be focusing on transportation and shipping.

That next trip to Mexico I spent fortifying my relationships, bringing with me more money and gifts from the States that fit my new associates' wants and needs. I found some more contacts that worked directly in the laboratories and ones associated with Mexican shipping. I found Mex Post to be the most efficient means of shipping my product back home. Mex Post is the Mexican post office, which I thought was the easiest mode of exporting my steroids. It wasn't that difficult a task. I found most of the people working at the Mex Post were women, and when I went to send my first box on my second day, I immediately began to cultivate my relationship with a few women employees, one being the manager of the facility. I was so friendly with them that I ended up going to some of their family affairs. After my first package was sent and relationships built, I was no longer standing in line but was rather going to the post office manager's office, and she was handling the mailing personally. I was never even told to open them before sending. This was all well and good, but the final hurdle would be the American authorities and our postal system. I began to find the opening of my packages was a hit or miss entering the United States.

The land of opportunity. People say the United States of America is the land of opportunity. I say a man makes his own opportunities in life. The world is the land of opportunity, if you know what you want and have the balls to make it happen.

* * *

"Senor, senor," the taxi driver said to me, awakening me from my reminiscing.

"Yes," I said, wondering what the taxi driver needed my attention about.

"Two miles to the border," my driver said as we had agreed to ahead of our trip.

I was now two miles from the border of Belize and Mexico. I knew there to be a heavy military presence on the border, especially on the Mexican side. Mexico always had the illegal immigrant and drug problem, but then there were the rebels. Zapatistas, a revolutionary leftist group formed for political and military power, formed in the southernmost part of Mexico of Chiapas. They ventured outside that area so the Mexican military had their hands full with all sorts of issues.

I began preparing myself mentally and otherwise for this next step of the journey. As detailed as I was, the X factor was always prevalent. I got out my papers and laid a hundred-dollar bill in the middle of my passport. Being from New York, I figured this was a way I could possibly make my crossing into Mexico go a bit smoother. Mexico was and still is the land of opportunity and opportunists. Generally speaking, a healthy majority of the police, military, and government officials had their hands out for the greasing. While the power and money trickled downhill at an infinitesimal rate, nearly everyone in Mexico was for the greasing. Even if you were not doing anything illicit, it made sense to offer a nominal "fee" to an official. Just because you're not doing something illegal doesn't mean the powers that be in Mexico won't create something ominous for you.

We approached the apex of a small incline in the road. Just below the near-mid-morning sunshine, I saw a number of vehicles off in the distance blocking traffic from flowing to and from Mexico and Belize. This was it; there were no turnoffs or side roads to take. Regardless of what I wanted, my decision was already made, and I was going to see it through.

On the downslope of the apex we were about half a mile from the border-crossing roadblock. I was prepared but had some butterflies in my stomach. I felt the butterflies, but I was preparing my mind more to what lay ahead as I saw clearer the picture that was ahead. Both sides of the border had their troops guarding the coming and going into their respective countries. I began taking in my assessment of the Belizean forces, which constituted one troop carrier and a couple of jeeps. The Belizean side also had their own structure that appeared about half the size of a Quonset hut.

The Mexican side was heavily populated even from my vantage point, where I couldn't see the entire force. The Mexican forces were larger in number for many reasons, one being that most activity flowed north, not south. They had a troop carrier as well as a couple of jeeps along with a couple of Humvees with M60 mounts. As I was about a couple of hundred yards away, I noticed two M60 machine gun nests flanking either side of the road on the Mexico side. The Mexicans as well had a building on their side about the same size as the Belizean forces had. A hundred yards out, and we began to slow down due to a drop in the speed limit as well as the multitude of large bumps in the road to prevent vehicles from going more than a couple of miles an hour at a time. Both sides had their vehicles staggered in a way to not be in the crossfire if things were to get to that extreme.

We began our crossing over the first set of speed bumps, and I could see the outline of the faces of the military personnel. As best as I could, I took mental notes of how many were on either side. I counted eight Belizean army members, not counting those that might be in their hut. I didn't see fully the Mexican side, but roughly, I counted twenty-five members of their government's troops even though I couldn't clearly see all. That was enough to deter most activities from getting out of line.

We slowed to a crawl as the Belizean military signaled for us to stop. I could see that the officer was a captain accompanied by two enlisted personnel. The only military personnel I had seen in

Belize had been at the airport, and this captain looked familiar. As it flashed through my mind, I realized it was the same officer that was at the airport when I passed. I only saw him for a few seconds when I passed him by in the airport, but that was him. He was in an office and on a cell phone as I passed by before pressing the red light on the customs checkpoint. No such thing as a coincidence for sure, and I was stuck in the back of this taxi with nowhere to go. The captain had his eyes fixated on me as we came to a halt. He looked at my driver for a brief moment and asked a few questions to him in regard to me, our route, and what our cargo was. The taxi driver gave him his papers, and oddly enough, he didn't request mine. The captain barely looked at my driver's paperwork and handed it back to him. He again stared at me and waved his hand for us to cross. I assumed that this checkpoint was mere formality and that the Belizean military let the Mexican side deal with whatever came next. Even with the shade from his cloth-style military hat covering his eyes, I felt his gaze upon me. I didn't want to stare but had the uneasy feeling that the captain was staring at me the entire time as I passed by through to the next obstacle. What the hell was that that just happened? I wasn't even spoken to, and no papers were checked. What the hell was he doing here? Hell, all I know was I was passing through to Mexico, but what exactly lay ahead for me in Mexico, I had no idea. Would I be arrested there? Was a deal made to take me into custody from the Mexican authorities? I had no time to think of what-ifs, just act and react.

The Mexican side appeared to be more of a hurdle than the smooth sailing I just experienced. We went over a few more speed bumps, and in between two large bumps was where we were made to stop. On the driver's side of the taxi were three Mexican military, one officer and two enlisted. The right side of the taxi had a couple more enlisted men standing a few feet away, all with their patented tough-guy stares and blank faces. Even with the temperatures climbing, these soldiers donned full military gear and had a razor-sharp focus. The officer flagged us to move to the right-hand side of the road, escorted by the two soldiers on our right, about thirty feet away from the machine gun emplacement manned by two soldiers. There was nowhere to go with the open road in front and back and the jungle off to the right, which would have to be cleared by over one hundred yards of open terrain before reaching. The Mexican officer, a lieutenant, wanted everyone to know, including me, that he was in charge of this crossing.

The enlisted men carried their M16 rifles across their chests at the ready while the lieutenant had his .45 holstered at his hip. The lieutenant had sunglasses covering his eyes, but his presence was that of an officer in every sense of the word. He commanded his men with his stern silence. Standing about six feet tall, he was lighter skinned than the others, and while lean, he was far from skinny. The lieutenant approached the driver's side of the taxi, his stoic expression intact and on full display. In robotic fashion, he lifted his sunglasses, revealing his hazel-green eyes. There was a brief moment when nothing was uttered before he moved his eyes, one focused on the driver and the other assessing the American in the backseat.

"Afuera!" the lieutenant barked in a curt tone.

The lieutenant's right hand eased down to his holster as he gave his command, never once taking his eyes off my driver or myself. We both exited slowly out of the taxi and did as we were ordered to do. Both of the lieutenant's comrades flanking him moved their fingers to their triggers, expecting the unexpected. I exited the car as the driver did and stood just outside the car about four feet from the soldiers. The lieutenant didn't say another word—he only looked at us—and then finally, he gave me his full attention.

"Documents and papers!" the lieutenant ordered us both to produce.

I didn't make any sudden movements and knew to have the required papers ready for him to inspect. Instinctively, the driver was of the same mind-set as he had his paperwork waiting in his hands. The lieutenant was methodical about his business and didn't spend much time on the taxi driver's paperwork. He gave it back to the driver then turned his attention toward me. I didn't even wait to be asked for anything as I slowly reached out my hand with my paperwork in it, offering it to the lieutenant. He didn't even look at my paperwork before he began demanding the driver to open the trunk of the car and ordered the two soldiers on the passenger side to inspect the trunk. The lieutenant then walked without one word back to his building with my passport in his hand. I had no idea what was going on, and the taxi driver turned and looked at me as if to say, "You must have done something or are in trouble for something."

We stayed out in the sun for about ten minutes while the lieutenant was in his office before he returned.

"Where are you going?" the lieutenant asked me directly, still holding my passport in his hand.

"I'm going to Cancun for vacation," I replied, knowing he was going to ask me if it was for work or vacation.

"How many days will you be there?"

"Two weeks," I said quickly.

The lieutenant didn't say anything as beads of sweat began to roll down my forehead. The heat mixed with the stress of the day had me a little overheated. The lieutenant looked into the taxi and saw my luggage before asking another question, still not relinquishing my papers.

"Is this all the luggage you have?"

"Yes," I said, again not wanting to have any more words with the lieutenant than I absolutely had to.

"Bien, you can pass, and have a safe vacation in Mexico," the lieutenant said as he handed me my passport and papers.

"Thank you," I said, outstretching my hand to take hold of the papers.

The lieutenant didn't let go of my papers right away. I felt him not wanting to relinquish them as his steely hazel eyes looked at me intently. A few seconds of this, and I felt his grip release. With my papers in my hand, the driver of the taxi and I got in the car and began making our way over the next series of speed bumps on our way into Mexico. I didn't even move much once inside the taxi and wasn't truly relieved until the rear view was clear of any government forces. I looked inside my passport, and the hundred-dollar bill I laid in there was gone. Not only was the money gone, but my papers and passport weren't stamped at all. I thought it odd, but then again, I choked it up to corruption on some level. These checkpoints are always a dangerous venture, and even for those doing things the correct way, it's still a crapshoot at times.

CHAPTER 3
THE RETURN

PROLOGUE

Sitting outside a restaurant on the beach of Playa del Carmen, Armando took in the sun's empowering rays as he spoke on the phone and ate his favorite dish of ceviche, a seafood medley of raw fish in citrus juices and onions, washing it down with the perfect accompaniment, a michelada, a beer served with lime, assorted sauces, spices, and peppers with a chilled tall salt-laden-rimmed glass.

"Bueno!" Armando said, speaking into his receiver, sipping on his michelada.

Armando was dressed in his impeccably maintained military fatigues. Creased and ironed to perfection, it was indicative of his personality. Everything he did was razor-sharp and impeccable.

"I appreciate you looking after our guy. I'll see you next week. We have much business to discuss." Armando finished his conversation and hung the phone up.

Armando finished his seviche and michelada, and like his personality, he never rushed anything. A true planner, he always seemed to be three or four moves ahead of everyone else in the game.

Armando stepped into his armored Humvee and, with his two underlings, was beginning to get onto the road when his phone rang.

"Güero, I'm glad you made it! I know you had to spend another day there. Hahahaha. I knew you all too well, my old friend. It's in your DNA. Good, very good to hear, my friend. Get settled in, and I'll be waiting for you." Armando hung up the phone only to take another phone out and make a call.

"It's me. Yes, yes. The work will be completed on schedule. Of course, have I ever let you down before? My man never lets me down."

Armando hung his phone up and lit his after-meal cigar as the ocean wind blew the smoke in all directions.

THE RETURN

"Drive on this road for about twenty-five kilometers until you reach a pharmacy and rest area." I gave my driver his instructions as I sat in the back, taking in a deep breath and a sigh of relief.

I figured to be there in less than an hour and was thankful to squeak by that border crossing. A few nights in Tulum, and then I would be off to my final destination of Cancun, where I would make my home.

Mexico in 1997 was still a rather safe haven for criminals, felons, and fugitives from all walks of life and countries. If you were financially capable and/or connected with the Mexican police, politics, or military, you could make a decent life for yourself. Always prevalent was the danger of the double-cross or double-dealing, but isn't that always the case? You can either be the lion or the lamb. Being on the winning side of things is essential, but knowing who and where those sides are is crucial. Mexico's criminal landscape is forever changing and generally depends on politics, both national and international. Each Mexican president and presidential hopeful are controlled by a cartel. The cartels put their money, manpower, and munitions behind each candidate, making it their mission to get them elected. The same is done for the governors and so on down the food chain.

Currently, there's one political party that has been governing Mexico for close to eighty years, the Institutional Revolutionary Party (PRI), in power since 1929. The year 1994 saw the rise of the EZLN, guerrillas of the Zapatista National Liberation Army, with many a confrontation in the southern part of Mexico. The EZLN was born out of a rise in poverty in Mexico with the stranglehold the PRI party had had on the country for all these years.

The United States saw an opening to insert their influence on their southern neighbor in early 1995. The United States observed Mexico's floundering economy and stepped in. In the beginning of that year, the United States stepped in with a plan and pledges of aid. Although the American intervention saved Mexico's currency from collapsing, everything had its price. The North American Free Trade Agreement (NAFTA) took effect, and now the United States was firmly entrenched in Mexico. As history shows, US foreign policy is more than flawed and not truly born out of an inherent need to truly assist but in the ulterior motives of the powers that be. The officially stated goals of the foreign policy of the United States, as mentioned in the foreign policy agenda of the US Department of State, are "to build and sustain a more democratic, secure, and prosperous world for the benefit of the American people and the international community." Notice the first part is "benefit of the American people," when truthfully, it's the benefit of the select. History shows us that that hasn't worked well for the majority of those countries, i.e., Iraq, Iran, Guatemala, Vietnam, Cuba, Colombia, Nicaragua, Pakistan, Afghanistan, Somalia, Philippines, Chile, and the list goes on.

Not every nation on earth can function as the United States does. Mexico, although flawed in many ways, for years was a functioning quandary. Outside perception is that Mexico is the wild Wild West. On some levels, this is true and perhaps won't change, but there's a method to Mexico's madness.

The percentage of Mexicans with any influence and control is 1 percent. The power from that 1 percent trickles downward at less than a snail's pace. Their main sources of income are oil (controlled by the government), agriculture, tourism, and drug trafficking and not necessarily in that order.

The drug trade fuels much of Mexico's economy. In the drug organizations, there are rules that are enforced. One such rule is that drug dealing inside Mexico is forbidden. The drug cartel bosses want anything in quantity to be exported and not for consumption, and the penalty for an offense to the rule is death. The United States and Europe are the major destinations for their products and ultimately where the money is. The cartels and politicians didn't want a society of drug addicts for one thing, and another, the money to be made in the lucrative US and European markets trumped anything that could be profited from in Mexico. The powers that be in Mexico knew that having a country of dependents was counterproductive to their desired end result: enjoying the illicit billions of dollars in proceeds.

Boundaries were generally respected, and territories understood. There were even some levels of cooperation among the cartels. That doesn't mean there weren't turf wars between cartels, because there were, but nothing that generally affected the country as a whole. Cartels shared or rented out their distribution routes. Especially when the cocaine trade became popular, the drug routes were transformed from marijuana routes to all-purpose drug routes with all drugs being transported. So while there were disputes, the law of the jungle always applied. One commonality is universal: nothing can or will stop the multibillion-dollar-a-year business that is the drug trade. One's safety wasn't always secured, but events in Mexico were fairly routine.

"Senor, the pharmacy is coming up." The taxi driver looked at his rearview mirror, speaking to me.

The driver came upon the pharmacy that I instructed him to stop at. I had the driver exit the vehicle and purchase a few cold drinks while I bought a phone card for the pay phone just outside. I lifted the receiver and dialed a number.

"Here. Hahahaha. I know I couldn't do just one night either. You know me so well. Okay, I'll see you in a couple of hours." As I said my last word and hung up, the taxi driver made his way back to the car.

I got back in the taxi for the remainder of the twenty-minute-ride to my hotel. Driving down some side dirt roads in the jungle, we came upon my hotel. The driver almost missed the entrance as there wasn't much of a sign or anything indicating the hotel was there. I instructed him to slow down as I knew where the entrance was, because I had been here on previous occasions.

The driveway was dirt and had to be taken slowly because it was meant for one car in and one out at a time. Thirty yards we reached the top of the upslope, and before we began heading down, I could see the ocean in front of me. The hotel was to my right and a little turnaround was ahead of us, where I instructed the driver to stop.

I exited the taxi and couldn't help but be mesmerized by the tranquility that was exuding from the entire property. No matter how many times I visited this paradise, I was still captivated by the magical harmony every time.

Right away, the turquoise water that was a hundred yards away caught my eye. There was barely any movement to the water aside from the light ebb and flow of the tide. The Eden-like retreat had five bungalows just off my right. The thatch-roofed huts were on large pylons protecting the structure from rising tides or fierce storms that the Caribbean produces. With the proximity to the ocean being only about seventy-five yards or so, any security from Mother Nature was welcomed. In front of the bungalows, closer to the ocean, was an outdoor restaurant servicing the guests and small staff of the retreat. I was so caught up in the magnificence of where I was that I didn't hear a voice calling to me.

"Hola," a soft older voice said, calling out to me.

I turned to see an older woman greeting me with open arms and a bright smile topped with a warm hug and kiss.

I reciprocated her greeting with a warm "Hello," smiling from ear to ear. The woman was the matriarch of the family that owned and operated the Hotel Diamond. She was the bohemian type, clad in sandals, baggy three-quarter-length pants, and a light hooded fleece jacket. Sandy was her name, and being in her late fifties, she was filled with energy, living her dream every day of her life.

"Bienvenido, T——. It's so good to see you again," Sandy exclaimed.

I first met Sandy a few years back when I was introduced to the hotel by her son, a Mexican television actor. Like most people in those days, I met him partying in the nightclubs of Cancun.

"Thank you, Sandy. I missed this place something awful."

"How long will you be with us?"

"As always, I plan for one period of time and know that's not the reality."

We both chuckled, knowing this to be the case. I paid the taxi driver, and Sandy began escorting me to my bungalow. Up the stairs we went, and inside was everything I remembered and then some. The decor was inviting and serene, as was every single aspect of the resort. The bed was king-size, encompassed with a large mosquito net. The source of light was either daylight or candles. There was a generator that was operational a portion of the time for the kitchen and mood music that filtered through the resort air. There was a small couch and sitting area in the bungalow that totaled about one thousand square feet. The entire bungalow was made of wood and was certainly a sound structure. The bathroom was tiled in small colored-mosaic style.

"Your room," Sandy said, presenting me with the key to my quarters.

"Feels like I'm back home," I said as I surveyed the one-of-a-kind living conditions.

"That's exactly what we want to convey, the homey feeling. Here's your room key, and shall I have some drinks brought up? A bottle of Tres Generaciones tequila, juice, water, and some fresh fruit?"

"You're acting like you know me," I said, laughing.

"I don't forget," Sandy said, smiling.

"I'm going to shower, so they can just enter and leave it here for when I get out. Thank you. Thank you, Sandy, for everything, and we'll have a drink together later on," I said, wanting to shower and get the dust off my body from the long drive.

Sandy excused herself, and I got to my much-needed shower. Sandy didn't know any of my affiliations, just that I was a friend of her family and that I loved their resort immensely.

The entire bathroom, which had an old-fashioned tub and shower, had tiny colored-mosaic tiles that, although must have been labor-intensive to lay, was just the sort of detail Sandy and her family used in the entire resort. The little stress I had left in me that carried through my day was slowly exiting as the shower and surroundings began taking effect. Toweling off, I left the bathroom to find my refreshments in full view, as I expected. Pouring myself a three-finger glass of tequila, I sipped it as I began to unpack some of my clothes, knowing that I would be spending at least a few days here and wanted to be comfortable. I withdrew some weed from the bottom of my suitcase and rolled myself a couple of joints, letting the ocean air-dry the rest of myself off. I put on some sunblock, protecting my Irish skin from the tropical sun, smoked myself a joint, sipped my tequila down, and ate some fresh fruit. I put on some swim trunks and tank top, and I was ready to venture out. Cigar in one hand, the other on my traveling case, I exited into the tropical sunshine. As soon as the sun hit me, I nearly forgot my water, and perhaps getting stoned before being totally prepared wasn't the best of ideas.

I walked to the edge of the beach, where the Caribbean Sea barely moved and could only be heard when up close. At the water's edge, I took a moment to listen to the rhythmic bliss of the ocean while puffing on my cigar and staring off into the turquoise abyss.

Walking down the beach, I heard the noises of the occasional indigenous creatures that inhabited the jungle and the lapping of the Caribbean waters. Miles of white sand was ahead of me, the vast Caribbean to my left, and the dense jungle to my right—the solitude was otherworldly. Not a person was to be found and not a care in the world. Moments like this were few and far between in my life.

I was passing a mile or so on my beach jaunt when I stopped dead in my tracks. I was caught up in my own mind-set, decompressing from my New York state of mind to this complete reversal of tranquility. I had my guard down for a moment, brought back by what I saw—a concrete structure cut out in the middle of the jungle. Talk about what didn't belong; this was spot-on. The structure had a concrete framework, the beginnings of a rather large home, but who would even want to construct this monstrosity in the middle of the jungle? I left the water's edge, making my way to the front of the structure. The structure blended in so well that it took me off guard. It was well camouflaged into the jungle and apparently hadn't been worked on in a few years at least. I didn't even know how the materials were brought here or why it was thought to be constructed here in the first place. There was nothing around for miles aside from the Diamond Hotel. I thought that whoever began this construction must have brought the materials in by sea, and that must have been costly. Judging from the sheer size of what was being built, though, it looked as if cash wasn't the issue.

Cautiously, I walked through what I surmised was the front doorway. There was a set of concrete-poured stairs leading to what appeared to be a basement. No houses in this region even had a basement, so the oddities continued. There was a staircase that led to the upper level of the would-be house. Immediately, walking through the front entranceway, I felt a heaviness in my soul. I couldn't quite put my finger on it, but my instincts told me something was amiss—that was for sure. I proceeded around to the staircase leading to what was to be the upper level of the house. The upper level was framed out of concrete as well, and what appeared to be the master bedroom was enormous. There was a spot for the Jacuzzi that would comfortably fit ten people. The upstairs appeared to have five bedrooms carved out. The entire structure appeared to be about eight thousand square feet, to be modest.

The uneasy feeling I had when I first passed the threshold slowly escalated into a dark, sorrowful evil, letting me know it was time to exit this would-be dwelling. I was just a foot outside of the entranceway when the heaviness that I felt entering began to depart from my body and my psyche.

I wasn't a few feet outside the dwelling when I heard a voice behind me.

"Leaving so soon?" the voice behind me said.

The voice was English with a touch of Spanish accent. I hadn't heard it in some time, but it was unmistakable. I turned to see my old friend Armando walking up from the cellar of the structure. Exiting the cellar, Armando was immediately flanked by two soldiers of the Mexican army.

I hadn't seen Armando in about fours years but remained in contact with him ever since our first meeting over seven years ago in Mexico City.

The two soldiers with Armando were in perfectly tailored uniforms, steely eyed, MP5 submachine guns across their chests, with trigger fingers on the ready. Armando had on green fatigues and a matching beret. On Armando's shoulders and beret, three gold stars, that of a full-fledged colonel in the Mexican military, were encrusted. This rank and involvement in the military was not known to me, but then again, I never asked, and Armando never spoke about it. His military service was never relevant to anything we were doing. When I met him back in 1990, he had his military hairstyle for sure, but I was only interested in arranging to purchase steroids and gaining contacts. In my life and that of Armando, the less we knew, the better, including events, and information was always on a need-to-know basis for everyone's well-being. Armando had a P7 German special forces handgun in his shoulder holster. You would rarely see a shoulder holster, but Armando was never cookie-cutter by any stretch of the imagination.

Armando's expressionless face grew into a wide smile as he approached me, his arms now outstretched. As we got within hugging distance, we wrapped our arms around each other and gave a brotherly hug as if making up for the years we hadn't seen each other. We kissed each other on the cheek and hugged again, and as we broke our grasp, Armando grabbed me by my shoulders and spoke to me.

"It's been a while, my brother. You look fantastic. New York has been treating you well, I see. I'm glad you're back and on a full-time basis, I trust." Armando knew I was, but it was always good to have validation.

"Full-time basis, my brother, full-time basis," I replied as I grabbed ahold of Armando's shoulders, encrusted emblems and all.

"So what's this all about?" I said, looking at the uniform and soldiers in tow.

Armando dropped his left hand behind him with his palm facing the soldiers. A third soldier emerged from the structure, walking toward us. The third soldier had black satchel in his left hand, approached Armando, and handed it to him. No words were spoken between Armando and his minions. Armando wrapped his right arm around me and walked me toward the surf.

"Let's take a walk and discuss your future," Armando said, walking stride for stride with me.

"Good by me. This place gives me the creeps anyway," I said with a little sigh of relief.

"The creeps? I didn't think anything gave you the creeps, T——," Armando said, chuckling and smiling.

We started our stroll onto the moist white sand. Reaching into my pouch, I pulled out a Cuban cigar, Montecristo Churchill, one of Armando's favorites as well as mine. I clipped the end of it, handed it to my friend, and lit it for him.

"Ah, nothing but the best. Thank you, T——. I trust the time between our last meeting and now, you've not changed much?" Armando said, puffing on his cigar, wafting in the ocean an earthy cigar-air mix.

I would let Armando give me the information he wanted to divulge at his leisure. I knew Armando wanted to see if my frame of mind or anything else was different from the man he met years back in Mexico City. I was never one to ask questions, and there sure were a lot to ask. Armando's uniform, the soldiers, clandestine meeting location, satchel in his hand. All in good time, I thought and never gave it a second thought past my initial thought of seeing new moving parts to my friend. Armando was never a man to do something without a well-thought-out plan of attack-and-exit strategy. Armando's choosing of this location would be revealed in good time, of that I was certain. I was enjoying my friend's company and enjoying the ambience of the location, minus the structure.

"I never change, my brother," I retorted with enthusiasm.

"That's what I was counting on. I've been needing some friendly faces around me lately. Ones I can depend on that conduct good business. Mexico is growing increasingly difficult to trust and depend on people. Too many here are swayed by the dollar, the whiff of power, and betrayal is now commonplace," Armando said as he puffed on his cigar.

"Mexico's not unique in that regard, my friend. Back home, I was going through some of the same shit. The value of someone's word is now almost a lost art form," I said to Armando, echoing his sentiments and relating.

Armando and I reached the water's lapping edge as we both faced out into the abyss of the Caribbean. We both puffed on our cigars and stood in silence. I knew I was reminiscing about back home and what I had been going through, still fresh on my mind, and I knew Armando was running through the same set of emotions in his mind.

"This is your home now, my friend. I have a welcoming gift for you," Armando said, releasing his right arm from around me.

The black satchel Armando was holding in his left hand he now raised up for me to take hold of. Before he relinquished his grip, Armando looked me dead in the eyes. It was a typical Armando look that made me realize that this was not only an important moment but also one I should take note of. Armando could say things without even uttering a solitary syllable. Perhaps that was why we became die-hard friends from the word *hello*.

I unzipped the satchel/gift as Armando looked on. Immediately I saw stacks of money, both Mexican pesos and American dollars. The money took up about half the satchel while the other side had a .380 automatic pistol with six silencers lying next to the gun. I looked up at Armando wearing a sheepish grin on his face.

"Take a look under the money, my brother," Armando said, knowing I missed something.

I reached back inside the satchel and moved the money to find three eight-by-five-inch blocks with the yellow markings C-4. Taking it all in for a few moments, I raised my eyes, finding Armando looking dead into mine. Armando was well skilled in the art of interrogation and character assessment. I knew this from the time we had spent together since we first became friends. He was looking for my first impression and reaction to what was being considered my gift.

"I remembered our talks from back in Mexico City. You thought I would have forgotten?" Armando said, as he was not only proving to me his memory skills were sharp but also reminding me of our friendship.

"You never forget," I said back in response as I zipped up the satchel.

"The C-4 works better than that black powder that you're used to back in New York. I was hoping you would be able to hone some of those talents of yours down here and apply your craft. Is everything to your liking?"

"Yes, it is," I said, short and sweet.

Armando then reached into his shirt pocket, taking out a white envelope, handing it to me. He held the envelope out and waited for me to grab ahold firmly before he let go. Armando was always serious and calculating, but it seemed he currently had a lot on his plate. Armando didn't relinquish his hold on the envelope for a few seconds even when I had grabbed hold of it. I felt him staring into my soul as I had full control of the envelope.

Opening the envelope, I found two black-and-white photos. While I reviewed the first picture, Armando began to give me information on what and whom I was looking at.

"There are two targets of interest. The photo you have in your hand now is the main target. Flip it over and you'll see the address listed is of his home in downtown Cancun."

As Armando went over the pertinent information, he saw the trepidation on my face. Armando sought to address the apparent concern that I couldn't help but show. While it was not necessary and I never required full-on details, there were always some details that truly needed to be spoken on ahead of time.

"Nothing to concern yourself with. They're only immigration," Armando said, trying to minimize the fact that the two targets were federal agents.

As I flipped to the second picture, I noticed it was another male in uniform, and Armando proceeded to tell me that this gentleman was the bodyguard of the first pictured man. Back home in New York, I was always very careful to make sure all "work" was sanctioned with very little to no loose ends that might arise. This was a very different situation. Aside from Armando, I knew no one else involved in either perceived side. I was flying blind here, and truth be told, I wasn't expecting this situation. Hell, I was just getting out of my situation back home, and I hadn't even laid my head down in Mexico, and I'm diving headfirst into craziness. Armando was helping me a little here in Mexico, but I wasn't expecting this to be what he wanted of me. I didn't want to show any more than that first reaction. I didn't particularly care about the assignment itself more than I wanted a change of pace in my life. *Here we go again,* I thought as I was briefed.

Armando began filling me in on the particulars that he felt I needed to know. He told me that the bodyguard would always be armed generally with a .45 or 9mm automatic. The main target carried a 9mm as well but lately had been feeling comfortable, and reports were that he had been unarmed at times. I didn't care what the reports were saying; I always considered my targets armed, and especially in this type of situation, I certainly considered them to be armed at all times.

I studied the targets' facial features, stature, and identifying marks. The main target was a taller man with thinner hair that was well-groomed. The bodyguard was a smaller man but with a large gut and was more unkempt. Both men wore the uniform of a Mexican immigration agent. I wasn't sure of their rankings, and in this particular case, it didn't matter much. Both men were distinctive in their own way and, combined, wouldn't be hard to point out in a crowd. The address was an easy one to burn into my memory—1217 El Dorado St. After saying the address a number of times to myself and flipping back and forth their pictures a few times, I put both photos back into the envelope and handed them to Armando.

"Finished?" Armando asked me, as he wanted a verbal confirmation.

"Yes," I said, positive I had the information stored in my memory.

Armando puffed hard on his cigar, exhaling the smoke, withdrawing the cigar from his mouth, and putting the end of the cigar to each picture one by one. He blew on the cigar and picture to make sure both would be burned to ash and thrown into the surf.

I was then verbally filled in on information that would be needed. Armando said they both worked at Cancun International Airport. Both men would almost always be together; hence, as I would find one, so would I locate the other. The bodyguard would always pick up and drop off his boss. The shorter man was referred to as the bodyguard not only because of his stature but also because of the fact that he was of lower rank and acted as such. The time these two would be at the airport varied, but usually, the shift was early to late evening or bright and early in the morning for the first flights into the airport. I came to find out that their schedules were dependent on the incoming flights from Central to South America. Armando proceeded to inform me that these two were the key role players in an international human-smuggling ring. The people were brought up on planes from South and Central America and then transferred to other members of the group in the pipeline for the ultimate destination of the United States. This had long been a steady and most profitable business. Like most illegal activities going on in Mexico, the end game was exporting the merchandise—i.e., drugs, humans, etc.—to foreign lands.

We both puffed away on our cigars as I listened to Armando speak. He wanted to know for certain that I was on board with what he had in mind, and he was laying it out to me. Now, Armando and I had had dealings before, but that was for steroids and certainly not on this level. I always knew Armando had connections and was involved on a grander scale, but I had no idea this would be on the agenda. We spoke about many things while getting to know each other in Mexico City, and I didn't open up about anything in particular. Armando was smart enough to get the picture, as was I about him. One of the reasons we became friends so fast.

"Everything in order?" That was Armando's way of asking if I was going to be on board with his plans.

"To the tee, my brother," I confirmed in response to Armando's query, not taking my eyes off his, nor his off mine.

"What's with the getup?" I asked with a particular smile and verbal jab.

I was now able to break the ice with Armando about his manner of dressing. The underlying question I asked would be what was really going on here with the uniform, soldiers, this location, him wanting me to kill people for him, etc.

"Oh, this?" Armando said, smiling, looking down at himself and his uniform.

"I've always been in the military even years before we met. My mother being a diplomat enabled me to rise quicker and take advantage of more opportunities. I worked the majority of my time in Mexico City, where I was cementing relationships and learning the ins and outs of Mexican politics and policies. Thanks to my mother, I have dual citizenship with Mexico and Panama, which has given me even more of a leg up in the military. I entered the army while studying political science at the university in Mexico City. I applied for and joined the military intelligence branch of the army, as I was told by my mother would be the most valuable asset in my coming years. I have been reassigned to the Yucatán Peninsula about six months ago, and upon my appointment here, I was promoted to full colonel. This tropical paradise is now my backyard," Armando said, giving me more detail than I expected and more than ever before.

Armando was now putting some of the pieces of the puzzle together for me, ones I had already thought to be a match but was getting confirmation only now. The one thing I was now certainly wondering about was why here in the middle of nowhere, and what about this structure?

"So what's the deal with this structure, and why are we meeting all the way out here?"

"Oh, that?" Armando said nonchalantly, looking at where he had emerged.

"That's Pablo Escobar's house. Or at least it was the beginnings of his house before he was murdered," Armando said matter-of-factly.

The year 1997 was just about over, and hands down, the most notorious drug lord had been dead for over four years. Pablo Escobar was that man, and in the later parts of his life, he was constructing homes around the world wherever he had a foothold in the drug trade and wherever he was expanding his business. Tulum was just such a place, but he was murdered before this home could come to fruition.

"Now we look after this house and territory," Armando said, staking his claim to not only this particular place but also to the entire Yucatán region.

Armando said *we*, but in reality, I knew Armando was the driving force here. As Armando was explaining the house and who it's previous owner was, I was now looking at the would-be house in a different light and perspective. Now, upon further inspection, I saw two soldiers on the top of the structure a little farther back. They were well camouflaged and on either side of an M60 machine gun nest. I was beginning to see the bigger picture, and the rest was self-explanatory.

"Let's get out of this sun. My uniform is attracting all this damn heat. There's a car parked at your hotel. It's yours to use as long as you need it. It's clean, and the paperwork is in the glove compartment. I had a license made for you. The keys and license are in your satchel," Armando said, walking me back off the shore and toward the structured and shade.

"What picture did you use for my license?" I said with curiosity.

"When you came through the Belizean customs, I had a picture taken of you and sent off to me. The picture isn't the best of quality, but it'll do for what's needed. The address on the license matches the one on the registration of the car. Consider both a gift for your new start here. Nobody will question your credentials, I've made sure of that. The address is an empty house owned by a bank controlled by us. The president of the bank is on our team. I was with you every step of the way since you got off the plane in Belize."

"Yeah?" I said with a curious look, wanting a little more clarity.

"Well, not in the flesh, but I had some associates keep an eye on you from the airport to the hotel and through the border."

I thought back to the airport and who might have been Armando's eyes and ears. Flashing through my mind, the one face I kept seeing time and again was that of the captain. First, the captain from the airport I passed by going through customs and then again at the border crossing Belize to Mexico.

"I see you remember now," Armando said as he laughed, seeing me recollect in my mind.

"Yes, I do remember now. There's no such thing as coincidences," I said, making sense in my head.

"No, no, my friend, there isn't. I have to protect my friend and my investment. We're going to do some big things here, T———. I want you to not only be a part and take part in events, but I'll be relying on you more and more in the years to come. Your loyalty and business sense is of great value to me. You know that I know how to reward those that have such qualities and parallel beliefs as I. I wouldn't have involved you if I thought you weren't the man I knew you to be. Mexico can be a very comfortable place for a man that has his priorities in place and his wits about him. The money in the satchel is for you to use for whatever expenses you incur and getting yourself settled in. After the New Year, I've arranged for you to meet a friend of ours, the local chief of police. He's a great asset and ally for us. He'll be expecting to see you, and he knows of our relationship. He's agreed to sell you the ecstasy he confiscates. It's another revenue stream for you and a fairly decent one. Enjoy yourself here for a few days, and I'll speak to you when you're all settled in Cancun."

"Thank you for everything, my friend. It's so good to be back here and with you. I'm looking forward to a new chapter in my life."

Armando and I hugged, kissed each other on the cheek, and said our good-byes.

"Hey, T———," Armando said.

I got about ten feet going in the direction of my hotel when Armando called to me. As I spun around, he threw in a comment that was meant with a double meaning, like a lot of our comments were.

"Spend a few days with that girlfriend of yours."

I nodded in agreement, and I knew the double meaning. Armando wanted me to know he was well-informed about myself and whom I associated with. Armando sure had changed in these last four years. Well, I wouldn't say *changed*, rather escalated and elevated. I came to Mexico to escape New York and all the madness that was taking place there. Armando agreed to help me here in Mexico, and I knew that nothing was free—it never is. I didn't know the extent I would be beholding to him. Now I knew, but at least it was laid out in front of me. These weren't things Armando could speak about on the phone even if it were possible to do so. He had to see me face-to-face and look into my eyes to see me for me. It had been some years since we last saw each other, and much can change in that time. Aside from selling steroids in the United States—and now ecstasy here in Mexico—I stayed clear of the drug trade. It was apparent that Armando was involved in at least the protection aspect of the drug trade. Armando knew I would be selling ecstasy, which was why he made arrangements for me and the chief of police to become acquainted. The chief he was speaking of was the chief of the regular police. In Mexico, there were various chiefs. The local chief was the one I was going to meet and do business with. There were a few federal police chiefs—the PGR, which was the equivalent of our DEA, and the PJF, which would mostly be acquainted with the FBI. I was to cut the chief in on the sale of all ecstasy he provided. Armando was on it as well, especially for making the arrangement. When the numbers broke down, it was well worth it. I received my product for free and split the dollar amount sold three ways. I was also receiving protection, at least on the state level. *What's better than this arrangement?* I thought. Back in New York, we had some similar protections, but nothing out in the open like this, and the difference back in New York was here, I was the main guy.

Walking back to my hotel, I puffed on my cigar as so many thoughts raced through my head. I for sure had lost the buzz from the marijuana I had smoked and was looking forward to a drink and some more weed. As the thoughts were racing through my mind, I was sorting them like a high-speed computer. This exchange with Armando had me thinking about the last time I was in Mexico City with him.

* * *

Summers in Mexico City were always hot. The relief from the heat would begin once the sun retreated behind the horizon. I had an apartment with my Mexican girlfriend at the time. I had a few girl-friends during my years in Mexico City, but this last one was a great match for me. She molded to my lifestyle and was very unobtrusive. I was with her for about a year, and she maintained my apartment when I was back in the United States.

Business was very good, and I spent my summers in Mexico City when possible. I made other trips as I could, when I could, but the summers I enjoyed most. I sent packages from Mexico City to the United States frequently, and all in all, I couldn't complain.

One particular evening, toward the end of the last summer I spent in Mexico City, Armando stopped by my apartment to get me. We were going out to get a bite to eat in an area known as La Zona Rosa in Mexico City. This was where the nightlife happened in Mexico City. It had nightclubs and restaurants and was the in spot at the time. We dined outside on some typical Mexican food, although my serving was more on the bland side.

"After we eat, I'm going to stop by my cousin's place and get some weed," Armando said.

"Whatever you need to do," I responded, knowing Armando liked to smoke a little, and it wasn't out of the ordinary.

I had smoked a few times when I was younger, but not in recent years; it just wasn't my thing. I had always been told and taught by my associates/mentors back in New York that this was not tolerated. The powers that be frowned on drug use or involvement of any kind. I knew there were guys that partook in it but not me and not the majority of the people I associated with.

Finishing our meal, we were underway and en route to meet Armando's cousin. We drove about twenty minutes until we came upon an old cobblestone street. Nearly halfway down the block, driving in Armando's Volkswagen, we came to a stop and parked. The street wasn't residential, but it wasn't industrial either. There were a few businesses with apartments on the top and looked a little like some of the neighborhoods back in New York. We both exited the car to no sign of movement on the street. I followed Armando's lead out of the car and about twenty paces until he stopped directly in front of the location. The location had a door that was designed for the vertically challenged. A normal doorway stands about seven feet in height. This door was no more than four feet tall at best. About three feet up was a slot like the old speakeasies had back in American Prohibition days. Keeping in the tradition of those days, Armando knocked on the door. A couple of moments later, the two-by-two-inch slot opened partially, revealing an eye and part of a nose. It was hard to make out anything else besides the eye, partial nose, and dark complexion of a man. Armando didn't say anything, letting me know the man recognized Armando if not expecting him to be there. The eyes from the slot were fixated on me. I totally understood because at this particular time in Mexico City, Americans were scarcely seen. No Americans were in any of the locations I had been conducting business in, or living in, for that matter. Hell, seeing an American in this part of the city at this time of night would have raised more than the eyebrow, which was now being raised, looking at me through this tiny peephole. The immediate thoughts running through my mind involved why Armando's cousin would be behind this door that appeared to be about four inches of thick steel. The door was designed to not only keep people out but also to barricade oneself in, making it impossible to bust it down with regular methods.

The few seconds of the Spaghetti Western showdown was up, and the sound of the security locks inside being undone seemed to take forever. The steel portal opened, and true to form, it was every bit four inches thick at the least. Armando entered first, ducking down as I followed behind. I raised my head and was immediately met by the eye that stared at me through the peephole. The man had his 9mm pistol in his right hand, and his cold stare was trained on my eyes, waiting for anything further from me, one way or the other. The inside was dimly lit with single lightbulbs hanging from a single wire in the ceiling. The lightbulbs attempted to light the single long hallway leading from the front door to the back. The hallway was just wide enough to fit two normal men walking side by side. From what I could see, the hallway appeared to be at least fifty feet if not more. Lining the hallway every ten feet were men with automatic weapons in staggered formation. These men were rough, expressionless, and none too happy to be seeing the likes of me in their midst. The door behind me closed shut with a loud thud and then the securing of all the locks.

This situation was like so many I had found myself in and would find myself in for years to come. The situation was one that required a cool head, quick reactionary thinking, and very careful vocabulary.

"El Güero, está conmigo." Armando broke up the tension, letting everyone within earshot know that I was supposed to be there.

Armando's vouching for me, I think, was more for me than it was for the men who had their eyes trained on me. The doorman, whose importance was unclear at the time, led the way down the armed corridor. No words were spoken; everything seemed to have been worked out ahead of time because I couldn't imagine I would be allowed in this environment if it hadn't. Passing each armed tough, I kept my eyes moving forward, feeling their steely eyes trained on me every step of the way. The hallway was rough, as if it were just dug out. There were no comforts here. This was not a place anyone wanted to spend more time in than necessary.

After forty-five paces and ten armed toughs, we reached a room off to our right. There was no door, just a concrete entranceway. I followed Armando and the doorman into the room. The room, which was lit fairly better than the hallway, was about fifty feet by fifty feet, void of any furniture, and apparently, this was not a location of residence or for conducting regular commerce. It fit with the hallway and lighting as if it were just a staging area.

Four men stood in the middle of the room and, like all the others did since I entered, had their eyes transfixed on me. With us in the room was a large tarp that covered something of which I neither knew nor, at this point in time, cared to know about.

"Que onda, guey?" Armando spoke a Mexican slang equivalent to our version of "What's up, man?" to the men, one of the men in particular.

The men greeted Armando with outstretched arms of a hug and warmth with a certain degree of respect and reverence. The first man Armando greeted differently than the others and vice versa; they hugged with more warmth and kissed each other on the cheek, a sure sign their bond was deeper than that of the others.

"Orale, Pepe." Armando broke the embrace and spoke to the one man that everyone's body language was deferring to.

Pepe's appearance wouldn't lead you to believe he had any stature different than that of the other men, but there was a presence about him that was unmistakable. Pepe's clothes were Mexican country, but what stood out was his belt buckle, which was blinged out. Pepe's boots were polished to a shine that was blinding. He wasn't much over five feet, six inches tall but stood out. I guesstimated Pepe's age to be in the early thirties, a decade more than I.

There was tension ever since I walked up to the miniature door to this location. I felt a heaviness in the air, and I was only here for material support. Pepe was looking at me with a hard scowl, as had been everyone else I encountered here. I thought, *This is really a lot to go through to get a bit of weed, and I don't even smoke.*

"Ese guey es El Güero," Armando said to Pepe, introducing me.

Pepe's scowl turned 180 degrees like a lightbulb went off inside his mind, recalling an apparent conversation he and Armando had previously had.

"Ese guey es El Güero?" Pepe mimicked Armando.

Pepe stepped forward and greeted me with what shocked me, a bearlike-hug grasp, grabbing with both of his hands on my shoulders. What left a resounding impression was his hands' strength and intensity. Pepe spoke with every inch of his body even if words weren't uttered. My eyes were locked onto Pepe's, but I still had my eyes on the other four men, looking for any sudden movements. There weren't many places to go besides back through the maze of armed toughs or the closed door at the back of the room that led to a certain unknown. The other men settled back into a more-relaxed nature as their threat assessment pacified. Once Pepe was okay with my presence, everyone else acquiesced to me being there.

"El Güero," Pepe said again in a smiling approval and acknowledgment of my presence.

My Spanish was still in its infancy, and I didn't want to start down a road that I couldn't see the end to. I could understand a decent amount of Spanish by now and spoke some but preferred my native tongue especially in a situation where an ill-timed word might be misconstrued. Apparently, I was being referred to as El Güero (the American), a name that I earned in my first day in Tepito with Armando a few years back. The nickname that Armando started would stick with me for years to come and would be carried with me even thousands of miles away in other countries.

"Pepe, nice to meet you," I said while Pepe still held my shoulders.

"My cousin says you do good business," Pepe said in his barely audible English, but he wanted me to know he had some bilingual skills.

"For a few years now," I responded, nodding and looking in Armando's direction.

"You want to buy mota?" Pepe said, turning around.

As Pepe spoke and turned around, two of the men pulled back the tarp that covered the pile. Underneath were bundled packages all the same size, about four inches thick and about a foot long. *Mota* is one of the Spanish slangs used when referring to marijuana. I looked at Armando to find him waiting for my response, as was Pepe and the remainder of the men in the room. I could tell Armando was gauging my reaction to the question and situation. Armando never did anything without purpose or cause, and this was a typical Armando move.

"I deliver to Washington, DC. You take from there, and you take two hundred pounds a week. Price is two hundred dollars delivered," Pepe said to me before I could respond, adding some more information in order for me to make a more-intelligent decision.

I knew what to say but waited about fifteen seconds so I could formulate the best way to convey my message without offending anyone. This is a perfect example of why one should always think before speaking, acting, or reacting. Words and actions are crucial, and the most important ones require in-depth thought, not reactionary thought. While I was in the steroid business, I didn't consider it to be drugs even though some might consider so. I considered myself not to be in the drug business, although some of the old gangsters back home and the US government thought differently.

"I'm not in the mota business, but I will make some calls back home and see if there's interest from anyone there. I'll let Armando know what I find out. It's a good business, I know, just not my business," I said as diplomatically as possible.

My response was acceptable for everyone. I wasn't locked into a definite answer but let Armando and Pepe know the ultimate answer wasn't mine to make. The possibility was there to conduct business, and I never wanted to close any door even if it weren't in my particular field. An associate of mine and the man who became my best friend back in New York, Anthony, was in the game—or at least around the game—and was the only man I knew and trusted enough to have a conversation about the weed offer. Anthony was into all types of business dealings. Gun running, extortion, gambling, robbery, assaults, loan-sharking. And he was also in the steroid dealings with me. I brought Anthony into part of my business to handle the packages coming in while I was in Mexico. Anthony was a rising star in the Italian underworld, with his home base being the Bronx, New York. Anthony and I became close since the first day we met, playing college football. We were inseparable ever since our first encounter. Anthony was in the Navy Seals until a freak accident had him leaving the navy and heading back to the Bronx to pursue his next options, football and the Mafia. Anthony and I had many similarities, to say the least. I knew Anthony's people back in the Bronx were somehow involved in the drug trade. To what extent or what drugs, I didn't know for fact, nor did I care to know.

"Bien, muy bien," Pepe said with content.

Pepe and Armando spoke to each other, ending with Armando taking about a quarter of a brick of weed with him as we all said our good-byes.

There are no such things as coincidences. Being in this spot with these people under these circumstances had so many intertwining meanings. Armando wanted to show me off to his cousin and the other men in the room. Armando wanted his cousin to know he had connections in the United States, a most-coveted connection for Mexicans in any illegal trade—or legal, for that matter. Pepe wanted me to know about his capabilities, among them the ability to export tons of drugs into the United States regularly uninterrupted. Pepe was also showing his authority among his men and to his men that he could command audiences and was valuable. Everyone was there to show and prove, and I was the linchpin. Armando and I never really spoke about the real reasons for this meeting because truth be told, there were too many to go around, and it was part and parcel to the lifestyle. There are always so many moving parts to everything.

The time I spent in Mexico, Mexico City in particular, from the early nineties to midnineties was quite enjoyable and an all-around great learning experience. Armando and I grew quite close, and I considered him to be my other best friend. What made Anthony and I close were the same things that drew Armando and I together, our commonalities. Our love of weight training and our business, weaponry, beautiful women, great food, and cigars were just some of our bonding moments. Our beliefs fell in line with one another, which was the true cornerstone for me. Respect, awareness, business savvy, intelligence, and understanding were inherent from the first time we met. Had Armando, Anthony, and I ever ran in the same place together, God help the world, because we were all like-minded. Armando was always impeccably dressed and had the air of someone of importance and upper class. He carried himself in a fashion that I couldn't quite put my finger on, but it was what I called ruthless, gentleman gangster.

The next morning, I made my way to a pay phone in Mexico City and dialed back to Anthony back home. Anthony was the only one I could call with such a question about moving drugs. I didn't want any involvement in the process, but like my nature, I didn't mind arranging the parties together to conduct their business. Anthony and I had prearranged times to call; they were to pay phones that we would use one time then move on. I told Anthony about Pepe's offer, to which Anthony told me to call back the next day with our prearranged phone. I did just that.

"Ant?'

"Yeah?"

"What's the word?"

"Can't do it," Anthony said.

"What do you mean you can't do it?" I said, never hearing that set of words coming from my friend's mouth before, especially knowing the potential dollar signs involved in it.

"We just can't do it. The Jews control the market," Anthony said in a definitive way.

"Jews? Since when are we concerned about a bunch of Jews?" I said to Anthony shockingly.

"That's the word I got. The Jews have been doing it since the beginning of time. If we start to move that kind of weight, it wouldn't go unnoticed and would be a problem."

This wasn't the time, place, or even my concern to get into it any further, so I dropped it. I just chuckled a bit as Anthony's response wasn't one I was expecting. I never knew Anthony to be concerned with much of anyone or anything. He did respect the chain of command, so I knew this information was valid and came from the top; otherwise, he would have been all-in on the weed.

I gave Armando the news I received, and there was never anything further spoken about it between us. Armando knew it wasn't my game but knew I would, at the very least, inquire about the proposition.

*　*　*

My entire beach walk back to the Diamond Hotel had me reflecting and putting into perspective what Armando and I had just spoken about but also, more importantly, what we didn't speak about. I knew I would have to do something to trade for what Armando was going to be doing for me with my new life in Mexico, but not to this extent. I was trying to slow my pace to a crawl and switch gears. A little ecstasy-selling here and there was about all I was thinking about. I was trying to stay under the radar, not man the radar station.

The car was right where Armando said it would be. I opened the driver's side door, got in, and opened the glove compartment. Everything was as Armando said it was. That's the value of a man's word, when it's vocalized and realized.

I drove to the nearest pay phone and dialed a woman I was seeing in Cancun. She had handled my living arrangements and some other minor things for me ahead of my journey here. She was my *girlfriend*, Paola, in Cancun. I had her come out to meet me at the Diamond and spend a few days together in paradise.

As was typical fashion, the few days turned into a week of massages, weed-smoking, ecstasy-taking, relaxing, and getting acquainted with Paola. I wanted some peace and quiet before heading to Cancun. While Cancun was enjoyable most times, it could be hellish at times. There was deceit, jealousy, and treachery afoot, and now with my new work needing to be done, I wanted as much calming solitude as I possibly could. I loved to party, something I only did in Cancun, so when I was here, I really let loose. Even before moving to Cancun on a full-time basis now, I had been gathering a reputation. I was known for the best parties, best ecstasy, and no-nonsense attitude. If you wanted something and I was able to oblige, you were welcome to it. The other side of the coin was, if someone stole or tried to steal from me, then I was known for dispatching with those foul issues expeditiously. I had been visiting Cancun on and off for the past three years, each time cementing more relationships and enjoying a different side of life than the organized chaos of New York. My time in Cancun was mostly personal, although there were times when I would arrange some steroid shipments back to the United States. Spring break was always a popular time for me to join the ranks of the partygoers that flocked to Cancun. One associate in particular I partied with in Cancun was the one that first introduced me to the partying Cancun scene. I was careful not to do anything in the United States that would put me in danger or take me out of character, but Cancun had no boundaries or system of checks and balances, at least not for me.

CHAPTER 4

CANCUN: BOTH SIDES OF THE FENCE

The outside setting appeared to be a ranch where Armando was sitting across from a rather obese man with half a dozen armed men just outside of earshot but close enough to act or react.

"A gringo?" The large, overweight man raised his voice.

Large in height as well as in weight, topping well over three hundred pounds, the man was dressed in jeans and a button-down shirt. There was nothing much to notice besides his belly protruding from the bottom of his shirt and the large sweat stains from under his armpits that changed the color of his blue shirt to a darker blue. He was in his early fifties, had a thick mustache, and was a hulking man that exuded dominance and confidence. He chain-smoked cigarettes and wheezed as he spoke. He was the epitome of gluttony.

"How do we trust in this gringo to do the work correctly?" the large man asked, sweating profusely, constantly wiping his forehead of beads of perspiration.

"Have I ever let you down?" Armando said in his defense as well as in the defense of the gringo that was mentioned.

"No, no, you haven't. I remind you that this is your responsibility, and if you tell me it's going to be handled, then I trust it will get done. You are responsible for the outcome either way." The large man sat back in his chair after speaking.

"You don't have to remind me. I'll handle my business as I've always had. He's my guy, and I wouldn't have brought him in if trust, loyalty, or capability were the slightest of concern."

The overweight man didn't speak for a few moments; his chest was heaving as his heart worked overtime to keep him alive. He took a long drag of a cigarette, exhaling as he broke out in laughter.

"Come here, my friend." The large man stood up and embraced Armando.

"Your cousin Pepe always spoke highly of you, which is why I had you transferred down here from Mexico City. Pepe mentioned something about this El Güero character. Pepe also mentioned that you were a man that got the job done, and so far, so good. This American is a close friend of yours, is he not? I won't interfere with your relationship as long as the work is handled. I'm going to hit the southern cartel where it hurts: their money and their protection. You being in an elite military group and not beholding to the regular military has all the advantages that I need. I've been second fiddle for too long, and the time is right. Once their allies and funding sources are depleted, I'll be the one in power."

"El, Señor De Todo. Salud!" Armando said, standing up, clasping a glass of tequila, toasting the overweight drug lord.

El Señor De Todo was originally from the northern part of Mexico and always thought he should be the one in power among any and all cartels in Mexico. He had been biding his time, but the years of patience was running out as he thought he should be the head cartel boss in all of Mexico.

CHAPTER 4

CANCUN: BOTH SIDES OF THE FENCE

The road to Cancun from Tulum was relatively smooth. The Volkswagen Armando left me was taking the bumps and potholes in stride. Cancun and the surrounding areas were still up and coming, and the road construction was done when it was totally necessary and only to the areas that would matter the most.

As I passed a sign that read Cancun International Airport: 10 K, many memories began to flood my mind. I had traveled this road for both business and pleasure, and now I was here permanently. The thought of all I had left behind in New York hadn't hit me yet, and I knew it wouldn't for some time. I thought it to be a slow process of adapting. I never let my mind go to the past for any long period. I always had to think forward, many steps forward. It's the true definition of *survival instinct*. Moves had to be made, and decisions taken. I made my decisions without regret and without second thought. It wasn't until I made my conscious decision to leave everything behind that I began having flashbacks in my mind.

* * *

At first, my trips to Cancun were strictly for vacation purposes. I wanted an escape from the craziness that was New York, and being in Cancun, I could let my guard down, decompress, and recharge my inner batteries. I was never able to let my guard down, and it took me nearly my entire first trip there to do just that. I never partied before like how I would in Cancun, and that took getting used to as well.

My entire life, I found business wherever I went, and Cancun would be no different. I had been shipping steroids back from Mexico City some years before but had stopped that connection as other opportunities presented themselves, and I took advantage of those—more quantity, cheaper pricing, and nearly zero risk. I found in Cancun a way to ship the steroids back again with minimal risk and sending quantity. I found cruise ships debarking from Miami to be ideal. Cozumel was one of their stops on a typical three-day jaunt. I arranged an elderly couple back in the United States to take this trip. We would meet in Cozumel, a short ferry ride from Playa del Carmen, after a short drive on the same road I was traveling now. I would package up the steroids in gift boxes and then make my forty-five-minute drive from Cancun to the ferry and over to meet the couple. Timing is everything, and in this venture, it was perfect. When this particular boat my old couple was on reached Miami, it would dock at the same time as another cruise liner. This meant that 1,600 tourists would be debarking at the same time, and at best, there would be a drug dog there to sniff out packages. With steroids undetectable in that manner, it made the trip quite easy and have very low risk. Nobody would hassle an elderly couple on a three-day excursion, especially with no forewarning. The sheer number of passengers and crew made it impossible to handle any other way than the way they did. Had they done it another way, it would've been too time-consuming and would have cost way too much money for the personnel needed.

Once they made it safely off the boat, they took their motor home ride back up the East Coast and await my return. The motor home was the easiest and most comfortable way for the couple to travel, and it gave me enough time to enjoy my vacation in Cancun. I had to use this method of smuggling steroids as the United States

Customs had been tracking my travel for some time now. I had to be innovative and have outside-the-box thinking. This to me was the easiest of all.

One such vacation/business trip to Cancun had me leaving through John F. Kennedy Airport on a direct flight to Cancun. I overstayed from my original two-week ticket, as I usually did. At Cancun International Airport, I bought a ticket to return right before the flight was to depart. I just barely made this flight that had me connecting in Houston on my way to New York. Houston was a very short flight from Cancun. Now, mind you, I just purchased my ticket in Cancun some hour and a half prior to getting into Houston. I had barely stepped through the door of the plane to the jet bridge when five agents, drug dog in tow, were there to greet me, so to speak.

"Mr. H——, come with us please," one agent said at me.

I didn't pay the agents much attention, break my stride, or give any outward signs of taking me out of my character. I wouldn't say this was normal or typical, but the hassle I got from law enforcement when traveling outside the United States sure was. Being questioned, searched, frisked, and followed was all part and parcel to me returning home. I always expected the unexpected and conditioned myself never to panic or fold under whatever pressure came about. I was careful to know what authorities had and didn't have on me regardless of where I was and what I was doing. I had always been and always would be a great planner, and preparation is vital. I never took the activities of the law enforcement personnel or what they said personally. I was aware they had their jobs to do, and the same as they had their jobs, I had mine. Mine was to be prepared, not get out of character, and complete the task at hand. In the worst possible situation, I would call my lawyer and let the process work itself out.

I do, however, enjoy bating agents and law enforcement at times and having a bit of what I call fun and busting their balls. I'm quite sure they enjoy the same sort of thing on their side.

"Cute dog," I said, bending down to pet the drug dog.

"Don't touch the dog!" the dog's handler yelled out at me.

"I didn't know I couldn't touch him. He looks so cute," I responded to the handler.

I knew I wasn't supposed to touch the dog, but I couldn't help myself. I wanted to get a rise out of them and knew the dog wasn't going to pick up anything on me, so why not have a little of what I called fun?

I was escorted by the five agents, two in front, two behind, and the dog handler off to my right. It was about five minutes of this escort until we reached the customs area, where a slew of other agents were waiting for me to arrive. I didn't need to retrieve my luggage; the agents were kind enough to get it for me and already had it on the table in front of me as I approached.

"Anything you wish to declare before we begin the search?" one agent said, standing directly behind the table with his hand on the zipper of the first of the two pieces of my luggage.

"Nothing," I said back to the agent in fast order.

"I gave you the opportunity to come clean. I asked, and since you said no, if we find something, we're going to charge you," the same agent continued to say.

The agent made it seem that it would give me a pass if I came clean and ratted myself out. I knew they had procedures to follow, and I wondered how many people in this situation would rat themselves out, thinking the feds wouldn't charge them and would just simply let them go.

I stood there in silence as they rummaged around my bags. I didn't even give them the respect of eye contact and acted as if they didn't exist.

"We got 'em, we got 'em!" an agent declared about five minutes into the search.

Now the customs agent had my full attention as I wondered what the hell he had. I knew my packages had already made it safely back to New York, and I never traveled with anything that would jam me up. Then I saw what the commotion was about. In the agent's outstretched left hand, he held up three Cuban cigars. I totally forgot about those and never even gave it a second thought when I was packing. I was in Cancun for a month and bought a box of cigars when I arrived. I smoked all but the ones this agent was now holding up in the air like he won a gold medal.

"What about these?" the agent asked, showing off the cigars as if he just found a ton of cocaine in my luggage.

"I didn't even know they were there," I said matter-of-factly.

"Well, they are illegal. We can charge you with possessing them, and that carries possible jail time and fine. There's still an embargo, and it's against the law."

Holy shit, you can't be serious! This do-gooder was really telling me this. The way he shouted out, I thought for sure he would bust my balls over the cigars.

"We're going to have to confiscate these," the agent told me.

"Okay" was all I could muster, not knowing what to say but knowing I should say something in response.

When a passenger goes through United States Customs, even an American citizen entering the United States, he or she is almost void of any rights and is at the mercy of individuals who make judgment decisions, one way or the other.

Just when I thought the fun was over, another agent began directing me to go with two armed agents to another room for a secondary body inspection. I was getting a little weary of the cat-and-mouse game. They knew I didn't have or travel with anything, but I was on their turf, and it was their game with their rules.

"I have a connecting flight," I said, knowing I wouldn't get any sympathy or leeway but was saying it anyway.

"You can get another flight," one agent snapped back at me with content.

No further words needed to be said on either side as I followed one agent and the second close behind me. We didn't go too far until there were two doors in front of us, about twenty yards from the inspection station. The agent in front of me opened the door to the left. Upon entering the room, I noticed it was void of any personality and any furnishings. As I entered the room, I heard the door close behind me, leaving me inside the room with the two agents. Immediately, I was instructed to place my hands against the wall with my palms down and to spread my legs. This was the proverbial "assume the position." I was told to look straight ahead as their search was just beginning.

One agent began the pat-down and started from the top of my shirt going down my back and around the front of my chest. The second agent was just off my right, out of my peripheral view, but I knew he was there. Both agents were armed and apparently serious about their work. The pat-down got to my groin, where I thought it an optimal time to bust balls. I turned a few inches to the right with my head, hands still firmly in place on the wall.

"Find anything?" I said as the agent frisking me hit the inside of my groin.

"Face the wall and don't fuckin' move," the second agent chimed in fast.

As he spoke, I saw his hand reach for the 9mm on his right hip, preparing to draw his weapon.

"Take it easy. It's not that serious," I responded as I assumed the position again to their liking.

"Don't move, and shut your mouth," the agent to my right said.

I figured, if I were missing my flight, I might as well get a rise out of the two agents. Needless to say, I missed my connecting flight, and they found nothing.

I ended up flying through Houston International a few times to varying degrees of scrutiny. That was enough times to never have me travel through that airport ever again.

I was always curious about what information was on the other side of the computer when my name was entered in as I reentered the United States. Apparently, no matter when I purchased my ticket, be it weeks in advance or just before my plane left the runway, I would hit the system at the speed of light, and for sure, I would be having some interaction with authorities in the United States.

* * *

As I passed through the hotel zone with my girlfriend, Paola, the sights of tourists in their shorts, tank tops, and bathing suits were quite welcoming. I enjoyed privacy and tranquility, but I also wanted to party. First things first, I wanted to get settled into my new place and begin my tropical existence.

Ten kilometers into the hotel zone, and I reached the place Paola had rented for me. I prearranged this move with her before I left New York. The location was prime beachfront real estate, a two bedroom condominium with a large community pool right on the beach. Paola had the keys for me, and we made our way to my unit. Paola followed my instructions to the letter. The unit was on the top floor, an end corner unit. We entered, and it was better than I expected. I immediately went to the terrace and opened the sliding doors. The fresh salt air began filling up my condo. I couldn't wait to watch the sunset and feel the ocean's breeze, listening to the waves of the powerful ocean hit the shoreline.

The kitchen was just right for me, with a coffee machine and grinder. I had always been serious about my coffee. I knew food-shopping was in order, but that would wait until tomorrow. The two bedrooms were done just right with classic Cancun furnishings. The master bedroom was quite spacious, with a large dresser perfect for what I had in mind. I was having a locksmith come and change all my locks. The same locksmith would be doing the floor safe. I was having the floor safe and locks done through a friend of Paola's. I wanted the safe installed under the large dresser, covered by a rug. It would make getting to all my supplies a hassle, but it would be less likely found by the casual eye. I unpacked my clothing and waited for the locksmith to come and change the locks on all the doors. I had a phone installed for local calls—under another name, of course—and paid that bill for what amounted to a year in advance as well.

I never told Paola or anyone else my exact date of arrival; I never wanted anyone to have my schedule. After the brief tour of the condo, I placed my luggage in my bedroom and went to the property office in the downstairs lobby. I paid a year's rent up front and in advance through Paola, but I wanted to introduce myself to the manager so he would know it was I who was there and he would not have to guess or have cause to interact with me. I made it clear that I wanted anonymity and made sure I was dealing with one person and one person only. I paid the year's rent in advance not only because I wanted limited interaction but also to strike any and all deals that I cared to. Cash is king in any venue, and especially in

Mexico, cash certainly is king. I got the condo semifurnished and paid for as I didn't want to spend time furniture shopping. In case I had to leave quickly, which almost always was the case, I wanted to make a clean break. I didn't want a lot of things holding me down, girlfriend included. The only thing left to do was some food-shopping, but that could wait until tomorrow. There were some other odds and ends needed to complete my residence, but those could wait as well. It was getting later in the afternoon, and I wanted to drop Paola off at her place and pay my respects to her kids. Paola and I spent time together, but I wanted a separate residence even though we spent most nights together.

The house Paola was living in, I rented as well. I had never seen it before today but was pleasantly surprised when I saw it. A split-level downtown with a nice garden and sitting area in the front. It was directly across a private school. That was where her two girls were going to school, and the best feature was, the house was on top where the teacher lived. The teacher would look after the girls while Paola and I partied or took short trips together. In the condo on Sundays, I would have Paola and her girls over to enjoy the beach, pool, etc. I had two places, as that was just typical for me to do, but also, I wanted to keep my work and home life separate. Keeping my two worlds apart was something I consciously did my entire life. Having those two worlds collide, especially when your home life is square and the complete opposite of your professional life, can be disastrous and flat-out unnecessary. As much as I tried, though, the two at times would meet up and not in a favorable manner. My family chose their lives, and nobody chose that for them. I left my family behind, coming to Mexico, which I knew would eventually come to my mind at a later date. Perhaps it was the selfish side in me that didn't allow me to think of my family and what they went through with my lifestyle. I told myself it was my life to live when in reality, my life and actions affected others in ways I couldn't see or understand in the moment.

Paola was in her midtwenties and worked at a local nightclub, selling wristbands to tourists. The wristbands allowed the partygoer to enter the club and exit the club without paying again and showed the security that they had paid their cover charge for entering. Paola's family was well-known in certain parts of Mexico, as her mother was a senator from a state about six hours north of Cancun. I called it a fishing village because that was what it looked like to me when I finally made it there to visit. In fact, the city itself was very old, with its majority having cobblestone roadways with amazing architecture.

This time of year for the nightclub scene was considered their slow season, so Paola could take off some nights here and there and not have it affect her or the club. She was able to get a few evenings off in order to do what she and I did best, party. I left her to arrange her daughters and get prepared while I went back to my condo and relaxed before the evening's festivities.

I took a long hot shower and rested before ordering Paola and I some dinner. I would certainly need the energy for the night I knew I would be having. The next day, I had planned nothing until the afternoon to early evening as I knew this night would take me into the wee morning hours. Tomorrow, I would be distributing the ecstasy I brought with me—well, the majority of it anyway. I wanted to keep a certain amount for my parties, which became legendary in the Cancun area and beyond. The quality of my ecstasy was above reproach, and it was coveted by the local dealers I knew. The months before I made this final trip to Mexico, I made quantity deals with a couple of local distributors for when I returned, tomorrow being that day. Aside from having a reputation for parties and good ecstasy, I had a reputation as being no-nonsense. The no-nonsense reputation would grow and take on varied forms as my time in Mexico marched on.

I always had a private table for my parties regardless of what nightclub I frequented. There were two major clubs for nightlife in Cancun—at least for me and my needs there were two. There were other clubs, but nothing that fit my party, music tastes, and style. Other nightclubs would come and go in Cancun, and some I wished stayed because of the atmosphere, but then again, that was probably why they didn't stick around that long, because it was for a select group and not for the masses. Those clubs were for the after-hours scene, which was a direct result of the growing ecstasy demand and use. The techno, house, and trance music wasn't the norm for the majority but created a nice niche for me and the others who dealt ecstasy.

I was friendly with the majority of the staff of the clubs and always had a security guard from each club watch over me. It wasn't something that was done by me but just something that came about. Everyone has reasons why they do things, and I didn't much care why; it was a great service to have. I frequented the clubs quite often and always treated the staff and everyone else the way I would like to be treated, and that went a long way.

Being that Armando had set me up with the chief of the regular police, I didn't have many concerns when it came to being harassed by law enforcement. There were, however, various forms of law enforcement in Mexico as there were in the United States and anywhere else for that matter. I was only protected directly with the local police. I had connections in the other areas as time went on, but I knew firsthand that nothing would touch me on the local level. Then there was the military that protected the drug shipments. Now, not every member of law enforcement and the military was on the take, but it seemed like that to me. Until I saw Armando in the uniform and him giving me direct information that the military was in cahoots with the cartels, it was all pure speculation and hearsay.

Mexico was it for me. I found myself free of the restraints, constraints, and politics of my associates back home. I felt I could ease off on being on guard 24-7. The process didn't take place overnight; I was a work in progress. I didn't realize how wound up and on edge I was until I didn't need to be. One thing that helped me was the ecstasy. It made me actually feel things. Over the next few years, it was a blessing and a curse to begin to feel. I went through waves of emotions and revelations. Keeping them in check at times was a chore.

Paola was prompt, right at seven in the evening. I opened the door, and she flat out looked amazing. I knew she was coming over, and she always advised of such so I wasn't taken off guard of someone knocking on my door. I didn't like knocking on my door or unexpected company. She was dressed in short shorts and a small top with platform shoes; Paola was ready to party. She always dressed appropriately with clothing that highlighted her assets, her assets being her small waist, thick smooth legs, flat stomach, highlighted reddish-blond hair, a smile that warmed up any room, and rather large round ass, my favorite of all body parts.

Paola leapt into my arms, wrapping that smooth skin around me as if she had been starved for affection. She was brimming with excitement, showing me the outfit I apparently bought for her. Her tanned body brought out the colors of her outfit and colors of her hair. The food hadn't arrived yet, and I couldn't wait to begin christening my new condo. Christen it we did, every room and the balcony.

"The condo's great, hon. Great choice and perfect location," I said, now really settling into it and seeing it from a calmer perspective.

"I know exactly what you like, mi amor," she said, looking at me with those almond eyes and sly smile that would melt the most hardened of men.

I counted out fifty ecstasy pills from my bundle and placed them in a candy container; that part of my party was in order. Most of the pills were for my party, and the rest was for sale. While selling the pills led to money, my main concern was to party and enjoy many of the vices I couldn't back home. The ecstasy, I used as a form of tipping. Whether it be the waiters, security, managers, and even owners, at that time in Cancun, people were working to get ecstasy, and hence, the middleman was cut out.

The safe that I had installed earlier in the day was crucial. It wouldn't be the biggest safe by any stretch, but it did the job for the things that mattered most. I had a rather large armoire in my bedroom, and there was a small throw rug underneath that covered the four legs of the armoire. I moved the armoire and slid back the rug to reveal my safe. The third number was locked in and confirmed; my safe was open. One foot long and five inches deep, it was solid enough for these purposes. I had my suitcase next to me and began to withdraw the ecstasy, the silencers, the .380, and the C-4. I arranged my tools for my toolbox and locked up everything, nice and tidy.

Our food arrived as we had just finished our first sex session. Just in time, as we were both hungry and wanted some food in us before heading out.

Paola and I took a taxi to our first location of the evening. We were now in the heart of the hotel zone and nightclub area. Our first stop was an outdoor bar where a lot of people's preparty would take place. It was a great central place to meet up and then, a little later in the evening, move to whatever nightclub or party was the place to be.

The bar was facing the street, equipped with tables, and had wraparound stools for sitting. Most nights it was standing room only but not crowded and always had a great flow to it. The large awning covered most of the bar with the exceptions of a bunch of tables on the outsides. This was also an amazing place for those that liked to people-watch.

This particular bar's owner was a jovial man, quiet in some ways, noisy in others. He certainly had a weight issue; the issue was, he was so fat he could sweat in an igloo. This gentleman also had some ties to a cartel. I heard rumors, but it wasn't my business, and he and I never had any business together. I never charged him for anything, and that was just as I wanted it.

The manager greeted Paola and me and escorted us to our table at about ten in the evening. I got along with everyone, even the ones I didn't particularly care for. Summoning a waiter to the table, the manager ordered a round of drinks for us, on him. As the drinks returned, I handed Paola, the manager of the bar, and myself an ecstasy pill.

"T——, thank you very much," the manager said, popping the pill.

I had Paola open her mouth and threw a pill inside, and then I the same. The three of us raised our glasses and toasted to each other as Paola and I kissed.

We took in the sights, said hello to a bunch of people, and settled in as the ecstasy began to take effect. The second round of drinks was brought by the manager. He leaned in to tell me these were compliments of the owner, Saul.

Paola and I took the drink and went to Saul's table to thank him and pay our respects. It was the end of the year, and Saul was still sitting there with a handkerchief in his hands for the intermittent sweat-wiping.

"Bienvenidos, welcome back T——, Paola," Saul greeted us, standing up.

I didn't want Saul getting up and overexerting himself. Saul enjoyed his life in every regard. His overindulgences bordered on gluttonous. I knew Saul liked ecstasy and handed him one along with his acquaintances, times two. "Why have just one woman when two works so much better?" was Saul's motto. Saul was charismatic in a quiet way, and his flash and tastes had women flocking to him.

"Very good, T——. These tachas [Spanish slang for ecstasy pill] are like the others?" Saul asked regarding my reputation for always having the best ecstasy.

"Yes, without question," I said confidently.

"Then we're going to have a great evening," Saul said as we all took our pill, the second one for Paola and me.

Paola and I had a few laughs with Saul and both his women before we headed back to our table. Not long were we seated than the manager came back to the table and asked if I wanted to meet some people that wanted to buy some ecstasy. My immediate response was asking if they had the money. The manager snickered a bit before very confidently saying yes. I excused myself from Paola and followed the manager past the midway point of the bar, and a group came into view. I saw a semicircle of men donning a cream-colored type of relaxed, classy matching attire. I counted ten men in all and figured that was a lot of security for any "normal" group. I could make out that each of the security detail had clear earpieces in their right ears as well as matching black pouches. I got a closer look at the cloned security as the manager and I walked up on the table.

The manager began his introductions of who was who as one of the men stood up and greeted me with a smiling face. The bar manager introduced me to Andres, one of the three men at the guarded table.

"Please sit down." Andres pointed to a seat at the end of the left-hand side of the table. "This is my brother Mario and my cousin Ernesto," Andres said with pride.

"Good evening." Mario reached out his hand to me, and with a smiling embrace, we met.

"Nice to meet you," Ernesto said lastly.

Ernesto was on the far end, Andres in the middle, and Mario seated next to me. With all the pleasantries out of the way, Andres invited me to a drink. I hadn't concluded or even began a conversation about the ecstasy they were supposed to be interested in, so I politely declined. I needed to be focused on my new trio and the cast of ten that watched over them. My initial ecstasy high was evening out as I was unsure of these men and the situation. My New York ways were still well intact and expected the unexpected.

Mario was Andres's younger brother, who appeared to be about twenty-two years old. Mario was slimmer in build than the others, dressed in designer clothes, with jet-black hair parted in the middle blending down to just shoulder length. My first impression of Mario was he was full of life and youthful exuberance. It made me think of an excited boy on Christmas morning.

"This is my cousin Ernesto," Andres said, grabbing Ernesto's shoulder, showing a different kind of respect between the two.

"Nice to meet you." Nodding a bit, Ernesto extended both hands across the table, and we shook. He was more even-keeled but certainly matter-of-fact.

Ernesto was about twenty-two as well, had chiseled facial features and short hair spiked up. He too was impeccably dressed and grooming in line.

Andres began to lead the conversation as both Mario and Ernesto deferred to Andres. The security detail didn't seem to have much concern about me.

Andres was older than his brother and cousin by a couple of years. Andres was deferred to by the other two and was comfortable in his role. He was about my height but a slim build. Dark brownish black hair and professionally groomed from the manicured hair, manicured hands down to the custom designed clothing that stood out in any crowd. His tone was educated and well versed in the art, of negotiation and diplomacy.

"Do you have tachas?" Andres leaned in a bit, asking the question all three wanted to know.

"You have the money?" I replied directly and without pause.

I knew why I was there. I was asked to come speak to these men and was told they had the money, so my reaction indicated that. Andres sat back, taken aback by my words. Then he chuckled and laughed, followed closely by his brother and cousin.

"I don't know what's so funny," I said in a lower tone, not aggressive or confrontational. My eyes never left Andres's. As he was the spokesman of the group, we were dealing with each other.

"The money is no problem," Andres said, withdrawing money from his front right pocket.

There was a wad of dollars and pesos. He extended it in my direction and asked me how much. I told Andres the amount for each, and he told me eight. Andres was looking at me as if to be waiting for me.

"Right here at the table?" I said, answering the question on Andres's face.

"Yes, right here. Nobody's going to bother us," Andres said in between chuckling with sincerity.

I didn't hesitate at all. With Andres's confidence and my overall comfort in my surroundings, I took out my ecstasy container. I tapped out eight pills as Andres chimed in.

"These are the elephants?" Andres said, referring to the shape and type of ecstasy pill of mine he had apparently taken before.

"Yes, they are," I said.

Ecstasy came in all different shapes and colors and were molded into shapes and symbols. There were some that really stood out, like my elephants and some others. Some types were copied and were an inferior product, but that was some years later. I had elephants the last time I was in Cancun, and apparently, Andres had obtained them and knew of the quality. So when Andres asked for elephants, I knew exactly what he was speaking about and where he got them before.

"Very good. I had those before, and they are amazing," Ernesto said in his excitement.

Andres and I exchanged pills for money, and everyone was more than pleased with the results of the transaction.

"Will you be around later?" Andres asked me as he gave his brother and cousin two pills each.

"Yes, I'll be in the club later on," I ,said pointing to the club exactly next to us.

"Great, we'll be there as well, and we'll probably want more," Andres said, feeling confident they would be in need.

I stood up with business concluded, and we all said our good-byes. Andres, Ernesto, and Mario seemed to be decent people. I enjoyed their getting right to the point and conducting business well. I left the table and made my way back to Paola and then our evening together. The manager of the outside bar met me before I arrived at my table.

"Hey, how did it go?" the manager asked me with a bit of a smile on his face.

"Great," I said. "They had the money, and all went well. Thank you."

"Do you know who they are?" the manager asked me with a bit of a puzzled tone in his voice.

"No, I don't. All I know is their money was good," I said, wanting to get back to my evening.

"That's the president of Mexico's two sons and their cousin." The manager now let out what he had been dying to tell me since the beginning.

Now the scenario with the ten men, earpieces and all, was making more sense. The lack of concern from Andres or the other two men about anything regarding the legality or otherwise. Truth be told, the status of the men didn't faze me at all. Celebrities, musicians, politicians, whatever the case, I never got starstruck. Actually, they were the ones that wanted to hang around the gangsters, not the other way around. They had their status but were enamored with the status that the gangsters had and the star power we wielded. My lack of caring or expression to the manager's information took him aback as I headed back to my table with Paola. Just in time as well, as my high was just beginning to hit me again and I could see the look on Paola's face as hers was well in effect. A few other people had joined our party, and it was time to move on to the next leg in our journey.

We went next door to the nightclub and walked in, bypassing the long line that was typical of a Cancun weekend evening. I never paid for a cover charge to enter a club, not here in Cancun or any-where I went. I began saying "Hello" to all the club employees along the way, from the people selling club wristbands to the waiters, man-agers, and security. The manager of the club greeted me and led us to our table for the evening's party. Paola let the staff know we would be spending the evening partying here, so we had our table all set for us by the dance floor; she knew how to party, all right.

My party was in full effect; bottles of water and pitchers of juice with vodka were brought over by our waiter, and the manager led the way. Drinks were poured, and the fun began. I would say about an hour or so into the evening, the manager came back to my table. This time, he was armed with the same waiter and another bottle of vodka and accoutrements.

"T——, this is from Andres," the manager told me upon seeing my face, because I didn't order anything yet.

I thought for split second, then it came to me: the Andres I had met a little earlier in the evening. I leaned my head back, follow-ing the manager's gesture with his well-manicured right hand. There I saw the three men from earlier, the president's family, their faces painted with smiles and a sense of joy. Andres lifted his glass to me and gave a slight nod. With the salutations of Andres, Ernesto, and Mario, the manager looked at me in a funny way, as was everyone else who recognized it. The collective feeling among the locals here in the club was that this type of event was rare, if at all. The first family got whatever they wanted and didn't ever show this side of grati-tude, least of all involvement with anyone outside their tight circle. I grabbed my glass and bowed my head while I toasted to the three. I then returned to my party. I felt everyone wanting to ask me multi-ple things, but nobody spoke. I didn't say anything; quite frankly, it wasn't abnormal for me.

The next time I had to use the restroom, I tapped out ten ecstasy pills more. I enjoy a mutual respect and understanding, and the first impression is always the most lasting impression. I placed the pills in a napkin and began walking. I stopped at Andres's table and greeted my three new acquaintances. Passing them off to Andres, I shook everyone's hand and gave a bear hug all around. I didn't spend much time. A pass and go as I say. Plus, I needed to get to the restroom; the water and drinks were going through me.

I walked back from the restroom, and as I passed back the same way, Andres stopped me and thanked me. I played down his appreciation and told him, "My pleasure. Enjoy your evening, and thank you again for the bottle."

What I truly loved was keeping people guessing. Both sides guessing who I was, what side I was on, who I was associated with, or whatever. The less someone knew about me or what I was about, the safer I would be. Walk silent and act accordingly.

I knew Mexico was ruled by a select few. The power was central and understood. The benefits that came from that few were otherworldly. I saw firsthand all that I had been feeling and seeing over my years in Mexico.

I made it home in the wee hours of the morning with enough time to get some rest and recharge a little for the day's affairs.

It was business as usual in Mexico the past year, and the People's Revolutionary Party, or PRI Party, had been going strong for eight decades without relinquishing power.

Today I had to meet with two main people that I would lean on later as close allies. The man I was meeting first today, Sebastian, I had been introduced to by Paola before on my last visit here. I chose the top-two dealers in Cancun and intended to stabilize the market. I learned that the less confrontation among dealers, the better off everyone would be.

The meeting was at Sebastian's house. He had been a full-time dealer after leaving the police force. He was the equivalent of our state troopers. His move to Cancun also had him shifting lines of work full-time.

"T——, how are you?" Sebastian answered the door after I rang the bell.

"Sebastian, what's up?" I responded as we shook hands and hugged.

Sebastian was about my age, late twenties, and had thick, curly black hair and the warmest persona one could have. He always made you feel welcomed and comfortable. He was about my height and was average in weight and stature. Sebastian was modest, modest in his surroundings and every aspect of his life. He wanted to stay under the radar as I did. We entered Sebastian's house, and he took me on a little tour before we spoke on anything else. I preferred relationship-building as well. I wanted to know more about this man as we were about to enter a business relationship.

"A very nice place you have here, Sebastian," I said as we were just about to finish our tour and small talk around the house.

"T——, thank you for that, and thank you for coming down here and meeting me today," Sebastian said, being the consummate gentleman.

"My pleasure, Sebastian," I said as Sebastian directed us to the office area of his house.

"How's Cancun been?" I asked a general question, which leads the person answering to speak on what it is that's on his or her mind.

"It's a bit slow right now, but spring break will be here soon, and the Mexican season starts as well." Sebastian wasn't going to tip me to anything besides something vague—a man after my own heart.

Sebastian opened his desk drawer and pulled out a stack of money. It appeared to be a mixture of Mexican pesos and American dollars. I followed suit by taking out a bundle of five hundred ecstasies.

"I don't need all that," Sebastian said after seeing me with the large bundle.

"Let's talk," I said to Sebastian as he stopped counting money. "How many do you want?" I asked nonchalantly.

"A hundred will work."

"How's the scene down here these days?" I asked, wanting to know any other tidbit of news I could take with me.

"There isn't much product around, especially being a little slow. One hundred works for me," Sebastian let me know again.

"If you'll allow me, I'll leave you with four hundred more. I don't want you to go back and forth, and it will allow you to spread yourself out a bit."

"I don't mind if you don't. I have some other areas I want to get into, and having quantity will certainly help that end," Sebastian said, rethinking his initial response.

We mutually agreed on this and knew it was beneficial on both sides. Sebastian had the reputation of being a good businessman and a man of his word. I got that sense from him and knew this would be a good investment for me and would limit the amount of time I would have to carry pills and limit the amount I would have to hold. On top of that, Paola had introduced me, and so far, she had been on point with all her contacts since I'd known her.

Sebastian had his own clientele, and I knew his rarely clashed with the second man I was to meet after this meeting concluded. I left Sebastian's house and made my way to my next appointment and drop off. The second man was more into the rave scene and kept his sales in Cancun but ventured out to Tulum, Playa del Carmen, and other areas.

My second meeting went without a hitch, and I was able to unload some of my supply and collect some cash.

The week after I met Andres and company, I was having some diner out near my condo. There were several excellent eateries nearby, which allowed me to walk back to my condo and walk off the feast I would be served. At the beginning of my meal, in walked Andres and his cousin Ernesto.

"T——, how are you?" Andres and Ernesto said as they noticed me and approached my table.

There were only five security personnel with them, as I came to find out the larger security presence was needed when they went nightclubbing, which was quite often. The more public and unpredictable the location, the more security was taken with them.

"No need to get up, T——. We don't want to interrupt your meal," Andres said as he held his hand out, wanting me to keep seated.

"Nonsense, Andres. Anything I can get you to eat or drink?" I said, already standing up and warmly greeting the two.

"No, thank you. Very kind of you to ask, but we're expecting some company soon. I'm glad we ran into you." Andres visibly showed his enthusiasm, as he always did.

"Really glad," Ernesto said, backing up and emphasizing Andres's comment.

"You wouldn't happen to have any more of those elephants from the other night, would you?" Andres eagerly inquired of me.

"It just so happens that I do have some."

Andres's English was near perfect, while Ernesto's was a little rougher around the edges but certainly a lot better than my Spanish. Most of these elite families in Mexico or those with the means sent their children off to be educated in Europe and the United States. These three—and in particular, Andres and Mario—were no exception.

I reached into my pocket and saw Andres's obvious expression of excitement. I didn't even ask either of the men how many they wanted. I tapped out a bunch, probably about six, and handed them to Andres. Andres reached for his money, and I held my hand out now. I let him know his money wasn't necessary and that these were on me.

Andres put them into his pocket, paused for a second, then said, "T——, I have a question to ask. Well, more of a favor than a question."

"What's on your mind, Andres?" I asked, knowing this was the exact position I wished to always be in, the driver's seat.

"I'm going to be leaving with Mario to Mexico City, and Ernesto is going to be staying here in Cancun. Most of the security detail will be leaving with us, and I wanted to know if you might be able to watch Ernesto, you know, keep an eye out for him. I know we don't know each other too well, but I see how people respond to you, and I know you have some experience when it comes to bodyguarding and protection. Just your presence will be the best deterrent for those wanting to do him harm. It's not easy for us to trust anyone, and in the short period of time, we feel you would be best suited to watch Ernesto's back. Can you watch out for Ernesto while we're away?"

It's true; I had only known these three for a very short period, but we'd bonded and had a mutual respect for one another.

"Of course I would," I said without hesitation in response to Andres's question.

"Good, here's my number and Ernesto's as well. What's your number so we can keep in contact?"

We exchanged numbers, and I was now in direct contact with the Mexican first family. I was always able to maneuver my way into some unique positions in life, and this was another one of the maneuver jobs. I never plan to have these relationships; they just come about. It's a matter of putting yourself in the position and then letting your character come through.

"Great, we'll speak tomorrow and arrange everything," Andres said as we hugged and went about our evenings.

Just as my dessert was arriving, so were Andres and Ernesto's companions—four of who appeared to be models, all dressed up for an evening on the town. I finished my tiramisu and espresso and now my after-dinner drink of Grand Marnier. To my surprise, one of the women from Andres's group approached my table with my drink in one hand and hers in another.

"Mr. T——," the woman said, placing the drinks on the table, mine in front of me.

"May I sit down and have a drink with you?"

"Of course you can," I said, getting up and pulling her chair out for her.

Before sitting down, I saw Andres with that smiling face on him, and I appreciated his gesture. We had some small talk, and when we were about finished with our drink, I asked the waiter for the bill. I was told there was no bill and that it was handled already. I nodded in Andres's direction, and he confirmed with raising his glass. My new companion and I didn't need to have stellar conversation or any hesitation. We both got up. I went over to say good-bye to Andres and his table.

The next day, I received a call from Andres as he was on his way to the airport with Mario. The girl he sent me had just left, and I thanked him for sending her. He laughed and asked if I enjoyed myself. *Immensely* was the word that came to mind. She was both passionate and in the moment.

Collecting favors has been a lifelong hobby of mine. I prefer favors more than any other form of payment. The key is collecting them from those that are capable of understanding the idea of a favor and being able to repay when that favor is called in. Merely taking cash for a service or act isn't always the best action to take. Andres wanted me to know they weren't around, so I would be calling Ernesto in a couple of hours when I believed he would be awake. Even a couple of hours after Andres's call, Ernesto must have still been sleeping.

The sun was going down, and I was just now leaving the gym close to my condo. My phone rang, and it was Ernesto, returning my call from earlier in the day. It appeared Ernesto was on vampire time, as were much of the Cancun residents that partied. We made arrangements to meet at Saul's outside bar, where we first met. We agreed on nine in the evening. That gave me plenty of time to relax and prepare myself for this security detail.

I was the first to arrive and did so at about eight thirty. I wanted to see who was around well ahead of my nine-in-the-evening meeting. Andres was correct; I had a lot of experience with bodyguarding. I used to do that for the old-timers back in New York as well as other personal security and nightclub bouncing.

A few minutes to nine, and a black SUV pulled up. It was still quite hot out, but I dressed in all black with black sneakers in case I needed more traction whatever venue I was in. My instincts told me this was Ernesto and his security detail. I was given no specifics on anything aside from watching Ernesto and that not much security would be available this evening. I saw one bodyguard exit the vehicle and open the door for Ernesto, who was sitting in the passenger seat. I was waiting to see who else would emerge, but as the two approached me, I became aware that this was it.

"T——," Ernesto said, approaching and giving me a hug. "T——, this is Geraldo. Geraldo, T——," Ernesto said, introducing me to his lone bodyguard.

Right off the bat, I got a good vibe from Geraldo. There was no jealousy or ill will. More to the point, the sentiments were opposite. He was very glad to see me and join forces with him tonight. Ernesto sat at his table, and Geraldo and I began to speak as Ernesto ordered some food and a drink.

"How did you get this job?" I wanted to begin vague and see what Geraldo would offer, as my curiosity was more than piqued.

"I'm in the military. All of us are military that guard the president's family."

"What's the requirements for being on the presidential family's detail?" I was curious about their training; I wasn't not only curious, but I also wanted to know his skill set just in case there was an issue tonight or in the future.

"I'm an expert marksman," Geraldo said and stopped with marksman.

"An expert marksman?" I said with disbelief.

That took a few moments to process. Geraldo was all of about five feet seven and maybe a 170 pounds, not much of an imposing figure.

"There's no other requirements aside from that?" I said, still in disbelief that that would be the sole reason for being able to protect the president of Mexico's family.

"We all have to be in the military and pass all the background checks," Geraldo said to me, perhaps trying to make it seem like there was more to the protection detail that there really was.

Now Andres wanting me to be here and watching over his cousin made more sense to me. We would be in a crowded, dark nightclub and who knew where else, and the whole marksman thing wouldn't cut the mustard at all. My skills in threat assessment and hand-to-hand fighting are what was needed for this evening. I asked Geraldo what he wanted for the evening as this was his turf and it seemed more his game to call than it was mine. To my surprise, Geraldo deferred to me, and I didn't hesitate. I told him I would lead the way, and he'd follow up behind. I would also escort Ernesto to and from any bathroom trips or places he needed to go. I wanted Geraldo to watch the table and make sure nobody interfered with the drinks. We were going to the club next door, and I knew my way around the club and who was who. We entered the nightclub around eleven that evening. We got a booth with a great view of the club and with good exit points if needed be. The people around that night and those that heard about that night really didn't know what to think of me now. *Why is this American here, and how does he know these people?* Another aspect to this was the fact that the Mexican first family had such a grip on the country that my being here with them added another aspect of the "Who's the American?" Quien es El Güero?

The evening coming to an end, I followed Ernesto's black SUV back to the presidential compound in Cancun. This compound was usually inhabited by the president's children and various relatives but seldom by the president and/or his wife.

Ernesto called me the next morning on his way out of Cancun and back to Mexico City. He thanked me for a peaceful evening as well as inviting me to fly with him this day or any day I chose. I came to find that not only Mario and Andres had their own private planes, but so did Ernesto. Now, I could imagine that the children of the president would have their own plane, but the cousin was a stretch.

I was glad Ernesto rang my phone in the morning, as I had some errands to run and get my day started. I had my safe installed on the first day, and now I wanted to add a little more security to my establishment. In the hallway outside my door, I placed a small camera that was invisible to the naked eye but gave me a clear line of sight who exited the elevator and who was approaching my door. I linked the camera to my laptop computer so I could monitor my hallway security from inside my condo or remotely if needed be. It also recorded anyone that appeared on camera so I could see who came by when I wasn't around.

Dusk was settling in, and I had to square away my condo and prepare for the evening. I first went to secure my valuables and arrange what I needed for the evening's events. The newly installed floor safe was a true blessing for me. I went into the bedroom to move back the armoire and get to my tools. I turned the combination-style dial until the third number locked in and my safe opened. I withdrew my .380, two of the four silencers, and two fully loaded magazines. I closed the door to the safe, spun the combination style lock a few times, placed the rug back over the safe, and put the armoire back in its place.

My next order of business was to pick out the appropriate attire for the evening. A black-on-black hooded jogging suit with matching black sneakers would do the trick. I reached into my dresser drawer and took out my Velcro watch and another Velcro strap. I put on my jogging suit and fastened the holster for my .380, which fitted snugly on the small of my back. I had widened the holster a bit in order to accommodate the silencer once fitted on the barrel. I placed my watch on the inside of my right wrist and laced up my sneakers.

Looking on the inside of my right wrist, I read the time—6:49 p.m. I put on a pair of thin black gloves and wiped down the gun and magazines of any fingerprints. I withdrew the bullets from the magazines, wiping them down before reloading them. I clicked in one of the magazines, loading the .380 from below and chambering a round. The first round that would exit my gun was a hollow-point round. I wanted the first bullet to inflict maximum damage. A hollow-point bullet is an expanding bullet that has a pit hollowed-out shape in its tip often intended to cause the bullet to expand upon entering a target in order to decrease penetration and disrupt more tissue as it travels through a target, basically maximizing tissue damage, blood loss, and/or shock. The bullet was meant to remain inside the target.

This particular .380, a SIG Sauer, I particularly enjoyed. Each magazine clip held seven shots with one bullet in the chamber. Armando sure listened and retained everything we spoke about those years back in Mexico City.

The first magazine was loaded and ready. I placed the second magazine and second silencer in my black pouch along with a Velcro strap. I checked my watch again—6:59 p.m., plenty of time.

The drive I had timed at thirty-five minutes in the worst of conditions. I left plenty of time for a couple of surveillance drive-bys and waited.

It was 8:53 p.m.; time for one last look around and prepare myself. Unzipping my pouch, I took out one of the silencers, withdrew my pistol from its holster, and screwed on the silencer clockwise with the necessary four rotations until it was flush on the barrel. I leaned forward and secured my weapon in its holster. I withdrew the Velcro strap and used it to secure the remaining clip to my left wrist. I'm right-handed, so I needed my spare clip on my left wrist for faster reloading if necessary. Each silencer was capable of expelling seven shots with little more than a thudding sound. After the seventh shot, the packing inside the silencer would begin to blow apart, making each successive shot nosier. My targets were two, and I wanted to be prepared in case I needed more rounds.

As I stepped out of my car, the tropical sun had long since retreated, pulling with it the tropical heat. I pulled the hoodie over my head, leaving enough room as to not obstruct my peripheral vision but enough to cast doubt about my facial features.

El Dorado Street wasn't lit properly, with some trees staggered on both sides. Only a few cars were parked on either side of the street from Calle 11 to Calle 12, where I now stood. A few minutes before nine, and there had been barely any movement on El Dorado Street for the last hour and change. The neighborhood was upper middle-class, with houses surrounded by manicured hedges and gates shielding them from the street. Most occupants parked their cars inside their gates, although some used the streets.

I reached inside my hoodie, clutching my St. Jude medal, the patron saint of lost causes. I began the prayer that I learned as a kid, had stuck with me through adulthood, and I believed comforted and protected me. With my eyes close, I began.

"Sacred heart of Jesus, have mercy on me. St. Jude, worker of miracles, pray for me. St. Jude, the helper and keeper of the hopeless, pray for me."

My eyes open now, I saw a pair of headlights making its way down Calle 11 and stopping just in front of 1217 El Dorado Street.

I crossed the street and began jogging the hundred yards to the black Mercedes that just turned of its headlights. It was the same black Mercedes I'd been tailing the last few days.

Routines can be one's downfall; comfort, another means to a person's demise. When a criminal or individual that operates outside the law becomes complacent in his or her success, this is the time when he or she is most vulnerable and open to being taken down, overthrown, and/or vanquished.

From my last few days of surveillance, I knew the driver of the Mercedes would exit first and open the passenger-side door for the second occupant.

I was now fifty yards away, and the passenger placed his right foot down on the curb. The air was stagnant, and I could feel beads of sweat forming under my hoodie. My heart rate rarely passed one hundred beats per minute, and now was no different. As the passenger's left foot hit the curb, the driver held the door open with his back to me. I quickened my pace, keeping it just under a sprint. Timing is everything, and luck plays a large part especially after all the planning has been computed to the slightest margin.

Both targets were now on the sidewalk, and the passenger-side car door closed. I was less than twenty-five yards out, and I saw the passenger already had his keys in his right hand to open the gate leading to his house.

Twenty yards out and either the driver heard me or felt my presence approaching. I steadied my breathing as the driver's threat assessment didn't seem to elevate. I blended into the affluent community, and it wasn't uncommon for someone to be jogging this time of the evening.

Fifteen yards out and I eased my right hand back, withdrawing my pistol. I eased my arm upward from my running pose. Coming within seven yards, gun in hand, I had my targets in full view. The driver of the Mercedes was the same man in the photo Armando showed me on the beach in Tulum. His boss was a foot away from him, with one foot inside his gate, having just opened it. He too was a dead ringer for the picture Armando presented me.

As my left foot landed on the pavement just feet from my two targets, I steadied my pistol parallel and fired my first shot. The first muffled shot struck the bodyguard in the upper left side of his chest inches from his heart. The force of the bullet's impact mixed with his instincts spun the bodyguard around to where his torso was facing me full-on. I fired two more times, striking the bodyguard center mass and dropping him backward, his head landing in the thicket of bushes shielding the house from the street.

As the bodyguard was in the midst of his fatal collapse, I landed my last stride, bringing into full view my main target. Standing in the walkway of his entrance, he fumbled for his weapon holstered in his shoulder holster. The few moments of shock gave me the advantage I needed. All my main target could see was his bodyguard falling, and in an instant, he came face-to-face with me. With his hand barely on the butt of his weapon, I discharged a round, striking him in his upper chest. Rapid succession and two more bullets followed suit, hitting their mark dead center. My main target fell backward into the walkway leading to his front door.

I took no time in making sure both were deceased. I tapped the bodyguard in the head with a single shot, walked over to his boss, and followed suit. A quick assessment, and I knew there were no witnesses. An envelope peeked out of the main target's inside breast pocket. The envelope was flush with money. A brief search of the corpse showed another cash flush envelope. The bodyguard likewise had a similar envelope on his lifeless body. I put my .380 back in its holster, with one round remaining.

I exited the entranceway, surveying my surroundings. Nothing was out of the ordinary, and thankfully, nobody was around. I jogged just short of a sprint down El Dorado to my car. I put on my seat belt, started the engine, put the car in drive, and drove down El Dorado with a quick view of the work I had just completed. A left-hand turn on Calle 11, and I made my way to the main boulevard. A mile down the boulevard, I pulled over to a secluded area where the land met the jungle water. I discarded my gloves and spent silencer in a bag, tied it tight, weighed it down with some rocks, and threw it deep into the murky, crocodile-infested waters.

I walked a few minutes more and broke the gun against the rocks and threw the gun pieces in different parts of the same water. The last thing I wanted was a gun that could potentially tie me to any murder, landing me behind bars and throwing away the key..

Back at my condo, I emptied the money from the envelopes. I thumbed through them all together, and from a rough count, it was in the seventy-five-thousand region. The cash was a mixture of pesos and dollars in larger denominations. I stripped down naked and put all my clothes into a plastic bag along with my sneakers and anything that would leave any trace evidence on me. Whatever these two guys were into, it was lucrative to say the least. I placed the clips and remaining rounds in the safe along with a majority of the money. I left out a couple thousand pesos for after I showered up. I scrubbed myself down good in the shower, toweled off, got on a fresh pair of clothes, gathered up the bag of work clothes, and left the condo. I lit a cigar and enjoyed the evening breeze of the Caribbean night. I took the long way to the downtown area, bypassing the side of town I was just on. I had some food-shopping to do and no better time for me than late at night, when nobody was around. I dumped the clothes I had in various dumpsters around the shopping center. I made plans to spend the next day with Paola, so I needed some food cooked and needed to replenish my condo's supply. I would be cooking a feast for morning breakfast and then to the beach for some tanning.

It was a typical sunny Cancun morning, and Paola and I had finished eating and were now just getting settled on the beach. With our bellies full, the warm Mayan sun began recharging our bodies. I carried two phones on me now, one for my regular, everyday life and the other I used to communicate with just one man, Armando. I was about an hour into tanning when my phone rang. The ringtone made me know it was Armando calling me.

"Yeah," I answered, never wanting to speak too much on this phone, or any phone for that matter.

Armando told me quickly what he wanted to say, and then I hung up without even saying anything else. I didn't want to say anything on the phone, or I wanted to say as little as possible, especially after last night's events. "Baby, you need anything? I'm headed inside for a bit, getting some more water and refreshing my drink."

Paola never questioned me; she never wanted me to lie to her, and I never wanted to formulate something to mask what I was doing. I wanted to protect Paola from anything I was doing and shield her from the other part of my life that made up my existence.

"Yes, mi amor, another orange juice, please. And make it a mimosa."

"One mimosa coming up," I told Paola, bending down to give her a kiss before departing.

I made it back to the condo, packed a bowl of weed to smoke, and began squeezing oranges for our drinks. A small surveillance camera I had installed in the hallway pointing to the door of my condo would give me a little heads-up about people coming to see me or someone paying me an unwanted visit. I had the camera hooked into my laptop so their picture would show on my computer screen. There was a knock on the door, and looking at my laptop's camera view of my outside door, I saw Armando. Even with his hat pulled down, I knew it was him, especially since I was expecting him. I flipped my computer down and went to the door.

"Come on in," I said, opening the door for Armando, giving him a hug and kiss on the cheek.

Armando was casually dressed but, as always, was impeccable. Being well dressed was part and parcel to his character. He was meticulous about everything; some would say anal, but I would say cunning and calculated. I closed the door behind Armando and locked it. I used the remote to close the blinds in the house to keep any wandering eyes out.

"Something to drink?" I asked as I continued my drink preparations.

"A bottle of water would be great," Armando said, looking parched.

I took a cold bottle of water out of the refrigerator and turned to hand it to Armando only to see him laying a newspaper on the counter. I handed Armando the water and looked at what he wanted me to see. I saw what Armando wanted me to see now, the reasoning behind it I would find out in his time.

"Dos agentes de inmigración fue asesinado." Two immigration agents assassinated.

That was the headline of the leading Mexican newspaper. The headline wasn't the most provocative part. Mexico, like a lot of countries, loved to show the gore in detail. Two agents were shown in full view, blood in the walkway, bodies with bullet wounds, pools of blood, and near exactly what was in my mind's eye. The United

States was more reserved with showing bodies in their publications, but Mexico showed the whole enchilada.

I continued to read the paper as I saw Armando out of the corner of my eye open a bottle of tequila and pour a couple of glasses. The article said how these were two immigration officials who worked at the airport. Not much information was given aside from that. The murders happened last night, so I was sure more would be coming out in the days ahead when other facts and data were brought to light. Armando slid one of the two glasses over to me and lifted his to me in a toast.

"Salud," Armando said, raising his glass, toasting to me.

"Salud," I responded, drinking my toast.

Armando finished his drink first, and before I could do much of anything, he was reaching into his inside jacket pocket. The envelope he withdrew was thick, so thick it couldn't be sealed.

"Message sent and received, loud and clear. These two"— Armando pointed to the two corpses in the newspaper—"were the major players in the pipeline of illegal immigrant smuggling. Their network from South America through Central America came through Cancun with its final destination, the United States. Cancun International Airport was the main passageway for the illegals. That's where the money would be collected and then later distributed. Greed was their downfall. They began sharing less and dabbling in stolen artifacts and drugs."

I don't know what the real truth was, but I wondered why Armando was sharing this bit of information with me. It wasn't like him to mention anything unless it had a purpose, so I waited to see what this purpose might entail. I looked inside the envelope, and there appeared to be about fifty thousand dollars. *I tell you what,* I thought, *I know I wanted to be retired, or at least not as active, but I wouldn't mind taking jobs like this every now and again.* Back home most jobs I never even received payment for. They were more out of duty and advancing up the importance ladder than they were about paid work.

"You want to tell me something else?" I said to Armando, sensing he wanted me to say something.

"There's a loose end," he said bluntly.

A loose end, I thought. *How could that be.* I was quite careful about not leaving any evidence or being seen. I knew nobody was there before I was, and afterward, I couldn't see a single soul around anywhere. I flashed back in my head about what could be loose.

Armando saw me struggling with my reflections of mind and told me, "Now that these two are out of the way, there's another person involved. We didn't know exactly who it was or what their role in the operation was. We only knew that there had to be someone else pulling strings and using these two as the fall guys, as the case may be."

The *we* Armando kept referring to was another unknown for me. I somehow knew the *we* had several meanings, twists, and turns. Armando never gave me clarity on the *we* part, and I didn't much care to know. Even if I asked and were told an answer, it probably wouldn't be true anyway, so why bother having that information or lack thereof in my head?

"The chief of the judicial federal was one of the first on the scene. This case could have gone to any jurisdiction, but why them, and how did the chief get to the scene so quickly? From what I hear, the chief is taking this case himself and being the lead investigator on it. We believe him to be the silent partner in this scheme, but nothing tangible yet," Armando said, looking for my reaction.

Armando didn't say for sure, but even him just giving me that little bit of information was enough to seal the chief's fate. Armando wanted to see my level of interest or hesitation. I didn't waiver or show any signs one way or another and stood stoic. I knew where Armando was going with this, and it had my name written all over it.

"We don't know too much about the chief except that he's ruthless, a stone-cold killer, and mixed up in a number of rackets. He's normally surrounded by his goon squad. They are all detectives under his command that do his bidding, both legally and illegally. They operate all hours of the day but mainly in the evenings, which is another reason why the chief was one of the first on the scene last night. I'm sure with these two being eliminated, the chief is even more on point and on high alert."

I knew Armando was gauging my thought process, so I wanted to bring this conversation to a halt, speaking my mind. "Nothing's too difficult. The chief isn't immune to anything those two weren't. It's quite simple—weakness. Everyone has at least one. This is just a little more delicate than the others but totally doable," I said, reassuring Armando I was on board and, even more to the point, already beginning some early planning stages in my head.

"This is no rush. We have to let the opportunity present itself. Let's enjoy this victory today, and we'll work on this next move. Chess, not checkers, my friend. Now go on and get back to your day, and we'll catch up again," Armando said, ending the conversation.

"Hey, before you go, I'll be needing another gun like the last one. You know exactly what I like and need."

"I sure do," Armando said as he withdrew another .380 from underneath his shirt.

Armando handed the gun to me, concluding our meeting for this day. I showed Armando out and placed the new gun in its rightful place, the floor safe, along with my new stack of money. I finished off the drinks, smoked a bowl of weed, and headed back to rejoin Paola.

"Back baby," I said, leaning down and handing her her drink.

"Just in time. I'm thirsty, mi amor," Paola said in such an alluring tone and sexiness.

We took in some more sun, sipped our drinks, and enjoyed the serenity as I slipped into a slumber right there on the beach. My body needed rest more than I knew.

* * *

The houses on this suburban Long Island town were of decent size, a few thousand square feet roughly. The night air was cooling off from the late-July summer heat. I exited the expressway and lifted the visor of my helmet, letting in some fresh air. The peaceful sky was clear, with stars filling it. The moon was three-quarters of the way complete, bringing some light to the darkness. Light wasn't exactly my best friend this evening, but circumstances are what they are. I was hoping there would be enough cover of darkness to aid me this evening.

The first of the four stop signs I approached had me looking for 637 Valley View Drive. A few minutes after passing the first stop sign, I was driving down Valley View Drive. The quietness of the neighborhood wasn't disturbed by my motorcycle. My cruising bike had normal pipes on it and was quite quiet. Halfway down the block, I saw house number 637 on my right-hand side. The number 637 was prominently displayed over the top of the attached garage, which was almost like my beacon. I continued down Valley View to the stop sign, made a right, and parked. I had a clear line of sight down the entire block in all directions. I didn't see anyone about, which was a bit odd, being it was only ten at night on a beautiful summer evening. Fourth of July had just passed, and the intermittent fireworks could still be heard from time to time. I took my helmet off while continuing to look about to see signs of any life. I kept my leather jacket on as I wasn't planning on staying long, and in case of a fast getaway, I would only need to put on my helmet and go. I unlocked the compartment underneath my seat. This evening, prior to being here, I constructed a bomb consisting of three sticks of dynamite. I wrapped the sticks together with electrical tape and attached a timer to the sticks. My timer was a crude small clock but was more than effective. It took me just a minute to carefully connect the timer and wires to the device. I didn't want to be traveling with the device fully armed in case something was to happen on the way to do my work. The last thing I needed was a bomb going off under my ass while on the expressway; that wouldn't have turned out well for me. Device armed, I looked around to see if I could see anything out of the ordinary or people about, and there was nothing that I could see. I would usually do at least a day of surveillance on a location before I finished a job, but this one was not one of those situations. I locked up the seat and put the keys in my front right pocket in case I needed to get them out fast and go. I also left my helmet on the back of the motorcycle. I put the bomb under my jacket and walked down Valley View, going back the direction I had driven down. Crickets and heat bugs were all I could hear as my walk began. Maybe it was just me and the tunnel vision I had, but those crickets sure sounded noisy.

I reached inside my shirt and took out my St. Jude's medal. Holding it in my gloved right hand, I closed my eyes briefly to pray. "Sacred heart of Jesus, have mercy on me. St. Jude, worker of miracles, pray for me. St. Jude, helper and keeper of the hopeless, pray for me."

That prayer, along with many others, had been ingrained in my subconscious since before I could remember. Once a Catholic, always a Catholic, at least in some regards, that is.

My target was coming into view, a beige two-story home with an attached garage. There were multiple windows on all sides, which wasn't an optimal situation. The nonoptimal sides of this job began to add up. I scanned the house and knew where everything was. My head kept going to my surroundings and if there was anything that had changed from when I began my walk. My worst nightmare was someone walking a dog and coming upon me or someone just taking in the New York summer evening.

I approached the target house and began walking down the driveway. The left-hand side of the house had two lights on, one on the top left and one on the bottom, which appeared to be a living or family room. The right-hand side of the house was dark and was the perfect cover for me. The driveway led to the car garage that had another living space over the top of it, all attached to the house. I was forty paces down the driveway, and the coast was clear. I stepped off the driveway to the right of the house/garage. To my delight, there was a large propane gas tank. I withdrew the bomb from under my jacket. I was relieved to see the metal tank there. I didn't know where I would be placing the device or how I would ultimately place it. The information I got was that there was a garage attached to the house, and I thought that would be an ideal location. I was prepared to tape the bomb to something or attach a magnet if I were able to find a metallic structure to fasten it to. Sometimes I would use both just in case one failed. I had placed bombs in many locations and on plenty of different surfaces. Relatively speaking, this was a piece of cake. Once the device was fastened securely to the tank, I set the timer. I gave myself fifteen minutes to make it clear of the location, at a safe distance, and nowhere where I could be associated with the event.

This was the time of uncertainty, and there was no turning back. I couldn't be certain nobody was out or peeking through a window and seeing me. The best I could do was stick to my plan and hope for the best. There were many uncertainties in this type of work; I didn't know who was in the house, who might walk by, or how much propane was in the tank. I didn't concern myself with any of those factors, especially who was in the house and who would be collateral damage. A job is a job; the less thought I gave it, the better off I was.

With every assignment I accepted, my knowledge on explosives grew. My curiosity began when I was a kid making homemade pipe bombs. When I met Richie in Brooklyn, he began honing my skill set as I became a fast proficient. Typically, I used black powder, and on the rare occasion, I used bombs that had metal objects inside, like tacks, nails, etc. The majority of the time, jobs were meant to seem natural or unassuming to the public eye. Arson investigators aside, most of my work was never brought to light. Sometimes Richie was with me, but aside from that, I was always alone.

It was 10:13 p.m. when I made my first step away from the device. I had until 10:28 p.m. until the bomb would go off, and I budgeted it as plenty of time for me to be far enough away. I kept my pace even and had my head on a swivel, looking for anything out of the ordinary. I made it to my motorcycle, put on my helmet, keys in the ignition, and started the engine. I retraced the path that brought me here from the expressway. I stopped at the final stop sign and looked at my watch before getting on the expressway—10:26 p.m. The route back to where I needed to go had me driving parallel to 637 Valley View Drive just four blocks from the expressway. Just as my motorcycle was parallel to the house, reaching fifty miles an hour, I heard the explosion. Mind you, I was wearing my helmet, doing fifty miles an hour over four blocks away, and through the wind of the evening, I heard the explosion go off.

The noise was louder than I anticipated, and I wondered how much damage was inflicted. Apparently, the propane tank was more on the full side than empty. I was still in the experimental stages with using the dynamite along with other incendiary devices.

The newspapers the next day didn't fully label the explosion in any definitive manner. The paper quoted investigators as investigating the cause of the blast but said it had something to do with the propane tank. The paper also said there was one fatality in the blast, my target.

Through the heat of the explosion, I didn't think that there would be any remains to my device, but then again, I couldn't be sure. If authorities thought it was an accident, they might not even look too hard. There was so much debris to sift through the odds were in my favor. Unless the target was shady or known to be involved in illicit activities, a quick scan would be all authorities cared to do.

Sure enough, this blast was determined an accidental death. Many factors played in my favor; the neighborhood was not on any radar, and in the early nineties, bombings weren't much on law enforcement's radar either.

* * *

A kiss on my lips was an enticing way to take me out of my slumber. I must have really been knocked out because I had some drool on me, and the sun was already on its way down. My body knew it was time to shut down, and after smoking some weed and a couple of drinks, my body gave in.

"Babe, you looked so peaceful sleeping until you began moving around like you tend to do. I thought a soft kiss would help ease you out of your sleep. We're you having one of those dreams?"

"Yes, I was, but it was not as bad as the others, or at least that's what I think," I said to Paola.

I didn't want to, nor could I, explain to her what I was dreaming about. I called them dreams, and that was what I told myself. It was easier and more functional for me to dismiss or deny what I just relived in my dreams. I would go as far as to say I was haunted by my dreams, but *haunted* in regards to a foreshadowing of something to happen in my future. At times my sleep would be interrupted by what my mind saw. I never dreamed like this back home, but now when I had more time to relax my mind, the dreams became more frequent. As I took certain drugs, my mind was more at ease to let thoughts and feelings enter it. My dreams consisted of things I hadn't ever thought of. Sometimes they were events I already forgot about, sometimes old friends or associates that passed on. At times I felt like I was being haunted. What was the most frightening was that events in my present triggered events from my past. Sometimes they were events that were about to happen or would happen. I would find myself trying to piece together the dreams after I had them and then try to figure out where they made sense in my present. I didn't know if they were premonitions, a blessing, a curse, or karma. My unconscious state was wrestling with my past and, at times, haunting my present while foreshadowing my future. I was given reminders of who I am, who I was, and who I was becoming. There were times when I dreaded going to sleep. Partying with drugs helped me at times, allowing me to sleep, but the other side was, when I would take hallucinogens, the outcome wouldn't always be favorable for me, opening my mind up. There was a drug called Nubain that worked well but was highly addictive. Nubain is in the opiate family and is quite effective. Bodybuilders would use it to train through injuries, doctors used it for pain management, and I used it after weeks of straight partying. I wanted uninterrupted rest, and Nubain allowed me to sleep straight through and not dream or wake up. It wasn't a drug to do regularly; I did it a few times a year.

I kissed Paola back, letting her know she could wake me up like that anytime. We gathered our belongings, and my mind was still trying to understand why I had that dream of over seven years ago. I hadn't even thought of that bombing since the night I completed it.

Decisions we have made in our past have lasting results that affect our lives as we proceed through it. One key to living with the decisions we make, at least for me, is to make intelligent, well thought-out decisions, to weigh all the possible outcomes, to balance the risk-to-reward factor, and to then own your decision, good, bad, or indifferent. I have made my decisions without regret. Regret forces the mind into the past without the ability to focus forward. For me, regret will sidetrack me, and if I live in the past, it can turn out deadly for me, not conducive to my survival at all. Perhaps there will be a day when my mind goes to those what-ifs, but not now and not anytime in the near future. I've owned each and every one of my decisions and have no regrets.

I had now been in Cancun for about six months and had a follow-up meeting with Sebastian. He let me know he was in need of more ecstasy, and we needed to square away our previous balance. We met again at Sebastian's house. I made it down to his house and knocked on his door.

"T——, come on in, my brother. How are you?" Sebastian and I hugged each other, and he was apparently very happy to see me and vice versa.

"I see you've been busy rebuilding your home," I said, seeing that Sebastian had been doing some major changes to his house.

"Yes, I have. I'm thinking of starting a family in the next few years, so I'm preparing for that. I'll need more room here, that's for sure."

"Well, you're doing a great job, and I certainly want to see the finished product when you're done."

"That you will. Come, let's sit down and have a drink. What can I get for you?"

"A beer and tequila if you have it," I said as if Sebastian didn't have tequila.

Sebastian laughed out loud, knowing what I had just asked was a funny thought and meant in that manner. A dark beer and tequila poured, Sebastian and I had our small talk. I was getting the feeling that Sebastian wanted to tell me something, but the words weren't coming out of his mouth.

"Sebastian, is there something you want to tell me?" I said, breaking up the small talk.

"Yes, there is. T——, I think there might be a problem," Sebastian said almost sheepishly.

"What kind of problem is that?" I asked now that Sebastian had my full attention.

"There seems to be a problem with Joaquin," Sebastian said the name and then sat back as I was running through emotions in my mind.

Joaquin was a man in his early twenties that worked the night-club scene but also partied a lot with me. I'd known him for a couple of years now, and he spent a good portion of the past six months partying with me. Joaquin was a slight man, had dark hair, and always dressed well but not one for reaching into his pocket when the bill came around.

"Joaquin, what about Joaquin?' I asked now with curiosity.

"Joaquin wanted to speak to you and tell you himself. He said his uncle had a message he wanted delivered. Joaquin was hesitant in conveying the message and came to me to ask me my advice. He knew you and I were close and didn't know how to approach you. Joaquin doesn't know you supply me, just that we were mutual friends."

"Who's Joaquin's uncle?" I said, hardly being able to hold back my brewing anger.

"The chief of the judicial federal," Sebastian said, half not wanting to tell me.

Sebastian made it clear that he had nothing to do with any of this. Sebastian had everything to lose and nothing to gain in betraying or setting me up. I wasn't going to show Sebastian my true feelings, although I was sure some were so close to the surface that he knew how I felt. Nobody wants to get a message second- or third-hand, let alone someone in my line of work. Sebastian knew this all too well himself.

"A message, huh? Joaquin never told me of this uncle. No problem, though. I'll speak with Joaquin and see what this message is."

"T——, be careful. I don't trust Joaquin and, least of all, his uncle."

"Thank you for your concern and the heads-up. So let's round out our business. I'll handle Joaquin and his uncle."

Sebastian and I concluded our business with me getting paid the balance for the ecstasy I left him some months back and me leaving him another bundle of five hundred pills. We finished our drinks, and no other word of Joaquin came about. We spoke about family and other aspects of our growing friendship.

Sebastian and I parted ways, and I could feel the anger on my face. The anger slowly started to turn to a sly smile as I formulated the resolution to my new issue. This was my way in. Never look a gift horse in the mouth, and patience is most certainly a commodity in high demand. I thought to myself, *Killing two birds with one stone, so to speak.* Sometimes in life you're given gifts, and then there are gifts on a silver platter. I accepted my silver platter.

A few days passed before I reached out to Joaquin on a local pay phone. I let a couple of days pass to formulate the best plan and calculate my words without emotion. I wanted to make sure the information I received from Sebastian was on point and do some more digging into Joaquin and his uncle. I had the information that Armando gave me about the chief, but now armed with this new twist, I needed to delve deeper into the chief to see all the angles.

"Hey, it's me," I said into the receiver of the pay phone, having dialed Joaquin's telephone number.

I didn't want any names over any open telephone line. I learned that as a kid in New York. Never, under any circumstances, speak about anything of note regarding business or anything that could place me to any criminal or criminal activities.

"Not too bad. I saw our friend and got your message," I said with no change of inflection in my voice.

There was a pause in Joaquin's response time, but he couldn't hold back his reaction, stuttering a bit, and I calmed him with my reaction.

"So what's this message?" I said matter-of-factly. "Two thousand a month?" I asked, wanting Joaquin to repeat what he just told me.

"Tell him I'm interested in meeting, and you set it up. My only condition is that you be there when we meet. I don't know your uncle, and I would feel more comfortable if you were there to facilitate the meeting. I'll call you tomorrow morning to get all the information from you."

Joaquin's entire demeanor was now of comfort and confidence. Being that he didn't hear anything out of the ordinary, he agreed with everything I said in hopes he and his uncle would get whatever it was they wanted.

"Hey, brother, thank you for all your help. One word of advice, don't use the phone to convey the message. I suggest you see him in person. There are too many ears listening. All right, thank you again, brother. I owe you one," I said, making it sound as if he were doing me the favor.

Owe him one indeed. Shake me down! I'd never been shook down in my life, and I'd be damned if I'd be shook down here in Mexico by a two-bit cop trying to be a gangster. From what I had gathered, this cop, fed, agent, whatever, somehow got wind I was selling ecstacy. Since the information and message came from Joaquin, then Joaquin was the one I'd hold responsible. The old adage "Don't shoot the messenger." No problem—I wouldn't.

I called the following morning, as was scheduled. Joaquin was quite full of himself. In his mind he had facilitated the deal where it squared him with his uncle and ingratiated him to me for making the connection. Joaquin gave me the information that ten that evening worked for the meeting. The location was a restaurant where the gluttonous chief would feel like he were on his own turf, knowing the location and being familiar with its surroundings. I knew the location as well and thought it to be ideal for what I had in mind. I knew the chief would be coming with Joaquin, and I was told that he would be with the chief's driver as well. So now there were three in total that I knew I had to contend with. Typically in Mexico, men of authority, power, or status have a driver, so this third person was almost a foregone conclusion. The driver doubled as their security, although I had yet to meet a driver in Mexico that was able to secure a damn thing. The chief's driver was one of his underlings, so I expected some level of competency but nothing that made me overly concerned.

Now that I had the details of the meeting that evening, I began hashing out my plan and finalizing the details. My preparation had already begun with some surveillance of the chief and his driver. I saw their mannerisms and demeanor firsthand. They were a cocky bunch, having little regard for public displays of power and dominance. The driver was in his midforties, six feet tall, with a bit of a protruding stomach. The chief was shorter in stature and carried himself as if he were ten feet tall. With a thick mustache, the chief looked like he never missed a meal in his life. The couple of days of surveillance prior to me making the initial call to Joaquin revealed that restaurants were key to what this group was doing. They either met at them or shook them down or both. The chief had his hand in a lot of different pies, and his brute show of force mixed with his job title left people little alternative but to heed his demands. While this job for Armando meant one thing, for me it meant another. It wasn't important for me to let Armando know I had a personal stake in this; rather, I would let him think I was doing this solely for him and whomever was pulling Armando's strings.

Right after my call with Joaquin, I went for a meeting with Sebastian. Trust among people is typically a one-way street; trust among criminals is a foolish endeavor. Having someone with something to lose, who was partially invested, and as the saying goes, has "a dog in the fight" gave me more insurance that he or she wouldn't betray me. Sebastian already gave me the heads-up about the chief and Juaquin, which so far he had been right on point. Sebastian benefitted from me prospering, and I didn't see a move where it would be the other way around. Sebastian and I had a great business relationship, and on a personal side, we saw eye to eye on all matters. My purpose on stopping by to see him was to ensure his loyalty was intact and that he had some of his chips in the pot.

Sebastian was going to assist me without even realizing or understanding my motive. He was indebted to me already, and the deal I had made for him was sweet. His part wasn't totally necessary, but it was enough to have him involved and his silence in place.

Back at my condo, I was preparing for the evening's festivities. My preparation began hours before the rendezvous. I knew what my targets looked liked, knew the restaurant layout, researched all the possible routes to and from the restaurant, and attempted to compute every possible scenario. I retrieved my tools for the evening. Uncovering the safe and opening it, I stared at its contents. I withdrew a block of C-4 from the bottom of the safe. I also withdrew a small clock, some wiring, the new SIG Sauer .380, two loaded magazine clips, and two silencers. I had a hefty magnet in the closet that I was going to use to attach the explosives to and my trusty masking tape in case I needed that for any sort of backup. I knew I would have little time to place the explosives, so time would be my biggest enemy this evening. I didn't believe the gun was necessary, but I needed that with me just in case. I didn't know if I was going to get another crack at these guys and wanted to make sure I had not only a solid plan but also a backup plan just in case. My backup plan had to be just a solid as my plan A. I was heading into some unknowns with these people, so I couldn't rely on just one means to complete my work. The chief was no idiot, and he had been proven to be a survivor in this jungle.

Now for my dress. I had a standard-issue outfit I used, which was something dark, preferably black and long sleeve. I certainly needed something to cover my head and, sometimes, face. In this instance, a nondescript hat would do the trick. I had a thin pair of black gloves that I needed to not show the color of my skin as well as to not leave a fingerprint to trace my identity with. I completed my outfit with black tennis sneakers devoid of any logo or markings. I couldn't forget my St. Jude's medal, something I never took off and something I knew I would be leaning heavily on this very evening. I placed all my items in a black satchel and wouldn't return home until business was handled one way or another. I would be gone all day, so I packed plenty of food and water. I needed to be sharp and on point and not have my mind thinking about food or drink.

Watching the chief in his natural habitat was key to figuring out how to complete my work. The drive to Lopez Portillo Boulevard wasn't too hectic. A straight shot for me from the hotel zone, and I was there. Thank God for air-conditioning because today was a scorcher out. I parked my car on the opposite side of the street from the PJF (Policia Judicial Federal) headquarters. The distance was about seventy-five yards away, giving me full view of the headquarters and whoever came and went. It wasn't quite noon yet, near guaranteeing that the chief wouldn't be at his office just yet.

The PJF building was concrete, taking up a majority of the block. When I saw this structure, the only word that came to my mind was *bunker*. The left side of this structure was equipped with an underground entrance. Four-foot-by-three-foot concrete pillars staggered the length of the building minus the entranceway leading under the building. The pillars were placed to prevent a vehicle or otherwise from crashing into the building. For good measure, there were two guards at the entranceway to the underground and one guard at the front entrance. The guards were in a uniform of all green and looked every bit the menacing deterrent. Armed with MP5 machine guns at the ready, they had the demeanor of being on high alert. One more guard with the same dress, armament, and demeanor guarded the large double doors to the front entranceway. Just above his head and the archway were bold capital letters PJF.

I had a small pair of binoculars that fit in the palm of my hand in case I needed to get a close-up of anything. I had a pretty good vantage point, but the added clarity of vision was a blessing. The front of the building had two SUVs parked, which only blocked part of my view but nothing that was going to interfere with sight.

Just shy of two hours passed, and a green SUV pulled up to the front of the headquarters. It turned down the driveway, but only halfway, before stopping on the downgrade. The SUV didn't alarm any of the men guarding the building; on the contrary, the men expected the SUV to be arriving, at least that was what their body language was showing. The dark tint of the SUV's windows concealed its occupants, but apparently, they were known to the guards. The driver's door opened, and a man in his midforties opened the door. He moved around to the passenger side front door and opened it. I couldn't see who had exited the passenger side of the SUV. I put my binoculars up to my eyes to see if I could get a glimpse of the passenger. Before I could see who emerged, the guard on the passenger side snapped to attention. The passenger door opened, and at first I couldn't see who it was, and then the figure who emerged was easily noticeable by the protruding belly that cascaded over his beltline. The arrogance of his walk was unmistakably that of the chief of the federal police. The SUV was neither under the building nor in the street, signifying to me that the chief's stay at the headquarters would be short.

The fat fuck had arrived and was now on my radar, with the showdown imminent; so far, so good. The only one missing was the piss-ant nephew of his, Joaquin. I never made my work personal until my personal life, self-preservation, and assignment intersected.

Thirty-five minutes since my target entered the headquarters, four agents exited the front of the building, and down about half the block just behind the SUVs, they entered a red Chevy Impala with tinted-out windows. With two agents in the front and two in the back, the Impala pulled out and double-parked exactly in front of the headquarters. Not too long after, the chief emerged with his bodyguard taking the lead. The bodyguard opened the door to the passenger side of the chief's SUV, closed it, and got behind the wheel. As the car backed out of the space, the chief took the lead with the red Impala following behind as their wheels began to roll.

I pulled out from my parking vantage point, driving down Lopez Portillo Boulevard parallel to the chief and his cronies. The next traffic light, I was able to make a U-turn, always keeping a steady eye on the two vehicles that just passed me. I sped up, positioning myself fifty yards behind the red Impala. It was much easier to follow two cars than it was one; they were making my job a lot easier. I was never more than about five car lengths behind the two vehicles at any time. They might be greedy cops, but they were still cops with instincts.

Most of my day was spent watching the crew bounce from one location to the next. They collected their shakedown payments, visited other locations, intimidated others, "investigated" locations, and gorged themselves with food they didn't ever have a bill for.

The number of agents the chief traveled with was a normal occurrence, from what I gathered. I didn't know if it had always been the case or if it were a result of the two immigration agents that I had previously dispatched with. I did find it odd that the chief was out handling his business personally. Perhaps he was a control freak, perhaps he didn't trust any of his crew to do the right thing, or perhaps he wanted everyone to know who was in charge, especially in light of his two allies being gunned down. Losing people, in that fashion, that are supposed to be under your protection leads others to perhaps have independent thought. For a man like the chief, perceived lack of power, control, and strength can be a fatal perception. Weakness and vulnerability aren't conducive to staying on top or continuing to breathe. I didn't see the chief as the type of man to simply retire or relinquish anything without going out in a blaze of glory. Get caught slipping, and you just might find yourself on the front page of the *Cancun Gazette*, sprawled out in a pool of your own blood.

The sun began its descent below the horizon, and with the heat slowly declining, the chief and his posse returned to their lair. Another session of sit, watch, and wait was in store.

At 7:30 p.m., the sun well tucked away, my vantage point was clouded by the darkness that had since fallen. I could see the target vehicles still in the same position as they had been since returning. I was growing concerned that my prey had exited through another way or without me seeing them.

By 7:47 p.m., I saw two men strutting down the front steps to the headquarters and into the chief's vehicle. The ritual was the same as the chief had with his bodyguard: one man held the door open for the other then went to the driver's side to get behind the wheel. Even with my binoculars, I was still only 90 percent sure it was the duo I was supposed to be meeting with later in the evening. Now, I was certain these two were on the move yet again. This time, it was just the two lone men and nobody else in tow. The time line was still in effect except for Joaquin not yet with his uncle. There was still plenty of time left before our scheduled meeting, so no sense in a change of plan.

It was 8:19 p.m., and the SUV I was tailing made it to the restaurant where the meeting was set to take place. The chief and bodyguard were quite early, but still, there was no sign of Joaquin. I passed them by as the bodyguard was parking the SUV right in front of the restaurant. I didn't stop my car but passed them by, looking for an advantageous parking location across from the eatery. Just as the occupants exited the vehicle, I confirmed that these were the ones I had been following during the day. I now had the visual confirmation I needed. Who appeared to be the manager of the restaurant met the chief and his bodyguard at the front entrance to the restaurant, and there was a brief conversation before the manager led the two a table just outside the double doors separating the inside and outside seating of the restaurant. I had been driving by slowly enough to notice the movements of the two but not enough to be noticed. I drove around the block one time, looking for the ideal place to park.

The spot I wanted and thought most ideal was taken. There was a spot about one car behind the space I wanted and not too much off the mark. I parked my car on the opposite side of the street. I didn't notice any hit squad or countersurveillance I thought the chief might have had lying in wait for me, but there was nothing so far. There was plenty of time to still have some of his minions arrive, though. I knew the premise of us meeting was to arrange a payment schedule for the shakedown, but I didn't know if the chief had an ulterior motive or not.

The chief was a good hour and a half plus early for the meeting, so this was the first red flag for me. The second was, Joaquin was nowhere to be seen yet. The side of the street I parked on was a series of businesses, most of which were closed, which left scattered parking on both sides of the street. The left of the restaurant was a flower shop, and the other bookend to the restaurant was a mobile phone business. There was just enough foot traffic to not give me away but enough where my line of sight wasn't crowded. Most stores and businesses were closed or in the midst of closing, and by the types of businesses that were here, most would be closed when the scheduled meeting was to take place. As this was going to be a little more public than I cared, my options were limited, and time wasn't my ally. There was a good chance someone would see me or, at the very least, remember me for a later interview with the authorities.

At 8:32 p.m., Joaquin came striding into the restaurant. A minor sense of relief came over me. I wasn't going to call this off at all; it would've only made my circumstances on all sides more complicated. Joaquin sat at the chief's table with his back to the street. Food had been ordered, and the beers swilled between the three.

By 8:47 p.m., I noticed three beautiful women walking the street, approaching the restaurant. The SUV was blocking my full view but just for a few brief moments. As the three lovelies came into view, I saw them enter the restaurant, and the three men I was watching got up and moved some chairs around so the women could sit down with them. The chief ushered over the manager, and shortly thereafter, a waiter showed up with more drinks for all. The three women were dressed in various lengths of short skirts and short tops, showing as much skin as was tolerable for public consumption. From their four-inch-plus heels to their well-styled hair, these women meant business.

At 9:17 p.m., forty-three minutes away from our scheduled meeting, a second round of drinks was ordered for the girls. I reached my right hand behind the passenger's seat of my car and grabbed ahold of the black satchel I placed there when I left my condo this morning. I unzipped it while looking around to make sure there were no wandering eyes on me. Nothing was out of the ordinary, or at least nothing had changed since I first arrived at the restaurant. Slipping on a pair of thin black gloves, I began my final stages of preparation. I peered into my bag of goodies, and without withdrawing anything, I went to work. Attaching the receiver for remote detonation to the C-4 wasn't difficult. To the other side of the C-4, I mounted a large powerful magnet enabling my explosives to be placed solidly on any metallic surface without concern it would disengage in an inopportune time. The chief's SUV had a particularly strategic location for placing my device. I did my homework on the placement and, in one instance, did a walk-by, peeking at the undercarriage. The SUV was lifted enough off the ground for me to slide under the rear of the SUV and attach my device to the metallic undercarriage. I had little time to work with once I made my move to place the device. Everything had to be done here in my car prior to the placement. I withdrew the C-4, .380, one silencer, and one magazine clip. Keeping my eyes peeled and without looking at what I was doing, I attached the silencer with ease, counting the number 4 in my head. Four full turns, and the silencer was safely in position on the end of the barrel. I loaded the clip into place and racked a bullet in the chamber. I placed the gun in my holster at the small of my back and continued on with the process, now that my plan B was ready just in case plan A went horribly wrong. I withdrew the now-fitted bomb and placed that at my feet, out of the view of a wood-be onlooker. I zipped up my satchel and placed it back behind the passenger's seat. Looking at the table of the chief, bodyguard, and their newfound lady friends, I noticed everyone's attention was directed at one another. The ladies were engaged in cozy conversations, having now coupled up with each of the three men. Joaquin didn't look like someone that was simply conveying a message; he was an active participant in this scheme to shake me down. It mattered not at this point; my mission was clear, my mind focused, and my hands steady.

I would need more protection this evening than I did on most any other. I needed comfort and calm. I slowed my breathing, took a few sips of water, and with my right hand, firmly took hold of my St. Jude's medal, holding it in the palm of my hand. My eyes closed, I prayed.

"Sacred heart of Jesus, have mercy on me. St. Jude, worker of miracles, pray for me. St. Jude, helper and keeper of the hopeless, pray for me."

At nine twenty-five, I pulled the black hat down over my head and face a little bit more, snug enough to not fall off as easily and low enough to cover some facial features. I picked the C-4 off the floor and tucked it under my shirt. I exited the car, looking around briefly, pretending I was checking for traffic before crossing the street. All my acts I wanted to appear normal and smooth. I took my time, waiting for the traffic to pass me by. I saw headlights approaching and got an idea. As the approaching car was just about upon me, I began walking out, using it as cover so that the line of sight from the restaurant to me was blocked. I crossed the street without notice, and my timing was spot-on. I reached the SUV, crouching down just a few inches so as to make sure I wasn't seen by anyone inside the restaurant. I knew that the trio's attention in the restaurant was directed at the women and not much else. It was the wandering eye I couldn't factor in. Crouched now, I pretended to be tying my shoelace and took a final look around. With nothing out of place, I dropped to one knee, reached under my shirt, and withdrew the bomb. I pulled out a small antenna from the side of the receiver attached to the top of the bomb. With a small click, I felt the bomb leave my hand and attach itself to the undercarriage of the chief's SUV. It was directly under the gas tank, which I knew would make the explosion that much more intense. My heart rate was steady and my nerves even-keeled. The antenna was about three inches long when fully extended but thin and very hard to see, especially in the evening. I stood up nearly fully, and the entire process of attaching the device took about fifteen seconds. The full sense of the phrase "Calm, cool, and collected" fitted me well.

It was 9:29 p.m., and I was back at my car, opened my door, and turned on the ignition. As cool as I was, I was still sweating a bit and needed the air-conditioning to bring my core temperature down. I reached behind the passenger's seat and unzipped the satchel. In my bag of tricks, I withdrew a throwaway cell phone and attached a one-use-only throwaway SIM card. There was one call I wanted to make, and I needed to make it while still having eyes on my prey. This now was the most important time. I couldn't let these three out of my sight because if I lost them and the device was found, it would make my chances for a successful second hit significantly harder. It would also alert my prey to the fact that it was I who was after them, and it will put my life in jeopardy.

"Hey, it's me. I know the meeting is set for 10:00 p.m., but with this traffic, I won't make it in time. I have an idea. The way leading to the hotel zone is clear, and it won't take you long to get out this way. How about I get a table at Café Cubano and we enjoy ourselves there? I can set up a table, drinks, and supply the party favors. I also brought with me a payment so we can all start off on the right foot."

I watched Joaquin's face the entire time. I knew that changing the meeting place and time would be touchy, but to attract them was a free party that might do the trick. I didn't want to show my face at the restaurant, especially in light of what was about to go down, so I figured this could be the best solution to my plan.

"I don't think that'll be a problem at all. Let me ask."

Joaquin covered the receiver while I saw him convey my message to the chief. The chief's facial expression was first pissed off, and then as Joaquin's words continued, the chief looked comfortable. I saw the chief nod in agreement with the change of plans.

"No problem. We'll see you there. We'll close this out and then head on over."

The payday and party were too tempting to not agree to. The gluttonous group couldn't turn down free party favors, drinks, Cuban women, and money. A false sense of security, inflated ego, pride, gluttony, and an overall belief that one is at the top of the food chain are optimal breeding grounds for the tumbling from power. The chief had all these qualities in spades. He ran around Cancun imposing his authority without impunity, and other agencies gave him plenty of leeway. The chief was ruthless and created a lot of enemies, the problem being his enemies were too weak to act on their hatred and too scared to defend themselves. Those people that were unaware of their weaknesses made easier targets.

Café Cubano was a small jazz club just inside the hotel zone from downtown. It was near the party zone and had some amazing Cuban beauties that serviced the clientele—*serviced* was the operative word. I chose Café Cubano as the spot because I didn't want the women who were currently sitting at the chief's table to accompany them. I made sure Sebastian ingrained in the women not to get in the SUV with the men, just some drinks at the one location. This party I had planned for the trio was by invitation only.

"Great, I'll have everything prepared for you guys when you arrive," I said, watching Joaquin and the other two men laugh and carry on.

I saw the three men excuse themselves from the table and from the ladies. I cut my engine off so they would not need to look in my direction at hearing an engine run. No check paid, and the trio headed for the SUV. I breathed a sigh of relief that Joaquin joined the bodyguard and his uncle. Now, this hurdle had been overcome, but I wasn't out of the woods yet. I had never used C-4 before, and this was a hell of a way to experiment with it. I was familiar with how to use it, but this was some serious on-the-job training.

By 10:04 p.m., four minutes after my regularly scheduled meeting with this bunch, the SUV's engine turned over, and the wheels began to move. I slumped down in the seat of my car and made sure my hat was pulled down enough to shield my face from any outside view. I eased my right hand forward and turned on the ignition to my car and waited for the SUV to leave its parking space. Once it was on the move, I sat up, put on my seat belt, put on my left-turn signal, and pulled out, making a short U-turn to follow the SUV. I blasted the air-conditioning and made sure all vents were squarely on me. The target SUV was ahead of me, approximately thirty yards ahead, and there were three cars in between us. I could make out the top of the SUV above the other cars and used it as my beacon through the traffic. The bodyguard was still a cop, and I didn't want to spook him in any way, so I kept my distance. We came to a stop, and I used this pause to reach behind the passenger seat and grab ahold of my satchel. I opened the satchel and withdrew a small metal box about four inches by three inches and about three inches deep. The top of the box had a small light and switch. From the front of the box I withdrew an antenna of about three inches. Traffic picked back up, and my wheels followed suit.

I clearly saw over the Volkswagen Beetle in front of me the SUV's roof, which was making a right-hand turn. I could feel my pulse quicken as I lost sight of the SUV as it turned. I was too far away to remote-detonate, and now even if I could, I needed to have a visual. It took me a full minute until I was able to make the right-hand turn, the same as the SUV had done. My heart dropped as I made the turn and there was no SUV in sight. I knew where the SUV was going because I set the location, but there was more than one route to take. I sped down, passing two blocks, turned right down a two-lane roadway, came upon another light, and turned right past a large apartment building. As I turned right, I saw the SUV and exhaled with delight. The SUV was now two cars in front of me and was switching lanes. I applied my foot to the gas pedal and began my pursuit. This stretch of road opened up a bit and would last about a mile until it intersected with the main road to the hotel zone. I knew there was one last light at the corner intersection that the SUV would have to take. If all went right, that would be my kill zone.

One hundred yards to the their final turn, I placed the detonator in my lap, keeping my eyes glued on my quarry. I began to close the distance and took hold of the detonator box with my left hand, steadying the steering wheel with my right.

Fifty yards, and I closed in behind the SUV, making sure no other car would interfere with my work. I was also trying my best to not have much collateral damage. I was making sure no other cars came between me and the SUV. While there might just be other casualties besides those in the SUV, I couldn't concern myself with that. We were going about forty-five miles an hour and knew our speed would have to soon slow down ahead of the turn. Sure enough, with the traffic light now coming into full view, our speed began slowing. Forty, thirty-five, thirty, twenty-five, twenty, fifteen, ten, and the SUV came at a full halt in the far right lane, waiting to make the turn down the main boulevard. I was now about twenty yards behind when I stopped my wheels. I flipped the switch to the detonator to see the green light turn on. Just as the SUV's wheels made their turn, I pressed the button, being at what I thought was a safe distance of twenty yards behind the SUV. In the same instance, the C-4 was ignited, and the loudest noise that I'd ever heard rung my eardrums.

The SUV jumped in the air, lifting in a fiery explosion. Lifting a good fifteen feet in the air, it was split in two, jackknifing and spewing shrapnel in all directions. I felt pieces of the jackknifing SUV hit my car. I could see the entire inside of the SUV was engulfed in flames as it began its fatal descent back to the ground.

A car approaching the scene in the left lane next to me locked up its brakes, skidding over the median, landing its axle half on and half off the road. Parts of the SUV surpassed the height of the traffic light, touching the burning metal to the wires of the light.

As it careened to the ground, three of the SUV's wheels were on fire as the fourth blew clear off or melted; I couldn't quite see where it was. What appeared to be Joaquin fell out of the backseat. I say "appeared to be" because I couldn't tell any physical appearance, just that it was the backseat, and Joaquin was the only one back there, so I assumed it to be his burning body. There wasn't any motion to the burning body as the fire sucked the life out of him. About a full minute or so passed as the wreckage and debris settled into place.

I accelerated a little and gave enough birth to the burning wreckage as I pulled alongside parallel to what was once the driver's side of the SUV. What was left of the bodyguard was on fire and motionless. The chief didn't fare much better, as parts of him were blown in all directions. I felt some shrapnel hit my car again as there was another minor burst coming from the SUV. I wasn't concerned with any damage my car took, just only with making it away from the scene. I drove on, weaving my way around burning debris and body parts. Nothing was recognizable, not a body or even the make of the SUV. All I could think to myself was *Damn, that C-4 is some powerful shit. My old-school black powder's got nothing on this stuff. If I had this back in New York, I would've probably been on America's most wanted.*

My work was completed, what with twisted, burning metal in all directions along with three burning bodies. I didn't make eye contact with any other pedestrians or people inside vehicles. I didn't think anyone else was injured or killed, but I couldn't be sure. I wasn't sticking around to figure any of that out either. I was going to leave those stories to the newspapers.

Two birds with one stone, I thought as I made my right turn and headed back to my condo. The visual of the trio not too long ago at the restaurant, having fun, toasting to one another, and plotting on me put a smile on my face. Now the visual of them, their burning bodies, was priceless.

Clipping a Romeo y Julieta, I puffed my way back to my condo. I stopped near my condo to inspect my car under a streetlight. I heard my car take on some damage and wanted to see what damage it incurred. From the brief near-midnight inspection I spotted some dings in my paint job but nothing that stood out or could be attributed to the flaming crime scene downtown. The morning sunshine might reveal other issues, but for now, I was confident none of the damage could link me to bombing. Stowing away my gear in my safe was the first order of business. I showered up with a nice long, steady stream of hot water. I fixed myself something to eat, smoked some weed, and had myself a stiff drink, taking in the evening moonlight before turning into bed.

The next day, I had a small get-together at my condo. My typical get-togethers were usually women in various stages of undress. A couple of my male "friends" joined in, partaking in smoking some weed, dropping ecstasy, eating psychedelic mushrooms, taking acid, and/or drinking. There was always a smorgasbord of drugs to be had and never a lack of variety or quantity. This day, I limited myself to smoking some weed and having a drink. I didn't want to be out of sorts as I had a feeling that I would be hearing from Armando, and I wanted a semicleared head, keeping my wits about me. I would get into the other festivities when I knew I could truly enjoy it.

Not too far into the afternoon, and the distinctive ring of my *work* phone rang. I excused myself from my guests to answer the phone. Out on the balcony and with the door closed, I answered.

"Yeah. Thirty minutes? Good," I said, always wanting to keep words short on the phone, especially this phone.

I hung up the phone and stared off into the blue sky before opening the sliding glass balcony door, taking a moment to process the dialogue and tone of voice I just heard. Armando's voice and inflections gave me some cause to be concerned. I was hoping that this wasn't one of those times where the powers that be attempted to decide or had already decided whether I was an asset or I was a liability. Continuing to be needed was the key, but not knowing if I was was the gray area. The best I could do was strap up, say a prayer, and meet Armando.

I retrieved my .380 and silencer from my safe, loaded a full magazine, chambered my first round, screwed on a silencer, and placed it in my holster on the small of my back. I went to say good-bye to Paola. I put on sneakers, had on swim trunks and a T-shirt that covered my gun, and quietly excused myself from the party.

As I stepped onto the concrete outside my building, the heat from the sun intensified as it bounced off the pavement. Immediately I put on a pair of sunglasses to keep the glare of the sun from affecting my vision.

Across the street, past our assigned parking spaces, next to the newly built mall was a dark black SUV. The SUV had tinted windows that screamed some type of law enforcement. As it idled in the heat, I assumed this would be my rendezvous.

Reaching for the door handle of the passenger side of the SUV, I opened it carefully. As I did, I saw the usual smiling face of Armando but with his finger to his mouth signifying for me not to talk. That's the universal code meaning someone may be listening and to not say anything of note, if anything at all. I followed his lead as I closed the door behind me and Armando drove off.

Less than five minutes of a very eerie drive, of which the only sounds came from the radio playing loudly, and we were at a deserted beach cove. In between two dunes with a view of the ocean, Armando put the SUV in park, turned off the engine, and exited the vehicle. I waited for Armando to exit first. I didn't know what was going on and didn't want to turn my back on him. His actions were making me concerned, the same concern I was trying to escape back in New York. We were in between a couple of hotel properties that were in the middle of being constructed. It wasn't until we were well clear of the SUV that Armando began to speak. The entire drive, my focus was on Armando's movements, hands, and anything out of the ordinary.

"I didn't want to speak in the car." Armando broke the ice.

Well, that was quite evident, I thought but still wanted to hear what it was that had Armando on high alert.

"Getting paranoid?" I said in jest, trying to put a smile on Armando's face.

"Not paranoid. Cautious, especially after last night," Armando said quite quickly.

Armando was neither smiling nor in a joyous mood. We were always able to find levity in everything, even in stressful times, which was why this was a concerning moment for me.

"What about last night?" I said, wanting Armando to speak frankly and come right out with whatever it was that he wasn't yet sharing.

"The spectacle last night was a bit public, and the fact that a civilian was among those deceased is involving interest from other authorities. The initial inquiries are coming in from some unusual places," Armando said but still with not a lot of clarity and showing me the front page of the *Cancun Gazette*.

I took the newspaper from Armando's hand and began to read the front-page article. It was in bold letters, the English version, "Another two federal agents murdered this year and in a violent fashion." It went on to say, "This time, civilians were murdered as well. The violence is seeping into our everyday lives." Again, the gazette showed the carnage of the last evening and did so in typical grand form. It was almost what was in my mind's eye that I saw firsthand.

"Spectacle? No offense, but what did you expect when C-4 is involved? I had never used this stuff before, but I knew it wasn't going to be pretty, and you knew it as well. As far as the civilian, that's collateral damage, as far as I'm concerned, and a bonus on my part," I said to Armando, making sure he knew my tone was direct and serious.

"I'm not blaming you for anything or criticizing the manner in which it was done, but why was the civilian a bonus?" Armando's tone and mood changed; he was now curious.

"That was the chief's nephew Joaquin. He and his uncle had a plan to shake me down and extort me. Joaquin was no innocent bystander, and he was my bonus. It was my way in to make sure I could handle the job for you. The chief would have been near impossible to get to, especially as quickly as I was able. His crew was always around, and they were deep in number. You know that more than anyone. The other civilian that was killed, well, that's just tough luck. Now I came here to get away from craziness, not change locations and have the same craziness."

"Hey, like I said, I'm not criticizing you or how you went about your business. I'm just talking here friend to friend. We're trying to figure out how to deal with the fallout and why my people are getting immediate and enormous pressure."

"Armando, you knew I came here to start a new life. This is not the life I wanted to live. Yes, selling ecstasy was part of it but not all the extra crap. I love doing favors as you know, but that's really it. I want to be left out of whatever it is that is going on. You're my friend until the end, and I'm depending on you to cover my ass and keep me safe. I, in turn, will do the same for you. This is why I took the work you asked of me. Since the day we met, I never said no to you and always followed through. I'm in a foreign land here and have enough issues back home. I prefer not compounding them here. My suggestion is to use some of those press contacts you have and flip the story in your favor. I don't know the ins and outs, but have the press link the chief to whatever shady business dealings are appropriate."

I didn't think I had to vocalize my thoughts, but apparently, I did. The first part of Armando's concerns started to sound like a horrible recurring nightmare. I could only hope that a scapegoat wasn't needed, and who the hell was the *we* Armando was referring to?

"I appreciate all you've done, and more than that, I appreciate your friendship above all. I know you wanted a slower pace of life, and I can appreciate that. That's a good idea to use the press in our favor. Thank you for everything, and I'll work my end."

"That's why you're intelligence, and I'm the invisible man," I said with a chuckle, but a serious chuckle.

I wanted Armando to hear me separate our two roles, which seemed to be intersecting—never a good thing. I didn't mind voicing input, but I needed to be in the shadows, where I thrived the most.

We hugged each other, but I was careful for Armando to not feel the weapon at the small of my back. I wanted to get back to my party, and instead of driving back, I told Armando I wanted to walk back. It wasn't far, and I love a good walk. I needed to straighten some things out in my head. What kept returning to my thoughts was what Paola and some others were telling me about a city that was about four hours north of here, Mérida. I had already been in Cancun for close to a year now, and it was past the party season. This would be the opportune time to see another part of Mexico and lie low.

It was becoming clearer to me who would make Armando this on edge. I didn't know for certain, but politics and the cartels had been intertwined in Mexico since the beginning of time. There was also a part of me that knew Armando was no fool and always had a sound plan of action.

Armando being misinformed didn't suit his character. He knew by eliminating the different rungs of the ladder, it would eventually lead to the top. I didn't really care one way or the other. Hopefully, this would be the last of it, and I could blend into the Mexican scene and not be a pawn in anyone's game of chess.

CHAPTER 5

CHANGING TIDES

PROLOGUE

"Yes, Father, I understand. I know to be careful. I've done that and doubled my guard. I know that as well. I've taken another precaution to make sure. You have more to concern yourself with than me. I'm in good hands, Father. Yes, Father, the same one I told you about months ago. Well, Father, let me ask you this: is it better to have someone like him with no ties, no allegiances, no dog in the fight or the usual people we go to that perhaps have hidden agendas, associations, or aspirations? This is what I've been saying, Dad, your presidency is coming to an end, and you need to keep your focus. Franco just came in. He's here. Don't concern yourself with this. I'll handle it and keep you informed if anything transpires. Okay, Dad, we'll talk later. Be safe, and I love you."

Andres's father's presidency had about a year left to it, and change was brewing in Mexico more than ever before and more than most would think possible. Andres's father knew of all the changes firsthand, but even if he were to let them be known, nobody could be prepared for what was to transpire. Many things were happening, and with the millennium just a couple of months away, change was on everyone's mind.

"Franco, tell El Güero to come in, and have him wait for me in the library. I'll be with him shortly."

C H A P T E R 5

CHANGING TIDES

The entrance to the compound was equipped with two steel gates fifteen feet in height and fifteen-foot high walls surrounded by multiple cameras, especially two focused on the steel entranceway itself. I drove up to the call box mounted on the post just shy of the entrance. There was another smaller camera mounted on the call box that moved as I did. Whoever was monitoring the camera had a clear view of me. I reached out and pressed the call button to notify the monitor of my presence. I looked directly into the camera as a voice came through the speaker.

"Yes," a hefty voice behind the call box said.

"I'm here to see Andres. my name is T——," I said, speaking and looking into the camera/microphone.

"Please wait a minute, sir," the voice quickly responded.

A couple of minutes had passed before the same voice came back and said, "Please pull in through the gate and pull directly in front of the house."

As the voice was giving me instructions, I heard a low hum and crackling sound as the steel gates began to open for me to drive through. I applied a little pressure to the gas and eased my way into the gates. The second my car passed, the gates began to close behind me. Ahead was a large fountain with a circular driveway with parking to my right and to my left. There was a huge mansion-like house in the middle of the property. I was told to drive up to the front of the house and not in the parking lot. There were already a number of SUVs and a couple of custom motorcycles parked, with more spaces available. The mansion was an enormous Spanish style, with manicured grounds on both sides. I could tell the property had roaming security along with a multitude of security cameras.

I pulled up the middle of the circle just below the cascading rows of steps leading to the large front entranceway. I cut my engine off and had barely stepped out of my car when two men in soft cream linen suits met me. These were the presidential detail outfits I came to know the first day I met Andres.

"Sir, please come with us. You can leave your car here." The two men waited for me to close the door of my car and follow them.

The stairs to the house numbered twenty, and at the top of the staircase were two large wooden double doors. Opening up, the doors led to a rather large foyer. Directly in front of me was a grand staircase split on either side that met at the top to the rooms on the upper level of the house. There was a room off to my left and another off to my right. The room to my right had double doors that were ajar, and from what I could see, it was the security room and monitoring center. The room to my left was where I was ushered into. It looked like a library or a study of some kind. Bookshelves lined the walls along with various pieces of art and art sculptures. The art sculptures looked like Mayan art, but then again, my knowledge of this type of art was limited, to say the least. The bookshelves appeared to be oak, which was special for this region; there were not a lot of oak trees in the Yucatán Peninsula. The light fixtures, paint, huge oak desk, and high-back leather chairs rounded out the class and elegance of the study.

"Sir, please wait here." The larger of the two security details pointed for me to wait inside and closed the door behind me, leaving me alone in the room.

I was admiring all the works of art and the collection of books when I heard a friendly voice I recognized. I turned to see Andres. It had been some months since I last saw him, and it appeared he was quite happy to see me.

"T——, my friend, long time no see," Andres greeted me affectionately with much elation.

I handed Andres a box of his favorite cigars, Cuban Cohíba Robustos. I enjoy a good Robusto as well; they pack a lot of flavor in a thicker cigar. Andres dismissed his security and closed the large doors, leaving us in the library alone.

"Thank you, my friend, and you know just what I like, you always have. Let's open this up and have one, shall we? That means that drinks are in order as well. Some nice cognac to go along with these should fit the bill. Either that, or do you prefer some tequila?

"I'll leave the drink situation up to you. You're the bartender. I'll clip the cigars, and you man the drinks."

"T——, my friend, I'm glad you could make it over. It's been too long since we last saw each other. How long has it been?

"It's been a good six months or so. I haven't seen you out. Have you been down here at all?" I said, not really knowing whether he'd been here or not as I'd been lying low myself.

"No, I haven't been here. I just arrived yesterday evening, and aside from my father, you were my first call. Here's your drink, and let's get these cigars lit."

Andres handed me my drink. It was a rare tequila he said he got from his father, who in turn got it from Mr. Castro, as Andres put it. We first took our drink, toasted, and sipped it. Doing shots of tequila is reserved for the tequila you don't want to taste and just get into your system as fast as possible.

Andres was dressed in casual wear, but it was still designer wear. The phrase "Only the best," well, that applied to Andres in every sense of the word. The Gucci sandals and Armani glasses and clothing—he was always impressively decked out. Andres walked over to his desk and took out a gold-plated lighter; hell, it might have even been pure gold for all I knew. He lit my cigar then his as we puffed away. The earthy tone of the billowing smoke danced on my taste buds, allowing a small amount of the goodness to flow through my lungs. Andres puffed on his cigar, pointing to a comfortable high-back leather chair on the other side of the desk, where he sat down in his chair. I took his invitation to sit down and enjoy the cigar in comfort. With Andres taking his position in his chair, there was a period of silence on both our parts. Andres filled our glasses again and seemed to want to say something but was still formulating the words. Andres had a careful mind, another quality I respected and found in common with him.

"T——, I haven't been in Cancun for some months because of some family obligations, but the underlying factor is all the violence down here. My father has been having growing concerns for my safety, especially while here in Cancun. I was so persistent to come here that he doubled my guard for me. I was hoping I could count on you to look after me here as well. I have Franco I can count on, but truth be told, I have more confidence in you. You don't have an ulterior motive or any kind of allegiance. You've always been a man of your word and direct. From our first meeting, when you said you didn't know what was so funny. Hahahahahaha, that cracked me up and made me aware of your character from the start."

"Yeah, what character is that?" I asked, half-knowing the answer but not the wording.

"No-nonsense, a man of his word that you would prefer on your good side," Andres said back without hesitation

"I'll take that," I said with a nod of agreement.

It had been some months since the chief was murdered, and it seemed both Andres and I were lying lower than normal but for different perceived reasons. I didn't correlate the two, and piecing things together now, the picture went from murky to clear. Not too long from now, Andres's father would be leaving office, and the little over a year he had left was going to go by quickly. When governments transition in Mexico, it's always a tumultuous time. This particular time in Mexico history, there was a different climate. The rumblings around Mexico and, especially, the Yucatán Peninsula were about change, change in regard to the seventy-plus years that the current political party had been in power, and Mexicans wanted to change to another political party.

"My father wanted me to stay close to him in Mexico City, especially these days. I don't know if you knew this, but the chief of the federal police that was murdered was a friend of my father's."

There you have it, I thought. The connection I was formulating was now confirmed. I didn't know the exact correlation between the president of Mexico and the now-deceased chief, but I had enough pieces. The chief was partnered with the two immigration agents I killed, so it wouldn't be a far stretch to think they all had common goals. Now I knew the president of Mexico wasn't involved in the day-to-day activities but was certainly benefiting on some levels.

"But you just couldn't keep yourself away, could you?" I said with a smile.

"I don't think what's been happening here has anything to do with me or my family. Anyway, I have you to look out for me while I'm here, and with the added guards, I don't see any call for alarm," Andres said but was obviously thinking about matters of security and his well-being.

"I'm humbled by your confidence in me, my friend, and I'll be available for whatever you need," I said to Andres in total respect and reverence because out of everyone in his life, he thought I would most assist him in his safety.

"Have you heard of anything about what's going on or noticed a change in how things are being run?" Andres asked, taking me a bit off guard.

Andres wasn't just being curious; he was gauging my response to see if I knew anything, heard of anything, or had thoughts one way or the other about the murders or who could have been responsible. I knew enough to never let my expression show. No matter what is verbally said, it's what your expression shows when a question is asked that is a telltale sign of your true thoughts and feelings. Whether he thought I had direct involvement or not, I didn't know, but he knew I was plugged into what was going on in Cancun and I might have information. Andres wasn't aware, or at least I didn't think he was aware, of my relationship with Armando. I was more than committed to Armando; our friendship was well cemented, and any information I would offer would be of no benefit to me at all. Armando and I went back almost a decade, and although I didn't agree with Armando's methods at times, especially about bringing me into this mess, I wouldn't betray my friends. Andres was a new relationship, and I never asked or wanted money to watch them, and aside from our first meeting, where they bought the first pills of ecstasy, money never exchanged either one of our hands.

Andres knew that I sold ecstasy, so I might know of something going on. Some people also knew of my relationship with the chief of the regular police, so I had to assume that Andres knew of that. Now that I knew of the new dynamics between the first family and the deceased agents, Armando, and the chief of the regular police, it was sufficed to say that they were on opposite sides. They might have been on the same side at one point, but it was obvious things had changed. I had to be careful about any information I gave and walk that fine line. If I were to offer information that wasn't common knowledge, then it would show I had either contacts that were involved or firsthand knowledge. I took the only route I could take.

"Some months ago, there was some commotion, but it's seemed to settle down," I said, saying it but not really saying anything.

"Commotion? Can you elaborate on that?" Andres said like a pit bull with a bone, not wanting to give it up, as he sat back and puffed his cigar, watching my reaction.

"The chief of the judicial federal was murdered, and the papers said he was blown up. I had seen him out and about at times, especially in the party zone, with his crew. You know Mexico better than I do, Andres. He could have been doing a number of things and maybe pissed someone off enough where his position in the police force had no bearing. If you're asking me if someone is targeting government officials, I would say no, but then again, that's my personal belief. You know Mexico doesn't operate like that. His death was related to something, but I don't know what," I said, not admitting or speaking of anything while saying that Andres knew about Mexico more than I did.

I saw Andres was deep in thought, processing my view, as vague as that was. Since Andres's father was the president, and with the obvious political aspects to this, I wanted to interject something.

"Since we last saw each other, I got another house in Mérida. What an amazing city it is. I've been hearing a growing movement of people wanting to change, especially coming from the younger generation. They want to change to something. I asked them what exactly they want to change to, and they simply reply 'Change.' It's apparent that they are fed up with how things are going for them politically. I wonder if the murders and all have anything to do with the opposition party and them wanting to change as well, but a more drastic type of change. The thing is that I hear it in Mérida more than any other place, but I've heard it here in Cancun as well," I said, wanting Andres to begin to think about a political twist and perhaps put his father and whomever else in that direction, away from me.

Mérida is a city about four hours northeast of Cancun and a place where the Spaniards first landed and settled. That first Spanish and early Spanish influence can still be seen today in the types of houses, the old Spanish colonials, to the streets and food influences. Some of the streets still had cobblestone to them, a feature I loved but no car or its shocks had a love affair with. I found Mérida a quaint existence and a great place to get away from the party and tourist part of Cancun. Not to mention the heat from the chief and other murders that was beginning to die down a bit, or at least I thought so. The houses were amazing, large and inexpensive to rent. I got such a big house for very little money. It had a slower pace of life than Cancun by a mile.

Again, there was a silence that lasted close to two minutes. I wanted my words to sink in before breaking the silence.

"I'll keep an eye out for anything out of the ordinary."

"Thank you, T——. You always have a different pulse on the goings-on here. My family and, especially, I appreciate your loyalty. I told my father that you have watched over not only myself but also his nephew Ernesto and been a dear friend to all of us. My father was thankful I found someone that was like-minded and one whom I could rely on. Mérida, huh? How's Mérida been for you?" Andres said with a look of pride as he spoke.

"My pleasure, my friend. We hit it off from the word *hello*, didn't we? Mérida's such a peaceful retreat from Cancun, and I absolutely love the architecture and history. I loved it so much I have been spending more and more time there. I always need my partying, and so Cancun is that for me, but I enjoy the slower pace of life at times, and Mérida affords me that."

This was a bit more on the radar than I was comfortable with. Events seemed to take on a life of their own and became unavoidable. I came to Mexico to start a new life. I would say, thus far, all I did was change the cast of characters. It was more laid back but was not what I envisioned it to be. The murders didn't bother me; it was all the other bullshit that came with it—everyone's agendas and partnerships that quite frankly had nothing to do with me. It was kind of like back home, except here was more of the wild Wild West, and back home, things were sanctioned more. Those were all just semantics; the bottom line, I wanted to sell a little ecstasy and blend into the background of Mexico.

I was careful not to ever reveal my true identity to anyone, not even Armando. My first name was all I ever gave to anyone, and sometimes, that would change. Andres, let alone his father, was certainly never privy to my real name. My concern was that no matter how careful I was to conceal my real identity, now that the president of Mexico knew of my existence, there was a possibility that I could be outed, and that I couldn't have.

"I was planning on going out this evening. Would you be available to join Franco and bodyguard? An extra set of eyes couldn't hurt, and I sure would feel a whole lot safer if you were around," Andres said, heartfelt.

Ain't this some shit? Andres wants me to protect him from me. This was probably one of the easiest protection details and assignments I ever had. Now I knew there were other possible threats, but the one Andres was concerned about was sipping tequila and smoking a cigar with him in his compound, just feet away from him.

"Again, I'm humbled by your confidence in me. I'm available on your time," I said as I raised my glass of tequila and toasted to Andres.

"Thank you. Someone who might want to do me harm might think twice with you around, T——. I'm starving. Let's go out to the pool. My chef has arranged lunch for us, and I arranged some company for us, all waiting out at the pool," Andres said with a smile and confidence about having others do his bidding, a lifestyle he wore well.

Andres always had women around and loved sharing them with me. It was the power, but more to the point, he loved to treat his friends with everything he was afforded. It came natural to him; while others looked at it as extreme extravagance, Andres wanted others to enjoy life on his level—well, a taste of what his level was like.

"I'm starving for food and company. Count me in," I said, having Andres lead the way.

Andres and I chuckled, taking our cigars with us out the back of the estate to an awaiting feast of females and fare. I followed Andres's lead and settled into a lounge chair. We were brought drinks and rounds of different foods, and the scenery of women in various stages of disrobe was right up my alley.

"Do you have some of those elephants, like the first time we met?" Andres was asking for the ecstasy pills he first bought from me.

"No, I don't have any more of those, but I do have great quality pills as always. I'll bring some with me when I return in the evening. I know just what you like," I said with positivity and understanding what kind of a high Andres enjoyed.

"You're the best," Andres said, clinking his glass with mine and toasting me.

Andres motioned for his main security guard to come over. This was Franco, who, since my arrival, was never too far behind. Franco wasn't overly muscular but was quite tall by Mexican standards at six feet, four inches. He certainly would stand out in the crowd and had a certain presence of no-nonsense about him. Andres treated Franco differently than the others, and the respect level was noticeable.

"Franco, this is T——. T——, this is Franco. You both have seen each other before but have not formally met. I wanted to introduce you both, especially since T—— will be going out with us this evening as an extra set of eyes. T——, I've already briefed Franco about you and our relationship. I think it's important that you both speak and get to know each other," Andres said, making the initial connection between us.

I could see Franco wasn't ecstatic about having a foreigner impeding on his territory. Franco had no say in the manner, unlike their security counterpart, the Secret Service, in the United States. Franco held his tongue for what he might have said differently, and we extended our hands at the same time to greet each other as Andres continued speaking, lending a little more credibility to the abilities and assets I had.

"T—— knows the locals here and has a firsthand, detailed understanding of the layout I'll be going out to tonight. T—— has more than enough experience in protection," Andres said, and it seemed as if he was already echoing what he had previously told Franco, just this time, he wanted it done in front of my face with Franco present.

Franco and I shook a firm handshake and exchanged looks of strength.

"Good, very good, both of you. My plan was to start at Saul's place and then hit the club next door and then that new after-hours place. The only place Franco isn't familiar with is the new after-hours spot. T——, I want you to brief Franco on the location and layout and your overall assessment of the evening. I'm going to take a dip in the pool and see about some of these lovely women here." Andres excused himself and joined the bevy of beauties in the pool.

I first began taking the lead as Franco stood looking at me, apparently to do just that, lead.

"Franco, pleasure to meet you. Andres speaks very highly of you," I said, wanting to praise Franco and not wanting to come off as a know-it-all or for Franco to have any perceived threats against his manhood.

"T——, thank you. Andres has spoken highly of you for some time now. I remember you that first day at Saul's and then again at the restaurant that day before we left to Mexico City," Franco said, letting me know he recognized me from the very first day, lending to his great memory and recognition skills, something vital for a man in the security business.

"That's very kind of him. You know the layouts of the first two places, but the after-hours club is something else. There are about forty steps leading to the second-floor club location. The club is about fifteen hundred square feet or so. When you enter the doorway from the long flight of stairs, there's a bar with a disc jockey booth at the end of the bar just off to your left. There's a bit of a platform where the booth sits on, giving them a clear vantage point overlooking the club. There's a small dance floor in the middle of the club that's sunken down, with tiered seating/tables surrounding it. There are two booth/tabled seating that fit six comfortably per table on either side of the restroom in the back of the club. Either side of the restroom would be ideal for us to sit in. It gives us a great vantage point of anyone entering the club or coming at us. There's a couple of ways to come at the booth/tabled seating, which is a small walkway along the top or directly up from the tiered floor leading to the bathroom and the dance floor. Now, for the downsides of the venue, the club has one way in and one way out. This is where the outside security must be extremely tight. The outside security should be our strongest link and where I would suggest you be with your men in order to make sure of the people who enter or leave the club. Whoever would plan on doing something would know this to be a suicide mission, so be aware of that fact. There's no possible way that someone would be able to enter, attempt to kill Andres, and ever think of making it out alive. Again, your presence, knowledge, and abilities are needed to ensure that no threat enters the club. The club is dark inside and doesn't lend itself to full sight lines. Whoever holds their life in such little regard would have to dispense with you and your detail outside before even getting in to complete their task. I also suggest two men just inside the club doors as well as another buffer between yourself and Andres and I. The parking in the front of the club has plenty of room to park the SUVs with four men watching them. We can use the vehicles as a way to cordon off the section in the front of the club and have a good look at who will be entering the club. The long walk up the stairs is another natural deterrent, giving people plenty of time to think or change their minds about what they might want to do to harm Andres. With you and at least a few men on the outside of the door and a couple of men with me inside the club should round out the security for the evening. I believe this scenario is our best plan to keep Andres safe. You're the ultimate decision-maker, and I leave it to your experience to decide what's best for the safety of the president's son."

I laid my plan out to Franco but also left the perception that he was the author of this plan. While the final decision rested on him, he also has some plausible deniability if something were to go wrong. He could blame it on me and my plan while also take credit for its success if all went well because he had the final say in the plan. If Franco were to change the plan, then everything rested on his shoulders, and that was not a comfortable place to be, especially in Mexico, with Andres's father to answer to. I saw Franco going through the permutations in his mind, formulating the response I was expecting.

"The plan sounds solid, and I lean on your experience at the club and knowing a lot of who's who to cut down on possible threats inside the club. I'll make sure all goes well outside, and those that enter will be those there to simply party and have fun. I'll do a reconnaissance of the club now and see what other security measures we'll be needing for the evening. Are you armed?" Franco said directly and without hesitation, and I answered him in the same fashion.

"No. I don't carry a firearm here in Mexico," I said with my response having many meanings.

My response was twofold, one to let him know I wasn't armed and for him not to begin to have ideas as to how I got armed here in Mexico and why I would be carrying a gun. The other part was to let him know that I was no stranger to carrying a weapon and that I had in the past but just not here. I planned on carrying my weapon anyway and didn't want to alarm Franco or anyone else that I was armed. I wanted the advantage in my favor and the element of surprise in case Franco or anyone else had thoughts of doing something, and I didn't want them tipped off that I was ready to defend myself and protect Andres with armed force.

Franco excused himself, his pride and manhood intact. I was unaware that Andres ventured back into earshot, and I didn't know how much he caught, but it was enough for him to comment on what Franco and I spoke on. Andres approached me as Franco left our sight.

"You spoke tactfully and succinctly. Nobody wants to feel threatened, either their machismo or their life. Franco is a prideful man that takes his job very seriously. From what I heard, your plan was well thought out, well prepared, and insightful. I could tell Franco appreciated your expertise, and the fact that you left decisions to him didn't fall on deaf ears. He understood what you were saying and what you weren't saying," Andres finished speaking and shook my hand in thanks.

"Thank you, my friend. At the end of the day, your safety is the only concern, and I'm here to make sure you leave as you came, in one piece."

I wouldn't say events were spiraling out of control, but events were certainly taking on lives of their own. My friendship with Armando was stretched to new heights. While the murders didn't particularly bother me, it was not what I wanted to do, although the last bombing I did enjoy and took great satisfaction in. I wanted to sell my ecstasy and mind my business. My friendship with Andres certainly was unexpected but had a genuine side to it that I enjoyed. Neither one of us had any agenda, just two men with mutual respect, sharing mutual likes in the finer things in life while me being able to provide a service that was needed that I enjoyed providing, bodyguarding. The issue I saw arising was that Andres and his family were at the opposite end of the spectrum as were Armando and his friends, which left me directly in the middle. A real-life Catch-22 for me for sure.

Bodyguarding for me came naturally. This nightclub event with Andres was just another assignment for me in a long list of assignments I had protecting and looking after people. Bodyguarding came naturally and had similarities to other aspects of work I did. I had to process threats and scan the area for possible weak points or spots of vulnerability, looking for that steely-eyed face in the crowd among the happy-faced partygoers. Someone's look or manner of difference in dress that stuck out is another potential sign of a threat. The key is being aware. Awareness for a man in my position is paramount, self-awareness as well as awareness of all that's around me.

Bodyguarding has many aspects that make it an art form and one that is coveted by both people in the public eye and those in the underworld who are in need of its services. Bodyguards deter the random acts of violence, but it's those that intend to do harm to an intended target that bodyguards are most valued for. The bodyguard must factor in the willingness of a perpetrator to inflict harm and damage on the protected, and so putting their own personal risk, safety, freedom, and life on the line to complete their task. It goes to the old adage "Never underestimate another person's willingness to do the unspeakable, especially if it makes no sense to you."

I wasn't what one would say a professional, but learning and honing my skills on the streets of New York gave me all the training and on-the-job education I needed. I was a big observer of people and their mannerisms, and I attribute a lot of that to my philosophy of less talk and more action. The less I spoke enabled me to analyze people and situations better. I worked as security in nightclubs, bodyguarding/collecting money for an escort service and their women, progressing to driving and bodyguarding the higher-ups of the Italian organized crime. I became more adept at my craft, and it became something I was known for. I could be trusted, kept my mouth shut, and did as I was told to perfection. I took John Wayne's mantra of the strong, silent type to the street level.

* * *

It was an early Sunday morning, and the sun was peeking through the cracks of the houses and buildings, reflecting through my windshield and into my eyes. I was on the move, having received an early-morning call. Bensonhurst, Brooklyn, was alive and full of aromas on this spring morning. I had my window down, puffing on a cigar, taking in the essence of Bensonhurst. The aroma of fresh bread and bagels being made was unmistakable. Coffee, cappuccinos, and espresso being served on nearly every corner were the lifeblood of anyone awake at this hour of a Sunday morning. The smell of the streets could only be understood when experienced firsthand. Bensonhurst,

Brooklyn, like all of New York City, is like no other place on the planet earth, the city that never sleeps.

Richie was very quiet, his typical routine before there was work to be done. The center console of my car had my coffee, dark and strong and this morning I made sure it was doubly strong. I knew how Richie took his, black and sweet, so I came prepared. With his meaty hand wrapped around it, he took hold and fueled his dependent insides. I wasn't seeking conversation and wasn't much of a conversationalist. Passing under the El Train, Richie sipped his coffee and, with his other hand, reached for the radio and blasted some rock tune. Richie leaned in and gave me some instructions in a matter-of-fact manner, a few inches from my ear, in a tone I could only barely hear, barely audible. Richie was quite cautious about being heard on any wiretap to the point of being paranoid about it—at least that was what I thought. One man's paranoia is another man's caution.

"We're meeting a captain," Richie whispered in my ear.

Immediately coming to my mind was a police captain. I thought of that because every Fourth of July, I was entrusted with making payoffs to the different police and law enforcement we had on our payroll. I delivered their agreed payoffs, from the beat cop to the precinct captain. The questions I had in my mind and knew better to keep to myself were, Why so early in the morning? And why did Richie want me to come heavy to this meeting? *Heavy* meaning "armed and ready to kill."

"I need you to stand there at the ready. If this meeting goes south, shoot 'em in the head," Richie said directly in his thick Brooklyn accent and, again, in a low tone when the music was at its loudest in beat.

Richie's breath mixed with coffee and cigarettes was horrible, but I knew he needed to speak closely and quietly. Now I had no problem doing as I was told—never had and never would. It was a little late for doing anything besides what I was going to do anyway, my job. I had no particular qualms about killing, and if it were a cop, oh well. I was in my early twenties and learning on the fly about the dos and don'ts of how to conduct myself in the organized crime life. I had been involved in criminal activities since my teenage years, but

I was progressing into different areas and territory that were ever changing. I admit I was a bit naive and had blind trust in Richie, but I had no other means of figuring it out besides him showing me the ropes. It was the politics I was unaware of, and I didn't want to rock the boat on anything. I knew that going around someone or speaking out of turn was always bad, so I followed the lead of someone I had trust in. That brought me in. Ricky was the boss over Richie and our entire crew. I seldom spoke to Ricky unless Ricky wanted it that way and wanted to direct me personally. It was understood, at least for me, that if Richie was directing me, then Ricky had given the go-ahead for whatever the work entailed. At the time, I didn't know murdering a cop was a taboo act; all I knew was I was called and Richie was there in the thick of it with me, so I had no reason to question a thing or even have a thought this was a bad idea.

Questioning an order or not stepping up when called upon was not only frowned upon but was also a good way to find yourself on the outside looking in. I voluntarily chose this life and accepted all that went with it. The structure and rules of the organization were to be adhered to, especially for an outsider such as me. By *outsider* I'm referring to not being born in this neighborhood and, more importantly, not being of Italian descent. Hell, I had zero Italian in me— not that I wanted any; I was proud to be Irish.

My particular skill set and willingness to do what others weren't willing to do fit like a glove in the underworld. Big, tough, zero hesitation, loyal, trustworthy, took any assignment given, intelligent, able to think on my feet, a quick study with a traceable past, and references that preceded me. One's name and reputation are some of the most important qualities built over time.

The wheels were already in motion, figuratively and literally. The point of no return had been crossed a long time ago, and I left my fate to the Lord and whatever his plan was for me when it was all said and done.

My .380 firmly tucked into the waistband of my trousers, I withdrew it along with a silencer. I turned the silencer on the end of the barrel until flush. I had the magazine already in and a round chambered. I made sure the safety was on again before tucking my piece back into my trousers. I pulled my shirt down over the top to conceal the slight bulge. We were getting close, and I didn't want to finalize the preparation at the location.

Richie directed me a few blocks farther, following underneath the El Train, a staple of many a Brooklyn neighborhood. As a rattling of a train passed overhead, Richie told me to take the next right off Eighteenth Avenue. Making the right, I was instructed by Richie to park the car about twenty feet down on the right-hand side of the street. I recognized the area and somewhat the location. Across the street and occupying the corner lot facing Eighteenth Avenue sat an Italian social club. Social clubs are places where guys meet, discuss their business, play cards, shot dice, plan their crimes, have their meetings and promotion-and-demotion day, and much more. Owning a social club was either a front for someone else or a sign of status in the organization. The promotion-and-demotion day was every Wednesday, where members would either get their promotions or demotions. Nobody ever wanted a demotion; those were tough things to go through and, sometimes, had not the healthiest of outcomes. You never wanted to fall out of favor with the powers that be. Falling out of favor could be that you weren't earning enough or there were some transgressions that were looked on unfavorably. There was always treachery around, and sometimes, you never knew why you were called to a meeting or being demoted. There was always one good reason; you just weren't earning enough money for the organization. "You're only as good as your last envelope" was the common saying. An *envelope* stood for an envelope of money. One had to constantly prove himself and stay in the good graces of those that had the power of life and death. I was excluded from this ritual because I wasn't Italian or a formal member of the organization. I maintained my distance from the politics of the organization, and my motto was to be seen as less as possible and, when called upon, to follow the instructions to the letter. Nonmembers were permitted to enter the club but with the invitation of a current member. Guys in the crew were allowed in and didn't have to be a member of the club, but a member of the crew, yes. Being called to the social club was almost never a good thing. You had to go, and while every boss and captain ran his or her crew differently, the majority of them would order your death if you didn't show up when called. Weakness is a disease that needs to be nipped in the bud early. If an order was passed down even for the slightest thing, like not showing to a called meeting, and it was disobeyed, action had to be taken, most times swift in fashion. You could get a beating, one of those demotions, or death. It all depended on the message the boss wanted to send. I avoided the pitfalls that were obvious and earned my respect through my actions and not a lot of talking.

A little cloud of concern began creeping into my mind about whom we were meeting with this morning. I began thinking this way because police, especially high-ranking police, avoided social clubs like the plague. With the addition of wiretaps, bugging, and constant surveillance, this was the last place I would've expected to meet a cop—and at this time on a Sunday morning. Social clubs were a constant target of law enforcement, and that too was a concern of mine as to who could be watching us this very minute. I stayed away from social clubs at all costs, not wanting to be on any law enforcement radar. I could meet guys in my crew elsewhere and always did. Now I was here at a social club, in broad daylight, loaded and ready kill.

With Richie looking about, I withdrew my car keys from the ignition, took a final sip of my coffee, and with my left hand, reached for my St. Jude's medal. With my eyes closed and reaching for comfort, I prayed.

"Sacred heart of Jesus, have mercy on me. St. Jude, worker of miracles, pray for me. St. Jude, helper and keeper of the hopeless, pray for me."

I sure needed some guidance and protection, and I had nothing else to fall back on at this point. It slowed my heart rate down and calmed me for what lay ahead. It brought my mind back to Easter Sunday. For this brief moment, I was back on the altar with Father Mathews, who was saying Sunday Mass. For us Catholics, Easter Mass is among the holiest of dates. I read the first reading, and the words seemed to just flow from my tongue. A few pews in front of me were my mother and father along with my two brothers and my sister. I felt a certain energy flow through me as if this were my calling in life. I was so at ease on that altar, and I could see the pride and joy my family felt upon seeing me there reading the Word of God. It was at that moment I knew what I wanted to do and who I wished to become. I was at an age where I wasn't tainted by any guilty pleasures or had any thoughts of criminal activity. I was in an all-boys Catholic school, still a virgin, still with a solid family base, and still naive about human nature and the ways of the world. I saw things and people for who they appeared to be. Naïveté only lasts for as long as it takes reality to set in.

"T——, T——. Fuck you doin'? You ready?" Richie said with his right hand on the door handle, looking at me with a stern look of conviction and anger.

"Yeah, I'm all set," I said back, having been snapped out of my moment of reflection.

"Get your mind right," Richie blurted out as he opened the passenger-side door.

I didn't need to respond, and Richie was right; this was no time for religious reflection or break from my reality. My reality was now at hand.

I followed Richie across the street through the sunbeams shining in between the buildings. Barely any traffic was on the streets this morning as I put a windbreaker over my shoulders. I wanted to make sure my weapon was concealed but also have another layer in case I needed to discard some clothing. I was just hoping not to be seen by Joe Citizen, but I was more concerned not to be seen by anyone in my crew or law enforcement. There were too many X factors that made this morning one I hoped I could look back on and laugh at.

All the careful planning, or in this case, the lack thereof, and all the precautions taken can all be thrown out of whack with just one odd variable. My only focus was to do as Richie said and hope I made it out of the club alive.

The social club was nothing to write home about. The corner lot that took up a little less than 2,500 square feet and looked every bit of a place that had been there since the beginning of the century. The paint was a fading light blue in color and could have definitely used a fresh coat.

Richie and I made it to the front of the club, a large door on the right-hand side and a large three-foot-by-five-foot tinted window. The window was tinted so dark no matter if you were ten feet away or right up on it, there was no way you would see anything inside the club. There was no signage to know what the club was, but everyone from the neighborhood knew what the club was and who frequented it.

I had never been to this particular social club, although I had been by it before and was certainly aware of its existence. I heard it belonged to a high-ranking member of our crime family, but I was not sure of the exact owner or if rumors were true or not.

Richie reached for the door handle, I a few feet behind. The door cracked open, and I took a deep breath, not knowing what to expect on the other side of the doorway.

One step inside, and the aroma of cigar and cigarettes was the first attack to my senses when I exhaled and inhaled again. It took me a few moments, and then my eyes adjusted to the dimly lit room, a stark difference to the Sunday morning brightness just the other side of the doorway. I could now see the right-hand side of the club had four small booths and, in the middle, about a half-dozen tables and chairs surrounding them. The left-hand side of the club was a full bar with seating. The bar reminded me of the Prohibition style I saw in the movies. *What a fitting style for this joint,* I thought in my head. There were two doors at the end of club just in front of us. One looked to lead to a bathroom and the other to a room behind the main room Richie and I were now in. In between the two doors sat a jukebox that gave light to the back portion of the club.

Richie and I hadn't made it but twenty feet into the club when the door to what I thought was the back room opened. Two men emerged and exited the back room with purpose and eyes fixated on us. As the two men traveled the fifty or so feet to meet us, Richie and I slowed our pace down to almost nothing.

The two men walked in staggered formation, the man on my left a few paces behind the man on my right. The man in the front appeared to be in his early fifties, dressed in black slacks, collared shirt, and suit jacket, again appearing to be all in black or dark colors. The gold chains around his neck stood out for me, and getting closer,

I saw one had a gold herringbone chain with a gold Italian horn attached. I could see he had a couple of gray streaks in his jet-black hair, and as he got closer, I saw that his stature was about five feet, nine inches tall, perhaps five feet ten, and medium build.

The man who was a couple of strides off his right shoulder was a bit taller than that and even a bit taller than me, standing a little over six feet, one inch tall. He had a larger-than-average build; although not muscular, he had a presence to him and a hitch in his walk. I guessed it was either a sports-related injury or hazardous work-related injury.

Richie stood his ground with me positioned a few feet off his left side shoulder. As the two men approached us and stopped just a few feet from us, I realized the man in the lead looked pissed off—his body language and facial features just screamed it. The scowl on his face was the telltale sign, but that wasn't needed.

"You brought a bodyguard with you, huh?" the lead man said to Richie.

Richie's words of "We're going to meet a captain" were resounding and echoing in my brain. The man who was in front of us was a captain, all right, but surely not a cop; he was a captain in the Mafia, a position of extreme power and just a couple of slots beneath the boss. My comfort level hit an all-time low. I shouldn't even be here, let alone armed, and even less, with orders from Richie to kill these two guys. The order was to kill the captain if things went bad, but I knew it would have had to include the other man. And who knew who else might be in the back room? My gut feeling was that this hit wasn't sanctioned by Ricky or anyone else up the food chain of command. I had already violated multiple rules and felt my odds of surviving dwindling by the second. By the looks on the men's faces, I wasn't supposed to be here, and another rule 101 is to never go to a sit-down or meeting armed. Now I didn't know what this was because I trusted in Richie, but the fact remained, here I was, armed and ready.

Richie responded to the captain that I was his guy, to which the captain said for me to go over there, pointing to the bar area about fifteen feet away, and show his guy my muscles. I looked at Richie for approval, still playing the role for Richie. Hell, in for a penny, in for a pound. The fact is, I didn't know this captain or the other guy. I didn't even know if he were with our family or what. Richie nodded in agreement, which infuriated the captain even more. I could see the captain growing incensed, and I stepped away as the captain's guy moved with me over to the bar. I was now a few feet away from the captain's man, him being off to my left and about a half step off my left shoulder. I had my hands folded in front of me and my hand ready to slide onto the trigger. I now got a good look at the man I would be killing first. His nose appeared to haven been broken at least once, and he definitely looked like the captain's muscle. My hands were steady, and my right hand rested just on the butt of my .380. I knew it would take me about two seconds to withdraw my gun and discharge a few bullets before anyone knew what was happening.

As I looked at this scenario, it appeared I was the only one that was aware of the severity of this situation. The captain's guy had no idea I was a couple of feet away with my hand inching to the trigger. He paid me no mind and was concentrated on Richie and the captain. His body language was nonchalant, and I surmised that it didn't even enter his mind that first, I would be there, secondly, I was armed, and thirdly, I was on orders to kill.

The captain was busy berating Richie just out of earshot. With some music in the background and the distance, all I was looking for was a sign from Richie to act. Based on their hand gestures and facial expressions, the meeting wasn't going well for Richie. My hope was that cooler heads would prevail, as my career and life were flashing right before my eyes.

Five minutes had come to pass, which felt like an eternity, and still, no sign from Richie. I felt relief, but I wouldn't be fully relieved until we were out of the club and a safe distance away.

Next thing I knew, the captain and Richie hugged each other, and the captain slapped Richie on the face, but not in anger, more of a sign of affection of not to do that again. The Italians loved speaking with their hands to communicate their emotions and words. Richie returned the affection without the touching of the captain's face.

Hugs and kisses on the cheek, and all seemed right with the world, but not in my world by any stretch of the imagination. I eased my hand off my gun and took a deep sigh of relief.

As we exited the social club, my heart left my throat and returned to the middle of my chest. I was directly behind Richie and tried formulating what I wanted to say. Richie still looked out of sorts and remained quiet. This was no time for me to mention anything or show any perceived sign of weakness that could be construed as lack of heart. Richie was so temperamental that I refrained from saying what was really on my mind.

"Everything got worked out?" I asked as we reached the car and before we got in it.

"Yeah, just a misunderstanding. It all got worked out," Richie said as he went to open the passenger door to the car.

I didn't want Richie to know how I really felt because that wasn't needed and wouldn't have done any good, especially with him. I waited until we had stopped the car and got to our location before I continued my thoughts and words. Speaking in the car was always a no-no; cars were bugged with listening devices all the time.

"Hey, Rich, perhaps a little heads-up—"

I was cut off speaking.

Before I could finish my sentence, Richie gave me a glare. Whether it was his adrenaline still on full tilt or maybe it was just his character, I knew to cut my sentence short. We walked a bit from the car and had our walk and talk about the neighborhood.

"I didn't want you having needless information. I wanted you calm, with a clear head, and focused. If you had any information on your mind other than what you did, they might have sensed something wasn't right. Your demeanor and frame of mind was the most important thing there, and the less information you had, the better off everyone was. Know what I mean?" Richie said, but it was rhetorical, as he wasn't waiting for any words from me; he was just speaking and I, listening.

That was right where Richie left things, and while I first thought I should be more informed, what Richie had said was right. The entire situation for me was wrong, but I might have acted differently had I known more. Richie's managing of me in that situation made sense even if the situation itself was completely fucked up. Murdering a Mafia captain, a member of his crew, in their club no less, was unexplainable, and Richie wasn't going to offer any more information to me than he already had—a misunderstanding was all.

Richie's state of mind lately was a bit off than in the years I had known him. It was getting to the point where his actions were irrational, at least to me they were. Richie used to be more calculating and was a big planner. This situation was another of his more-recent moves that were a bit wild, and for Richie, that's saying something, because he had always been wild. A street term we used, *cowboy*. A *cowboy* is not something someone wants to be referred to. A *cowboy* is someone that is out there, operating on his own terms without direct permission from his crew boss or anyone further up the chain of criminal command. A cowboy does not respect the chain of command and does not follow the rules.

The following morning, I was awakened by a knocking at my apartment door. This was not a normal occurrence as nobody, with the exception of a couple of people, knew where I lived. I had an apartment in Bensonhurst, Brooklyn, the one Ricky had arranged for me. I looked over at the clock that read six thirty-six in the morning. Although I wasn't too concerned, if it was law enforcement, I would be concerned. Law enforcement would've been way more vocal and probably knocked the door down, their usual routine. I wasn't one for using a cell phone unless they were cloned, and even then, I used those usually once and threw away the phone and broke up the chip inside. Most of my conversations were face-to-face, on cloned phones, and/or on pay phones, of which I used my device for making free calls.

I lifted my .380 from the nightstand next to my bed, got up, and flipped off the safety. I slipped into a pair of sweatpants and made my way to the knocking at my door. I leaned into the peephole, pistol in hand. To my relief, I saw the scruffy face of Artie. Artie was Ricky's right-hand man and ran the daily activities at Ricky's shop. I opened the door, with my pistol down at my right-hand side.

"Sup, Artie?" I said before inviting him in and letting my guard down.

"Ricky needs to see you."

Being sent for is never a good thing, and while I was in good standing with Ricky and the organization, there was always that space in my mind that had doubts. I invited Artie in, making sure not to turn my back on him anytime just in case.

Artie stood about five feet, nine inches tall and looked like an auto mechanic, but that was just one side to him. He was a bulldog in every sense of the word in his early forties. He was thick and stout, had hands like steel mitts and a bit of a belly, but most in the neighborhood did. His scruffy face and clothes that always made him look like he was working on a car were all part and parcel to his persona and cover. Yes, he worked on cars but was mainly the eyes, ears, and day-to-day man at the shop.

I knew that Artie showing up at my door at this time was something not ordinary, and it was a matter of importance for everyone involved. It was rare that Ricky requested me directly without Richie, and this was the first time Ricky sent Artie to get me. To say it was unnerving would be an understatement.

"Come in for a minute while I get ready," I said, walking with Artie inside my apartment.

"I brought you coffee, dark and strong," Artie said, handing me mine as he held his.

"You're a good man, Artie," I said, wasting no time in lifting the lid and taking a gulp. "Ahhhh, the nectar of the gods," I said, taking another sip.

Ricky must have been in a hurry to see me; for one, the hour was early for anyone in our crew, and two, he didn't even want me to waste any time stopping to get coffee or even thinking of brewing any.

I put on a T-shirt, brushed my teeth, left my gun, and grabbed my keys, following Artie outside. I didn't know exactly where we were going, but that was of no consequence. I didn't have an option, so it was irrelevant. Being called to a meeting was never a voluntary act.

The usual meeting spot was the shop, and it was not more than ten minutes from my apartment. Artie parked half a block away, and we walked the rest of the way, sipping coffee, with very little spoken besides the usual bullshit.

Artie lifted open the steel garage door to us being greeted by Tara and Brutus, the two resident pit bulls. Not long after that, Ricky went down from the office at the top of the stairs. All I could do was stand there and wait while playing with Brutus. Tara was Ricky's dog, and nobody played with her but him.

"T——," Ricky greeted me with a kiss on the cheek and a big hug.

Ricky wasn't the formal gangster, and by that I mean wearing suits and all the typical things one thinks of when they think gangster. Ricky was definitely hands-on though, no doubt about that. Unless he had something formal to attend, he was in the trenches with us and in everyday wear. Jeans, dress slacks, the casual shirt or T-shirt were what I typically saw him in. Ricky wasn't about the flash that most gangsters flaunted around. Probably one of the reasons he never spent a day in jail before. He didn't speak much, but his presence was commanding.

"Come, T——, walk with me," Ricky said, putting his right arm around my shoulder and leading me outside the garage.

This was another one of the walk and talks. It was the most optimal when sensitive talks needed to take place, and in this day and age, everyone in the criminal world needed to be careful of anyone listening to conversations. We made it about a block and a half away from the garage before Ricky began his conversation with me. He knew I didn't have a bug on me and didn't need to frisk me or strip me down as Artie would have already taken care of all that.

"T——, thank you for coming in. I wanted to speak to you about Richie."

This wasn't a good thing but more for Richie than it was for me. I had a funny feeling this conversation was going to take place at some point, just not so soon, and maybe not in this particular manner. I don't know exactly what Ricky wanted to speak about in regards to Richie; it could've been any number of things, but being that not twenty-four hours prior I was in a social club, armed and ready to kill, I assumed it was that. There was a pause as Ricky let me think a moment and let thoughts sink into my head.

"You need to stay away from, Richie," Ricky said in his usual blunt manner, keeping his hand over his mouth as he spoke.

Now, this wasn't the place for me to say a word; instead, I just listened and took advice and direction. It was always best to listen and digest than it was to blurt something out, especially when I didn't really know what Ricky was speaking about. Not knowing any of the real variables of what he was speaking about, I waited for further conversation.

Ricky was a very cautious man, and so when he spoke, he kept a low tone and put his hand over his mouth so if anyone was watching, they couldn't read his lips about what was being said. Artie saw me nearly naked and did not give me time to put on a wire even if I had an inkling to do so; Ricky was sure I wasn't a risk to him. Nothing was foolproof, but all the preventative measures that could take place usually were, especially in my crew and among my associates.

"I know he's your friend and he's responsible for introducing you to us. Richie's got a problem. Well, he's got a lot of problems."

Oh shit, this isn't going well. Ricky never spoke to me like this, and when someone like Ricky mentions that someone has a problem— not just one, but many—that's the kiss of death, so to speak. My hope was that it didn't effect me at all, or at least minimally. By now we were about five blocks away when Ricky gave me the bombshell.

"Richie's got a problem with drugs."

Drugs, I thought to myself, were never a good thing, especially with Ricky and our crew. I never thought that Richie had a problem with drugs, but as it sank in, I began going back in my mind about Richie's behavior and the progression it was taking for the worse. I especially knew how Ricky felt about anyone in our crew being involved in drugs, whether it was the business aspect or the taking of the drugs themselves. Some in the underworld turned a blind eye to the drugs, and some dealt it with permission, both taking their share of the profits. When the drugs came to the surface and became a problem, the punishment was typically death. Even if were tolerated, death was the usual outcome, because why take a chance? The punishments by law enforcement were so severe it made turning rat or informant a viable option for those facing extensive prison sentences. Once a problem arose with the drugs, it was damage-control time. While the dealing of the drugs was tolerated by some, the consumption of drugs was a universal no-no. Being an addict in our life was just plain stupid and made no sense to me, but it did happen more often than I knew and, apparently, closer to home than I thought possible. Being a liability was the worst you could be. Hell, it was tough enough just trying to stay in favor when doing the right thing. No self-inflicted craziness was necessary for me.

"He's not in his right frame of mind. Ever since Antonio was released from prison, he and Richie have been teaming up," Ricky said, more forthcoming than ever before.

Antonio was the boss's nephew, the one Richie brought to my restaurant when I was having the issue with the trio of jerk-offs and Mr. Florida, the wannabe gangster. Richie was in a tough spot. He wasn't a made member and was supposed to be under Ricky. Antonio was a made member and, being the boss's nephew, certainly had more leeway than Richie did. Richie didn't have any direct family members that were made members, so there wasn't even a lifeline there to grasp. Just because you grew up in the neighborhood, worked in the neighborhood, and was friends of made guys didn't give you a pass. Richie knew this firsthand. Why he left Ricky and went with Antonio was unknown, but I would guess it had to do with Antonio's charisma and the fact that he was in the drug game, and Richie was taking the easy way out. Ricky's crew made money, but there was nothing like the drug money. The money you could make in the drug game a week would take you months to make doing other hustles.

"They both have addictions, and Richie never really asked to move crews. He slowly began changing his allegiances and type of business," Ricky said with a touch of bitterness.

I knew that Richie was with Ricky and knew that Antonio was in the mix somewhere, but I didn't know all the dynamics. I knew that Antonio was in the same family as all of us but in another crew. Antonio, from what I heard, had his own crew and, being the boss's nephew, was afforded certain luxuries. Antonio did his seven years and had a lot to prove. Even from Antonio's mouth at my restaurant, he said he wanted to claim what was his and make up for lost time. Antonio was in the drug game, and it didn't matter much what anyone thought of it because it was permitted by the boss. Proving he could keep his mouth shut and bring in large envelopes weekly was a large factor in his staying in good favor. The strikes were mounting against Richie, and it had come to this.

"T——, you've been loyal, dependable, and a trusted asset for us, me in particular. From now on, you're to report directly to me," Ricky said, making me feel more at ease that I wasn't the problem.

Ricky didn't have to tell me twice. Ricky knew about the steroids but wasn't concerned about that. He knew I barely even drank, let alone take or deal drugs.

"I know you were at a meeting yesterday morning. Knowing you, I know you were armed," Ricky said as we came to a stop some blocks away from the shop.

I didn't know how to react and couldn't muster a single word. I knew that meant death for me, and so I couldn't say I was and didn't want to say I wasn't and lie. Ricky saw my face, and that was an expression hard to hide. My transgression wasn't intentional, planned, or even my call, but still, nonetheless, it was my transgression. Good thing we stopped for a moment because I was frozen in my tracks and was having an out-of-body experience.

"T——, keep walking with me. I'm not mad at you, and nobody else is either. Richie's our problem now. He's created a lot of enemies in a short period of time. He's been collecting the money from the jukeboxes, slot machines, and arcade games. That's not the problem, though. The problem is, he's been skimming off the top from the collections. Not just those collections, but he's been out there under our flag and shaking down people who aren't involved in our thing. He's been bringing unnecessary heat down on us with civilians that aren't afraid to run to the cops and talk. Between these offenses, the drug habit he's picked up and his changing allegiances within the family, without permission, he's run out his welcome and fallen out of favor. The skimming had gotten so bad that he was called to a sit-down to explain himself. Richie called you to back him up. Whether he thought something was going to happen to him or just in case, he brought you to that meeting. That captain you saw remembered you from the fireworks show when you were with my father and the other old-timers. The captain was there as well and remembers you. He's heard of your work and knows your reputation. He knows what kind of man you are and how loyal you are. He also knew that Richie probably didn't tell you why he needed you there and, more than likely, lied to you about everything. The captain respects you and didn't want that to be the place to bring everything to light."

"The captain you saw yesterday morning knows of your work and allegiance. My father, myself, and few others had a sit-down yesterday afternoon, and you got a pass. He was impressed by your loyalty and set of balls. You're not in trouble at all, actually the contrary. You've been reassigned to me, and we have some jobs that are right up your alley."

I looked at this as a good thing. I was now reporting directly to Ricky, another rung up the food chain, and I was noticed by some powerful people in the family and complimented for characteristics that meant a lot in this lifestyle, loyalty and balls.

"The first piece of business is, we're giving you an escort service to run. We also want you to drive the girls and make sure they're acting accordingly. You're to drive them, collect the cash, and then drop it off at the end of the night. Hey, and, T——, no fucking the girls, all right?"

"Yes, I understand," I said.

No fucking the women who were getting paid to do just that. Ricky must have bumped his head. I was still trying to figure out if Ricky was serious about that. I knew he rarely joked, and I was hoping this was one of his rare moments of levity, but that wasn't the case. I didn't even think he thought that was reality, but I guessed he had to say it.

"When do I get started?" I said with curiosity and enthusiasm.

"Tomorrow night you'll be on. I have a beeper for you and a cloned phone for emergencies. When we get back to the shop, I'll give you those. Let's keep walking," Ricky said as we continued walking.

We had made it to a couple of blocks behind the shop when Ricky stopped me and leaned in really close with his hand over his mouth for sure on this one.

"We need you to see someone," he said and then stepped back from my ear.

Ricky usually referred to things as *we*. By *we* he meant the organization. When I was sent to "see" someone, it usually meant that the person being seen was warned before or was a case where the person being seen was unwilling to conform to whatever the organization had planned. A beating, bombing, whatever the case, the person being seen wasn't going to be the same again.

Ricky looked around as if to double-check there was nobody watching. He reached into his pocket and pulled out a photograph and handed it to me. He didn't say anything; like many things in Ricky's life, words were at times not only unnecessary but also not prudent.

"You got the image?" Ricky said, letting me hold the picture for a minute while I ingrained it into my memory banks.

"Yeah, I got it."

"Good," Ricky said, taking hold of the picture again.

Ricky reached into his pocket and withdrew a lighter. With his right thumb, he ignited the lighter and put it to the corner of the picture. Once the picture was lit, he held it upside down so the flames would hunt for oxygen and burn the entire picture to ashes. He threw the remains on the ground and stomped them out, spreading them around so as to never let it be known what we had both just looked at.

"This guy's been a thorn in our side and won't back off. He's a fire marshal who's been giving us a hard time for some months now. He's making it increasingly difficult to operate our fireworks operation, this costing us money."

I knew there had been a change when we had our operation spread out now to more facilities. We had been doing a lot of moving around, but I didn't know the reason why. The change in how we did things was a direct result of this fire marshal. It was up to me to deliver the payoffs to all the cops, and especially around the Fourth of

July holiday, I went around to various cops' houses with an envelope of cash and bag of fireworks for them and their families. Everyone got a delivery, from the beat cop to the precinct captain. Even the fire department chief got his payoff. After our annual fireworks show was completed, we had the fire department come out and lay water on the smoldering piles of spent fireworks just in case there was something still live or burning. Our show was in a fenced-off playground next to Richie's house. It gave us a secure and safe location to give the neighborhood some joy on our nation's birthday. I made sure all those firemen were taken care of as well and nobody had a cause to get their feathers in an uproar or speak out of turn about anything we were doing.

"Nobody can reach this guy?" I said with a puzzled tone. I said it that way partly out of bewilderment because it was always business as usual and nobody until this guy had busted our balls. The other part was, I was hoping to avoid my participation, if at all possible.

"We tried all the way up to the precinct captain and the fire chief. This guy is some kind of do-gooding crusader or somethin'. He's been approached and warned by the precinct captain himself to keep his fuckin' mouth shut and take the money. He said no, that it was his job and it wasn't right. Some kinda bullshit like that he said. This fucker's costin' us money."

That was all anyone had to say about it. Costing us money. That was "end all, be all" in the underworld. The bottom line: you were never as good as your last envelope, and the cash always had to keep flowing at all costs. Heads would roll and, in most cases, figuratively roll.

"Understood," I said with not much else to say on it.

My one word let Ricky know I was in, but then again, I never turned down a job. With that, Ricky handed me a piece of paper. I opened it to find two addresses written on it. I studied them, already putting them to memory, as I knew I wouldn't be taking that piece of paper with me past this point.

"The first is his home address, the other his girlfriend's address. He's home with his family most nights, but one night a week, he spends with his girlfriend. There's at least one day during the week

330

where he's at his girlfriend's, sometimes two days. It shouldn't take long to get his pattern locked down. he's a creature of habit," Ricky said with conviction.

I memorized the two locations and handed the paper back to Ricky. It was apparent that Ricky had done his homework on the marshal. All that was left was to make the problem disappear and to continue business as normal. Just as Ricky did with the photograph, he lit the paper with the marshal's address on fire and stomped out the burning ashes.

Continuing our walk, Ricky expressed his thoughts on Richie. Ricky knew it was a thought in my mind. Ricky also knew I wouldn't speak on anything, so he wanted to be the one to speak on it. He wanted my mind focused on what I needed to do and my new position as well.

"I'll handle Richie. He'll understand that you're with me now. He should be thankful you've saved his life," Ricky said while accenting the word *thankful*.

Ricky wasn't the crew boss for nothing. He wanted to know if I was going to have problems with Richie not being in the picture anymore. I didn't have options. Ricky wanted to see if I had issues with it. I sure didn't and knew it was out of my hands.

Our walk and talk was now over, and back at the shop, Ricky gave me a pager and cloned phone that I would exchange every couple of weeks or whenever necessary. Artie drove me back to my apartment as I thought about the last bit of my conversation with Ricky. Richie was probably marked for death yesterday, and on some level, I think he knew it; otherwise, why drag me into the mix? Richie knew he was violating multiple Mafia laws and had been for some time now. Richie's drug use, dealing, skimming, bringing me armed to the club to kill a mob captain were just the transgressions I knew of. Any one of those transgressions was a death sentence. A man makes his own way in this world, but Richie's and my friendship had now come to an end. He used me to spare his life with no regard for mine. My life could've ended that day or even today, and I wouldn't have known why I was killed. When a situation like attempting to kill a made member of a family and, especially, a man with the captain's standing in the family for something you did wrong, being killed quickly wasn't going to happen. Your death would be long and tortuous in order to deter others from even thinking about violating laws or making a move.

Now being under Ricky, I didn't associate with Richie any longer. I would be busy with the escort business, the other bit of work Ricky had for me, my steroid business, and much more. Richie helped me get this far, and I appreciate that, but he violated not only the laws he laid out for me but also the laws of friendship that I held true.

A couple of weeks after Ricky and I had our conversation, I was enjoying the escort business and building my surveillance of the fire marshal when I heard through the grapevine that Richie had been murdered.

Richie's barely recognizable body was found in the trunk of an abandoned car near the East River. His body was bound in a plastic drop cloth and left on display to give a warning to all those who would think of getting out of line. From what I heard, he was tortured with dozens of ice pick wounds, none of which would have been fatal. He was ultimately shot in the head and then in his face. Richie had a hundred-dollar bill stuffed near down his throat, another symbolic gesture of his greed. The powers that be wanted to make a statement in this killing and wanted it done in a grand fashion. When someone is killed in the mob, generally speaking, either the body will never be found, or if found, it means it was meant to be found. Everything happens for a reason, and there are no coincidences. Richie's funeral, of course, was a closed-casket one and off-limits for any of us to attend. It was a private affair for his family and relatives, and even that service had a limited number of attendees. It was apparent that Richie had run his course with not just us but many in his blood family as well. To be honest, I didn't feel one way or the other about Richie's death. I didn't think about it past hearing it the first time. I considered us associates and friends, but really, I had no friends. I had Anthony, and he was murdered. Richie and I were close but grew distant as he moved in a different direction. I had respect for him even when he walked me into that social club. It might sound odd, but I respected the balls he had; he was just missing smarts.

Ricky was correct when he said the fire marshal was a creature of habit. In the two weeks since I got the assignment, I had been tracking the marshal and all his moves. I found the marshal to be a worthy adversary; even though he didn't know he was mine, he certainly was for me. Whether it was his survival instincts that kicked in or the collection of colleagues and others telling him to back off, he was aware of his surroundings. He changed his moves often, but there were certain aspects he just wasn't willing to change. The marshal was seldom alone, and he thought he was zigzagging and being cautious. However, there was one aspect of his life he was either unwilling to change or was just unaware was a weakness, his girlfriend. Time and patience will inevitably show a person's weakness. The age-old weakness so many men succumb to was the same one the fire marshal showed, women.

The house of the marshal's girlfriend was the ideal location for my plan. The marshal drove a Crown Victoria, and because he was married, his girlfriend's house was the only place he didn't have someone accompany him.

My plan was to use explosives I would place on his car. The marshal's house wasn't ideal. He had a garage, and his car was always parked inside. His girlfriend's, however, had no place for inside parking; hence, he was forced to park in the driveway or the street.

The girlfriend's house was located on a cul-de-sac in Staten Island. The marshal was there during the daytime, but that wasn't the most opportune time to strike. The only possible time would be his usual Friday-evening tryst. The marshal stayed until about ten in the evening, leaving me enough hours of darkness to have my plan enacted.

The third Friday evening of working the escort business, I called in to have someone cover for me. I wasn't getting any pressure to complete the assignment, but every day this guy was able to work, we were losing money, so I knew this had to happen sooner rather than later.

Friday was now here. I stopped by the shop and picked up a nondescript auto from Artie. There was one route that the inspector would take from either his family home or office in Brooklyn to his girlfriend's house in Staten Island. This route he always chose because it gave him the shortest travel time, enabling him to have more time to spend with his girlfriend. The previous two Fridays showed him passing by a certain point anywhere between six and six thirty in the afternoon, depending on traffic. I would position myself there from five thirty just in case he was early. I wanted to make sure nobody was following him or watching his back. Even though there was nobody with him or tailing him, it didn't mean it was always the case.

At 6:22 p.m., my target passed me by and was en route to his den of iniquity. I let a few cars pass me by before pulling out of my space and following. I knew where he was going, so it wasn't important that I be right up on him. I gave myself enough room to make sure he wasn't being followed or escorted.

It was 6:47 p.m., and my target had pulled up to his girlfriend's house. I didn't turn down the street right away but rather waited for darkness to settle in before I moved anywhere. I was on the main street he would have to come out of when exiting, one way in and one way out.

By 8:35 p.m., I waited for darkness to fill in the warm June evening. I drove down the block of the marshal's girlfriend and parked my car about two hundred yards away on the right-hand side of the street. I made sure the inside lights of this car were disabled so that when I exited, no light would shine upon my face.

For all the bad characteristics and demons Richie had possessed, he taught me a lot. He taught me a lot about the lifestyle, the dos and don'ts, and most importantly, he taught me about how to use explosives. I had always been interested and practicing with explosives since I was a kid. Whether it be gasoline or pipes filled with small traces of black powder, I had an early start in the art of explosives. No coincidences for sure. When I met Richie, I discovered he too was a lover of explosives; we were kindred spirits. Out of all the people I could have met, I met the one man who had some of the same interests as I. Not everyone had a flair for explosives, and to be honest, aside from Richie, I didn't know another guy in life that was as adept in the art of explosives. I didn't know of another that even had an interest in it like we had. I found it to be an art form the making of the explosive to the placing and timing. Richie lost sight of why he was in the life, and he let his demons take over his desire to excel in organized crime.

Richie was the first man ever to teach me about the placement of a bomb for maximum effect. For instance, the positioning of an explosive on a windshield wiper, facing downward, would explode into the engine, where gas was stored, making it quite effective. The windshield was a simple placement, merely by walking by and, in one motion, placing it. I tell you what; it worked and worked well. He taught me a poor man's timer, which is a cigarette placed on the end of a wick. Break off the end so there's no filter, light the one side, and when it burns down, it will ignite the fuse. He went into detail about remote destinations as well, and that too was very effective. I didn't know I could use the remote from a remote control car to rig an explosive, but sure enough, he was right. I particularly loved the placement under a gas tank. The only issue was making sure the device would stay put and not jar loose, but I made sure it would never do that. I had two methods to ensure it stayed until I was ready to press the button or flip the switch. I used a powerful magnetic device attached to the bomb as well as a powerful adhesive tape. These were things I'd miss about Richie, our commonalities, which he had long forgotten about. In a moment of honesty, though, I was glad to see him go. He took a lot of my secrets with him, and that's a good thing.

At 8:43 p.m., I scanned the neighborhood from the safety of my loaner car. I didn't want anyone to place this vehicle with me in any regard, which was why I had Artie manage this one for me. I knew it wouldn't be reported stolen until at least Saturday morning, so it gave me ample time to do my work. Before leaving my apartment and heading over, I constructed the marshal's present. It contained two large metal casings filled with black powder, the equivalent to four sticks of dynamite. I had the tubes welded together in order for them to go off simultaneously for a more powerful punch.

I had a large magnetic device attached to the explosives so I could attach it to the metal undercarriage of his Crown Victoria. I already attached the remote-detonation timer. The distance for ensuring I could remote-detonate was fifty yards. As long as I was within this distance, I would be able to activate the explosives remotely.

All clear as I checked again the surroundings. I exited my car, looking about to see if a wandering eye was on me. I walked down the right-hand side of the street into the cul-de-sac. Wouldn't you know it, someone on the opposite side of the street began walking her damn dog as I made it fifteen feet from my car. I had the explosives tucked under my sweatshirt and my hood covered my face, but my concern wasn't being seen as it was how long this dog-walk would be happening. This was an older lady, and I was hoping she wouldn't be out for one of these extended walks. I still had less than two hundred yards until I reached the Crown Victoria, so I slowed my pace to a bit of a crawl, hoping that wouldn't alarm her or anyone else around.

I was getting close to the marshal's car when the old lady ducked back into her house. It was just in the nick of time, or I would have had to do another lap and put timing off.

It was 8:56 p.m., and I came upon the Crown Victoria parked on the street, a much easier target for me. The house had a few lights on inside, and the porch light was on but didn't shine down to where I stood by the marshal's parked car. There were some streetlights active, lighting up a little bit of my area, but the risk was minor. The key to placing the bomb is to act natural and be quick. Nonchalantly, I kneeled down as if to tie my sneakers. I was directly next to the right rear quarter panel of the car, and on my way down, I pulled out the explosives and dropped to my back, rolling underneath the vehicle. The device easily attached to the tank underneath, and I made sure it stayed put with some extra-adhesive tape. I extended the antenna on the remote and rolled back out from underneath the car. My total time was less than thirty seconds, and I was all set. This was my first time using a remote-detonation device in real action. I had tested it before but not in practical use.

There was a lot riding on this. If this didn't go right, it wouldn't go right for many people. For me it would be a failure, and the device would most likely be found. What would come down on the organization would be intense. As they say, shit rolls downhill, and I was right there to catch it. I was surely sweating, what with the heat of the summer, and while I wasn't nervous, there were more X factors involved in this job than in my past works.

I made it back to my car and turned the engine over. I turned all air jets on me and blasted the air-conditioning. I sat there for a few minutes, taking in the cold blast before putting on my seat belt and leaving my position of observation. With the car's headlights on, I rolled the wheels out and was on my way to my next location. I was going to be a few blocks away on the route I had tracked. If all were the way it had been, the marshal would be passing by me in less than an hour. That gave me plenty of time to calm myself and wait. I left the car running but turned off the headlights as I sat, parked in a prime location to see the marshal pass me by. This time of night and in this suburban area, there weren't many cars coming or going, so when a car passed, I was always looking to see if my target was on the move.

It was now 9:55 p.m., and if all was correct, I should be seeing a pair of Crown Victoria headlights approaching my location. I would see them in my rearview mirror as I parked on the right-hand side of the road, making my ability to follow the marshal smooth.

Being immersed in this lifestyle, I found out that there was little that brought me comfort. I slept but didn't really sleep soundly. There wasn't anyone I could confide in without incriminating myself or looking weak for speaking on it. I had to internalize everything and store it inside me. Gone were the days of innocence, and in times like this, I reached for the only part of me I kept from my past, my St. Jude's medal. My grandmother gave it to me when I was a child, and perhaps, she saw something in me that made her gift this to me. I know it sounds hypocritical to pray at times like this, but it's what I found comfort in, and truth be told, I feel that it had protected me from harm. The hypocritical part came as I did it before committing some really heinous acts. Blasphemy, hypocrisy, futility, whatever, it was me.

My thoughts brought me back to my senior year in high school. My feelings about embarking on a calling in the priesthood were all but gone. Since my freshman year, I had seen many things but blindly dismissed them. An all-boys Catholic school was where I went, and like most things in religion, it was blind acceptance. I chose to find all the good things in the priests and, for the majority of my time, ignore all the negative aspects my eyes saw but my brain and heart were unwilling to process logically. Our priestly principal had been abusing boys for years. Those that entered his office and were looking for guidance, well, some of them found a different sort of guidance, but it wasn't priestly or holy. While there were rumors, those rumors later turned out to be fact. The sexual acts between the priest and students looking for guidance were such a breach of trust on all levels. It was a mere hushed rumor until the year after I graduated, when it became a known fact. As students, we joked about it. Back then, it seemed a joke as we saw it through youthful eyes, never thinking it could be a reality. A priest breaking his oath and vows for such an act was beyond any of our comprehension. I guess that was what he used to prey on those that were vulnerable. If my desire to become a member of the priesthood wasn't doused before I left high school, it certainly was when I heard that news. So many of the priests I saw and admired slowly showed me the human side of man. I still remained religious even after I left high school, but the desire I once had in my heart went away when the human side of man was shown to me time and again. I was dedicated and driven. When I slowly began to see and feel that those I idolized weren't holding to their vows, I felt betrayed and disheartened. Why would I dedicate my life to a calling that showed so much hypocrisy? The vow of chastity, of poverty had been trampled on. Though it was not committed by all the priests, it was enough to make me not want to join the vocation. I wouldn't say my choice to move in the direction I was in now was validated, but what I experienced made my conscience easier to handle in times like this. I closed my eyes and, with my sweaty right palm, held on to the medal and prayed.

"Sacred heart of Jesus, have mercy on me. St. Jude, worker of miracles, pray for me. St. Jude, helper and keeper of the hopeless, pray for me."

It was 9:59 p.m., and a set of headlights coming up from behind me snapped me out of my thoughts, bringing me back to my reality. A few seconds later, my target passed by me. I caught a glimpse of the man in the photograph Ricky showed me a few weeks ago, the same man I was about to introduce to the afterworld. I put on my seat belt and let the marshal get a little ahead of me before I turned on my headlights and moved into the road behind him from my parking space.

The marshal made a right-hand turn just as my headlights went on. I followed with the same right turn about fifteen seconds behind him. I was just far enough away to not be on his radar but just close enough to make sure he never wrote another report on any of our fireworks operations.

I kept my left hand on the steering wheel, and with my right, I leaned down and opened the glove compartment. Retrieving the remote detonator from the glove box, I placed it on my lap, pulling out and extending the antenna. I followed the marshal through a series of rights and lefts, closing the distance to the expressway. My remote was the usual length of about three inches thick and six inches in length.

We entered the expressway and soon saw signs for the bridge that would take us to Brooklyn. I kept checking my speed and distance from the marshal's Crown Victoria. I was careful not to let anyone come between him and me—not a simple task on a Friday evening.

At 10:06 p.m., the Crown Victoria was in perfect position. A tollbooth was less than a mile ahead, and the time was now. My speedometer read fifty-five. I applied my right foot to the accelerator, closing the distance between me and the Crown Victoria. Sixty-three miles an hour, and I was closing the distance. Seventy-five yards and closing now. I switched to the right-hand lane from behind the Crown Victoria still in the middle lane next to me. I didn't want any debris to hit me and hoped that being in a lane over, I could avoid such a thing. I had no idea how this whole thing would go but thought being directly behind the explosion wouldn't be the most prudent of actions. My stress levels were at a premium now. I had no backup plan, had never used this method of explosives when it counted, and the consequences, good or bad, had me sweating even with the air-conditioning on full blast.

I put my finger on the switch and flipped it. Nothing happened, the light on the box was still red and not green. Either I was out of range or the signal, for some reason, wasn't connecting. My heart picked up the pace a bit as I eased my right foot down on the gas pedal a bit farther. *Fuck, what the fuck happened?* I thought. I was going about sixty-five miles an hour now and gauging about forty yards out from the Crown Victoria. I took a brief glance down and saw a green light. Not hesitating, I flipped the switch, and no sooner had my index finger moved when the Crown Victoria exploded.

The explosion had me ease off the gas and apply the brakes, not to a screeching halt, but enough to slow my closing distance. I looked behind me so as not to get rear-ended, and thankfully, the next car behind me was a few lengths back and applying the brakes as well. I literally saw the rear end of the Crown Victoria lift off the ground and become engulfed in flames. Either the placement of the explosives was spot-on or the marshal had a full tank of gas or both. The surrounding traffic began to react, and I heard wheels screeching to a stop and collisions around me. I turned the wheel of my car hard to the right, moving my car off the third lane and into the service lane close to the going off the road. I was trying to avoid not only the pieces of metal blown in my direction but also the larger pieces of burning metal that could seriously damage my car and perhaps keep me from leaving the scene. I also had to contend with the other motorists, who were careening into one another and causing more of a logjam. Not only were burning metal pieces being spewed all over, but the gasoline from the tank was like a flamethrower shot in different directions. I could feel metal pieces banging off my car, and I was just hoping I could drive through this maze of carnage. I was able to slow down to just about a complete stop, and then finally, I was parallel to where the Crown Victoria was burning, or at least the majority of it was burning. I was going about fifteen miles an hour when I passed the main wreckage and then sped up, maneuvering through the burning rubble. There were about half a dozen cars that made it through along with me; the remaining cars were in varying degrees of wreckage and disablement. I couldn't see how anything that was once alive and breathing would be alive and breathing through that. The amount of damage that was done and the intensity of the fire were so different from anything I had seen or done before. I sped up to the speed limit, and in less than a minute, I was at the tollbooth. The stunned tollbooth worker didn't even stop us to ask us for money as we went through. We were just waved through, and I wasn't arguing. I made sure my sweatshirt was covering the majority of my face in case there were pictures taken as cars went through the tollbooth.

I passed through the tollbooth and heard the sirens off in the distance. Someone must have called this in fast or there were units in the vicinity. I could just barely see the flashing lights of the first responders as I passed over the bridge back to Brooklyn. Other responders were passing me in the opposite lanes, going from Brooklyn to Staten Island. I was at the highest point, going over the bridge and driving in the right-hand lane, and I tossed the switch out of my window and down into the deep, murky waters below. Not too far off the end of the bridge, I moved through Brooklyn to a local diner, where I parked the car. I took a few moments to gather myself, thinking that I was lucky to make it off the bridge and be in one piece. I opened the glove compartment and withdrew the cloned cell phone. I dialed the only number I ever did from this phone and waited. After the third ring, a friendly voice answered.

"Yeah," the voice said.

"Done," I said.

Ricky and I were the only two on this call, and these were brand-new cloned phones that had not been used any other time before or would be again. The cloned phones came about because a part of our crew was stealing the signals from passing-by motorists that were using their phones at the time. We cloned their numbers and placed them on a chip into our cell phones so the calls would look like they were coming from other people's cell phones when in reality it was us using them.

There was a pause of dead air after I gave Ricky the word he had been waiting for the past few weeks.

"You all right?" Ricky asked, knowing the job was done but then wanting to know if I was safe and in the clear.

"Perfect, just hungry is all. I'll meet our friend in an hour, but all's well," I said

I had to let Ricky know that all was well. I knew he would be worried about the job, me, and the aftermath. He had to be prepared for any potential backlash from this public display. I didn't know how Ricky was going to feel about the media coverage that would come from this, but I couldn't concern myself with that right now. I also wanted to give Ricky a time for me to meet Artie back at the shop and get rid of the car I used. It was obviously damaged from the blast and could be linked to the bombing. Artie's job was to take it to friends of ours and have it scrapped.

"Good. See me in the morning," Ricky said, hanging up the phone.

I went into this diner that had the most amazing pastrami on rye I had had a craving for the entire evening.

* * *

CHAPTER 6

BETRAYAL

PROLOGUE

"**A**gent Coppola, this is Francisco de la Cruz from the Procuraduría General De La República in Mexico City," the voice from Mexico said.

"Yes, sir, what can I do for you?" Agent Coppola said as he read a report on his desk.

"Well, it might be what I can do for you. I'm charge of the fugitive task force here in Mexico and have received some information about an American living here in Mexico that might be a person of interest for you."

Agent Coppola put the report down and was now taking a deeper interest in the conversation. Agent Coppola knew that there was no formal extradition between the two countries, and cooperation between the two was almost always one-sided. Just getting a call wanting to help was both rare and unexpected.

"Yes, I've heard of you. You've trained here in the States before, haven't you?" Agent Coppola was beginning to recollect the past in his head.

"Yes, at your location in Quantico, Virginia. I'm there every year for training and coordination with my counterparts in your government."

"So to what do I owe the honor of this phone call, Agent de la Cruz?" Agent Coppola asked, not wanting to expose his eagerness.

"I've been tracking someone who's been living in Mexico for the last few years. He's an American citizen, and from what I've gathered, he's from New York. Rumor is that he's got some problems there in the United States. I don't have a name on him, only his first name.

He's not down here legally, from what I gather. Before I pursue this matter further, I wanted to know if this was of interest to you," Agent de la Cruz said without giving all the information he had, not knowing what direction this might turn.

"What's the man's first name, and do you have a photograph of the man?" Agent Coppola asked; he wanted to see if this was someone on his radar or even worth further investigation.

"His first name is T——, and I'm faxing a picture now to the fax number you have listed."

"T——, you say? Let me check with my secretary about the fax. Can you describe this man to me while I'm waiting for thee fax?" Agent Coppola's eyes gained even more life, and he sat up in his chair. "Dorothy, there's a fax coming through. When it does, can you bring it to me right away? Thank you." Agent Coppola cupped the receiver as he spoke.

"He's about six feet tall, muscular, and athletic, is always at the gym or associated with being in the gym, has short dirty-blond hair and, I believe, blue eyes. I'm in Mexico City now but heading back to Cancun, where he'd be known to be. I have some other business to attend to there and was going to see about speaking to him or detaining him."

Agent Coppola wondered if this was the same man as the one he lost a few years ago and had been on his mind quite frequently. As Agent Coppola's thoughts were racing, in walked Dorothy with the fax from Mexico City.

Once it was in Agent Coppola's hands, his eyes lit up like a Christmas tree, and he could barely hold back his emotions. Agent Coppola had to hold back his excitement as he didn't know who Agent de la Cruz was, what his affiliations were, or if this was even Agent de la Cruz on the phone.

"Agent de la Cruz, are you still there?" Agent Coppola asked, gathering his composure.

"Yes, I am. Did it come through all right?"

"Yes, it did, and this man looks familiar to me. I'll have to run this by some old photographs to make sure it's the same person. I would ask you this, please don't approach him yet. If this is someone of interest, we would want to be there when he's apprehended. Is that a possibility?" Agent Coppola said, knowing that anything could happen and wanted to be on the ground when it did.

"Bueno, I'll wait for you. I'll do some more surveillance. When can I expect to hear back from you?"

"I'll be in contact with you before the end of the day and before you leave to Cancun. Is that a time frame that works for you?" Agent Coppola said, barely holding back his true energy.

"Perfect for me. I'll call my people in Cancun and have them hold off on anything until I hear from you, and I'll get more information ahead of any actions taken."

"Thank you very much for the call, Agent de la Cruz, and I look forward to speaking further with you later."

Hanging up the phone, Agent Coppola called for Dorothy to enter his office. There was no need to hide his enjoyment and excitement any further.

"Dorothy, call the team. We're going to Mexico."

CHAPTER 6

BETRAYAL

I found my peace of mind and solitude in Mérida. This quaint old Spanish city was perfect for me. I still maintained my condo in Cancun for when I went back to collect money, re-up my people with ecstasy, and get my party on. The last time I was there was the day I saw Andres and escorted him out with Franco. I got one of the feelings I would get from time to time. I can't explain the feeling; it's just a feeling that comes over me, directing me to act. This particular feeling was that Cancun was no longer a safe place for me to live, at least not full-time, and I always listened to my gut feeling.

My girlfriend and I had split up but remained friendly—relationships had never been my forte. We spent the millennium in Mexico City, and without any worldwide disasters taking place, we rang in the New Year in style. We were invited to the house of a couple we met in Cancun some months before while partying. He turned out to be the nephew of a politician who was supposed to become the next president of Mexico. We got along quite well, and I was looking forward to the smooth transition from Andres's father to my new friend's uncle as the president. Life is about relations and relationships. I was always careful to build mine the right way. Even though the outcome wasn't always the way I wished it to be, I made sure I did the right thing when at all possible. Just as I met Andres and his family, I met my new friend I spent the millennium with in Mexico City. The great common denominator was ecstasy. Those pills have a natural effect on people.

My ecstasy business was going well, and my inventory was dwindling to the point where I was going to need to purchase some new material soon. I still had the chief of police in Cancun, but I wasn't there much and hadn't seen the chief for a good six months. I certainly would make that a trip the next time I went to Cancun, which, I was thinking, might be about time.

I was always looking for quality product at a good price and had grown my connections since being in Mexico. One of my new connections was a gentleman in Amsterdam that was a good connection with a wide array of product. Another connection I developed was from Medellín, Colombia. Colombia was a better location as far as geographically and timewise. It was closer to Mexico, and the shipping routes were faster. The only caveat was that more eyes were on packages, what with people coming to and from either country. If you knew people in the government or shipping facilities that were friendly to your cause, then Columbia was a much better way to go. The authorities in Colombia and Mexico were easier to bribe than the ones in Europe. I requested some samples be sent from Columbia, and after receiving them, I and a few others sampled the material. We partied at my house in Mérida, where I could control the music. Mérida wasn't the best location to have an all-out party in regards to the best music quality. I invited a DJ I knew and had him spin for us. I wanted to make sure I experienced the pills properly and not with some Yucatán music that would most certainly bring my high down. I didn't mind the occasional party at the local clubs, but I enjoyed my after-hours party, and this night was going to probably carry over into the morning. My lab rats loved the pills, and we all enjoyed our night/morning.

My home in Mérida was of decent size. I would say it was about two thousand square feet inside, and the outside was probably just as big. Three bedrooms are inside with a nice-sized kitchen, living room, and dining room to round out my living quarters. The back-yard was amazing, filled with fruit trees like lemon, papaya, and kiwis that gave me year-round fruit every morning. I had a little casita in the back as well as a full bar for entertaining or just enjoying the serenity in comfort.

Now that the party was over, I rested the entire next night. In the morning, I wanted to be fresh for the series of phone calls I knew I would be making. I used to be excited to get to Cancun, but increasingly, I was becoming comfortable in the peacefulness of the Mérida.

Before anything, I wanted to have myself a fresh cup of strong coffee and sit outside as the morning began to take shape. The fresh air mixed with the strong aroma of dark roasted beans was heaven for me. Sometimes it's the little things that count and the little things that are needed in order to even out the other aspects of life that are less peaceful. These early Mérida mornings are quite priceless.

Somewhere between my second cup of coffee and my wandering daydream of nothing important, I heard the distinctive ring of my phone. It wasn't my usual phone; it was the distinctive ring of the Armando line, as I recalled it in my head. I knew I wouldn't be able to answer it before Armando would have hung up, so I let it ring out and finished my java. My feeling was that this call was important both for me and for Armando. Armando never called me just to chitchat.

"Hey," I said as I reached my kitchen and made the call and spoke into the receiver. "No, I'm good, just having my morning coffee and enjoying this amazing weather. Of course I'll be able to make it. I'll leave first thing in the morning. Lunch works for me. I look forward to it, my friend."

I hung up the phone, thinking that by this time tomorrow, I would be leaving my peaceful existence for what I felt would be a more-than-interesting time in Cancun.

I took a long bath in my on-suite Jacuzzi tub. I had to gather my thoughts before heading out and make some phone calls. I didn't know what Armando wanted, but I knew it was something I probably didn't want to know about or look forward to hearing. Being in Mexico for nearly three years had me slowing down and not wanting to speed back up anytime soon. The only good thing would be that I wasn't there for some time and I had a lot to do once there. I had to stop by my condo, collect the mail, collect money, replenish my two dealers, see the chief of police, grab what pills he had, and pay him.

I planned to call Colombia in about another hour. That call I would make from a pay phone. The last I spoke to my people there, they were going to send the samples, which were right on point, and the deal was they had twenty-five thousand of the same type ready for delivery. The only thing I knew was that I would be able to have my delivery within three days of the call. The other details I would finalize today on this call, if I were interested in moving forward with the deal.

I took my long walk to a pay phone about twenty minutes from my house. There were other phones closer, but the distance didn't bother me and just in case the call was intercepted, I had some added protection from authorities attempting to figure out my exact location. As I made the call, the plan was agreed that Cancun would be the drop-off point. The amount of traffic coming in and out of the airport lent to a mishap less likely taking place. My people in Columbia said they could arrange a drop-off in Cancun much easier than other locations. I didn't ask and I didn't care.

The two-cigar ride back to Cancun went off without incident, with me having a full agenda and arriving right before lunch. My meeting with Armando was to take place soon. We had agreed that I would be changing cars with him. I wanted a different car so as not to stay on anyone's radar and to keep whomever might be watching guessing. Although every car Armando traded in I didn't pay for, I wanted this to be the last one. I was just having some different feelings, and I wanted to not be dependent on Armando or anyone else. I had enough money now, and with my being in Mérida nearly full-time, I knew my life was moving in a different direction. Lately I was becoming a little complacent in my activities. I felt my complacency more as I began approaching Cancun. I was feeling that Mérida had softened me a bit. Coming back to Cancun, I needed to bring a little bit of the old me back, if for nothing else but self-preservation. These past few years, the meetings Armando and I had didn't last as long as those days in Mexico City, when we would be with each other all day at times. It was more of a friendship back then, and I longed for those days. I believe we were both on different agendas now and moving in different directions. I was slowing down, and Armando was full steam ahead.

I made it to my condo to find everything in order. I wanted to freshen up a bit before heading to meet Armando. I found bills, but they were all credits, as all was paid up months in advance. I took myself a shower with my appetite getting stronger by the minute.

Armando wanted to meet downtown. For the first time in some time, our meeting was going to be in public. Armando chose the bullring as our meeting spot and for good reason. He loved the tacos at the bullring, another similarity he and I shared, the love of good food and, for sure, great tacos.

I pulled into the dirt parking lot in front of the bullring to find not many cars around. The next bullfight wouldn't be for a few hours, giving us plenty of time to enjoy ourselves like the old days. I arrived ahead of Armando, parked, and made a beeline for the taco joint inside. This place was always open, a testament to the quality and special taste of these delectable treats. I placed a double order of tacos de cabeza, cow's head. This was my favorite of all the taco varieties, and if Armando would be late, I certainly would have eaten his order and placed more.

Being late wasn't Armando's style, as he pulled up just as the double order was placed. Armando was by himself and behind the wheel of a nondescript Chrysler Neon.

"Que onda guey?" I said as Armando approached me.

Armando looked different, not in his manner of dress, but rather in his demeanor. I could tell right away that something was off in his behavior. I knew it would come out during our conversation, so there was no need to address it now.

We slapped each other's hand, pulling each other in and hugging. I gave him a kiss on the cheek as Armando did the same in return. We separated, and the reason for Armando's different demeanor became evident.

"What's your last name?" Armando said with stern conviction.

I did not expect this from him. Hell, we had known each other now for almost a decade, and he never asked me or inquired about my identity ever. There are certain things that you just don't ask or care to know. Names aren't important to conducting business, and if one of us was to volunteer information, that's one thing, but requesting information that wasn't volunteered, that's another thing entirely.

"Why?" I asked, not really knowing what else to say.

I was rarely taken out of my character, and even more rare, I was never caught off guard. This was one of my rare moments.

"What's your last name?" Armando said, not wavering from his first words.

Armando wasn't a man to be questioned even by a friend. Armando was a lot of things, but a man that liked to be questioned wasn't one of them. He spoke with purpose in all areas, and this was certainly one of those times. I was in a bad way and had no way to answer besides the truth, good, bad, or indifferent. If I lied to Armando, then our relationship would never be the same; especially if he already knew the truth, then lying wouldn't matter. If I told the truth and Armando somehow used it against me now or in the future, I would always have to be concerned about it. I didn't hesitate in responding once he asked; I knew all the angles and most of whatever the possible outcomes could be. The one thing I wouldn't do was lie, not at anytime in our relationship and not here and not now.

"H——," I said, speaking no matter what came next.

"Hey," Armando said with a pause, wagging his right index finger in my direction, "a friend of mine was just asking about you." But then he did not offer anything further.

Armando had a look on his face as if he were putting a puzzle together and were coming up on the last few pieces. Nothing good would ever come of any of Armando's "friends" asking about me. Armando's friends were powerful, and for any one of them to ask for me by my real name wasn't looking good for me.

"A friend of yours?" I said with inflection in my voice, only being able to muster these words in the same tone as I was thinking.

"Yeah, a friend of mine I ran into yesterday was asking questions about you. I didn't know your last name. All he knew was an American from New York who works out in the gym, frequents the club scene, was muscular, and he was ultimately describing you. He was asking if I knew where you were or had any information about you. He mentioned your name, but since I never knew your name, I never even put anything together. It wasn't until I saw you just now, pulling up, that I began thinking my friend might have been asking about you."

"So who's this friend?" I stopped Armando right there, wanting to know who the hell was asking details about me and knew my name.

"Oh, he works for the PGR here in Mexico. He's in charge of finding fugitives and people that are wanted by foreign governments. He's friendly with anyone who's anyone in Mexico. From nightclubs' personnel and owners, restaurant owners, hotel owners, staff, and regular people. Those on both sides of the fence he's either friendly with or intimidates. He's trained at the FBI school in the States but works for the Mexican government."

"What did you say?" I said with much curiosity.

"I told him that I would meet with him later tonight. He wanted to see what I came up with," Armando said.

"Can we meet after that meeting, and let me know what he says?" I asked, wanting some clarity on the situation.

"Yeah, of course we can. Let's get some of these tacos in us. I see you ordered already, and I'm starving," Armando said, not skipping a beat, having gotten the answer to what was on his mind.

"Let's get to it. These are the closest tacos to those from Tepito," I said, not wanting to dwell on what I couldn't control and not wanting to let Armando see my true concern.

With the tacos served, I ordered us a couple of drinks, a chillada for Armando and a michelada for me. My palate had always been a bit blander, so all the spicy stuff wasn't for me. Armando and I had some small talk, and when the drinks came, we toasted to our friendship and dug into the tacos. It wasn't long before we ordered another round of drinks and tacos. We enjoyed ourselves for the first time in I didn't remember when. It felt good to just enjoy my friend, even with whatever it was hanging over my head now. I had to trust that my friend would do the right thing and have enough pull to work it out. The worst-case scenario was, he could give me a heads-up and tell me what was happening, and I could get to a safer place.

"How long are you planning on being in Cancun?" Armando asked.

"A few days at least. I need to see the chief and handle some other odds and ends. Maybe we can see the chief together if you want to make an evening out of it."

"I tell you what, let me speak to him and see what he has on the schedule, but I'm sure we can do tomorrow night, if that works for you."

"That works out perfectly for me. Tomorrow it is. Just confirm with the chief, and we'll get together. Let him know I'll take whatever it is he has on hand."

I enjoyed this time with Armando and made plans to meet around ten that evening. I tried not to think about what this so-called friend of Armando's was after, but it was hard not to. A few beers consumed and our bellies full, we began to say our good-byes.

"T——, this is your new ride," Armando said, handing me the keys to the Neon.

"Very nice. You know, it's just like me, not too flashy but nice enough to handle a road trip with. Thank you, my brother, I appreciate it," I said, giving Armando a hug and accepting the keys, handing him the old ones.

We parted ways as I had some people to meet and phone calls to make. I tried to keep myself busy and my mind off whatever information I would receive from Armando that night. I drove off in my Neon to continue the rest of my day.

I called Medellín from the first pay phone I came across. Phone cards in hand, I called to see what time frame was available for the shipment to arrive. I didn't want to know details, just a time frame, so I made sure I was available and not schedule anything else. I was told with assurance that this set of ecstasy would arrive in two days' time. I hung up the phone and continued to make my rounds around Cancun. I met with Sebastian and my other distributor. I rarely had issues with people not paying me, and the ones that tried to test my toughness figured out in short order that was not a route to take.

I collected twenty-five thousand dollars and along with the fifty thousand I had in my floor safe. I had enough to cover my upcoming purchase. The amount the chief of police would bring tomorrow wouldn't be anything substantial, and I prepared on having money ready for a few hundred at least.

It was getting to be about that time, and I called Armando to make plans to meet. Armando said he would drive to meet me as his meeting with his *friend* was over. The thirty minutes until I met Armando seemed like hours. I couldn't really do much and smoked weed to calm myself a bit.

Thirty minutes was up, and we met outside the mall near my condo. It was closed, so not many people were around.

"Hey, my brother," I said, greeting Armando.

"So I spoke to my friend, and the first thing he did when he met me was ask about you again."

"And what did you say?" I said, eagerly awaiting a positive response.

"I told him you weren't here and that you were in Monterrey."

Monterrey is a city in the northern part of Mexico and probably one of the farthest points away from Cancun as one could get.

"So what did he say?"

"He remained adamant that you were here in Cancun and that he knew it. I repeated myself that you weren't here and you were in Monterrey."

"He took that?" I said, wanting to know more.

"Of course he did. I'm the godfather to his son. Today was his son's birthday, and I threw him a party."

"Did he tell you who was asking about me?"

"All he said was some feds from the States were asking about you and that they were planning on coming here to get you."

I was trying to process how the fuck this came about and why would the feds now be interested in me. And who tipped them off? What I was going to do next was the immediate thought that came to mind. I couldn't say anything at all. I was trying to say something, but nothing was coming to mind.

"Not to worry. I got you, my brother. My friend works for whoever pays him the most. He gets paid by the PGR, the FBI, and by those that don't want to be handed over. There's always a deal to be made, and this one is on me. This is why we build lifelong relationships and always do the right thing. T——, you've done the right thing for me here, and now it's my turn to reciprocate. I'm not saying be careful or watch out now, but I'm saying this avenue is a dead end. Whoever is coming for you is going to be pissed off and go home with their dicks in their hands," Armando said, laughing and slapping me on the shoulder.

I felt a bit of relief now that I had some more information. Now I could be better prepared and get back a little to the old me and keep my head on a swivel. I was getting too complacent, and quite frankly, I was losing the edge that had been keeping me alive and free all these years. I truly thought that I could come here and start a new. The fact of the matter was, I was a fugitive. I was wanted, and I needed to act accordingly. I needed to be better prepared and act less like a friggin' tourist. I was acting like so many of the marks I had erased, being too comfortable in my success and complacent in my daily routine. The few years and perhaps all the ecstasy I had been taking softened my survival skills. That would come to an end at this moment, right here and right now.

I knew Armando had my back, but did he truly have my back in every regard? Was Armando trading me in for something more for himself, making me his bargaining chip? Was Armando just using this as a means for me to continue to do his bidding? Did Andres or his father find out it was I who had killed their allies? Did I wrong someone here in Mexico aside from the ones I was associated with? Why was Armando's *friend* all of a sudden on my case and had all my dead-on, correct information?

"Thank you, my friend, I can always depend on you as you can always depend on me," I said to Armando, reaching out to hug him.

Even if Armando was responsible for this or not, I didn't want to think I had changed anything about me, especially in regards to him. I knew what I had to do now, and it began with cleaning up my tracks and changing my living arrangements.

"Come on, let's go meet the chief and enjoy ourselves a bit," Armando said as we drove downtown to meet the chief.

I didn't know we were meeting the chief that night, but I had enough money on me to take care of him, and I needed a drink at least.

Meeting the chief that night, I was able to get about five hundred pills, a little more than I expected, and gave him the money right then and there. I also gave Armando his customary taste. We met at a closed bar downtown where we could talk and conduct our business without any prying eyes on us. I didn't want to have to come back again and pay them both their cut. I wanted less interaction with both of them at least until I could get a better grasp of who was against me. The chief came to the meeting bearing gifts, some guns for Armando and one for me, a gift that was typical of him. I really liked the chief; he was a man of his word and, for me, a man of respect. I was sure there were countless people that had the opposite feelings toward him, but that's life. Just as I knew there were people who felt the same about me on both sides of the coin. The chief brought me a special gun, which I appreciated and was quite astonished that he gave me one. He took out a case and opened it, sliding the opened case to me. It was an old-school Thompson submachine gun. I looked at him, and he said it was for me. I looked at Armando, and he sat back and smiled with appreciation that his friend thought of me. Hell, we had known each other for three years now and had done some great businesses together. I assumed the chief was showing his appreciation. I was a bit overwhelmed as I loved weaponry, something all three of us had in common. Apparently, the chief and Armando were running guns from Mexico down to Central and South America, and the chief came across this and thought I would appreciate it. The chief was correct; I certainly did appreciate it and marveled at it. I thanked the chief as he sat back in his seat, joyous in my excitement of my new gift. I had a feeling the chief and Armando were doing some deals together, but guns, I wasn't expecting. I saw part of the shipment that the chief had confiscated and arranged for Armando. Armando's ability to transport them with impunity meant a perfect partnership with smooth transactions.

Our evening concluded, it was a bit after midnight, and I needed to get some rest ahead of a long day tomorrow. I had my first dealings with the Columbians in another day and needed to be sharp for this transaction. The Columbians were known for their shrewd business dealings, and I had to be at my peak form to be able to make sure nothing went awry. I was pleased to get my Thompson, but there was nowhere to really conceal it in my condo, so I had to place it in my closet in its case.

A full night's sleep, and the next day, I spent cleaning up loose ends. I was prepared for my first transaction with the Colombians and eager to complete this transaction and leave Cancun.

I was off to the airport in my Neon. I made it to the airport, where the flight would be arriving in moments. Cigar in hand, I parked my car and positioned myself just outside the airport exit, where the passengers would be exiting from. I dared not enter the airport as that certainly wasn't prudent. I made the call at the scheduled time to make sure the courier had left. My instructions were to go to the airport pay phones and call. I didn't have any other information on the transaction and would receive my instructions then. I called to Medellín and was told to call back in fifteen minutes.

The sun was extraradiant this morning, and I was glad I sprayed an extra layer of sunscreen on me and had my hat on. The hat was to protect me from the sun's rays and attempt to conceal some of my looks. I was at the airport, and who knew who would be walking out of it? After the ordeal I just went through with Armando the day before, I was concerned that I would run into someone other than my courier. I couldn't change the plan and didn't want the Columbians to think anything besides smooth sailing. Try to explain to a Colombian on the first transaction that the meeting had to be changed or delivery postponed; I knew better and just had to be on high alert.

"She did? Okay, great. Okay, okay, dirty-blond hair, red top, red skirt. Okay, I got it. I'll be in touch shortly. Thank you. Likewise," I said into the receiver, calling back fifteen minutes later.

The airport was never a good place to be at for a man in my position, a fugitive. A friend of mine whom I met in Cancun about a year or so earlier was in the same type of scenario as me. He was a fugitive wanted for cocaine trafficking, murder, and a slew of other charges. We hung out often in Cancun, and while I knew part of his story, I really didn't believe most of it. He told me stories of being one of the largest cocaine distributors in the United States. He was in his late twenties and didn't seem like someone that would be in that position. He went on the run when guys in his crew were arrested, and ultimately, most got lengthy prison sentences and one, the death penalty. With my friend being the boss, he would have certainly received the death penalty. He told me tales of arranging all the drug stashes in every major city in the United States. I'm talkin' aircraft hangars filled with drugs. He would travel from city to city and make sure all was well with the locations and supply. He told me a tale of being hooked up with some major players in the game. One of those players was the head of the international police. Factoring in my friend's age, the fact he told me about his legal issues, that he was a fugitive, the entire story I thought was part true and quite embellished. He decided he needed money and left to go work at the airport, selling timeshares and—get this—in his real name. He surrendered his real passport to immigration in hopes of getting a legit Mexican work visa.

We became close in a short time, and I couldn't talk him out of what he wanted to do. I did tell him to never make any decisions without me, especially if it meant going anywhere to meet anyone. You can only advise people so much and give advice that's for their best interest. Ultimately, it's up to them to make their own decisions as men. Unbeknownst to me, my friend got a call from immigration that his work papers were ready. He didn't tell me about it and left the airport to get his papers. His eagerness and whatever else going through his mind made him have a crazy lapse of judgment yet again. I had some people at the airport watching him, but when I got the call that he had left their care and went to the immigration office, it was too late. I called the immigration office, where I was friendly with the chief of immigration. He informed me that my friend walked in, gave his real name, and was arrested. I couldn't believe it, and the chief of immigration didn't know he was with me. By that time the feds in the United States were notified, they were already in a private plane and were headed to Cancun. I felt horrible. I even made plans to break him out of the airport jail. I sent some people over there to see if it was possible. The word I got back was, they couldn't even get within a hundred yards of him. My guy at the airport told me there were more agents there with letters on the back of their wind-breakers than he could count. My friend that was apprehended and I became so friendly in a short time. This event left a mark on me that I thought about often after he was sent back to face his music. When I read about it in the papers the next couple of days, sure enough, he was telling the truth about all of it and more.

I couldn't help but think of my friend being flown back and facing his past back home. I didn't care what he did or didn't do; I knew him for how I met him. He was someone I called a friend, and the sad thing about me calling people friends was, that the friendship was usually short-lived. Just the hazards of the lifestyle and why I had friends I could count on one hand with room to spare. My senses were on high alert, and I couldn't wait to get out of this place. My Columbian's didn't know my situation, it wasn't there problem." It was safer for me to be here to get the courier than any other scenario. I just didn't want to spend any second here longer than I absolutely needed to. I had people I could call if I got jammed up, but Mexico is Mexico, and you never know.

I clicked the receiver down, and from the information I got, she had already landed and would be exiting soon. I got the description of her from the other end of the telephone call. I pretended I was still on the phone and dialed the phone to make it seem as if I were still busy speaking. I didn't want to rouse any more wandering eyes than needed be. I had my eyes peeled for the exit, looking to see who would fit the description I just received. I was sweating outside for about twenty minutes when from out of the shadows of the airport came my courier.

Five feet, nine inches tall, dyed dirty-blond shoulder-length hair that was styled very well. Her skirt was formfitting, ending just above her knees. Her long legs ended perfectly into four-inch heels that had her towering over many of the Mexicans that she passed by.

Her top was three-quarters in length, showing a few inches of her midsection, which was totally flat and tan. Her top had a plunging neckline that couldn't help but show the outline of her enhanced DD breasts, perfect in shape, form, and size. All her skin was a perfect bronze color that made the red in her outfit pop that much more. I stepped toward her as she approached the phone booths where I was standing. She had but one suitcase that she wheeled behind her.

"Aracelli?" I said as she was but a few feet from me.

"Yes, hello," she said, smiling, with a distinct Colombian accent.

"I'm T———. Pleasure to meet you," I said, extending my hand.

Aracelli ignored my hand and gave me a hug while whispering in my ear, "No need for a handshake. We should know each other more than a handshake." She hugged me and kissed me full on the lips.

I didn't know why she did that, but I went along with the act. I grabbed a hold of Aracelli's suitcase, walked back to the pay phone, put in a phone card, and dialed back Medellín. I let the person who answered know that Aracelli was with me now, and I put her on the phone to confirm. I was told by the voice on the other end of the phone to take good care of her. That I was certainly planning on doing regardless. I didn't notice a ring on Aracelli's finger, so I was under the assumption she wasn't married, and with her being a courier, I didn't know what her connection was to my connection. I was sure it would all play itself out as we went on. My main focus was getting the hell out of the airport and having her checked into her room. I didn't want her staying with me just in case something went wrong with either her or me. I showed her to my car and opened the passenger door for her. I closed her door, put her luggage in the backseat, got in, and drove off.

"How was your flight?" I said, attempting to make small talk.

I wanted to gauge her attitude and demeanor as we pulled off. I would be spending some amount of time with her, and we still had to conduct business. I wanted to conclude our business as soon as possible and anything after that was extra.

"My flight was okay," Aracelli said in her broken English.

Her accent and broken English made her even that sexier to me. My mind was on business, but I couldn't help but have flashes of personal feelings.

"How many days will you be staying?" I said, still making my small talk but trying to figure out my schedule as well.

"I'm staying two nights. They didn't want me flying back right away as that would raise unnecessary suspicion," Aracelli said directly, and it made sense.

We had some more small talk, and the drive to the hotel wasn't that long. I pulled into the long entranceway to the hotel, where I had made reservations. Pulling in, I noticed the sign read "Welcome to the Ritz Carlton." I pulled to the front steps of the hotel. Before my car came to a stop, a bellhop was already approaching my car. He opened the passenger side, where Aracelli sat.

"Welcome to the Ritz Carlton. Will you be parking long-term or short-term?" the bellhop said in a polite manner.

"Short-term," I said as I exited the car. "I'll be about half an hour or so." I wanted him to know so he could park my car accordingly.

The bellhop and Aracelli exchanged a few pleasantries, and he took her suitcase with him. The look on Aracelli's face said it all, as she was surprised to be staying here. Not that the hotel wasn't of her caliber, but it was what I chose for her.

I chose the Ritz for a few reasons. One, it was only a few hotels down from my condo, and it cut down on driving time for me lessening my risk. The Ritz being this exclusive would eliminate the majority of the negative incidents that could occur in a less-prestigious hotel. This being my first business dealing, I needed it to go smoothly and put my best foot forward.

I checked Aracelli into her room with her name. I had just reserved the room with straight cash. I didn't want to be linked to her, on paper anyway, and wanted her to look as if she were a tourist on her own accord. I knew a few of the hotel personnel, and they allowed me to pay in cash. She and I both had keys, to which she had no complaint about.

Up in the suite, I tipped the bellhop, and once we were alone and before Aracelli could ask about the transaction, I told her I would return in thirty minutes with the money. I didn't want to go to the airport with seventy-five thousand dollars; that would have been just plain stupid. She said she would freshen up after her flight and thirty minutes would be a good time for her as well. I excused myself from the suite and went down the elevator. I was quite excited about the upcoming transaction and eager to complete it. The airport really had me unnerved, bringing back thoughts of the friend I lost to the feds.

I returned in just about thirty minutes and went straight to the suite. I knocked first to be polite and then entered the suite. I announced myself so Aracelli wouldn't think it was hotel staff entering. Aracelli called for me to enter the bedroom. I went in with my satchel of money, and she had a suitcase lying on the bed. She looked at me and saw I was carrying a satchel. She in turn opened her suitcase, and in the bottom of it, hidden, was a compartment where the ecstasy was situated. I was quite impressed with the false bottom. The compartment was well manufactured, and I would've never thought it was there. She took three bundles out that contained my part of the deal. I opened the satchel and withdrew the stacks of money, eight of them, seven stacks of ten thousand each and the last one of five thousand. She thumbed through the stacks and counted them out as I looked through the pills she brought. She finished counting and said everything was good. She put the money where the pills were and sealed it back up. I agreed everything was in order now.

"Good," I said.

"Very good," Aracelli said, smiling and just as sexy as hell.

I placed the pills in the satchel and sealed mine up. Business was concluded, and I knew that Aracelli would have to make a call back home to give them the word that she was in possession of the cash. I too wanted her to make that call so my connection knew my part of the transaction was completed. I was still responsible for Aracelli, but the majority of things were handled. All I had left to do was entertain her for a couple of days until she returned. I didn't know how Aracelli felt, but I wanted to enjoy some of the amenities of the hotel, especially in light of what Armando had told me. I knew the Ritz would be a safer place to enjoy myself and hide out.

"I suggest we go make the call to your people and let them know all's settled."

"Yes, I agree. Let's go do that," Aracelli said in agreement.

As we were walking down to the hallway, I asked Aracelli what she had planned for her time here. I didn't know if she had other people to meet or what was on her agenda.

"Plans? I have none. I've never been to Cancun and don't know anyone here besides you," she said it to me in that sexy accent of hers.

"Okay, let's handle this call, and I'll walk you back to the room afterwards. I have a couple of errands to run, and I'll be back in the early evening. If I can make some suggestions, get yourself some of our sun outback by the pool and beach. The water is amazing and so peaceful. Order whatever you wish, and we'll have dinner together tonight. I'll call you about thirty minutes before I come back over. If you need anything else, there's a fantastic boutique in the lobby, and the concierge can arrange whatever else you might require that's not here. If you're hungry, there's plenty of restaurants to grab a bite at, and they deliver right to you wherever you wish. Just make yourself at home, and let's plan on, about seven, I'll be back."

"Since you thought of everything, I'll enjoy the day and wait for you to call for our dinner date," she said, smiling, and reached for my hand as we walked out to get the car.

"She's all set. Yes, she's here with me right now. Okay, here she is," I said, speaking to the same person I had always spoken to back in Aracelli's home country.

"Yes, everything, and yes, he's treating me well," she said, looking at me with a lustful gratitude.

She spoke a little longer then hung up, and I drove her back to the hotel. I wanted to get these pills back to my condo, count out a couple of bundles for my two Cancun dealers, and get them situated. This time, though, I told them that when it came time to pay me, they might need to take a trip to see me wherever I might be. I thought I would be in Mérida, but I didn't want them to know a definite location just in case one of them was the person ratting me out to the PGR. That issue was still not resolved, and so far, it could've been anyone for whatever reason. I hated having loose ends, but the only alternative was to cut everyone out, and that was no alternative for me. I now had to see how my people I knew reacted to what I said and threw some tests out there, all the while not letting on that I was testing them. Letting people have information or disinformation was a good way for me to calculate who was on what side and who was betraying me. I had to begin narrowing down who attempted to offer me up. It started with the people I supplied. I dropped off their bundles and laid down some information to see what returned.

By the time I made it back to my condo, it was getting to be about six in the evening, and I had to shower up, get dressed, and enjoy my evening with Aracelli. I brought a little overnight bag with me and some party material. I was getting pretty hungry and was looking forward to having some supper with my newfound Colombian friend.

I got dressed and called over to the hotel to tell Aracelli I would be there in about thirty minutes. I asked if she needed anything so I wouldn't have to leave once there.

I valeted my car and, this time, not in the short-term parking space. I would be spending at least the evening here. I stopped in the lobby and ordered some drinks to be sent to the room. I was in need of stiff a drink, looking forward to that and smoking a large joint to unwind.

I gave my polite knock and then put my key in the slot. The light turned green, and I turned the handle, opening the door. The lights were turned down dim with candles throughout the suite. Adding to the ambiance was some soft music playing in the background. I was taken aback by the spread of food that was waiting for me. There were bottles of red and white wine on the table along with a bottle of champagne chilling next to it. This really stopped me in my tracks, and I took it all in. Out of the corner of my eye, I saw Aracelli appear in the doorway between the living space and the master suite.

Speaking of being stopped in my tracks, now my mouth was hanging open. I thought she was gorgeous when she was wearing the skirt and her midsection was showing, but this blew my mind. Aracelli, in the doorway, was wearing a turquoise lace outfit that showed enough to make me speechless and left enough covered to have my imagination going bananas. Her outfit was complete with garter belt and four-inch heels. My imagination was running rampant, and she knew it. She stood with a champagne glass in each hand.

I must have been staring for too long because she made the move to come to me when usually, it would've been me that made the move. She walked right up to me, leaned in, and kissed me full on the lips, and I let her do the work. Her lush lips and the hint of lip gloss was a perfect mixture. She tasted so good as she broke the kiss and handed me my glass of champagne. I didn't even want to say a word and ruin anything.

We clinked glasses and toasted to each other. I took a sip of champagne, and she did the same, with us both never losing eye contact. I didn't know if the clinking of the glasses or the sound of her voice toasting me snapped me out of my fog, but I was back.

"You must have read my mind today," I said, taking another sip of champagne.

"Not all of your mind. I'll let you fill in the rest," Aracelli said as she again showed her quick wit mixed with the type of personality that more than attracted me.

My type of personality was the A-type personality. The attractive part was that she could maneuver in my world, assertive and confident, but when it came time to meld with me, she succumbed to my strong personality and knew how to treat me. Aracelli was exactly the type that I found attractive not only in looks but also in her personality, which was a perfect match for me.

A knock on the suite door interrupted us, and then I remembered I had some drinks coming up. I took them right at the door. Now we had plenty of drinks, ecstasy, and weed. With the food she ordered, we were bunkered for at least the evening.

I had Aracelli roll us a joint—rolling them was never my strong suit. She looked sexy rolling with her manicured hands. I didn't know if it was me or what, but everything she did was sexy to me. We hadn't even been together a full day, and I already didn't want her to leave. A woman that understood my lifestyle, let alone me, was such a hard commodity for me to find. I'd found a few, but then my lifestyle always seemed to catch up with the relationship, eroding it. Either I had to go on the run, I got arrested, my work consumed me, or I lost interest in some manner. Now here was Aracelli, who got me, obviously understood the lifestyle, and I knew, in a couple of days, she'd be headed back to Columbia and I would be back to what chose me.

Aracelli lit the joint, took a drag, leaving some of her lip gloss on the end, and handed it to me as she leaned in and exhaled her smoke down my throat. We finished the joint and proceeded to sit down and pick through the food that she ordered. It was a great collection of meat cuts, seafood, varieties of fruit, some desserts, and plenty of water and freshly squeezed juices. In between dinner and the effects of the weed, I asked her if she had someone back in Colombia. She told me she did have someone, and before she could finish, my mind began to wander. She then said that they had a child together and he was killed a few years ago. I told her I thought that was terrible and didn't want her to elaborate on any of that. I just wanted to make sure I wasn't stepping on any toes before I got knee-deep into something.

"This is the first time I've been out without him. My cousin thought it would benefit me to come here to Cancun and spend some time to enjoy myself. I put everything into my child and haven't done anything for me since my husband's death."

"Who's your cousin?' I said, eating some steak.

"Rafa," Aracelli said directly.

"Rafa?" I looked at Aracelli, hoping that she was going to laugh or say something besides that.

"Yeah, Rafa. It was his suggestion that I make this trip. He told me about you and that you were a very good man. He told me you would be able to make me forget about the last few years and get back to the old me.

Rafa was the gentleman I met in an after-hours party in Cancun. He was at a table next to mine, partying with what I discovered was his wife. I offered him my table for partying as well. We all ended up partying until sometime the next afternoon. He was really cool, and we got along from the word *hello*. I got a great vibe from him and his wife before we even said a word to one another. I didn't know too much about him. The next day, before we said good-bye to one another, he offered me his number and gave me a couple of pills that he had. He also said that he had a good connection and would be able to deliver. So here we were in this moment, and I was with his cousin. I didn't know much about Rafa, but I knew where he was from, and he was no slouch in the underworld game. I had tons of respect for him and his wife and certainly didn't want to have anything interrupt business or offend him. Aracelli put all my concerns to rest, and we got back to us.

"I'm glad my cousin sent me," Aracelli said as she leaned in and kissed me passionately.

Now that all my concerns were answered, I turned my full attention to the woman that just kissed me. I reached into my pocket and pulled out a couple of the ecstasy pills she brought. I had her open her mouth and take one and I, the other. Our meal was over, and we knew we would be nibbling for nourishment throughout the evening. I put on some house music as we had drinks and waited for the ecstasy to take effect. Our room looked out over the ocean, the balcony giving us fresh air as we smoked another joint. The first puffs were taken, which triggered the ecstasy, kicking our evening into high gear. We spent the next thirty minutes kissing each other and exploring each other's bodies. Aracelli was passionate, and with the atmosphere, the drugs, the anticipation, and the years of not allowing herself pleasure, she was unleashing it in waves. I was more than a willing recipient. Our passion soon made its way to the bedroom.

I laid her on the king-size bed, slowly making my way through her lace lingerie. I slipped her garments off, negligee, bra, panties, garter belt, leaving on her heels. She reached down to undo her heels as I intercepted her hands. Not a word was spoken, and not a word was necessary. I took mental notes of all her curves, doing well to take my time and savor the moment. Aracelli had taken care of herself even amid all her pain and anguish. Everything about her was perfect. Her skin was smooth and evenly tanned, her hands and feet manicured and pedicured to perfection. She had just enough perfume to entice me without me being overwhelmed by the aroma. I'd agree; the ecstasy had my senses enhanced, but the attraction for me had been there since the airport.

Aracelli's enhanced breasts were topped with nickel-sized brown nipples. More than anything, I was enthralled by her ass. It fell perfectly into my hands with plenty to keep me busy for hours on end. Her body responded to my touch, letting me know we were in sync.

It was nearly sunrise, and neither Aracelli nor I had even thought about sleep. Three ecstasies, more drinks, and weed certainly enhanced our marathon sex session. We were compatible in every way conceivable. We had another day and evening together, and if this first evening was any indication, then the send-off would certainly be bittersweet. I didn't want to think about the departure just yet. We watched the sun as it awoke, sipping juice, holding each other in silence. There wasn't anything to be said, and the moment was savored.

The entire rest of the day and evening was much of the same as we continued to just enjoy us. Nothing else existed besides us in this place at this time. She was leaving the following day, and that was a certainty. There was nothing I could do or say or even wanted to say to change that fact. What I wanted mattered not. I was getting used to the fact that when I would fall for something or put my heart into something, it would disappear. I would forget myself and the decisions I'd made. I would try to be someone else if even for a couple of days. Sometimes those days turned to weeks or even months. When my reality would come calling about the life I had chosen, it seemed I was always drawn back to that which I attempted to distance myself from.

These last couple of days had me making a decision that I had been on the fence about. I enjoyed Cancun, but for many reasons now, I didn't enjoy it as much as I did in years past. Questions began to arise in my head. What should I do, and how do I obtain the existence that I wanted? I decided right then to close down my condo, take everything with me to Mérida, and make that my home. Not many people knew I existed in Mérida, and I had fallen in love with it. Cancun was only a four-hour drive away, and the two dealers that I supplied had already said they would come to me, wherever that might be. Mérida it was, and I concluded my last couple of days in Cancun cleaning up the loose ends of bills and rental payments.

While I fell in love with Cancun, it wasn't my speed anymore and wasn't the safest location for me, or at least that was the feeling I got. I had enough money saved to last me some years, and I had enough product in circulation to keep with a steady influx of cash. I didn't know what the exact political landscape would be, but I assumed it would be business as usual with the reigning political party and my allies. I didn't let Armando or anyone else for that matter know about my plans to reside full-time in Mérida.

Aracelli and I planned on seeing each other again, but before anything, I had to find out who was against me. I had my plans in full swing with my dealers to see if they were the turncoats. The last couple was Armando and Andres. I had enough experience to know that more than anyone, the ones closest to you are usually the ones against you. I couldn't imagine someone else being able to sell me out, but it was Mexico, and I was the odd man out. Story of my life.

COMING SOON

THE SEQUEL

t's not that I didn't trust Armando, but I didn't trust Armando. Armando traveling in that larger Humvee made surveillance easier for me. I had to keep my distance as Armando would fully recognize what I was driving as he was the one that gave me my car in the first place. The entire drive back to Merida from Progresso I continued to run through scenarios in my mind. With all this information Armando just gave me about the Governor being on the run and Chief of Police being arrested I could no longer accept blind information. I was having that gut feeling that Armando wasn't telling me something. He might have been here to tell me about some news but true to form he had an ulterior motive and I felt it.

Reaching the city limits of Merida, Armando's Humvee drove to an Argentinean Steak House. I parked my car a couple of blocks away and began to walk. The newsstand on the corner gave me a great vantage point to the entire restaurant. The sun was at my back making it even that much harder for anyone inside the restaurant to see in my direction with any clarity. I picked up a Mexican Newspaper to see splashed on the cover, "The end for El Senor De Todo" (The Lord of all). The article read that The Cartel bosses body was found tortured, beaten and decapitated in an apparent bloody Cartel turf war. The photograph was graphic showing a note pinned to the corpse's headless body. The note read; here lies the old cartel. We are The New Cartel, out with the old and in with The New Cartel. It was signed El Pastor, (The Shepherd). I heard of El Senor De Todo before, going back to my days in Mexico City and wondered what he was doing in Cancun. Apparently he wasn't that welcomed there.

Somewhere between picking up the newspaper and finishing the gory article I missed a couple of vehicles pulling up to the front of the restaurant. I had to do a double take to make sure my mind wasn't playing tricks on me. Armando was no less than a hundred yards away from me meeting with Andres and the Commandant of the Judicial Federal Police (PJF) of Merida. I just saw Armando and he didn't mention this meeting. Not that he had to but it would have been nothing to do so, especially since he made me believe he came all this way just to watch my back. 'Watch my back?' Mexico and New York are one in the same. The three looked as if this wasn't their first meeting together. Armando and Andres definitely had a closer relationship. I know Armando, he and Andres had known one another well before this encounter. I took a brief moment processing the visual before knowing what I had to do. Tighten up and take the offensive!

A B O U T   T H E   A U T H O R

www.timharron.net

Having had the opportunity to travel extensively throughout the United States and the Americas the author has seen and experienced things that most of us have only witnessed on television. His blend of reality and fiction create a powerful world of philosophical action that captivates its audience.

Tim Harron was born and raised in New York, residing now in Las Vegas Nevada.

CPSIA information can be obtained at www.ICGtesting.com
Printed in the USA
BVOW08s0839050616

450753BV00001B/45/P

9 781682 896259